AN

ENGINEERED

INJUSTICE

OTHER TITLES BY WILLIAM L. MYERS, JR.

A Criminal Defense

AN
ENGINEERED
INJUSTICE

WILLIAM L.
MYERS, JR.

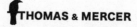

THOMAS & MERCER

Published by Thomas & Mercer, Seattle

www.apub.com

Amazon, the Amazon logo, and Thomas & Mercer are trademarks of Amazon.com, Inc., or its affiliates.

ISBN-13: 9781542046480
ISBN-10: 1542046483

Cover design by Damon Freeman

Printed in the United States of America

*This book is dedicated, first, to the men
and women who work for our nation's railroads.
You are the backbone of this country. It is my honor
and privilege to fight for you.*

*I also thank the team at The Myers Firm.
Pat Finn, Mike Kelly, Dominic Itri, Ivana Gonzalez,
Courtney Johnson, Kathy Ho-Piccone, Greg Lott,
Bill Smith, Steve Milone, Lisa Chalmers, Lisa Schmoke
and Ellie Moffat. That you work so hard, and care so
much, for our clients makes me prouder than I can say.*

1

Monday, June 16

The moment of truth.

It's 2:00 p.m. Vaughn Coburn, his client Raymond Harris, and Vaughn's boss Mick McFarland stand side by side at the defense table. The foreman of the jury is also standing, the verdict sheet in her hand.

It all comes down to this. Years of appeals, months of trial preparation, two weeks of trial, three days of jury deliberations. The foreman will read the verdict, and Ray Harris will either go free or he will spend the rest of his life in prison for a murder that Vaughn Coburn is convinced he did not commit.

Ten years earlier, Harris was convicted and sentenced to death for killing his five-year-old special-needs son, Jacob. The boy perished when the family's South Philadelphia row home burned to the ground. Harris and his wife escaped. Their ten-year-old daughter, Rebecca, was at a sleepover. The prosecution's theory of motive was that Ray had intended to kill his wife, Penny, who had recently threatened divorce. The DA told the jury that Harris wanted his son dead, too, because it would have been a headache to raise a child with Jacob's limitations alone.

The jury bought the story hook, line, and sinker, ignoring the testimony of friends and neighbors who swore that Ray had doted on Jacob, while Penny did everything she could to pass off the boy's care to others.

A longshoreman, Ray Harris was also an intimidating-looking man with tattooed arms and hands. Penny was an elementary-school teacher straight out of an Ivory Soap commercial. Ray never had a chance.

After sweating it out on death row for a decade, Ray Harris managed to get his sentence reduced to life imprisonment due to ineffective assistance of counsel. That same year, Vaughn's boss Mick agreed to represent Harris pro bono and persuaded the Superior Court that Harris's first attorney was so incompetent that his client deserved a new trial.

For the second trial, Mick hired a nationally renowned fire expert, the former fire commissioner of New York, now teaching forensic fire investigation at St. John's University. The DA hit back by hiring an equally distinguished expert. On the nontechnical side, Ray, ten years older, now looked more pathetic than tough. Penny's lined and aging face betrayed her as the hard-drinking party girl she'd always been. Plus, Vaughn and Mick presented evidence dug up by their investigator, Mick's brother, Tommy, that Penny had been running around on Ray for years before the fire and later bragged that his conviction "got him out of my hair" forever.

The trial turned into a knock-down, drag-out ordeal. The prosecution and defense teams are both exhausted. So are the jurors.

When the judge asks the foreman to read the verdict, Vaughn holds his breath. He hasn't been this nervous since he sat through the roller-coaster trial of Mick's law-school classmate, David Hanson, two years earlier.

The foreman looks at the judge, her face serious, hands shaking. "On both counts, of arson and murder in the first degree, we the jury find the defendant . . . not guilty."

The courtroom erupts and Ray Harris breaks down in sobs. Just behind him, his daughter, Rebecca, now twenty, is crying, too. Ray turns and they embrace, shaking as they weep.

Vaughn smiles at Mick. *This is what it's all about.*

Ray turns back to Vaughn and Mick and shakes their hands, pauses, then bear-hugs them both. "You guys . . . you . . ." Ray steps back and searches for the words to thank them, but Mick and Vaughn wave him off.

"Get outta here," Vaughn says. "Let Becky take you out for a steak."

Ray smiles, turns away, and joins his daughter on the other side of the bar. Vaughn watches them leave the courtroom arm in arm.

"Enjoy it," Mick says. "It doesn't get any better."

Vaughn blows out air. "I can't imagine what would have happened—"

"Yeah, you can. You've been there. We both have."

Vaughn nods. He's suffered through his share of guilty verdicts, first during his five years as a public defender, and now, for the past four years, working for Mick and his partner, Susan, at McFarland and Klein. But this verdict means something to him. He believed to his core that Ray Harris did not set the fire that killed his son. The way the man's eyes welled up whenever he talked about Jacob, his pain when he learned that his wife had run around on him, his naïveté in failing to understand how a jury could convict an innocent man. Vaughn read the man's goodness in all of it.

"Come on," Mick says, shaking Vaughn out of his thoughts. "Let's get back to the office, take our victory lap."

Fifteen minutes later, Vaughn and Mick enter their building on Fifteenth and Market Streets and take the elevator to the twentieth floor. Vaughn is surprised to see that the firm's secretary, Angie, is not at the front desk. Walking down the hall, he sees that the paralegals aren't in their offices, either. When he turns the corner, Vaughn sees why: everyone is in Mick's office watching the large, wall-mounted, flat-screen TV.

Angie sees Vaughn and Mick and shakes her head. "It's awful."

Vaughn walks into the office with Mick behind him. He looks at the TV and is instantly jarred by the image on the screen: a zigzag of wrecked train cars. Most of the cars tilt dramatically or lie on their sides. One is upside down. Another is so obliterated it's impossible to tell which side is up. Ahead of the passenger cars, the engine is smashed into a giant yellow railroad machine, the two vehicles forming a *V* that straddles the track.

An army of police, firefighters, first responders, and railroad workers swarms the wreckage. Passengers are crawling out of windows—or being pulled out—and carried on stretchers or limping along on foot. Some lie on the ground covered, or half-covered, by coats and blankets.

The Chopper 6 camera zooms in on one of the tilting cars. The top half of a woman's motionless body hangs out a window. Her face, arms, and torso are covered in blood. Two men carefully pull the woman through the window and lay her on the ground. She doesn't move. One of the men kneels down and lifts her arm, takes her pulse. He looks at the other man and shakes his head. The other man drops to his knees over the woman's body. The camera pans out and scans the rest of the scene.

"Where exactly is this?" asks Mick.

"North Philly," says Jill, the senior paralegal. "The Torresdale curve. The train was going to New York."

"Oh, no. Susan!" Mick's face is white. "She was going to visit her mother in New York." He races for the phone on his desk. He dials and waits. "She's not answering her cell."

"I'll call her apartment," Angie says, running out of the room.

"We have her mother's number in New York somewhere on the computer," Vaughn says. "I'll look for it."

"Andrea and I can start calling the local hospitals," says Jill.

Vaughn rushes to his office and pulls up the contact-management software on his computer. He finds Susan's information and dials her mother's number in Manhattan.

Candace answers on the first ring. "Is this Mick?" she says. "Are you calling about the train? I was just about to call down there. I think Susan was on it. Oh my God."

"This is Vaughn Coburn, Mrs. Klein. I work for Susan. We're making calls now. As soon as we find something out, we'll call. I promise. If we hear from her in the meantime, we'll tell her to call you yourself."

"Oh God," Candace repeats.

Vaughn's phone buzzes as soon as he hangs up. It's Mick, calling everyone into the conference room.

"Let's do this calmly and methodically," Mick says. "Angie, you keep calling Susan's numbers—her cell and her apartment. Call Amtrak and see if they'll confirm that she was on the train, or that she wasn't.

"Jill, Andrea, you start calling the area hospitals. Temple, Aria, Hahnemann, Jefferson, and Einstein. Get to the ER departments and ask if a Susan Klein has been brought in."

"Maybe we should *go* to the hospitals," Vaughn offers. "I'm thinking the emergency rooms might be too overwhelmed to be fielding calls."

"Good point. You take Jefferson and Hahnemann. I'll go to Temple and Aria."

"We should have Tommy go to the crash site," Vaughn says. "He knows a lot of cops. Maybe they can give him information."

Mick nods. "Good point. I'll call him."

Fifteen minutes later, Vaughn enters the Thomas Jefferson University Hospital emergency room. It's bedlam. Scores of people pack the waiting area. Some are crying; others are pleading with the intake nurses. Many are on cell phones, talking with relatives. Everyone is terrified.

Vaughn makes his way to the front desk, impatiently waits his turn, then runs Susan's name by the frazzled intake nurse. She checks her computer screen, flips through some papers.

"I don't see her name. But that doesn't mean she's not here. She could have just come in. She could have been admitted without any ID. I'm sorry I can't be more definite, but—"

Vaughn thanks her and leaves for Hahnemann, where he finds the same scene. He tries Susan's cell and gets her voice mail. He calls Angie at the office.

"I'm so worried," Angie says. "She's not answering at her apartment or on her cell. I can't get through to Amtrak. Jill and Andrea can't reach anyone at the hospitals."

Vaughn thanks Angie and tells her to keep trying, then calls Tommy. He's already at the accident site.

"I talked to some cops," Tommy says, "but they can't give me any information. They're not letting anyone near the crash except for the rescue people."

Vaughn tells Tommy he's going to keep running back and forth between the hospitals. Tommy promises to stay put at the crash site until he hears something.

It's not until hours later that Vaughn gets word—from Mick. "She's at Frankford Hospital. I'm there now. An ER doctor told me she has some serious injuries, though nothing life threatening. She's going to be admitted, but no one's allowed to see her. All we can do right now is go home, get some rest, check up on her tomorrow. I'll call her mother right now and share the news."

"I'll call the office, let everyone know," Vaughn says. He hangs up and exhales. He hasn't been so shaken up in a long time.

Late that night, in his apartment, Vaughn feels unnerved. He's sitting on his couch in front of the TV and watching the aftermath of the crash play out on the news. CNN, Fox, MSNBC, and the big three networks are all waist deep in the story. All three have reporters at the crash site.

In the studios, the anchors grill their talking heads—the transportation, railroad, emergency, and other experts quickly lassoed to dispense their knowledge. All the while, video of the wreck, its victims, and the responders plays ceaselessly on the wall screens behind the anchor desks.

Vaughn stops channel surfing, picks up his laptop, and opens the YouTube app.

Already posted are a dozen passenger videos of the crash. Many were taken inside the railcars after they came to rest. They show people trying to make their way out of the wreckage: a man trying to force his way through a door that's almost horizontal, a woman crying as she crawls over a pair of bloodied legs extending from underneath the wreckage of a passenger seat, two male passengers trying to lift an older woman in a business suit who's sitting spread-eagle on the floor.

Other videos show passengers, dazed and bloodied, being walked to ambulances—next to others being wheeled on gurneys. Passengers are shown sitting and lying on the ground, some wearing oxygen masks while scores more are loaded into buses to be taken to a local school.

Vaughn closes his laptop and focuses again on the television. He watches the reporters interviewing passengers trying to describe what they've just endured. The words "nightmare" and "chaos" and "hell" are used repeatedly.

"One minute, everything was normal," one passenger, a man in a ripped business suit, tells a reporter. "The next thing I knew, there was loud banging and the train was shaking back and forth. Then we tipped over and people were falling on top of one another. And everything just went flying through the air—seats, baggage, laptops, cell phones, you name it."

Another passenger, a college student, tells a pretty blonde reporter that he was traveling with his brother. He tells the reporter his brother's name, asks if the reporter has come across him. She says sorry, but no, and quickly makes her way to someone else.

Watching it all play out, Vaughn is overwhelmed by the horror and loss of it all. *How the hell could this happen?*

He's pulled from his thoughts by the ringing of his cell phone. He lifts it from the couch and answers.

"Vaughn? Is this Vaughn?"

"Yes. Who's this?" He recognizes the voice but can't place it.

"It's Kate, Eddy's wife."

As soon as Vaughn hears Eddy's name, his chest constricts. He knows instantly why his cousin's wife is calling him. He can't believe he hadn't thought of Eddy as soon as he heard about the crash.

"We need your help," she says, her voice unsteady. "It was Eddy's train. Eddy was driving. He was the engineer."

Vaughn struggles to catch his breath. His mind starts spinning a hundred miles an hour.

"Eddy told me that if he was ever in trouble, real trouble, you'd be the one he would call. He said you'd help him."

"Where is he? Where are you?"

"I'm at the hospital. Thomas Jefferson. Eddy's just getting out of surgery. He's in a recovery room somewhere. I haven't seen him yet. The doctors say he's hurt real bad."

That his cousin is even alive seems miraculous, given the condition of the locomotive as he'd seen it on TV. The whole front end was bashed in. The windshield was gone, busted out completely from the impact with the giant yellow machine the engine crashed into.

"All right. I'm on my way. I can be there in about fifteen minutes," Vaughn says as he starts rushing around his apartment, turning off the TV and the lights. Then the lawyer part of his brain kicks in, and he stops. "Kate, listen. Do you know whether Eddy talked to anyone? Did he talk to the police?"

"I can't imagine that he did. The man from Amtrak who called me said Eddy was unconscious when they pulled him from the engine and didn't really come to afterward. He only knew to call me because I was Eddy's emergency contact with the railroad."

"Okay. I'll be there shortly. Do you need me to pick anything up for you on the way? Have you eaten anything?"

"I can't eat. Just get here, please. I'm so scared. I know they're going to try and blame this all on Ed. But it's not his fault. It can't be. He's a good engineer, Vaughn. He's always safe. I know in my heart he didn't do this."

Despite her calm words, Vaughn can hear the panic in Kate's voice. *I hope to hell she's right.*

But whether Eddy is at fault or not, Vaughn knows he's going to do everything in his power to help him.

Eddy and Vaughn were raised like brothers in North Philadelphia. Their fathers—John and Frank Coburn—were thick as thieves growing up, and they wanted their sons to share the same closeness, especially since each boy had two sisters. So they saw to it that Eddy and Vaughn, born a month apart, spent a lot of time together. The elder Coburns took their families for joint vacations down the shore, had frequent picnics and cookouts together, and always visited each other for the holidays. When the boys were thirteen, Frank, a cop, took a bullet to the knee and had to retire. He had been a boxer while in the navy, so he took some of his disability money and opened a boxing gym in Kensington. Frank and John decided it would be a good thing if the boys—both short and skinny—learned to box together. Vaughn and Eddy took to it like gangbusters. They trained hard, jumped rope, ran, lifted, hit the bags, then each other. They got older, tougher, faster, smarter, and bigger. And better, too, though not good enough to become real fighters. But they were fine with that; neither boy wanted to get beaten up for a living, and they were both smart enough that they wouldn't have to. They both got good grades at Central High and won acceptance to Temple University.

And then, with one stupid move, Vaughn derailed Eddy's life. Eddy went to prison. Then he went to hell. Vaughn went to law school.

2

Tuesday, June 17

On the way to the hospital, Vaughn calls Mick at home. It's after midnight and it takes Mick some time to answer. Vaughn quickly explains his cousin's situation and asks Mick if he's ever faced anything like it.

"No," Mick says. "But I know a lawyer who handles a lot of civil cases against the railroads, on behalf of injured employees. I'll call him and get back to you with what I find out."

Vaughn thanks Mick, apologizes for the late call, and hangs up.

The Uber drops off Vaughn in front of the hospital. He calls Kate, who tells him she's in a waiting area off the surgical intensive care unit on the seventh floor of the Gibbon Building. "They just brought Eddy up. Visiting hours are over, but they let me see him for a few minutes. He looks awful."

Vaughn can tell Kate's about to cry. "I'll be there in a minute. It's going to be okay."

When Vaughn exits the elevator, he sees Kate in the hallway and does a double take at the size of her belly. She sees him looking and says, "Eight months."

Vaughn didn't even know Eddy and Kate were expecting; he'd fallen out of regular touch with them once Eddy and Kate moved to north New Jersey a few years ago. Normally, he'd offer his congratulations but, given the circumstances, he just smiles uncomfortably. "Come on," he says, taking Kate's arm. "Let's go to the waiting room and get you off your feet."

Once they're seated, Vaughn asks Kate to tell him what she knows.

"Probably not much more than anyone else who's been watching the news. I only know that Eddy went to work in the morning and that he was going to drive one train south, from New York's Penn Station to Union Station in Washington, then drive another one back. He left the house about three—"

"In the morning?"

She nods. "Our place in New Jersey's about an hour outside Manhattan. Eddy's first train leaves New York at 4:40 a.m. He does the round-trip and usually gets back home by about four in the afternoon. Anyway, it was about 12:30 and I was dusting the living room when I saw on the TV that there had been a train crash. I freaked out and tried to call Eddy. When he didn't answer, I really freaked out and called his boss at Amtrak. He sounded upset and said that it might have been Eddy's train that crashed. He said he'd call me back as soon as he knew anything. He didn't call back, but an hour later two men from the railroad showed up at my front door. I got hysterical as soon as I saw them. I thought for sure they were going to tell me Eddy was dead. They didn't say that, but they couldn't tell me what kind of condition he was in—just that the engine was badly damaged, and the first responders hadn't been able to force their way inside yet. So they stayed with me, and we all waited for, like, three hours. The two men were on and off the phone the whole time. I called my mother and she came to my house and sat with us. Finally, one of the men got the call: Eddy was hurt but he was alive. My mother and I jumped in the car and drove here as fast as we could. She's getting us a hotel room right now."

Vaughn watches Kate closely as she machine-guns the story at him. A nervous person by nature, she's completely strung out right now. When she pauses to catch her breath, he says, "I have to ask you some questions about Eddy. Please don't take offense." Kate frowns, then nods okay. "First question: Is Eddy sober?" Vaughn's cousin had gone through hard times and had been an active alcoholic for a long stretch.

Kate doesn't hesitate. "Absolutely. He's been sober now for three years—since before we were married. No slipups."

"Good, good." Vaughn takes a breath. "Any other substance-abuse issues?"

"Zero."

"How about sleep? He gets up awful early. Has he been getting enough rest?" Vaughn remembers from speaking with Eddy a couple of years back that adequate rest time is a big issue on the railroad, that it's as important for railroad engineers as for truck drivers.

"Eddy is very conscientious about that. He's in bed by nine most nights."

Vaughn pauses, trying to think what other issues might come up in the investigation. "What about the type of engine Eddy was driving? And the run? Was he new to either?"

"He's been doing the same run for, like, two weeks now."

"Two weeks . . ." Vaughn repeats the words. It doesn't sound like a long time.

"As for the engine, I don't know. I never really thought about it. I mean, Amtrak would train him on whatever they had him drive. Wouldn't they?"

Vaughn is about to ask another question when Kate's cell phone rings.

"What?" she screeches at the caller. "I don't believe it. Just drive on past. Don't go inside." Kate hangs up, then looks at Vaughn. "That was my sister. She was going to pick up some clothes for me from our house. She says there are two news vans parked outside."

"Jesus," Vaughn says. If the reporters are outside, then Eddy's name has already been made public.

"They're going to hound us, aren't they?"

Vaughn nods. He knows the press all too well from his experience with high-profile criminal cases. As intrusive as the media can be in those situations, he knows they'll likely be ten times worse for a story as big as the train crash. On the far wall, the crash coverage plays and, before long, as Vaughn feared, the anchor pulls up Eddy's photograph and identifies him as the engineer of the doomed train.

"Oh, no. Oh, no." Kate puts her hand to her heart.

Vaughn walks over to the television and turns it off, then comes back to Kate. "You and Eddy are going to have to find somewhere else to live for a while. Someplace not too close to your home."

"Look at me." She places her hands on her belly. "I need to be near my obstetrician."

Kate starts to cry and Vaughn reaches out, gently touches her shoulders. "Kate, listen to me. You're going to have to be strong. For the baby, and for Eddy. Do you hear what I'm saying?"

"This isn't right," Kate says, her sadness turning to anger. "This should be a happy time for me and Eddy."

Vaughn lets Kate talk herself out, cradles her in his arms until they both nod off to sleep.

The first rays of sunlight are making their way over the horizon when Kate taps Vaughn's shoulder. "I'm going to walk down to Eddy's room and check on him," she says. "One of the nurses is going to let me."

Vaughn watches her leave, then turns on the TV. Anderson Cooper is at the crash site, interviewing a police officer as still photos of the wreckage flash on the other side of the split screen.

Vaughn decides to get himself and Kate some coffee. He takes the elevator down to the first floor and exits into the lobby, where he's approached by a short, heavyset man in an ill-fitting suit.

The man looks around as though he's checking to see if anyone is watching. "Are you a relative?"

"Excuse me?" Vaughn says.

"Are you here for the train victims?"

"Who are you?"

The man extends his hand, offering a business card. Vaughn takes it and sees it's for a local personal-injury lawyer. "We're the best firm in town when it comes to train accidents," the man says. "And we're going to make those Amtrak bastards pay for what they did to your . . . to all the passengers."

Vaughn turns away, exits the building, and walks to the Starbucks on Thirteenth and Chestnut.

Fifteen minutes later, he's back in the seventh-floor waiting room, sipping coffee with Kate. She tells him that because of brain swelling, the doctors are using drugs to keep Eddy in an induced coma.

Vaughn tells Kate he's going to the office. "I need to do some research, talk to some people. I'll come back here as soon as I can, later this morning."

Vaughn reaches into his pocket and pulls out some of his own business cards. "In the meantime, I want you to give my card to Eddy's nurses, or to anyone who might come up here and ask about him. You tell them that Eddy and you have representation, and that any questions for either of you are to be directed through my office. If someone you don't know comes up to you, don't tell them anything. Don't offer any information about Eddy, and don't answer any questions. Okay?"

Kate says she understands. They hug, and Vaughn leaves the waiting room. He takes the elevator again, and this time it stops before it reaches the lobby. An attractive young woman enters and stands next to him. She looks up at him with big blue eyes filled with empathy.

"Are you here for one of the passengers?" she says, extending her arm to offer a business card.

"Really?" Vaughn says, not moving to take it. "Already? You people can't even wait a full day?"

3

Tuesday, June 17, continued

A short time after he leaves the hospital, Vaughn is back at his desk, his eyes on his computer. Mick hasn't gotten back to him yet about the NTSB, so he decides to look it up on the Internet. What he sees when he opens up Google surprises him: paid legal ads soliciting for victims of the train crash. The titles include "Train Accident Lawyers," "Philadelphia Train Crash," "Philadelphia Train Crash Lawyers," and "Train 174 Accident."

The first ads are for two well-known Philadelphia personal-injury firms: Day and Lockwood and the Balzac Firm. Vaughn clicks the top listing, which takes him to Day and Lockwood's website. It opens on a page with the banner heading "Train 174 Information." The section describes the crash, then continues with a detailed exposition about rail transportation and an exhaustive review of US train crashes over the past hundred years, the role of the NTSB in investigating railroad disasters, and the Federal Railroad Administration's (FRA's) oversight of the rail industry.

Vaughn clicks out of the Day and Lockwood site and onto the ad for the Balzac Firm. Balzac's website also includes a discussion of the Train 174 accident that includes an overview of rail litigation and the railroad industry as detailed as that of the Day firm's, and Vaughn is impressed that they have been able to put together such compendious expositions in such a short time. He clicks on a few more ads, which lead to websites with much shallower discussions of the railroads. The only thing common to all the ads—something only someone looking really closely would notice—is that none of them include any claim that the law firm has ever actually handled a train accident before.

"Hey."

It's Mick, who knocks on the door as he enters. The clock at the bottom of Vaughn's computer screen tells him it's 7:30 a.m. "I just got off the phone with Derek Kalin. He's the lawyer I told you about who handles a lot of employee-injury cases against the railroads. He told me the accident will be investigated by the NTSB out of Washington. The way it works is the agency dispenses a 'go-team' consisting of specialists led by an investigator-in-charge, or IIC. The go-team is separated into different working groups, and they each partner with representatives of the railroad's track, signal, and operating divisions."

"When will that happen in this case?"

"It's already happened. The go-team has set itself up at a hotel near the airport. That's where they're interviewing most of the passengers and crew. There, and 30th Street Station."

"Does the crew have to speak with them?"

"Yes and no. The agency has subpoena power. But a person can invoke the Fifth and refuse to talk." Mick lets the words hang in the air. "What's Eddy's condition? Will he be able to talk to the investigators?"

"No idea. Kate says he's badly injured, but I don't know the details. I'm headed back over there now."

"Here," Mick says, handing Vaughn a piece of paper. "It's Derek Kalin's phone number. He has information for you on other passenger train crashes. Give him a call."

Vaughn thanks Mick, who says he's going to wait at the office until visiting hours at Aria Hospital, where he'll visit Susan.

Vaughn mentally kicks himself. He'd been so immersed in what was going on with Eddy that he'd forgotten about Susan. "Did you learn anything new since yesterday?"

"Her mother called me last night. Susan has a broken arm, two cracked ribs, and lots of bruising."

Vaughn exhales. "I'll join you up there after I see Eddy and Kate."

He leaves the office and heads back to Jefferson. The seventh-floor waiting area is packed when he arrives, but he doesn't see Kate. He finds her leaving intensive care. She looks sick.

"Eddy has swelling of the brain," she says, fighting back tears. "Plus, a ruptured spleen and a bruised liver. His right leg is broken in two places. And his face . . . it's all black and purple. The swelling is so bad, I hardly recognize him."

He hugs her gently—as best he can, given her swollen belly.

"Is he awake?"

She shakes her head. "They want to keep him sedated. So he won't move."

"Where is your mother?"

"She called from the hotel a little while ago."

"Okay. Why don't you go to the hotel yourself, get showered, and join her for something to eat? Maybe take a nap afterward?"

"I can't leave here."

"Yes, you can. And you need to. From the sound of his injuries, Eddy's going to be here awhile. If you're going to stick by him, you'll need your strength. And so will your baby."

Kate resists some more, but Vaughn eventually persuades her to leave. She starts to walk down the hall, then turns back. "Since you're going to represent Eddy, you're the one who should have these," she says, handing him a half dozen business cards. Day and Lockwood, the Balzac Firm, and others. He puts the cards in his pocket, thinking that they wouldn't have bothered with Kate if they had realized her husband was the engineer.

An hour later, Vaughn walks into Susan's room at Aria Hospital. Mick's already there. So is Angie.

Mick's brother, Tommy, the firm's investigator, is there, too. He's sitting on the HVAC unit in the window, his muscled arms crossed, a serious look on his face. He nods at Vaughn but doesn't say anything.

On the television, a local politician who'd been on the train describes the accident to Joe Scarborough and Mika Brzezinski on *Morning Joe*.

"Hey," Vaughn says to Susan, reaching out for her hand as he approaches the bed.

"Hey." She smiles.

"How do you feel?"

"Like I was in a train wreck." Her smile turns to a grimace, and Vaughn can see that she's in pain.

Vaughn looks over to Mick, who says, "Susan was just sharing with Angie and me what it was like after her railcar came to a stop." Vaughn glances at Susan, who looks first to Mick, then to Angie, then to Vaughn. She takes a deep breath.

"I was completely disoriented. The car was on its side, so the ceiling became the wall on my left, and the seats were hanging sideways on the right, though some had crashed down. When I came to, I was sitting on a busted-up window. Along with glass, there was ballast—railroad rock—everywhere. It came flying into the car once it flipped onto the side. It was like shrapnel. A lot of people were hit by it. I think that's how I got the gashes on my forehead." Susan pauses, leans over, picks up a cup of water, and drinks. Then she sets down the cup and continues.

"Everyone in the car had blood on them. Everyone's clothes were torn. Some people were standing, helping other people get up. Some were crawling. Some were just sitting there in a daze. I'll never forget one of them. It was a woman. I'd noticed her getting onto the train. She was blind and she had a seeing-eye dog, a German shepherd. She was very well dressed, in a business suit with expensive shoes. I remember thinking that I admired her, that it mustn't be easy making your way in the world as a blind person. But she'd obviously done very well for herself. She took a seat across the aisle from me, in a chair that faced me. Her dog sat right by her." Susan closes her eyes for a moment, to gather herself.

"When everything came to a stop and my eyes cleared, I saw her. She was sitting on the floor, leaning against the wall. She tried to stand, started reaching around to grab onto something to help lift herself up. The whole time, she was calling out, 'Clyde! Clyde!' I was confused at first because I thought she'd been traveling alone. Then I remembered—the dog. She was crying out for her dog. I looked up and down the railcar, hoping to spot him for her. But he wasn't there. The dog was gone. He was just . . . gone." Susan begins to cry, and Mick and Vaughn each take hold of one of her hands. Angie strokes her hair.

When Susan's sobs subside, everyone directs their attention to the television, where the NTSB is conducting its first press briefing. One of the NTSB's five board members, Richard Olin, stands before a forest of TV news microphones emblazoned with their identifying logos: Fox News, Fox 29, Channel 6/ABC, 10/NBC. A tall man, broad shouldered, with salt-and-pepper hair, Olin is flanked by six members of the NTSB go-team. Like him, some are wearing short-sleeve polo shirts with the NTSB logo; others wear the NTSB pullover jackets or emergency vests.

Olin begins by introducing himself and giving a short synopsis of his experience. He takes a moment to extend his sympathies to the victims of the crash and their families. Vaughn listens closely, and he can tell that Olin is sincere; the man clearly cares for the people whose lives have been shattered by the tragedy, and he is serious about the business at hand.

Olin explains that the NTSB is the federal agency whose mission is to investigate accidents, determine the causes, if possible, and issue safety recommendations to help prevent similar accidents in the future. "Our purpose at the crash site is to gather 'perishable' evidence." Olin defines this as "evidence that would become unavailable with the passage of time." Olin identifies the investigator-in-charge as Nelson Wexler and states that Wexler and the rest of the go-team will investigate every aspect of the crash: the track, the train—including its braking system, recorders, and mechanical condition—personnel, and procedures.

Olin pauses, then gets down to it. "What we know right now is as follows: At 12:06 yesterday afternoon, Amtrak Train 174, a Northeast Regional, left Philadelphia's 30th Street Station. The consist included one locomotive—an ACS-64 built for Amtrak by Siemens—followed by six coach cars, the first two of which were the business-class and quiet cars. Eleven minutes after leaving 30th Street, the train, traveling on Track 2, entered the Torresdale curve in Northeast Philadelphia. The maximum permissible speed through the curve is eighty miles an hour, and the train had, in fact, slowed to eighty going into the curve, and maintained that speed through the curve and onto the straightaway. Approximately fifteen seconds after leaving the curve and traveling eighteen hundred feet down the straightway, it appears the locomotive struck an Amtrak TracVac excavating machine.

"The TracVac was a brand-new machine used to perform a number of maintenance functions including the excavation and removal of dirt and ballast. The machine was one hundred and ten feet long, ten feet wide, fifteen feet high, weighed ninety tons, and was painted bright yellow. Amtrak had recently purchased the TracVac to replace similar machines owned and operated by a company Amtrak subcontracted to.

"A preliminary download of the locomotive's event recorder, the 'black box,' shows that before the crash the engineer did not apply either the emergency brakes or the regular braking system. Of course, an important part of our investigation will be to determine why."

Olin pauses for a moment, during which Vaughn glances at Mick, whom he finds looking at him. They're clearly both wondering the same thing: *Did Eddy really not try to stop the train?*

Olin explains that the TracVac was being used by the track department. It had been making ongoing repairs to a section of Track 1, which had been out of service for two days. The day before, no work had been done because most of the crew was sent to the Harrisburg line for emergency repair work. The machine should therefore have been parked on Track 1; why it wasn't was a mystery.

Olin opens himself up to questions. Because the questioners do not themselves have microphones, Olin has to repeat their questions before answering them. "The first question," he says, "pertains to the number of victims." Olin takes a deep breath. "There were two hundred and seventy-eight people on the train, including five crew members. As of now, there are twenty-nine confirmed deaths and two hundred injuries of varying degrees of severity."

The next question is why the engineer would not have seen the giant, bright-yellow, ninety-ton track machine and applied his brakes.

"That will, of course, be a main inquiry in our investigation."

"And what was the TracVac doing on a live track in the first place?" another questioner asks. Olin repeats the question and answers that this, too, will be a main part of the investigation.

Olin looks to his left and listens as another muffled voice asks a question. "The next question is whether the train had any cameras that would show the crash. And the answer is that the train had both a forward-facing video recorder and an inward-facing video recorder. The forward-facing recorder captures the track ahead. The inward-facing recorder films the engineer. Unfortunately, Amtrak and the engineer's labor union are currently in the midst of contract negotiations, so the cameras were turned off pending an agreement about their use."

In response to this last point, a chorus of moans wafts through the air.

Another question is asked off camera. Olin listens, then says, "The question is whether we have spoken with the engineer. Interviewing the crew—and passengers, of course—is a top priority. The engineer, however, was badly hurt in the crash and remains hospitalized. I just learned before the press conference that he has obtained legal representation, and our IIC will be reaching out to his attorney this morning."

Olin pauses to listen, then says, "The questioner asks what I can tell you about the engineer's experience and history with Amtrak. The engineer's name, as many of you know by now, is . . ."

Mick lowers the volume just as Olin begins talking about Eddy. Then he exchanges glances with Vaughn. "Susan, Vaughn has something he needs to tell you."

"The engineer's my cousin," Vaughn says. "His wife asked me to help them through this."

It seems to take Susan a long time to process what Vaughn has told her. When she finally grasps it, she doesn't look happy. "Honestly, I don't know how I feel about that." She turns away wearily.

"I understand. I really do," he says. "I don't know how I feel about it myself." He doesn't explain why he *has* to help Eddy, at least with the NTSB. How he owes his cousin. That would open a can of worms he doesn't want to share with anyone—expose a secret that's been buried for sixteen years. "I'll need to talk to him. See what he says."

Susan turns back toward Vaughn. "So talk to him. See what he tells you. Then we'll all discuss it. You, me, and Mick."

"It may very well pose a conflict," Mick says. "You representing the engineer, and Susan being an injured passenger."

There's a knock at the door. Everyone turns to see an older man, well dressed, professorial. "Hey, everyone," he begins, his voice serious and folksy at once, "I know this is a terrible time for all of you. I wouldn't bother you if it weren't urgent. There's word that Amtrak claim agents are scouring the halls, trying to get injured passengers into giving statements that would seriously undermine their rights, and—"

Mick raises his arm. "That won't be a problem. You're looking at a roomful of lawyers."

"Including me," Susan says, her voice making clear that it's time for the intruder to leave. He does so, and they hear him move to the next room down, where he knocks on the door.

"Is it legal for law firms to send runners to hospital rooms?" asks Angie.

Vaughn shakes his head. "Not even close."

4

TUESDAY, JUNE 17, CONTINUED

Mick and Tommy stay behind with Susan while Vaughn and Angie Uber back to Center City. As soon as they enter the firm's offices, paralegals Jill and Andrea and file clerk Ivana approach them in the lobby to find out how Susan is doing. Vaughn describes Susan's injuries and tells them she's in pain but her injuries will heal. He leaves Angie to share Susan's account of the crash. As soon as he sits down behind his desk, his phone rings and Angie tells him that Nelson Wexler of the NTSB is on the line.

Vaughn takes a deep breath and lifts the receiver.

"Mr. Coburn, we understand from Mr. Coburn's wife . . . Well, let me ask you first, are the two of you related?"

"He's my cousin."

There's a pause at the other end of the line, then Wexler continues. "Edward's wife told our investigators at the hospital that you are representing him. Is that correct?"

"It is."

"You understand that ours is not a criminal investigation. We're just trying to gather information to determine the cause of the accident and, ultimately, make some recommendations as to how to prevent this kind of thing from happening again."

"That's what Mr. Olin said at the press conference," Vaughn replies, though he knows it doesn't take a genius to foresee that any serious fault on Eddy's part could very well lead to prosecution, with so many people dead and badly injured.

"So I assume you'll have no problem producing Mr. Coburn for an interview."

"I certainly have every intention of cooperating fully with the investigation. Before I'll agree to make my client available, though, I'll have to talk with him myself. I haven't been able to do so because he's not regained consciousness since the accident. In the meantime, perhaps you wouldn't mind answering a few questions that I have."

"Such as?"

"Whether you found anything in my client's blood. I assume you've had it tested by now."

Wexler doesn't say anything.

"This has to be a two-way street," Vaughn says.

"Up to a point," the IIC says. He sighs. "Your cousin's blood came up clean. No controlled substances or alcohol."

Vaughn breathes a sigh of relief. "Thank you. I appreciate your sharing that."

"You were worried?" asks Wexler.

Vaughn hesitates briefly, then says, "Absolutely not." He's certain that Wexler picked up on the slight delay.

"Will you agree to have your client sign a HIPAA form, to give us access to his medical records?"

"I don't see why that would be necessary, given that his blood came up clean."

Wexler, a new hardness in his voice, says, "Mr. Coburn, it is absolutely imperative that we find out the cause of this tragedy. We have to exhaust all avenues of information, leave no stone unturned. Your client may not have been under the influence at the time of the accident, but for all we know he had a medical condition that caused him to lose consciousness. That's all we'd be looking for, really."

Vaughn considers this and tells the IIC that he'll discuss it with his cousin, if and when he regains consciousness. "In the meantime, I hope you're looking into how that TracVac came to be on a live track."

"Absolutely. We're pursuing that as well. We're looking at everything, just as board member Olin said in his press conference."

Vaughn and Wexler probe each other a few more minutes before Vaughn ends the conversation with a promise to call the IIC once he's had a chance to speak to Eddy. He leans back in his chair and closes his eyes. He's only slept a couple of hours in the past two days, and he's exhausted. But there's no time for rest, so he forces himself to open his eyes and stand. As soon as he does so, the phone rings and he presses the button for the speaker. It's Angie, telling him that ten calls came in while he was on the phone. "Producers from the news shows for Channels 3, 6, and 10, and Fox 29. Someone from Fox News. A freelancer who writes for the *Daily Beast*. Chris Matthews from MSNBC—he wanted me to make sure you knew he's from Philadelphia. And Wolf Blitzer, who wanted me to make sure you knew he's . . . Wolf Blitzer."

Vaughn drops his head. "Wonderful. Just wonderful." He pauses and thinks for a minute. "That didn't add up to ten."

Angie inhales. "There were two more. A woman called and claimed she had 'dirt' on Eddy. Said she'd keep it quiet if we paid her. The last person was a guy. He said he had relatives on the train, and if Eddy didn't fess up, he was going to . . . to . . . kill him."

"A *death threat*? Seriously?"

"He sounded serious. Should I call the police?"

"Absolutely. I can't have people calling here and making threats. Make sure Mick knows, too. And Tommy. Definitely tell him. Thanks."

Mick's brother, Tommy McFarland, served hard time in prison. Still has the prison tats to prove it. And is as solid as a brick wall. Tommy's the kind of guy you want covering your back if things get bad. And, as the firm's private investigator, Tommy has done exactly that. Many times.

Vaughn sinks back in his chair and rubs his eyes. *This thing is only one day old and already it's getting nuts.* He walks to Mick's office, where he finds Jill and Andrea positioned before the television. It's tuned to CNN, and the anchor is reporting that the NTSB has just released the names of the—now thirty-one—dead passengers. They include businesspeople, teachers, college students, a pregnant mother of three, an aspiring actress, and a retired New York police captain, among others. Many of their photos appear on the screen as their names are read. None of the names or pictures is familiar to Vaughn until the anchor reads the last name: Alexander Nunzio.

"Jesus," Vaughn says. He looks at Angie, who has joined them. Her face is white.

Alexander Nunzio is the twentysomething son of notorious Philly underboss James Nunzio, a.k.a. Jimmy Nutzo, one of the most bloodthirsty gangsters in the city's rich history of organized crime. Angie's a South Philly girl, and Vaughn has no problem reading the message on her face: Eddy'd better not be to blame for that crash.

But wait . . . Why would Jimmy Nutzo's kid be riding a train? Could his presence have played a part in the wreck? Could he have been a target? Vaughn shakes his head. It doesn't matter why. The kid is dead, and if Eddy has any real culpability, he'll find himself in a vise with the law on one side and outlaws on the other.

Back in his own office, Vaughn lifts the phone and dials Derek Kalin, whom Mick said had some background for him on past train crashes. They introduce themselves, and Kalin tells Vaughn there are three important and relatively recent cases he needs to know about.

"The first is the 2008 Chatsworth crash. There, a Metrolink commuter train collided head-on with a Union Pacific freight train in Southern California. Twenty-five people were killed, and dozens were injured. The NTSB decided two things caused the crash. The first was the engineer's failure to see and stop at a red signal because he was texting on his cell phone. The second was the lack of a positive train-control system that would have stopped the train short of the red signal."

Vaughn takes a deep breath. "And what did they do to the engineer?"

"Nothing. He was killed in the crash. The engineer also died in a second Metrolink accident in 2015. That train hit a pickup truck that'd become stuck on the tracks. The engineer appeared to have done nothing wrong." Kalin pauses here to take a drink of water.

"The third crash," Kalin says, "occurred in 2013 in the Bronx. A Metro-North train derailed when it raced around a sharp curve at eighty-two miles an hour. The speed limit on the curve was thirty. Four people died and seventy were injured."

"And the engineer?"

"Survived the crash. He claimed that he'd gone into a 'trance' before reaching the curve, and that he remembered nothing about the crash itself. It was later determined that he had undiagnosed sleep apnea, and the Bronx district attorney's office decided not to prosecute."

"I don't think anything like that came into play here," Vaughn says. The only times he's ever heard of his cousin passing out were when relatives told stories about Eddy being blind drunk. But the NTSB tested his cousin's blood, and it was clean.

The call ends and Vaughn sits back in his chair, thinking about the engineer in the Chatsworth crash. The one on the phone.

Were you talking on the phone, Eddy? Were you texting?

5

WEDNESDAY TO FRIDAY, JUNE 18–20

For Vaughn, Wednesday and Thursday rush by in a blur. The NTSB's IIC, Wexler, calls the office several times, trying to reach Vaughn to see if Eddy is awake and able to talk. More law firms post Google ads soliciting victims of the crash. Vaughn scours the Internet to learn what he can about the type of locomotive Eddy was driving and about the track machine the train crashed into. He even researches sleep apnea to see if it really could cause someone to simply lose consciousness.

The cable news channels continue their relentless coverage of the crash. The newest angle is that no one at Amtrak can explain how the TracVac came to be on Track 2 instead of Track 1, where it was supposed to have been stored while its crew was called to the Harrisburg line for emergency repairs. NTSB member Richard Olin offers this update at his Wednesday-morning press conference. Hours later, the mayor of Philadelphia goes before the cameras and criticizes Amtrak for lax safety procedures with regard to the TracVac. Then he rips into Eddy, saying, "There's no doubt the train's engineer was acting recklessly. He absolutely should've seen that huge track machine, and he absolutely should've stopped his train. There's no excuse in the world, absolutely none, for his actions."

On Wednesday afternoon, Vaughn makes his daily trip to Eddy's hospital room, where he encounters Eddy's parents and his two sisters—Vaughn's aunt, uncle, and cousins—his own parents, plus Kate's parents and siblings.

Later, in the hallway, Vaughn tells Angie over the phone, "You'd never know from the crowd and flowers that Eddy is the most hated man on the Eastern Seaboard."

Vaughn hangs up and is joined by Eddy's wife and Eddy's parents, who press him for details about the NTSB investigation and whether their son will face criminal charges. He tells them that everything is up in the air. "The NTSB's mission is to gather information and determine the probable cause of the accident. The agency doesn't bring criminal charges. But that doesn't mean that the DA or the FBI couldn't prosecute Eddy if evidence turns up showing that he was criminally negligent."

"That's ridiculous," Eddy's mother, Claire, says.

"Eddy would never take chances with his train," Kate chimes in. "Do you know he won a safety award last year?"

Vaughn exchanges glances with Eddy's father, Frank, and the two men walk down the hallway. Frank tells Vaughn in a quiet voice, "If you do find out something bad, give me a call. Me, not Claire. I don't want her to hear it on the news. I want her to hear it from me. You understand?"

Vaughn nods nervously. He's always been intimidated by his uncle. Frank Coburn is a big man, and serious. Vaughn can't recall Frank smiling more than twice in all the time he's known the man. A year older than Vaughn's father, Frank Coburn is the undisputed leader of the family. An ex-cop, Frank is the one family members go to when they have issues they can't resolve themselves—including when their kids get into trouble with the law.

"Yes, sir. I definitely understand."

Thursday evening, Vaughn's phone rings. It's Kate. "Eddy can talk tomorrow," she tells him. "They took him off the narcotics, and he's been awake since this afternoon. I asked him, and he says he's ready to talk to you." Here, Kate pauses. "He's really upset. He's learned about the crash from the TV, and he's blaming himself."

"Learned? Meaning . . . ?"

"He doesn't remember the crash. I asked the doctor, and he said that sometimes when someone has a head injury, they can't remember things."

Vaughn rubs his eyes with his free hand. He'd hoped that Eddy might have an explanation for why he didn't notice the track machine and stop his train. His cousin's amnesia would make things more complicated. And harder on Eddy.

"I've heard about that happening, too," he tells Kate. "And I certainly understand why he's upset. Just keep doing your best to reassure him, and tell him I'll be there tomorrow."

The next morning, Vaughn climbs out of bed after a fitful night. It's going to be a challenging day. First, he's going to have to talk to his cousin, get as much information as he can, and tell Eddy what he's facing. He also has to make a decision whether to let the NTSB question his cousin and to let IIC Wexler know what the decision is. And he has to feel out Mick and Susan on the whole issue of his representing Eddy. The past couple of days have made it clear to him that he's on thin ice, at least with Susan. She had come back to work on Wednesday with her arm in a cast and still in pain. When Vaughn went to her office to see how she was doing, she acted coolly toward him. He shared that with Mick, who said that Susan was still shaken by the crash and wasn't comfortable with their firm representing the engineer. "Quite frankly," Mick had told him, "unless something develops that shows Eddy to be completely blameless, I don't think Susan'll ever warm to you representing him."

Vaughn showers, dresses, and heads into the office. Visiting hours for the critical care unit don't begin until 11:00 a.m., and he wants to give Kate and Eddy some time to get ready to see him, in any event. He figures he can put in a couple of hours at work before heading to the hospital. He has other cases that he has to catch up on.

The look he sees on Angie's face as he opens the door to the office lobby tells him his morning isn't going to go as planned.

"You better go right back to Mick's office," Angie says. "Something's happened."

Mick and Susan are both there when he arrives; Mick at his desk, Susan in one of the visitor's chairs. They're both staring at the television. The split screen shows a CNN anchor on the left describing a horrific car crash, while on the right are photos of a police cruiser smashed head-on into a tree and a Ford Mustang bent-elbowed around another.

Vaughn shakes his head. "*Damn.* I knew this would come out. I just didn't know it'd be so soon. I should have gotten out in front of this."

"Eddy killed a police officer?" Susan looks at Vaughn, her voice thick with accusation.

"It was an accident," Vaughn says.

"He was drag racing," Susan counters. "The officer came upon him. Eddy and the patrolman both crashed. The officer died."

Vaughn closes his eyes, takes a breath. "I know. It was awful. Eddy was eighteen. He went to prison for three years."

"The reporter says that even before the accident, his nickname in high school was 'Fast Eddy.' I guess he had some kind of speed addiction?" She's glaring at Vaughn.

Of course that's how the press is painting it. But it's not fair. "He got that because of track. He was a sprinter on the track team."

Mick flips the channel to MSNBC, then to Fox. Both are running the same story. Vaughn knows it will headline tomorrow's *Inquirer* and *Daily News*. It's probably already on their web editions.

Mick's phone rings. He presses the speakerphone button. It's Angie. "Mick? Is Vaughn still in there?"

"I'm here," Vaughn says.

"Matt Lauer's on the phone. He wants to talk to you."

Fuck Matt Lauer. "No press calls."

Vaughn tells Mick and Susan he has to get to the hospital. If Eddy was upset last night, he's going to be beside himself now.

The minute Vaughn leaves the building, his cell phone rings. It's Kate. She's rambling at a hundred miles an hour. It takes Vaughn the whole ride to the hospital to calm her. Two minutes after Vaughn hangs up, he's racing through critical care. It's still well before visiting hours, but he doesn't care. The nurses don't seem to care, either; no one stops him.

When Vaughn finally enters his cousin's room, he finds Kate standing over Eddy, leaning down to hug him. Eddy's breathing is labored. His right leg is casted and raised into an elevated position. He has an IV and a catheter draining urine into a plastic bag attached to his bed. And Kate wasn't kidding about Eddy's face; it's the shape and color of a dark plum.

Vaughn waits a minute, then moves toward the bed. His cousin and Kate look up at him, and Eddy goes right at the car-crash story.

"It's not right they should bring that up," he says, working hard to push the words out of his misshapen mouth. "That happened sixteen years ago. And it wasn't my fault, you know that. They're making it sound like I deliberately ran that cop off the road. Like I'm some kind of cowboy engineer. I'm the safest guy out there. I don't take chances. You can ask anyone who works with me."

Eddy grimaces and falls silent, all the talking taking its toll.

"I know, buddy," Vaughn says, putting his hand on his cousin's relatively unscathed arm. "Kate told me you won a safety award."

"That's right," Kate says.

She proceeds to vent for another couple of minutes, and Vaughn lets her. He can only imagine what she and his cousin must be going through. He's going to have to be as sensitive as possible dealing with them. The whole family.

"I hear you," he begins. "The press are jackals. All they care about is ratings. Ratings and filling their airtime. They're going to climb all over each other to dig up dirt and play up every possible angle. That's what they do, and everyone knows it." Vaughn pauses to let his words sink in. "The thing is," he resumes, "you can't let it get to you. They don't know you—"

"That's right," Kate says. "They don't. And nobody watching knows him, either. So they're all going to believe this crap."

"Not the people who matter—family, friends, coworkers. Certainly not me."

Eddy grabs for breath, then says, "It wouldn't be so bad if I could just explain what happened. But I can't remember. I can't remember the crash. I can't remember coming up on that track machine. I can't even remember going into the curve. There has to be some reason I didn't stop the train. But I search my mind and all I come up with is shadows. It's all in my head, man. I know it is. I just can't find it."

Eddy drops his head, and tears begin streaming down his cheeks. Vaughn tells Kate he'll give them a few minutes together. He leaves critical care, uses the hallway bathroom near the elevators. As he exits, he's approached by a well-dressed man in his twenties.

"Are you all right?" the man asks. "You look upset."

"To say the least."

"It's been tough—on all of us," the man says.

Vaughn's about to ask the man whom he's there to see, but he's beaten to the punch.

"You're visiting someone from the train crash?"

"Yeah. You?"

"Quite a few," the man says as he extends his hand, offers up the business card. "A bunch of people have asked my firm to represent them. We're the best train-crash firm in the city, and—"

"For chrissake." Vaughn smacks away the man's arm and brushes past him.

Reentering Eddy's room, Vaughn tells Eddy that he's already spoken to the NTSB. "They told me your blood test was clear of alcohol and controlled substances. So you're good on that front. Now, what about your phone?"

Eddy and Kate exchange glances, then Eddy says, "What about my phone?"

"Is there any chance you were talking on the phone at the time of the accident? Or texting?" he adds, remembering the Chatsworth crash.

Eddy pauses. "My phone was in my knapsack, on the conductor's chair next to me. And it was off. Haven't they found it?"

"I don't know," Vaughn says, making a mental note to ask Nelson Wexler the next time they speak. "Any chance you have a medical condition that could've caused you to pass out? Or maybe you were sleepy?"

"No. And no."

"I already told you that," Kate interjects.

"I know, and I believed you. I just needed to hear it from Ed's own mouth, that's all."

Vaughn keeps on for another hour, questioning Eddy about everything he does remember about Monday. When he got out of bed and how much sleep he had. What he had for breakfast. What kind of mood he was in. Whether he'd fought with anyone that day. Whether he was upset by anything, preoccupied, or distracted for any reason. "Was there anything at all on your mind other than your job?"

"Hell yes, there was," Eddy answers, nodding at Kate's swollen belly. "My wife was eight months pregnant, and my run was taking me two hundred miles away. And, sure, that was on my mind. But it didn't distract me from my job. I followed protocol, dotted all my *i*'s and crossed all my *t*'s. Like I always do."

Vaughn nods, jots some more notes onto his legal pad.

"Who are *they*?" asks Kate, looking up at the TV.

Vaughn and Eddy follow her gaze. Vaughn walks over and turns the volume back up. The two men, it turns out, are a pair of well-known Philadelphia personal-injury attorneys. They sit elbow to elbow at a gleaming glass conference table behind microphones from Fox 29, and Channels 6, 3, and 10. The lawyer on the left, Geoffrey Day, sits ramrod straight in his chair. He's thin, with a ring of gray hair on the sides and back of his otherwise-bald head. Wearing a light-gray suit with a dark-gray tie and peering through gray-framed glasses, he looks more like an accountant than a personal-injury attorney. An accountant, or, from the look on his face, a middle-school teacher about to scold someone. To Day's right sits his polar opposite, Benjamin Balzac, a powerful-looking, heavyset man with a large head, thick black hair and beard, and brooding dark eyes.

Taking turns with their statements, the pair announces that they represent a number of victims of the train crash and that they intend to file a large group of cases in federal court. For the rest of the press conference, they take cheap shots at Eddy and at Amtrak.

"The primary cause of the accident," Day says with the dry certainty of someone stating the time, "was the engineer's inexcusable inattentiveness."

"There's no question that, had he been doing his job and paying attention," Balzac adds in his slow, baritone voice, "he would have seen the hundred-foot-long TracVac and stopped his train."

"The engineer's conduct," says Day, "was incomprehensible—"

"Criminal," Balzac adds. "And sadly consistent with his deadly driving history, which must certainly have been known, and flagrantly ignored, by Amtrak."

"Which brings us to the railroad's detestable and deadly choice to employ as an engineer an ex-convict with a history that proves he is addicted to speed, reckless with other people's lives, and perfectly willing to make other people pay the ultimate price for his mistakes. As the family of Officer Gonzales knows all too well," Day adds, offering the name of the police officer killed in the car crash sixteen years earlier.

"All in all," concludes Balzac, "the whole tragedy was an exercise in outrageous conduct, both by Amtrak and by its criminally culpable engineer."

Vaughn walks to the television and shuts it off. Turning back to the bed, he sees Kate stroking Eddy's lowered head with her left hand and rubbing her belly with her right, her eyes wet.

"Don't let those two get to you," Vaughn tells them. "They're just a pair of P.I. hacks grandstanding for the press. Drumming up headlines to reel in more clients."

Vaughn knows what he's saying is true, and he figures that, at some level, Eddy and Kate probably do, too. But the lawyers' words must still feel like gut punches to them. He spends some more time trying to reassure them, then takes his leave.

Vaughn leaves the hospital, and on the way back to the office he actually smiles at the transparency of Balzac's and Day's performances. *Paper tigers.* Still, he wonders why they're pushing so hard on Eddy specifically when it's Amtrak that has the deep pockets.

In any event, the press conference has given him an excuse to call someone he hasn't seen in a while. Someone who's been on his mind.

6

Friday, June 20, continued

As soon as he leaves the hospital, Vaughn pulls out his cell and dials the number from memory.

"Well, well. Vaughn Coburn," the woman says when she answers.

"How—"

"Caller ID."

"I'm surprised you answered."

"Don't be a smart-ass."

"I need your help."

She pauses. "I'm listening."

"Not over the phone," Vaughn says. Then he suggests they meet after work. "How about El Vez?"

"Butcher and Singer," she counters.

"Pricey."

"You're paying."

"Of course."

They hang up, and Vaughn smiles. *Erin Doyle.* It's been months since he last saw her, at a bench-bar conference. They had spoken for only a few minutes—just long enough for him to get ideas. But Erin had cut the conversation short, saying she had to go back to her office.

Vaughn sighs.

He was smitten the first time he'd laid eyes on her. It was the fall semester of his second year in law school. Erin, also in her second year, transferred to Temple from Widener. He made a number of passes at her, some subtle, others so brazen they bordered on slapstick. Finally, when Vaughn had all but given up, Erin made her own pass, and they quickly became an item. The first time they went out, he learned she'd grown up in a small town just outside of Boston and graduated from Boston University.

"Why Widener?" he asked. "If you wanted to come south, why not start out at Temple?"

"Widener was the only school that accepted me."

This surprised him. "BU was so tough that you couldn't get the grades? Or was it attendance issues?"

She smiled. "My attendance was great. At concerts."

Vaughn and Erin were hot and heavy for six months. Then came the summer. Erin went to Europe for a clerkship in a big American law firm with an office in London while Vaughn stayed in Philly and worked for a community legal service. They kept in touch during the break, but their calls grew less frequent as the weeks passed, until they eventually stopped calling each other altogether. When Erin returned to Philadelphia for the fall semester, they tried to rekindle things, but it didn't work. Erin talked on and on about visiting the great cities of Europe, the museums, the restaurants, the theaters. All Vaughn had to offer were his small trials representing the indigent. The sex was still good, if somewhat subdued, but there was a space between them that neither knew how to fill. So they split up. What made it worse was that Erin hooked up with Corey King, the son of a six-term congressman from western Pennsylvania who basked in his family's status as small-town royalty. King was also tall and handsome, one of those guys who seemed to exude charisma. And, like Erin, King went to work right out of law school for Geoffrey Day.

It's close to 7:00 p.m. when Vaughn enters the restaurant. Erin is waiting at the bar, and Vaughn pauses to take her in. She's wearing a crisp, blue business suit that accentuates her tall and toned physique. Her thick black hair is silky and drapes over her shoulders. From the side, he sees her strong jawline and the small profile of her nose. And when she turns her head in his direction, he sees the feature that never fails to amaze him: her eyes. Erin's eyes are the brightest green he's ever seen. They seem to give off their own light, sometimes to the degree that they could be fairly said to blaze.

Vaughn sidles up to her. "Macallan twelve year?" he asks, nodding at Erin's glass. The summer she lived in Europe, she developed a taste for single-malt scotch.

"You take me for a troglodyte? It's fifteen."

"I'll have a Blue Moon," Vaughn tells the bartender. "Just the bottle, not the glass."

As soon as the beer arrives, Vaughn pays the tab and they move to a booth along the east wall, beneath a cartoon print of dogs dressed up like humans and socializing at a bar. They exchange some small talk until the waiter comes and takes their orders. Then Vaughn gets down to business.

"I saw your boss's press conference," he says. "With Balzac. I get that they're trying to drum up business. But how does it help them to paint Eddy as an outright villain? Simple negligence on Eddy's part puts Amtrak on the hook for damages."

"For compensatory damages, sure." Erin pauses to sip her scotch. "The injured passengers' pain and suffering, economic losses, medical care, loss of limbs, disfigurement. Loss of life. And those damages will be vast. But there's an even bigger fish to reel in: punitive damages."

"But there's a cap on what Amtrak can be forced to pay," Vaughn says. "Two hundred million for all the claims combined, from what I read. And the injuries to the passengers are likely well above that already, at least that's what all the talking heads are saying. A jury award of punitive damages would be an empty victory."

Erin shakes her head. "So pretty you are, and so naïve. Caps can be raised."

"Not this one. There've been big train crashes before, and the victims had no luck persuading Congress to increase the cap."

"But this is Geoffrey Day and Benjamin Balzac you're talking about. Were you aware that the sons of two US senators work with me at Day and Lockwood? That Day's partner is the former governor? That Day and Balzac have each hosted fund-raisers in their houses for presidential candidates? That cap is going to rise, Vaughn, and when it does, the hate that Day and Balzac garner for your cousin will add eight figures to their treasure troves."

Erin seems to have more to say, but she stops herself. The amusement drains from her eyes, which are suddenly sad. "Vaughn, I'm sorry. For Eddy. For you. For . . . all of it."

Vaughn leans back, empties his bottle, and looks away.

They sit in silence for a while, until Erin says, "I know you come from the criminal side. You still do mostly criminal defense, right?"

Vaughn nods.

"Well, let me tell you a little about how civil practice works. Civil litigation is dominated from the top by a handful of glamour firms run by guys like Geoffrey Day. They get the biggest cases, so they win the biggest verdicts and settlements. They splash their windfalls on their websites and in the *Legal Intelligencer*. The small-firm lawyers read the headlines. When a big case walks into their doors, they're quick to hand it off to the Days and the Balzacs for the promise of fat, easy referral fees. The cases generate more huge verdicts and settlements and headlines, and the circle of life goes round and round."

"And they live like princes. Mansions, yachts, airplanes. I know. My bosses have referred cases to P.I. firms," he says.

"And don't forget the biggest trophies of all: the law schools."

Vaughn nods. "Starting with our own alma mater."

Twenty years earlier, Philadelphia trial attorney Jim Beasley pledged $20 million to Temple University, in return for which the Temple University School of Law became the Temple University *Beasley* School of Law. More recently, one of Beasley's protégés, Tom Kline, gifted $50 million to Drexel Law School, which became the Drexel University *Thomas R. Kline* School of Law.

"And ending with my boss's acquisition of the crown jewel."

Two years earlier, the legal community was stunned by the announcement that Geoffrey Day had made a "historic pledge" to the University of Pennsylvania, in return for which Penn Law, the commonwealth's only Ivy League law school, became the *Geoffrey Day* School of Law at the University of Pennsylvania.

"I bet Day's buddy Balzac threw him one hell of a party when Day bought Penn," says Vaughn.

"Are you kidding? Balzac was apoplectic when he found out. He was thinking about buying the law school himself. That's what my friend Laurie Mitzner told me, anyway. She works for Balzac."

"So those two aren't quite the fuck buddies they appear to be on TV?"

Erin laughs. "Hardly. Although something brought them together on this train case. Something that's not quite right. The associates at my firm all think so, and Laurie says people at her firm are whispering about it, too."

Vaughn lets the remark sit, and he and Erin pick at the food that's been getting cold on their plates.

"So," Vaughn says, "you clearly aren't fond of your boss, or Balzac. How can you keep working for someone like Geoffrey Day?"

Erin looks away, then back at Vaughn. She has anger in her eyes. "Day may pay me, but I don't work for him. I work for the clients. And say what you will about our firm, but the people who walk through our doors are really hurting. It would break your heart. Just the other day, I met with the parents of a five-year-old girl permanently brain damaged by careless ER doctors who failed to diagnose bacterial meningitis. That child has no chance at a normal life, and her parents face life-care costs that would bankrupt them were it not for me. And I wouldn't be able to mount the legal case it'll take to save that family without the financial firepower of a firm like Day's."

"And the other lawyers at your firm?"

"Most are like me. The younger ones, at least. They care about our clients and work hard—fourteen-hours-a-day hard—to fight for them." Erin pauses. "It's just . . . over time, as the successes accumulate, as the bonuses get bigger . . . it changes people."

Vaughn sees something flash across Erin's eyes and wonders whether she fears that her own success will change her. Before he can ask, she stops him with a question of her own.

"So what are you going to do? About Eddy?"

Vaughn shrugs. "What can I do? Other than walk him through the investigation with the NTSB and hope it doesn't go any further."

Erin nods. "I wish you luck. I really do."

Vaughn studies Erin. She's stopped talking, but he hears the unspoken "but" at the end of her sentence. *She hopes I get Eddy through this safely, but she doesn't think that's going to happen.*

Later, as they leave, Vaughn smiles and asks, "Hey, how about we—"

"How about we *not*." The words are harsh, but Erin is smiling. She leans in and gives Vaughn a friendly peck on the cheek. "It was good to see you."

They turn and start to walk away from each other. Then Vaughn hears his name. He turns back, hoping he'll see a familiar spark in Erin's eyes. But her look is deadly serious.

"Be careful," she says. "Day and Balzac might've been grandstanding, but they're going after your cousin for real. They'll do everything in their power to crucify him, and they won't let anything stand in their way. Or anyone."

7

SATURDAY TO MONDAY, JUNE 21–23

Standing at the conference-room table, Vaughn and Mick pore over Google Earth satellite images of the track leading up to, and through, the accident site. They're looking for some clue as to why Eddy didn't notice the huge yellow track machine and didn't even try to slow down the train.

"There's no way around it," Mick says. "The track ahead was clear. There's no visual obstruction blocking your cousin's view down the roadway. He should have seen the TracVac the instant he rounded the curve. How fast was he going, again? How far down was the machine?"

"Eighty miles an hour. Eighteen hundred feet."

Mick googles a solution to the math. "Which means he'd have had a full fifteen seconds to apply the emergency brakes. Probably not enough time to stop the train completely, but enough to slow it down, so that the collision wouldn't have been so catastrophic."

Vaughn exhales. "Something must've been going on inside the cab that took Eddy's attention away from the track ahead."

"But your cousin can't say what it was because he doesn't remember anything." Mick casts Vaughn a hard look. "Was he alone in the cab?"

"Amtrak only has one engineer operating a train. Not like an airplane, where you have a pilot and a copilot. It's a practice that some of the talking heads are taking issue with; they're saying that it's foolish to have a lone engineer."

"Any chance there was someone in the cab who wasn't supposed to be there? Like a friend or . . . ?" Mick leaves the rest hanging.

Vaughn blinks. "No way. I mean, I can't see it. Kate, Eddy's wife, is pregnant with their first child. I can see he loves her. And she dotes on him. There's been no talk of problems between them in our family." Vaughn pauses, then it hits him: "And Eddy was the only one they found inside the cab after the crash."

"Could someone have been there and left? Gone back to the passenger cars?"

"If they left, Eddy wouldn't have been distracted. He would have seen the TracVac."

"Unless he was knocked out."

Vaughn shakes his head. "Are you saying someone clobbered him and ran away? They'd still be stuck on the train. They'd be putting their own life at risk."

They go back and forth a few more minutes, then Vaughn leaves the conference room. He finds Mick's second-person suggestion, and the whole notion of foul play, to be far-fetched. In the hallway, he comes across Susan. She gives him a quick glance before looking away. The air between them chills as they pass each other.

Before returning to the office on Sunday, Vaughn drops in on Eddy. Kate's in his hospital room, and so are her mother and Eddy's mother, Claire. Vaughn asks them to take a break, go down to the cafeteria and get something to eat; he'll fill in. Once they're gone, he replays for Eddy the conversation he'd had the day before with Mick.

"No way," Eddy says, his voice stronger than the last time Vaughn spoke with him. "There was no one else there. No one from the crew. And no one . . . *else*."

Eddy's indignation is palpable, so Vaughn moves on. "The NTSB wants to interview you," he says. "I haven't committed one way or the other."

"I have no problem talking to them. Or anyone else. I want to help."

Vaughn frowns. "Of course, and if I do agree to let them interview you, I'll prep you ahead of time. The reason I haven't agreed already is that we don't know what the NTSB is going to find. And"—Vaughn pauses—"I don't want to say anything that could get you into trouble with law enforcement."

Eddy does a double take. "Law enforcement?"

Vaughn explains what he's learned about previous rail disasters. "In two of the three largest crashes, the engineers died. In the Metro-North crash, he lived, but it turned out he had a medical condition that caused him to pass out. That meant he wasn't at fault, so the district attorney decided not to prosecute."

"I remember that crash. The engineer raced through a curve. The press wanted to crucify him. And then, it seemed like nothing came of it. I never thought to find out why."

"Well, that's why. In your case, you also lost consciousness. But that probably happened in the crash, when you suffered your head injury, not before. Until we know why you didn't react to the TracVac, I'm hesitant to have you testify."

Eddy considers what Vaughn has told him. He closes his eyes and slowly shakes his head. After a moment, he looks up at Vaughn. "I just . . . there's nothing there, man."

Monday morning, Vaughn walks through the doors to the office just as Angie is hanging up the phone. It's only 8:30 and already she seems flustered. "You've had two calls today, not counting the news. The second one, just now, was that guy from the NTSB. Wexler."

"And the first one?"

Angie pauses to catch her breath. "Jimmy Nunzio."

Vaughn's heart skips a beat. "Nunzio?"

"It was his secretary, actually. Or someone who said she was his secretary. She told me that Nunzio wants to meet you. He's going to send a car."

"A car? I'm not getting in a car with that guy!"

"You'll have to tell him that yourself."

"Forget that," Vaughn says, walking away.

"They want you to call when you're ready!" Angie shouts after him.

Which will be exactly never, Vaughn resolves.

A few minutes later he's at his desk, finishing up his Starbucks slow-roasted ham-and-Swiss sandwich. He crumples up the wrapping paper, empties his coffee cup, and dials the phone. It takes a few minutes, but he's eventually put through to Nelson Wexler.

"Mr. Coburn, how are you?" Wexler begins pleasantly.

"I have one question," Vaughn says, getting right down to business.

"All right. What is it?"

"My client's cell phone. I assume you found it. I'd like to know where you found it and what you learned."

"We're still analyzing the phone. As for where it was found, we'd really like to talk to your cousin before—"

"That's not going to happen." Vaughn hears the hardness in his own voice and eases up. "Look, I don't mean to be difficult. I want to help your investigation. And so does Eddy," he adds. "It's just that I'd like some reassurance that there isn't some kind of time bomb out there that you know about and Eddy doesn't remember. I don't want to be setting him up for prosecution."

Wexler says nothing for a long while. Then Vaughn hears him exhale. "Okay. That's fair. Let me put you at ease. We haven't uncovered any type of smoking gun. Quite frankly, we're completely at a loss to explain your cousin's actions."

"You mean his *inaction*. His failure to see the TracVac."

"That's exactly what I mean. And as to his phone, we found it zipped up inside his knapsack. We're still studying it, like I told you. But our preliminary analysis is that he wasn't on the phone at the time of the accident, or before the accident. The last time he appears to have used the phone at all was before the train pulled out of 30th Street Station."

Vaughn exhales. *Thank God.* He tells Wexler that he's leaning strongly toward having Eddy talk to the NTSB. "Unless something happens to change my mind," he says. "I'll call you once my client is strong enough to leave the hospital."

Wexler says he's glad to hear that, and they hang up on good terms.

Vaughn mulls things over for a few minutes, then decides he'd better talk to Mick about Nunzio. When he arrives at Mick's office, he finds Tommy sitting in one of the guest chairs.

"Speak of the devil," Tommy says.

Vaughn looks at Tommy, then glances at Mick, who tells him, "We were just talking about you helping your cousin."

"Susan's never gonna like that," Tommy says.

"I don't like it much myself," Vaughn answers. "The press and the plaintiff's bar are making him out to be some kind of ex-con, speed-demon driver, and Eddy can't defend himself—can't say what really happened—because he has no recollection of the accident."

Vaughn catches something passing unsaid between Mick and Tommy, and it gets him hot. "Yeah, I know. The *I don't remember* thing is a classic defense maneuver. Very convenient, right? But the thing is, he really doesn't remember. I know because I can see him struggling to recall what happened. He wants to know what happened as much as everyone else. But he can't find the answer, and it's killing him."

Mick nods. "Well, it's early in the game. Memory is tricky. It can seem like it's lost forever, then come back in an instant. All it takes is something to trigger it."

"Yeah, and in the meantime, Eddy is being pressed for answers by the NTSB, the media, the public and now . . . Jimmy Nunzio."

Mick and Tommy freeze at the mention of the gangster's name.

"Jimmy Nutzo?" asks Tommy.

"His son was on the train," Mick says. "He was one of the passengers who was killed."

"I must've missed that," Tommy says. He's clearly wondering what Vaughn originally did: Why was a capo's kid riding Amtrak? He thinks for a minute, then looks at Vaughn. "That's not good—for Eddy or for you."

Vaughn purses his lips. "He wants to meet with me."

"Not a good idea," Mick says.

"I wouldn't meet with him," says Tommy.

"He's going to want to know what your cousin told you," Mick says. "But you can't tell him without violating attorney-client privilege. You also can't let him use you as a conduit to carry threats to Eddy."

"You ever hear what happened to Jimmy's fiancée, back in the day?" Tommy asks.

It's a rhetorical question. Everyone in Philly knows some version of the tale. Jimmy Nutzo was engaged to an Eagles cheerleader. A girl who grew up with him in South Philly. He wasn't the big boss back then. Just a soldier. A guy higher up in the organization moved in on the fiancée, and, after a time, they both went missing. After a month, the police received a call tipping them off to look in the basement of the Pini Funeral Home on South Broad Street. The funeral director didn't care, because, so far as he knew, all that was in the basement were some old caskets that had been gathering dust for years. But when the police searched, they found Jimmy's fiancée and her new beau naked, bound together with duct tape, their faces mashed up against each other's crotches.

"Yeah, I know," Vaughn says.

"Some people say Nunzio shot them, but he didn't. He just bound them up like that and left them. The coroner said they died of thirst and starvation. But not before vomiting, shitting, and pissing all over each other."

"What I never understood," says Vaughn, "is why he left them where they might be found."

"The whole point was for them to *be* found—exactly like that," Tommy says. "He was making a statement. He's probably the one who tipped off the police."

"You can't meet with him," Mick says.

Vaughn studies Mick, then looks at Tommy. He nods. Mick's right. Of course he's right. Still, he can't help wondering if maybe Nunzio's son being on the train had something to do with why it crashed.

Vaughn leaves Mick's office, then walks down the hall to his own. He picks up his cell and dials.

"You again?" says Erin.

"I want to run something by you."

"Fire away."

"You've heard that one of the passengers killed in the train crash was Jimmy Nunzio's son?"

"Of course."

"Well, Jimmy himself wants to meet me."

There's a long pause at the other end of the line. "Not the best idea in the world."

"My boss says the same thing. It might be a conflict of interest for me. As his son's beneficiary, Nunzio will be a plaintiff in the litigation against Amtrak and Eddy."

"Uh, there are other issues to consider, as well."

"Such as?"

"You know what he did to his fiancée?"

"Everyone knows that story."

"Vaughn, listen to me. Nothing good could come from meeting with Jimmy Nutzo."

"But what if it could? Hear me out." Vaughn pauses, then explains. "Right now, Nunzio thinks that my cousin is to blame for his son's death. He knows there was no booze or drugs in Eddy's blood; the NTSB reported that. But he doesn't know that Eddy's phone was off and packed away. He also doesn't know that Eddy won a safety award from Amtrak. I can tell him that."

"Or he can wait to hear it from the NTSB, along with their other findings."

"It could take months for them even to announce their preliminary conclusions. A year or more for their final report. I'm worried that Nunzio is going to rush to judgment and decide to punish Eddy himself. I might be able to persuade him to keep an open mind—"

"Or maybe you'll say something to piss him off. He supposedly has a hair trigger. He's a grieving father, for chrissake."

Vaughn considers this. "I think I have to try."

"I want to go on record as being very strongly against this. Unless I'm in your will. Vaughn?"

He hangs up his cell and lifts the receiver of his office phone. "Angie, what was the number Nunzio's secretary gave you?"

"You're gonna go?"

"Don't tell Mick."

8

MONDAY, JUNE 23, CONTINUED

Vaughn sits in the second-row seat of a black Cadillac Escalade. In the front are a driver and another man, both very large, both very tough-looking, both dressed in grays and blacks. Sitting to Vaughn's right is a true giant of a man. After a couple of sidelong glances, he realizes the large man is John Giacobetti, Jimmy Nunzio's infamous enforcer.

The Escalade is heading south on Broad Street. No one is smiling. No one is talking. Vaughn expects the driver to turn any minute onto some small South Philly side street and park in front of a dark corner bar, where he'll be ushered inside and taken to a back room that has no windows. As a criminal-defense attorney, he's heard about this sort of thing. But the Caddy keeps heading south, eventually making its way into the Philadelphia Naval Shipyard, which has been redeveloped into a bustling mixed-use campus.

The driver pulls the Escalade into a parking lot. Vaughn is escorted to a modern four-story building clad in brick and glass. He does a double take because he's actually been here before—last year, for a minor elective procedure. Jefferson Hospital has a surgery center in the building. The 76ers also have office space here. And so, too, apparently, does James Nunzio, the most infamous underboss in the Philly mob.

The elevator opens onto the third floor, and Vaughn's honor guard marches him down the hall to a pair of glass doors. Through the doors, Vaughn sees an attractive woman sitting behind a modern desk of blond wood and glass. The sign on the doors identifies the suite as belonging to Modern Innovations, Inc. Vaughn is escorted through the lobby, down a hall, and into a conference room. He was searched before he was put into the car, and now he is searched again. Two of the men leave the conference room, closing the door behind them. Giacobetti stays with Vaughn.

"Have a seat," says the big man.

Vaughn sits at the table, and Giacobetti sits next to him, between Vaughn and the door. Ten minutes later, the door opens and Vaughn is escorted to an office at the end of the hall. Vaughn takes in the room as he passes through the doorway. It is large and bright, and light washes through two walls of floor-to-ceiling windows. The furniture is tasteful and modern, constructed of light woods, as is the shelving built into the two interior walls. Vaughn is directed to one of the guest chairs. His guards arrange themselves so that one sits beside him, one stands behind him. Giacobetti takes up a position behind and to the left of the desk.

After a minute, the bookcase in the wall behind the desk opens, and James Francis Xavier Nunzio seizes the room. He is well dressed, in an Italian suit that precisely fits his trim physique. Though in his late forties or perhaps early fifties, Nunzio still has jet-black hair, neatly trimmed. His square jaw is clean-shaven.

Vaughn takes a deep breath and starts to stand, but a firm hand on his shoulder tells him to stay where he is.

Vaughn tries to read the expression on Jimmy Nutzo's face as the gang boss's eyes bore into him, but he can't, and realizes it's because there's no expression *to* read. Nunzio's face is set in stone. It betrays no anger or joy, no love or hate. Nothing.

"So, Mr. Coburn. Thank you for accepting my invitation. It's always a pleasure to meet with a distinguished member of the defense bar, even one as young as yourself."

Vaughn is surprised at Nunzio's diction. He was expecting the dialect and pronunciation of a South Philly "yo boy." But the gangster speaks with perfect pronunciation and no hint of an accent.

"I hope you don't mind," Nunzio continues, "but I've done a little checking up on you." Here, Nunzio nods to a manila folder sitting on the center of his desktop. "Raised in North Philly. Son of a barkeep, nephew of a police officer turned gym owner. Trained to box. Not a tennis-club-and-cucumber-sandwich man; that weighs strongly in your favor, in my eyes. Education: undergrad at Temple, my own alma mater, and Temple Law, where you were on Law Review. Career: two years with the public defender's office followed by five years in a defense firm. You're one of the good guys."

Nunzio pauses, and Vaughn can see that he's being studied. The gangster's eyes are dark and deep, and Vaughn senses a keen intelligence behind them. Keen—and predatory.

"Single, no children. Are you looking to get married?"

"Uh, no sir. Not right now." Vaughn does his best to keep his voice steady.

"Well, you never know who's going to turn the corner." Nunzio winks and Vaughn forces a nervous smile.

The mobster pauses a minute, leans back in his chair. He smiles again and says, "So, guess what I did this weekend?"

Vaughn looks at Nunzio, then at Johnny Giacobetti, then back at Nunzio. "I don't know. I—"

"I buried my *son!*" Nunzio lunges forward so quickly and slaps the palms of his hands on the desktop so violently that Vaughn leaps from his seat and stumbles backward, toppling the chair. Before Vaughn can do so himself, the man standing behind him rights the chair and presses Vaughn back down into it.

The darkness in Jimmy Nutzo's eyes makes Vaughn shiver.

"Twenty years old, my Alexander. His whole life ahead of him. He gets on the Amtrak to New York. Ten minutes out of the station, and he's dead. Dead!"

Nunzio eases back into his seat, takes a minute to compose himself, lower his voice. "My beautiful son is dead, Mr. Coburn, because he was riding in a train that your cousin decided to run into a piece of railroad equipment. I say he *decided* to do this because I don't see how this awful thing could have been done other than deliberately. The TracVac he crashed into sitting on the track, in open view, in broad *fucking* daylight. And your cousin, Mr. Coburn, not only didn't stop the train in time, he didn't even try."

Nunzio stops and glares at Vaughn for what seems like days. Then, "Tell me, Mr. Coburn, have I correctly stated the facts? Or did I get something wrong?"

Vaughn's heart pounds in his chest. He gulps hard and answers. "Everything you said is true. But there are some additional facts—"

"Best you tell me what they are. And hurry."

"Well, first, my client's blood was clean. He wasn't under the influence. Second, he wasn't talking on the phone, or texting. The NTSB confirmed both of those facts for me. What is also important, I think, is that my client—"

"Your cousin. *Fast Eddy*," Nunzio interrupts.

"He got that nickname from running track. Not the car crash."

"The car crash where he was racing down Kelly Drive, ran a cop off the road, and killed him."

Vaughn exhales. "He . . . he was young then, and—"

"So was my son."

Vaughn takes a deep breath. "About that . . . Can I ask a question? Why was your son riding on a train? Instead of—"

"Instead of in a limo, surrounded by guards? Because he wasn't like me. And he wasn't ever going to be. That was the plan." The mobster's eyes fix their gaze elsewhere, and, for an instant, he seems to be far away.

Vaughn is sweating now. This is not going well. "I know it looks bad. I get it. I really do. But Eddy wasn't speeding. He wasn't high, or talking on the phone. My cousin is a careful engineer. His coworkers will all attest to that. He won a safety award for—"

"Then what's the explanation? What's the missing piece of the puzzle here, Mr. Coburn, that makes this accident make sense? The piece that makes me stop hating your cousin, stops my head from filling with visions of awful things happening to him? The piece that maybe you and your cousin know but haven't shared yet with anyone else."

Vaughn glances at Giacobetti, then back to Nunzio. "I wish I had something to give you. The problem is that my cousin doesn't remember anything about the crash itself. The last thing he can recall is when he was entering the curve."

Nunzio stares at Vaughn, the gangster's eyes growing blacker by the second.

"The NTSB is looking at the crash from every angle," Vaughn continues. "Their investigation—"

Nunzio puts up his hand, stopping Vaughn cold. "The NTSB investigation will take a year, or longer. I'm not waiting a year to get justice for my son."

Vaughn opens his mouth, but nothing comes out. What can he say? What can he offer this notorious murderer to keep him from whacking Eddy in the very near future? His mind searches frantically for some small crumb. "Eddy's wife is pregnant. She's due any day." Vaughn pauses so the words can sink in.

"You're telling me I should overlook the death of *my* son because the man who killed him is going to be a father himself?"

"No. What I'm saying is that Eddy had a damn good reason to be careful. There's no way he was taking chances with the train."

Nunzio studies Vaughn. "I'm not waiting a year," he repeats. Then he nods his head, and the man behind Vaughn raps him on the shoulder. Time to go.

Vaughn rises from the chair. He turns to leave, then turns back. "I'll find out what happened, and I will tell you as soon as I know."

"Move fast, Mr. Coburn. As my own father once told me, 'Soon isn't always soon enough.'"

Vaughn's guards escort him out of the building. He expects them to walk him to the Escalade, but they turn away as soon as they deposit him on the sidewalk.

Filling the doorway behind him, Giacobetti says, "Mr. Nunzio's travel service only offers one-way trips."

Vaughn turns and begins the long walk to the SEPTA station.

9

Monday, June 30

The day had been bright and clear, perfect for shooting. Fifty-five-year-old Royce Badgett knelt on his right knee, lifted the rifle, and put his eye to the Bausch & Lomb Tactical 10x40 scope. The rifle itself was a semiautomatic M25 Sniper Weapon System developed by the 10th Special Forces Group out of Fort Devens, Massachusetts, and manufactured by Springfield Armory. Royce had fallen in love with the rifle when he used it in the Gulf War.

The M25's maximum firing distance of 980 yards would be more than sufficient for the shots Royce would be making. And he had absolute confidence in his ability to make the shots, even with the pain in his left forearm from his new tattoo and the too-close-for-comfort overhead buzzing from the drone.

"Whose fuckin' idea was it to have that damned thing flyin' over our heads?" he'd asked, his eye still raised to the scope.

The tall kid standing next to him hadn't answered. Probably afraid to. *Damned yuppies*. Royce didn't like the kid being there any more than he liked the drone. But the boss was the boss, and his orders were orders. Plus, there had to be a second man to make the phone call.

"Do it now," Royce ordered, and the kid pressed on his iPhone. After a moment, he talked into the phone, uttering the magic words

Royce was told he would say. Then, Royce fired. Five shots, at two-second intervals. When he was finished, Royce lowered the rifle and stood up. "Come on," he told the kid as the train whooshed past. A few seconds later, the air down the track exploded with the sound of the crash. Royce hadn't looked back; he had felt no need to watch the show.

Sitting in the Llanerch Diner, remembering it now, Royce remains pleased with his work. It was a complicated operation, and it went off without a hitch. The boss was satisfied, and Royce got the full $5,500 they'd agreed to. The only bad thing that happened was that his tattoo had gotten infected. He'd ignored it for a couple of days, hoping that rubbing alcohol and Father Time would do the trick. But the infection got worse, and he'd had to see a doctor, something Royce hated doing.

"The usual?" asks the waitress as she sets a coffee mug on the table.

"You bet, Ellen." Royce smiles. "With lots of gravy."

As Ellen walks away, Royce watches her ass; she's the best thing about the place. The diner is down-at-the-heels. But it's a local place, and that means a lot to Royce Badgett. It's also cool, Royce thinks, that they filmed *Silver Linings Playbook* there. Imagine Bradley fuckin' Cooper and that pouty girl from *Hunger Games* sitting at this very booth. Which made the Llanerch Diner his second connection to Cooper, as he had also played a sniper in the movies, and Royce had been a real sniper in the Gulf War. The third connection was that Cooper had been born in Philly, and Royce right outside, in Upper Darby.

Royce studies his reflection in the window. That girl he met the other week was right; he does look like Vladimir Putin. She thought she was insulting him, he could tell. But what she said was actually a compliment, because that little prick Putin was one tough son of a bitch.

Waiting for Ellen to bring his open-faced turkey sandwich, Royce stares at the tattoos on each of his forearms. The one he'd done a month back, on his right forearm, depicts geometric designs that almost look Egyptian. Unlike that monochromatic design, the one on his left forearm—the infected one—was done in several different colors. It depicts a deer head with a twelve-point rack. Royce chose that design in honor of a buck he'd taken the year before.

Royce came late to tattoos. He always liked them, just never thought to get one himself. Then, about two years ago, he passed a parlor on Frankford Avenue and thought, *What the hell.* He turned around, went in, and the next thing he knew, he had a big ol' American eagle on his chest. After that, he got each of his calves tatted. Then he had them tat his back with a saying: "Fall Down Seven Times, Get Up Eight." Royce liked that. It was inspirational.

Getting tatted always hurts like hell but, weirdly, Royce Badgett has found that he's come to like the pain. It makes him think of those crazy *Fifty Shades* movies all the housewives are getting wet over.

People are so strange.

10

TUESDAY, JULY 1, AND THURSDAY, JULY 3

Fifteen days after the accident, Eddy Coburn finally leaves the hospital. His head is bandaged, his right arm casted. His face is still swollen and discolored. When his wheelchair reaches the front door of the hospital, Eddy rises and walks gingerly because of the pain from the injuries to his internal organs and the healing fractures in his ribs. Vaughn helps him into the back seat of Tommy McFarland's car. Kate puts some belongings in the trunk and then slides into the car next to Eddy. Vaughn sits shotgun, and Tommy pulls away.

There's little conversation on the two-hour ride to the small farmhouse that Tommy found for Eddy and Kate in southern Lancaster County. With the press still surrounding their house in north-central New Jersey, they wouldn't be able to return there, at least for some time. Another reason Vaughn himself wanted them moved was the ever-present threat of Jimmy Nunzio—something Vaughn decided not to share with Eddy or Kate. They are under enough stress as it is. Fortunately, Tommy knows a guy who knows a guy who farms corn on a hundred-acre spread in Lancaster County. The absentee owner leases the land to a big co-op. No one lives in the farmhouse.

Tommy pulls the car off the winding two-lane road onto a dirt-and-gravel driveway. After a minute, the house comes into view. It's a two-story white-clapboard structure with a sagging wooden porch. The paint on the house is peeling. The small lawn is overgrown with weeds.

Vaughn senses Kate stiffen in the seat behind him. He can't see it, but Eddy reaches over and pats his wife's hands. *It'll be okay,* Eddy tells her with his eyes. Kate forces a smile.

Tommy and Vaughn unload the suitcases from the trunk and carry them into the house. The air inside is stale and musty and carries the faint smell of something dead. *Maybe a possum that found its way inside,* thinks Vaughn.

Eddy gingerly escorts Kate through the threshold and looks around. "Some dusting, a little paint, and this place will look like new," Eddy says. Vaughn looks at his cousin and says he agrees. They both know it's bullshit.

Everyone moves into the kitchen, where Tommy tries the faucet. Brown liquid smelling of sulfur sputters out the end. "Well water," Tommy says. His friend had told them the water was good for showering and laundry but not for drinking, so he's brought along several cases of bottled spring water.

Vaughn and Tommy stay for a couple of hours, helping Kate clean dishes, mop the floors, dust, and clear out the cobwebs. Because of his injuries, all Eddy can do is replace the light bulbs. After he's done, he sits around feeling useless. Vaughn glances Eddy's way every now and then, feeling sorry for his cousin and wondering how Eddy is going to hold up over time. What worries him most is that Eddy will fall back into the bottle, which is where he ended up after he was let out of prison. He's already spoken to Kate about it, and she agreed to reach out to him if she sees Eddy about to go down that road. Not that there's much danger right now—there's no booze in the house, and Eddy's in no shape to drive anywhere to get it.

With the sun about to set, everyone heads out to the front porch, where Vaughn and Tommy say their goodbyes to Kate and Eddy. Kate is going to stay at the farmhouse until she gets close to her due date, at which point she'll return to Philadelphia to stay with Vaughn's parents.

Vaughn turns to Eddy and says, "I'll see you Thursday." That's when Vaughn agreed to let the NTSB interview his cousin. Vaughn talked it out at length with Mick, the pros and cons of making Eddy available. On the one hand, you face the risk that he'll say something to inculpate himself, something that could be used down the road as a basis for criminal prosecution. Vaughn has decided that the risk is minimal, given that Eddy's blood was clean and his phone was tucked away at the time of the accident.

On the other hand, Vaughn decided, the *optics* of Eddy's refusing to talk would be terrible. It would look like he was hiding something. Talking to the NTSB would give the press something positive to focus on, at long last. It's a small thing, but they need every edge they can find in their battle against the personal-injury lawyers who want to make Eddy into a scapegoat. And the fact is, Eddy *wants* to talk to the NTSB, wants to help them figure out what happened. Wants to clear his name.

"Have you heard anything more from Jimmy Nunzio?" Tommy asks on the ride back to Philadelphia. Vaughn had fessed up to Mick and Tommy about meeting the mobster despite their strong advice not to. Predictably, Vaughn's decision made Mick angry, and he let Vaughn know it. Tommy, however, let it slide off his shoulders.

"No, and I don't want to." Vaughn thought for a minute, then said, "I'm hoping that if nothing else comes out that's bad for Eddy, Nunzio will let the NTSB do its job before he makes any decisions."

"I wouldn't count on that. Guys like Jimmy Nutzo don't sit around and wait for other people to get things done."

The way Tommy puts it stirs something inside Vaughn. "You think Nunzio will look into the crash himself? Do his own 'investigation'?"

"Why do you think he wanted to see you?"

All of a sudden, Vaughn wishes he hadn't parked Eddy in the middle of nowhere.

Two days later, Vaughn and Eddy move through the concourse at 30th Street Station. People stop and stare at them as they walk by. Two Amtrak cops leaning against the passenger-service desk straighten up and glower. Vaughn calls Nelson Wexler on his cell, and Wexler tells him to wait by the elevators at the northwest corner of the building. After a few minutes, the elevator doors open and an Amtrak police officer appears and summons them inside. They ride up to the third floor, where the officer uses his ID badge to get through the security doors. He walks them down the hall to a large conference room with a table big enough to seat thirty.

At the far end of the table are five men and a woman. Vaughn recognizes Nelson Wexler, who introduces himself to Eddy. The others identify themselves as NTSB rail accident investigator Albert Cruise; Dr. Mark Johansson, NTSB chief medical officer; Patrick Ellison from the Federal Railroad Administration; Jack Bunting, Amtrak deputy division engineer; Luke Jenkins, Amtrak general road foreman; and Emmitt Green, local chairman of Eddy's union, the Brotherhood of Locomotive Engineers and Trainmen.

Wexler asks Vaughn and Eddy if they want anything to drink. Vaughn declines. Eddy asks for coffee with sugar, and Wexler makes him a cup. Wexler walks to the other side of the table and begins.

"Would you start by telling us what you did that day from the time you woke up until the time of the accident?"

Eddy says he got out of bed at 2:45, left home at 3:15, and reported to work at 4:00 a.m. He left Penn Station at 4:40, on Train 151, arriving in DC at 8:20. "I had breakfast with one of the conductors, had my job briefing, and went over the Form Ds—those are the forms that tell us what tracks are out of service. Then we got on the train, Train 174, and left Washington at 10:10. We got to 30th Street Station in Philly at 12:01 and left five minutes later. The last thing I remember is heading into the Torresdale curve. The speed limit in the curve is eighty, and I reduced speed, so I was right about there as I entered the curve. That's the last thing I remember before the crash."

"What's your practice with respect to operating the throttle?"

"Depends. If I'm going slow, I gradually increase speed. If I'm already going fast, I'll accelerate to full throttle, then back off as I approach maximum speed. But I'd lowered my speed because I was going into a curve."

"What is the first thing you remember after the crash?"

Eddy pauses here. He closes his eyes and takes a deep breath. This part isn't easy for him. "I think I came to, for a minute, inside the cab. I was lying on what I thought was the floor, but it must've been the side of the engine. I was in a lot of pain, and I think I passed in and out of consciousness a couple of times. After a while—I don't know how long—I felt people pulling me out of the locomotive. They were talking to me, but I couldn't understand what they were saying. Then I was in an ambulance. And then, after that, the next thing I remember is waking up in the hospital. I'm not sure what day or time, but Kate was there."

Wexler continues his questioning, asking Eddy whether he experienced any mechanical problems with the train or the air brakes before the accident, what train traffic he passed on the way, and what he heard over the radio. Then Wexler turns it over to Jenkins, the general road foreman, who asks how long Eddy has been working that run, whether he felt comfortable with the equipment.

"That exact run I'd been working for about two weeks," Eddy answers. "And yes, I was fine with the equipment. I've driven the ACS-64s lots of times."

Answering other questions from Jenkins about his work schedule, Eddy says he worked five days a week, Friday through Tuesday, and that the day of the accident, a Monday, was the fourth day in his schedule.

The FRA's Patrick Ellison asks Eddy where he kept his cell phone during the run, and whether it was on.

"I always kept my cell phone in my knapsack, turned off," Eddy answered. "It's a firing offense to have it on."

"When was the last time you were on the phone before the accident?"

"I called Kate just before I boarded the train."

Ellison tells Wexler that's all he has, and Wexler nods to the NTSB medical officer, who asks Eddy how he was feeling that day.

"Physically, I felt fine. Mentally, I was a little stressed—and excited. My wife is pregnant, so I was thinking about that. And there'd been some break-ins in our neighborhood, so I was a little worried. That's why I called Kate right before we left."

Dr. Johansson asks Eddy whether he was on any medication that day, whether he took meds for any chronic conditions. Eddy answers no.

"Have you ever lost consciousness, or blacked out?"

"No. Never."

"Ever have vertigo?"

"No."

"Mr. Coburn, can you think of any reason you would have lost consciousness?"

Eddy pauses, looks around the table, shakes his head. "No."

Ellison of the FRA takes over again. "I want to talk about fatigue issues," he begins, and they spend some time on Eddy's typical sleep cycle, what time he normally went to bed and got up, whether he would wake up during the night. Whether he felt he got enough sleep. Whether he felt tired during the day. Whether he has sleep apnea.

To Vaughn, it feels as though the investigators are simply running through a standard list of questions, the tone of their voices neutral, not accusatory. For Eddy's part, he is doing well, answering the questions rather than evading them. It's obvious he wants to help.

Then Wexler passes the baton to Deputy Division Engineer Jack Bunting.

"So your phone was off and it was in your knapsack?" asks Bunting.

"Yes."

"You're sure of that?"

Vaughn glances at Wexler. The IIC had told Vaughn the week before that Eddy's phone was in fact found in the knapsack, turned off.

Today, Eddy already confirmed that was his practice. Bunting seems to be retreading the facts.

"Any chance you made a call to your wife *after* you'd begun the run, then put the phone away once the call was over?"

Again, Vaughn looks at Wexler, who seems as perplexed as Vaughn is by Bunting's questioning.

"Come on," Vaughn interjects. "You guys have the phone. You tested it. You already know the answer to these questions." Beside him, Eddy stiffens, and Vaughn assumes it's because his cousin is getting frustrated by the repetition.

"All right, let's shift gears," says Bunting, a large man with a dark farmer's tan. "You told us you didn't have any sleep disorders and that you were getting enough sleep. Would it be fair to say that you were awake and alert during the run from DC to Philadelphia, and then after you left 30th Street Station?"

"Absolutely."

"And you can't think of any reason you'd have lost consciousness?"

"None."

"And we know that once your train rounded the curve at Torresdale, it was straight track through to where your train struck the TracVac. And I think the NTSB investigators measured the distance from the end of the curve to the machine at eighteen hundred feet."

"Uh . . . okay."

"Can you think of any reason why, if you were facing forward and looking at the roadway ahead, you wouldn't have seen the TracVac?"

Eddy takes a deep breath, opens his hands. "No, I can't."

"So would it be fair to say then that you *weren't* facing forward and looking ahead, like you're supposed to do when you're driving a—"

"What is this?" Vaughn interrupts. "He told you he doesn't remember anything after he started into the curve. Your questions are starting to sound like a cross-examination."

"I agree," Eddy's union leader Emmitt Green chimes in. "You keep going down this road, and I will strongly urge Mr. Coburn and his lawyer to end this."

"All right, all right," Bunting says. "I've never been in one of these before, so maybe I don't know the ground rules. I'm just trying to get as much information as I can."

"So stick to asking for facts," Vaughn says. "Not speculation."

Jack Bunting nods, looks down at his notepad. "I only have a few more questions. They may be a little sensitive, but I have to ask them anyway."

Vaughn feels his hackles rise.

"I read—we all read—about your car crash when you were younger. In your job application with Amtrak, did you disclose that you'd been convicted of a serious crime and gone to prison for it?"

"Whoa!" Vaughn shouts. "What does his job application, or the auto accident, have to do with this?"

Bunting slowly turns his head to Vaughn. "Well, for one thing, it shows us whether your client is the type of person who tells the truth. He's asking us to rely on his answers to our questions, and I think we're entitled to have some background on his veracity. It certainly is relevant whether he's lied on his job application about having numerous criminal convictions, including a conviction for vehicular manslaughter. I think it's also relevant whether he disclosed in his job interviews that he had a history of alcohol problems."

With a sick feeling in the pit of his stomach, Vaughn now understands what's going on. Eddy must've failed to disclose all of this when he applied to Amtrak. And now Vaughn has failed to foresee this line of questioning. A huge blunder on his part.

How do I get Eddy the hell out of this?

His only choice is to instruct Eddy to plead the Fifth—which would look awful. Or he could end it.

"That's it," Vaughn says, standing. "We're done here. I brought in my client because he wants to do everything he can to help you figure out what happened. But this last line of questioning has nothing to do with the train crash, or what caused it. You've turned this from an inquiry into a witch hunt, and I'm not going to allow it. Come on, Mr. Coburn. We're leaving."

Vaughn glares at Wexler as he turns to leave. The look in the IIC's eyes shows Vaughn that Wexler is as upset by what's happened as he is.

"I'll call you," Wexler says.

"Don't bother," Vaughn snaps.

Vaughn catches a cab in the station's taxi line, and he and Eddy get in the back seat. "I am so sorry, Eddy," he says. "I led you right into an ambush. I should have seen it coming."

Eddy hangs his head and shakes it. "No. I should have known they'd ask me about my application. I didn't put any of that stuff down because my sponsor told me not to."

"Your sponsor?"

"The program. AA. He's the one who got me the job. He works for Amtrak, and he's pretty high up. He said they never check criminal records or substance-abuse history, so there was no point in tipping them off."

Vaughn nods. He gets it. Still, Eddy's dishonesty is going to look bad when it goes public. And it will.

Back at the office, Vaughn hands Eddy off to Tommy for the drive to Lancaster County. Then he goes into Mick's office and tells him what happened.

"I think you may be in over your head," Mick says. "This whole area of the law . . . it's just not something any of us have any experience in. We may have to bring in someone who's more familiar with the railroads and the NTSB. Or, you may have to hand the case off."

Vaughn's stomach sinks. With Susan so clearly opposed to him representing Eddy, he was counting on support from Mick. But Mick's confidence in him seems to be waning.

"Think about it. And get back to me."

Vaughn says he will and walks to his office, where he sinks into his chair and asks himself how he could have fucked up this badly.

Back at 30th Street Station, Jack Bunting sits behind his own desk, smiling. He picks up his cell and dials. When the other man answers, he says, "It was beautiful. It went down just like we thought it would. You should've seen the look on that little shit's face."

"Which one? The engineer or his lawyer?"

"Both of them."

"Good work. Get his job application and the other records to you-know-who to leak to the press."

"Already done."

"Ahead of the curve, as always. Good man."

Bunting hangs up. *Good man is right.* He's served the railroad for thirty years and done a damned good job of it. He's been the highest performer in every job he's held on his unfairly long trek up the corporate ladder. And what does he have to show for it? A meager $80,000 in a 401(k). And his pension, frozen two years ago, courtesy of Amtrak CEO Edward "A for Asshole" Plankton. Between the pension thing and a rising share of health-care costs, management is worse off than labor.

What a way to run a railroad.

"What goes around comes around," Jack Bunting murmurs aloud. Thanks to the train crash, his financial worries will be over.

In the meantime, he has to do something about Reggie Frye, the foreman of the track crew responsible for the TracVac. Frye was so obviously nervous during his own NTSB interview the week before that Bunting thought he was on the verge of confessing the whole plan. And since then, Frye has twice called Bunting, worried about the calls he was getting from reporters. Bunting told him to hang the fuck up on them, then asked why he hadn't left town as instructed. Frye whined that he didn't have the money to leave town and pressed Bunting about when he was going to be paid.

Bunting resolves to tell the boss about Frye the next time they talk and persuade him to have Royce Badgett make the idiot disappear.

11

FRIDAY, JULY 4

Erin Doyle sits at her desk in Day and Lockwood's sun-drenched suite in the Comcast Innovation and Technology Center. It is cluttered with briefs, pleadings, mail, and legal pads. There's a small clearing for the Apple laptop that sits directly in front of her. To her right are two windows overlooking Arch Street, forty floors below. Behind her is the interior wall on which she's hung her college and law-school diplomas and her framed admission certificates from the Commonwealth of Pennsylvania, the state of New Jersey, and various federal district courts. An assortment of struggling cacti sit in small pots on her windowsill. To Erin's left is the interior wall adjoining the hallway, made of glass. Geoffrey Day told his architects he wanted to be able to stand anywhere in the suite and be able to see the whole way through, to the sky. Which means that every moment of the day, Erin's painfully aware that anyone looking in the direction of her office can see what she's doing.

On Erin's computer screen is the draft of a pretrial memorandum she's been working on for hours. At the moment, however, her thoughts aren't focused on the memo or the case, but on Vaughn Coburn and his ill-fated cousin Eddy. The whole firm is consumed with the train crash and the many cases it has brought in. Early on, Day assembled a team of junior associates to research the law related to train crashes and the regulation of the rail industry. Day is desperate to get up to speed so that he can look like the dean of rail-crash litigation when he appears on television. It's also important that he be able to dazzle potential referring attorneys when they call to discuss handing off cases from the crash that they've picked up through relatives or happenstance. All of which is why the firm is hopping even through the holiday.

The firm's eight-person, full-time marketing department has been working on the crash night and day, constantly firing off press releases to the media and developing written brochures and pamphlets related to railroad law and train crashes. Before long, it will appear to the world as though Day and Lockwood is the epicenter of rail-crash litigation in the United States.

Geoffrey Day himself oversees a working group of senior attorneys— all male—whose main job is to gather evidence related to the Amtrak crash. The associates spend most of their days on the phone or in meetings interviewing witnesses: passengers, first responders, police officers, and Amtrak employees.

"I want to know more about this crash than the NTSB," Day announced to the team, or so Erin was told by Corey King, who has ingratiated himself into Day's inner circle. Corey thinks Day walks on water, and he's so obsequious that some of the other associates ridicule him behind his back, saying, "Every Day has his dog."

Erin had never seen Corey happier than the morning the crash of Train 174 blasted its way into the news. Geoffrey called all the senior associates into the firm's enormous main conference room to watch the floor-to-ceiling television screen. Junior associates and staff were allowed to watch the coverage through the conference room's interior glass wall. Corey sidled up next to Day, beaming at the twisted wreckage on the screen. Watching him, Erin couldn't believe that she'd ever dated such a jerk.

"Looks like your boy's cousin is going down."

"What the—?" Erin is stunned to see Corey King standing in her doorway, as though summoned by her thoughts.

"He lied on his job application with the railroad. He never told Amtrak about his criminal convictions or imprisonment. Never told the railroad he'd crashed a car and killed a police officer, or that he'd had trouble with alcohol. It's all right here," he adds, holding up a manila folder. "Geoffrey is calling a press conference about it."

Erin stares at King but says nothing.

"I mean, you can't say he doesn't deserve whatever he gets," King says. "He should never have been driving a train to begin with. And Amtrak should never have hired him."

Erin continues to stare until King becomes uncomfortable. "Hey, this is the biggest case in the firm's history," he says at last. "Do you know how many people were maimed and killed in the crash?"

Erin leans back in her seat, thinks for a moment, then says, "I'm working on a nursing-home abuse case. It was brought to us by the daughter of an eighty-year-old man who'd lain in bed in the same position for weeks at a time because the staff never turned him over. He developed bedsores. I saw them when I went to the nursing home with his daughter. She lifted her father's sheets, and there they were—gaping, gelatinous wounds, wet and foul-smelling with infection." Erin stops, lets the words hang in the air. "I'm seeing the same thing right now, looking at you."

Corey King's face turns crimson. He opens his mouth to say something but can't find the words. Instead, he snaps the manila folder to his chest, turns, and leaves.

Erin closes her eyes and takes deep breaths until her hands unclench. She'd always known what a conceited ass Corey was. But what he'd become over the years is ten times worse. She'd like to say she didn't know what she'd ever seen in him, but that wasn't true. What she had seen in him was what was visible to the eye: Corey King is drop-dead gorgeous. Six foot three with broad shoulders, dark hair, a swarthy complexion, and deep-blue bedroom eyes. Curiously, although he looks like a natural athlete, Corey isn't much of an athlete at all. Back in law school, he could play passable basketball, but that was about it. In many ways, he is the opposite of Vaughn. You could pass Vaughn on the street and never take notice of him. It's not that he isn't a good-looking guy— he is. Just not so much that you would spot it unless you looked closely. And in clothes, his thin, five-foot-ten frame isn't compelling. But back in the day, Vaughn with his shirt off was something different. He was rock solid, with six-pack abs and cut biceps. And when he sparred in the boxing ring, you could see what a tightly coiled spring he really was.

She and Vaughn had a good thing going for a while. But it fell apart when they came back to law school for their third year, in part because of the vastly different experiences they'd had over the summer. Vaughn recounted his tales of fighting for his indigent clients while interning at the legal clinic. He fairly glowed as he described how he'd helped people wrongly evicted from their homes or unfairly fired by employers. Vaughn became especially impassioned when he talked about advocating on behalf of abused children. In return, all Erin could offer up were stories of sightseeing trips she'd taken to European cities and museums. Her experiences seemed frivolous. Worse, she got the sense that Vaughn was judging her. It didn't take long for both of them to realize that whatever they'd had wasn't working anymore, so they broke things off.

After law school, though, Corey King seemed to become more and more Corey King every day. Finally, she couldn't bear to be in his presence, and she dumped him, rather unceremoniously, at the firm Christmas party. Then she took a cab to Vaughn's apartment and fucked him so hard the bed broke. The next morning, she told Vaughn she wasn't going to be dropping by anymore. And, with the exception of one or two—or three—times over the years, she'd stuck to it.

But now here she is, and fate seems to be pushing her and Vaughn into the same space. Or, more accurately, fate is pushing Vaughn and

Corey King into that space, and she is going to have to intervene to help Vaughn save his cousin Eddy.

But how, really, can she help? Or maybe the better question is: Why help? Eddy Coburn crashed a train full of people, killing dozens, injuring hundreds. And if Corey is right, Eddy was in a position to do so only because he'd hidden a past that included alcohol abuse, incarceration, and a driving record of reckless speed that led to someone's death. Vaughn's quest, it seems to Erin, is worse than quixotic. Not only is it likely hopeless, it *should* be hopeless, because Eddy is culpable as hell.

Still, she knows that even the devil deserves a good lawyer. Not because anyone wants the devil to win, but because everyone wants the system to be fair.

Erin nods to herself. Yes, she'll help Vaughn. Not a lot, just enough to level the playing field. Enough to make sure that Vaughn and his cousin aren't steamrolled. If Eddy Coburn is guilty, then so be it, and may he suffer the full wrath of the legal system. But if he's not guilty, if there's some other reason for what happened, then so be that as well— even if it means that Geoffrey Day and Benjamin Balzac have to look elsewhere for their sacrificial lamb.

Erin picks up her cell phone and dials. "It's me," she says. "We need to meet. I have some news about your cousin."

"I hope it's good," Vaughn says. "I sat with Eddy before the NTSB today and . . . let's just say it didn't go well."

Erin pauses. "I'm afraid it's not good news. But we should still talk. Come to my place," she says. "Around ten. I may have something for you to look at."

"You still in that little place on Pine Street?"

"No. I'm at One Independence Place, on Washington Square. I've been there for two years."

"Wow, it's been that long since—"

"Later." Erin hangs up and works until 9:00 p.m.

The office is almost empty when she walks down the hall toward Corey King's office. She glances up and down the hallway to make sure no one sees her, then she turns on the light to his office and walks in, closing the door behind her. She steps to King's desk and sees the manila folder lying right on top of his blotter.

Doesn't even try to hide what he's up to, the arrogant ass.

Quickly, she takes the folder to the copy room and runs the contents through the Xerox. She returns the folder to Corey's desk, then goes back to her office.

Thirty minutes later, the documents sit on the coffee table in the center of Erin's living room. Fifteen minutes after that, the doorman buzzes the intercom and informs Erin that Vaughn is in the lobby.

"Send him up," she says.

Erin greets Vaughn in her work clothes and waves him into the apartment. She escorts him from the foyer down a short hall to the living room, where Vaughn pauses to look around and take the place in. A gray thistle rug sits over polished wood flooring. A cream-colored sofa and love seat are positioned around a glass-top coffee table. There are two occasional chairs, in white leather. The light-gray walls are textured, and Vaughn reaches out and touches one.

"Venetian plaster," Erin says.

"Pricey, I'll bet."

Erin doesn't answer, opting instead to take Vaughn on a brief tour of the apartment. It's a two-bedroom corner unit with a balcony. A little less than twelve hundred square feet. On the eighth floor. Far grander than Vaughn could afford on his salary at a small defense firm. But as a senior associate at Day and Lockwood, Erin is undoubtedly pulling in some serious coin. Probably a mid-six-figure salary with a fat bonus on top of it. Vaughn feels a pang of jealousy, but not much of one; he's never been in it for the money.

In the kitchen, Erin pulls out a bottle of Longrow 10-Year and fills two tumblers. "I know you prefer beer," she says, handing Vaughn one of the glasses. "But you're going to need this." They make their way back to the living room and sit side by side on the sofa. "That's for you," she says, nodding at the folder on the coffee table.

Vaughn leans over, opens the folder, and begins to read. The first document is Eddy's job application with Amtrak. In answer to the question asking whether he'd ever been convicted of a crime, Eddy had checked "no." The documents underneath the application show Eddy's answer to be a lie. Eddy's criminal record shows his conviction for the car crash. It also lists a plethora of other convictions for petty offenses following Eddy's release from prison—public drunkenness, disorderly conduct, resisting arrest, assaulting a police officer. Half a dozen mug shots show Eddy at various times and in various stages of intoxication. One mug shot shows him with two black eyes, a fat lip, and no shirt. He looks like a street brawler, though Vaughn suspects the arresting police did that to him.

Vaughn knew from family lore that his cousin hit hard times after he left Graterford Prison, so these records are no surprise. Still, they won't go over well with the public. Nor will Eddy's post-imprisonment driving record. Two citations for running red lights, three more for speeding. Citations for inattentive driving, reckless driving, and driving with an expired license. Vaughn sees that all the citations were written during the period when Eddy had spiraled his way to rock bottom, before he'd made the decision to turn his life around. Before he had admitted himself into rehab, joined AA, met Kate.

"Jesus," Vaughn says, closing the folder.

"I'm sorry." Erin refills Vaughn's glass with scotch.

"Where did you get all this?"

Erin pauses, unsure how much to share. "Corey King. He came into my office, waved the file in my face, said your cousin was going down."

Vaughn feels dazed. "This is the same stuff one of Amtrak's representatives on the NTSB go-team cross-examined Eddy about. How is it that Corey King gets a copy? Is there some connection between your firm and Amtrak?"

Erin opens her palms. "You're asking the wrong person. Geoffrey Day has a special team of lawyers working the investigation, and I'm not on it."

"But Corey is?"

"Oh yeah."

"So he and Day are—"

"Connected at the hip."

"It wouldn't make sense for Amtrak to be helping Day get dirt on my cousin. Eddy was Amtrak's employee when he crashed the train. Anything bad that Eddy did gets imputed to the railroad in the civil litigation. It'd stick to them as badly as to him."

"Which," Erin says, "tells me that someone in Amtrak is acting as a mole, helping Day on the sly."

Vaughn considers this. "Has Corey ever mentioned the name Jack Bunting to you? He was the Amtrak guy at the NTSB interview of Eddy."

"No. But that doesn't mean anything. Corey doesn't talk to me about the firm's investigation. He only came into my office this afternoon to gloat."

They sit for a while without talking. Then Vaughn says, "I screwed up. I've only been helping Eddy for a few weeks, and I already made a major mistake. I never should've agreed to let the NTSB interview him. Once Bunting started going after Eddy, I had no choice but to cut the interview short and walk out. That's going to be leaked to the press, and it's going to sound bad."

"You were protecting your client. And it was your decision, not Eddy's, to end the questioning. So long as your cousin didn't actually lie to the NTSB, he'll be fine. As for you, cut yourself some slack. You're facing off against the government, the press, and the biggest P.I. firms in the city. You have one hand tied behind your back because your client can't remember what happened—or is telling you that he can't. You're wading through a whole new area of the law—for you. Pretty ballsy, if you ask me."

Vaughn forces a smile, grateful for Erin's pep talk. He takes a long sip of the scotch. "It won't take much more before this stuff starts to go to my head," he says, nodding at his glass.

Erin studies Vaughn for a moment, then lifts the bottle and refills his glass.

When Vaughn wakes up the next morning, his head is throbbing. So are his balls. He smiles at Erin, still sleeping, and reaches over, pulls a couple of strands of hair off her face. Then he leans down and gently kisses her lips.

Erin stirs, shoos him away with the back of her hand. "Coffee," she mumbles.

Vaughn laughs and gets out of bed. He walks to the kitchen, brews a cup of Starbucks Komodo Dragon on Erin's Keurig, and brings it to her in bed.

"Black, no sugar," he says as he sits the mug on the nightstand. Erin opens one eye, then closes it again. Vaughn leaves her and takes a shower. When he comes back, Erin is sitting up drinking the coffee.

"You and that scotch wore me out last night," Erin says.

"The hooch had nothing to do with it. The credit's all mine."

"If that's what you need to tell yourself, run with it."

"I'm not going to be running anytime soon. You wore me out, too."

Erin smirks. "Where's my morning paper? What kind of doorman are you?"

"Bossy as ever," Vaughn says. But he takes Erin's cue and walks to the front door to retrieve the *Inquirer*, which Erin's real doorman apparently leaves outside her apartment each morning. His stomach drops as he unfolds the paper and sees the headline: "Engineer Had Long History of Alcohol, Violence, and Reckless Driving."

"Son of a bitch." Vaughn stands in the doorway, still wearing only a towel, and reads the article. It's long and details most of what's in Eddy's criminal record. The continuation on page two carries the black-eyes/fat-lip mug shot and quotes an anonymous source claiming that Eddy and his "lawyer-cousin" stormed out of the NTSB interview rather than answer questions about Eddy's pre-Amtrak past.

Vaughn carries the newspaper back to Erin and turns on her bedroom TV as she reads it. The cable news channels are all broadcasting the story. Disturbed as he is by the negative press about Eddy, Vaughn becomes even more upset when the angle shifts to Vaughn himself and the firm.

"What do we know about the cousin of the engineer?" asks one of the guests on *Morning Joe*. "Is he a bona fide lawyer? And what about this firm he works for—McFarland and Klein? Are they some nickel-and-dime outfit?"

"Mick and Susan are going to flip when they hear this shit," Vaughn says to Erin.

She opens her mouth to offer up another pep talk, but nothing comes out.

What can she say?

12

TUESDAY, JULY 7

Geoffrey Day reclines behind his desk in his ergonomic Aeron chair by Herman Miller. Across from him sit Jason Rutledge, a third-year associate, and Samantha Evers, who's been with the firm for two years. Day called them to his office an hour earlier to discuss "important business." Since that time, he's ignored them utterly. The first ten minutes he spent dictating a letter. The rest of the time, he's been on the phone.

About thirty minutes in, Jason quietly asked if it would be better if he and Samantha came back later. Day's perpetually disapproving frown deepened into a scowl, and he turned to face the floor-to-ceiling windows behind his desk. Jason and Samantha traded uncomfortable glances, then looked down, pretending to be somewhere else.

Another thirty minutes later, Jason quietly removes his iPhone from his pocket.

"Am I boring you, Jason?" Day has now turned around and is off the phone.

"Oh. No, I—"

Day raises his hand, signaling Jason to stop.

"The reason I've called you both here is that I've been reviewing your work. Jason, I've read the deposition of the defendant doctor in the Crowley case. Samantha, I've looked over your questioning of the two department-store managers in the Dorman matter."

Day lets this sit while he slowly reaches for the Smartwater bottle on his blotter, removes the cap, takes a swallow, replaces the cap, and repositions the bottle.

Jason and Samantha watch every move, holding their breaths.

"Samantha, I thought I sat down with you before the depositions and discussed, in some detail, both our overall strategy and the key points you were to establish with your questions." Day pauses. "Or am I misremembering?"

"Uh, no. We met ahead of time and prepared."

"And yet, three of the seven areas I instructed you to cover especially thoroughly, you more or less skated over."

"Skated? No."

"No? You believe you adequately addressed the managers' notice of the defective flooring that caused Mrs. Dorman to fall and shatter her pelvis?"

On the defensive now, Samantha leans forward. "Yes. I was very thorough on the notice issues. I—"

"So you're right and I'm wrong?" Day asks incredulously, removing his glasses for a brief inspection, then putting them back on.

Samantha's jaw drops. "Well, what I'm saying is that—"

Day raises his hand again. He shakes his head, sighs, then looks at Jason.

"The defense attorney in Crowley—what was his name again?"

"Gallagher. Robert Gallagher."

"A good lawyer. Tell me, was he smiling when you questioned his client? Because he should've been. You let his client drone on and on in response to almost every one of your questions. You walked away from that deposition without a single crisp sound bite I could use to hit the doctor over the head with at trial."

"I . . . I thought the deposition went well for us. I got a lot of good information—"

"Information." Day spits out the word like a piece of gristle. "We have our own doctors on staff to give us *information*. What we need from the deposition of the defendant doctor in a medical-malpractice case are damning admissions and patently false excuses. Come on, now, that's Doctor Depositions 101."

Jason looks down. "I apologize. I'll—"

"What you'll *do* is read my own depositions of the defendants in the McSorley and Zimmerman cases. Better yet, watch the videos. Then, I want you to summarize the depositions, highlighting the places where you think I was especially effective."

Geoffrey slowly goes through the motions with his water bottle again, then turns to Samantha. "I'd like you to go and see Deborah Manning in HR."

Day pauses to observe Samantha's face collapse as she realizes what he's just told her. Looking much like a scientist observing a failed lab experiment, he reaches for the phone, signaling that the meeting is over. He watches the two young lawyers leave and close the door behind them. News of Samantha's termination will spread through the firm like wildfire, he knows. She's a popular associate, and she's made no secret of the fact that she graduated law school $200,000 in debt.

Day yawns. One of the necessary exercises in leadership, he's learned, is that, from time to time, someone's head has to roll. The atmosphere in the firm had been growing a little lax of late. What's needed now—especially with the influx of cases from the Amtrak disaster—is a heightened sense of tension, of urgency. So it's time to dust off the chopping block. Though Samantha is as capable as Jason—probably more so, truth be told—Jason's father is Senator Rutledge of Ohio, so Jason isn't going anywhere.

A knock on the doorjamb pulls Day from his thoughts. He looks up as his secretary, Kristen, sticks her head through the doorway. "It's one o'clock. Time for the press conference," she says. "The reporters have set up their microphones in the conference room, and the security desk downstairs called to tell us that Mr. Balzac is on his way up."

When Eva closes the door, Day cringes. The mere mention of Balzac's name turns his stomach. The thought of having to sit next to that boor makes him shudder. But one does what one must.

◆ ◆ ◆

Three minutes later, Vaughn Coburn stands before the TV in Mick's office, watching Day and Balzac give their second press conference. Mick sits at his desk, watching with him. The spectacle is just like the first episode: Day and Balzac sitting side by side behind a small forest of microphones. Thin-shouldered Day sits erect and waves his long-fingered hands with fluid, almost effeminate, gesticulations. Balzac, stocky with black hair and beard, hunches over the table, looking like he's ready to grunt.

Day begins by reading from Eddy's Amtrak application for employment. "The very first thing on this application," Day says, "is as follows: 'I certify that the information contained in this application is true to the best of my knowledge. I understand that false information or the failure to provide complete information are grounds for dismissal.'"

Day pauses and waves the six-page document. Then he sets it down, turns the page, and reads, "Question: 'Have you ever been convicted of a crime?' And his answer?" Day asks, his voice thick with indignation. "His answer? 'No.'" Day tosses the application across the table in disgust, then picks up a thick pile of papers. "Yet what do the public records show? That he's been convicted of *many* crimes, from killing a police officer racing his car, to disorderly conduct, assault, and any number of driving violations. Outrageous. Absolutely outrageous."

Day sits back, and Balzac takes over. "And that's only half the equation. The other half is Amtrak's own failure to investigate this convicted criminal before hiring him." Here, Balzac holds up his own copy of the job application. "This application expressly gives Amtrak the right—and here I quote—'to thoroughly investigate my past employment and activities.' But Amtrak didn't undertake any investigation. It simply hired this young man who, by the way, not only had a criminal record but also a history of alcohol abuse, and sat him down in the engineer's cabin of a high-speed train packed with passengers."

"Unconscionable," says Geoffrey Day.

The press conference continues for another minute before the local Fox TV anchor cuts away to give her own brief synopsis of the train crash. Vaughn sighs and turns to Mick, who does not look happy.

"I asked you last week to think hard about whether you should be representing your cousin in this mess. Have you?"

Vaughn takes a deep breath. "I have. And I think that as long as he's not facing any criminal charges, I can handle it. So far, all we've really had to contend with are a couple of strutting plaintiffs' attorneys—"

"And the NTSB."

"Which is just an investigatory agency. And which has been fair to my cousin, with the exception of a single member of the go-team. We've faced tougher scrutiny than this. So have our clients. In the Hanson case, the press was actively trying to sabotage your friend, and the prosecutor and police seemed to have personal vendettas against him. And against you."

Mick's face sours. The Hanson case almost destroyed him—and his family. "Look, I don't shy away from fights. Neither does Susan. You know that. This firm exists to fight. And you're right about the Hanson case; we were getting it from all sides." Mick rests his forearms on his desk, lowers his head. After a moment, he looks up at Vaughn. "All right. You can move forward with your cousin, for now. But if he gets charged criminally, we're going to revisit this. Understood?"

"Absolutely."

"In the meantime, I suggest you find whatever dirt you can on Day and Balzac. Have Tommy help."

Vaughn knows Day is playing by crooked rules from the fact that he somehow obtained Eddy's employment records, probably from a mole working for the railroad. Hopefully, Day's chicanery will prove his undoing.

"I'm going to call Arthur Hogarth," Mick says, referring to the legendary P.I. attorney. "And ask him to talk to you."

"Really? I thought A-Hog had a heart attack."

"Four of them. The last one was eighteen months ago. He's retired now and living in Boca. I referred some good personal-injury cases to him over the years, so I'm sure he'll talk to you if I ask him."

"That would be great."

"Give me a few minutes to give him the heads-up that you'll be calling. I'll e-mail you his cell number."

Vaughn returns to his office and waits until Mick's e-mail comes through. Then he dials Hogarth's number. A-Hog picks up on the first ring.

"So, you want to know about Geoffrey Day and Benjamin Balzac. What are you looking for?"

"Dirt."

"How long do you have?"

Vaughn chuckles. Then, without revealing Erin's identity, he shares her theory that Day and Balzac are going after Eddy to make him a scapegoat in order to prop up their punitive-damages claims. He also shares Erin's view that Day and Balzac want to get the $200 million cap on damages raised.

"Raising the cap's been tried before, without success. But Day and Balzac are both very well connected. Their tentacles reach into every hallway in DC. As did mine, until recently," Hogarth adds with a sigh.

"So, what's their background? Where did they come from?"

"Well, Day followed the traditional path of a big-time P.I. attorney. Right out of law school, he went to work for the most successful personal-injury firm in town. Worked hard at his cases, harder at office politics. Then, when the boss was least expecting it—right after marrying the man's niece—he left the firm and took twenty of its biggest clients with him. That's more than twice as many cases as I pilfered when I left my first firm. Day formed his own firm with that nimrod former governor of ours, Everett Lockwood. A good move because of Lockwood's political connections and his family money, which kept Day's firm afloat until the cases paid off. Day won some big verdicts. Made a name for himself. He was able to bring on some associates, who stole cases from their own firms, and after ten years or so, he was a major player. Now, he's got his name on our best law school."

"And Balzac?"

"Now there's a horse of a different color. Benny Balls—that's what they call him, you know—grew up in Upper Darby. He went to a small state college, then on to some law school in the Midwest. Rumor is he couldn't get into any of the local law schools—didn't have the grades. But Balzac had street smarts. I saw that right away and offered him a job when he interviewed. Everyone at the firm told me I was nuts, but I hired him anyway. He did well, at first. Then, I started to hear things about how he handled some of his cases. Don't ask me what—I'd rather not say. And he was always fighting with the other lawyers—and our staff. He bullied people. Finally, I had to fire him."

"How'd he take that?"

"Not well. But what could he do? I was one of the most powerful attorneys in the city, and he was still just a grunt. Not long after he left, I heard he'd hung his own shingle. For several years, he hustled slip-and-fall cases and low-end auto cases. My associates would run into him in discovery court from time to time and come back with stories about how rude he was to some judge or lawyer. Then, about five years out, he struck gold. He landed a medical-malpractice case and tried it to an eight-figure verdict. An enormous amount back then. I think it involved an amputation. You can look it up—the defendants tried to get the verdict thrown out, so there's an appellate decision. It's the McCord case, or McCrory. The money Balzac brought home was enough to lay the foundation for the firm he runs now. He bought that four-story brick behemoth on Delancey Street and filled it with associates."

Vaughn pauses to take in what Hogarth has told him. "On television, Day and Balzac act like they're best friends. But my source tells me they despise each other."

"They've been at each other's throats since the beginning of their careers. Day was the first associate to come to me and say I should fire Balzac."

"So *you* were the P.I. attorney Day left and stole cases from?"

"Right after he married my brother's child. The shit. I hired him and Balzac together. One fought openly with every other member of my team and disgraced the firm. The other used deception to earn my trust, then stole millions of dollars' worth of cases from me. They've spent the years since then battling me, and each other, for business."

What a nest of vipers, these civil litigators.

"If they're such antagonistic competitors, why are they working so closely together on the Amtrak-crash litigation?"

"There's only one reason: they believe they can get more of the cases by holding themselves out as a team. They may be the biggest P.I. firms in town—now that I'm gone—but they aren't the only ones. By presenting a united front—and making it seem inevitable that they'll control the litigation—Day and Balzac will dissuade other firms from trying to seize the litigation themselves."

Vaughn considers Hogarth's explanation. On the surface, it sounds plausible, but Vaughn senses there's more to it. "And just how much do they stand to gain from the crash?"

"The math's not hard. Even if the cap remains at two hundred million, the standard one-third contingency will generate fees of sixty million, the lion's share of which will likely go to Day and Balzac. And Day needs the money."

"Needs the money?" This surprises Vaughn. "Why?"

"Two reasons: Penn Law and Relazac."

The Penn donation Vaughn knows about. "What's Relazac?"

"A nationwide litigation that Day engineered against Glaxon Pharmaceuticals. He invested millions before the cases fell apart on him. Word on the street was that Day was about to go under but found a white knight at the last minute to float him."

Vaughn makes a mental note to ask Erin about Relazac, then weighs what Hogarth has told him about Day and Balzac. "Which of the two should I be more concerned with?"

A-Hog laughs. "That's like asking which to be more afraid of, a cobra or a rattler." He pauses for a moment, then says, "It's a close call; they're both predators. But I'd be a little more worried about Day. That's only because Balzac doesn't try to hide what he is. He's the rattler—no lack of warnings from that one. Day's the cobra, hiding in the grass, striking you before you know he's there."

Vaughn pauses, and while he's thinking, A-Hog asks, "How is any of this going to help you defend your engineer?"

"Honestly, I have no idea. But I feel like I'm on a sheer rock face, grabbing for any handhold I can find. So, thank you for taking the time to talk with me."

"Don't worry about it. And if you need any more help moving forward, give me a call. I'm bored out of my skull."

"Retirement's not what it's cut out to be?"

Hogarth snorts. "My doctor told me I had to give up working to save my life. Well, let me tell you something: saving my life is killing me."

Vaughn laughs, and they both hang up. He leans in to his computer, pulls up Westlaw, and finds the case A-Hog mentioned. *McCrory v. Hospital of the University of Pennsylvania, et al.* After a two-week trial, Balzac won a $12 million verdict for his client, a fourteen-year-old girl who developed osteosarcoma, a bone cancer, in her left leg. The leg had to be amputated to prevent the spread of the cancer. Tragically, the surgeon—Dr. Matthew Anderson—mistakenly amputated the healthy right leg. When he realized his error, Anderson told the girl and her devastated family that the left leg still had to be removed. The patient and her parents sued Anderson and the hospital both, and won.

The hospital appealed, claiming the jury had been improperly inflamed by emotion, but what amazes Vaughn is that the cause of the jury's passion wasn't because of anything that Balzac had done, but rather was the result of Anderson's own epic offensiveness on the stand. The record contained more than a dozen exchanges between Anderson and Balzac, and between Anderson and his own counsel, in which the surgeon insulted the young plaintiff, dismissed the seriousness of his mistake, and even laughed openly at the girl and her parents. Some of Anderson's more noteworthy remarks included: "That one wasn't going to be a runway model anyway," and "Well, she's too old for hopscotch."

Vaughn reads and rereads the appellate court's decision affirming the verdict. *What the hell went on at that trial?* Dr. Anderson's behavior on the stand made no sense whatsoever. He had to have known that his outlandish remarks would only provoke the jury.

Vaughn prints out the case. He'll reach out to Balzac's opposing counsel in the case to find out if something happened at the trial that sheds light on the surgeon's erratic behavior.

13

Wednesday, July 9

The neon-blue display on Erin's nightstand clock reads 2:15 a.m. Vaughn is on his back, Erin straddling him, her hips pumping rhythmically. Both of them are slick with sweat; it's a hot night in July, the temperature hovering close to ninety, and hot air flows through the open window. Erin's back is arched, her head back. Her eyes are half-closed. Vaughn and Erin grip each other's hands tightly, and he feels her nails digging into his flesh. Vaughn opens his eyes to watch her. He enjoys her firm breasts; her large, dark nipples; her thin hips; her plump, pink lips. Mostly he loves seeing the rapture on her face; Erin gets more lost in it than any other woman he's ever been with. For Erin, sex is an act of complete surrender. Not to Vaughn, but to something inside herself.

Erin begins to move faster, and her breathing speeds up. Her muscles tense. Her rhythm breaks into manic thrusting. She sighs, then moans, then groans, until, at last, she spasms and gasps. Vaughn climaxes with her, and they grind and crash against each other until they are spent.

When they're finished, Erin falls onto Vaughn and they kiss each other deeply. Vaughn's tongue tastes her salt. Her sweet musk fills his nose. Then she rolls off him, onto her back.

"Skinny V," she whispers, her nickname for him. "Except where it counts," she adds, more to herself than to him.

This was the third time Vaughn and Erin made love that night, and the fourth night in a row they've been together—and neither has let up, or wanted to. Only now that he's been with her again does Vaughn realize how much he's missed her. How stupid it was to let her go. What was he thinking? That the world was filled with women like Erin? That he'd have no problem meeting someone else with whom he'd share such passion?

Vaughn recognizes much of himself in her: the same animal that paces inside him, recoiling at the restraint required by everyday life.

Vaughn turns his head to look at Erin. Her breathing is steady now, and he knows she's asleep. He closes his own eyes and drifts off. But his worries don't let him rest long, and he's fully awake after just a few hours. Quietly, he leaves the bed and dresses. He walks to Erin's side of the bed, leans over, and kisses her gently on the forehead. She doesn't stir.

It's 5:15 a.m. when Vaughn leaves Erin's building, and the sunlight is beginning to leak upward on the eastern horizon. Even before the sex, the night had been a fun one. Erin baked ziti and he'd brought a bottle of red table wine. They laughed as they ate, then rented *My Cousin Vinny* and laughed even harder. Questions about the crash, the NTSB's investigation, and Day and Balzac spun around inside his head, but he did his best to push them down, to just take a night off, enjoy his newfound thing with Erin. It wasn't easy, but by the time they went to bed, he was feeling good.

Vaughn pauses on the brick plaza outside the building and takes a deep breath. The air is still hot and humid. Vaughn hears birds chirping across Sixth Street, in Washington Square. He doesn't notice the black Escalade parked against the sidewalk until its driver exits the SUV.

"Now this is interesting," says Johnny Giacobetti, walking around the vehicle toward Vaughn. "The engineer's defense attorney spending his nights with one of the crash victim's P.I. lawyers."

Vaughn stares as Giacobetti lets the words hang.

"So tell me," the enormous man continues, "are you pumping her for information, or is it the other way around? Or are the two of you just pumping each other, period?"

Vaughn's face reddens. He's pissed. He knows there's no way he could take this giant, but he could get in enough punches to make the thug remember him. "That's disrespectful," he says.

Giacobetti laughs. "We're talking respect now? That's good. Respect my business."

"Oh yeah? Exactly what is your business *here?*"

"Here? As opposed to that run-down little farmhouse in Lancaster County where your cousin is holed up? That's a good question. And the answer is that I'm not there right now because Mr. Nunzio hasn't made up his mind about your cousin yet. But he's thinking about it. Especially after those lawyers showed everyone what a liar your cousin is at that press conference."

"None of that had a goddamned thing to do with the accident," Vaughn says, trying to hide his alarm at the mobsters' discovery of Eddy and Kate's hideout. "All those hucksters are trying to do is whip up public sentiment against Eddy, and Amtrak. To get punitive damages down the line, if the cases ever go to trial."

"See, now that's where Mr. Nunzio would disagree with you. All of that stuff those lawyers said *is* important, because it has to do with whether your cousin is telling the truth when he says he doesn't remember what happened."

"Look, I don't know what to tell you. No one wants to know what happened more than my cousin—"

"You think?" Giacobetti interrupts. "I know about two hundred people who probably care more about why that train crashed than your cousin, thirty of which are dead and one of which is Mr. Nunzio's son."

Vaughn glares at the big man. He's more than a little nervous, but his patience has run out. "Where are we going with this? Are you here to knock me around, send me a message?"

Giacobetti laughs again. "Knock you around. That's a good one. As if Mr. Nunzio would waste time with that in this particular situation. No, there won't be any beatings at this point. But you're right about the message part. So here it is: 'No more surprises.' If any more information gets out that your cousin knows more than he's saying—that he really is to blame, which, to me, already pretty much seems to be the case . . ." Johnny leaves the rest of the sentence hanging.

"Yeah? Then what?"

The big man shrugs. "Do I really have to say it?" With that, he turns away, walks around the car, and gets in.

Vaughn watches the big SUV pull away from the curb, drive down Sixth past Washington Square Park, and turn left onto Walnut. He exhales once the car is out of view. "Shit."

Vaughn walks down Spruce Street, toward his own second-floor walk-up twenty blocks away on the 1900 block of Spruce. He's exhausted from last night, but after the exchange with Jimmy Nutzo's muscle, he needs the walk to clear his head. By the time Vaughn reaches his apartment, he's soaked with sweat. He takes a long, cool shower but still seems to be sweating as he towels off. He turns his window air conditioner down as cold as it will go, then fries himself some eggs. He doesn't turn on the TV; he can't bear to watch the news, can't stomach any more negative press about Eddy.

Vaughn eats quietly, the only sound in the small apartment the steady hum of the Frigidaire. His thoughts meander from his renewed relationship with Erin to his troubled past with Eddy to the tension at work with Susan and now Mick. He has to make this work out well for Eddy; he owes his cousin. But how? Even if the NTSB—given Eddy's inability to remember what happened and the lack of hard evidence—doesn't blame the accident on his cousin, and even if Eddy never faces criminal charges, Eddy's career is over. Amtrak will never take him back. And any other railroad would be crazy to touch him. In fact, why would *any* employer ever hire Eddy? And then, of course, there's the biggest problem of all: Jimmy Nutzo. The NTSB investigation, Eddy's future job prospects, even the possibility of jail, are thin threats compared to the cloud hanging over Eddy so long as the mobster thinks he's culpable. Vaughn shakes his head as the realization sinks in that the only way he can save his cousin is to prove that he was *blameless* for the crash.

"But that's impossible," he says aloud. There's no way that Eddy *can't* be at fault here. He had to have been distracted not to have seen the huge TracVac his train collided with. But what possible distraction could there be that would justify him taking his eyes off the track ahead? For a full fifteen seconds? None that Vaughn can see. The bottom line is that Eddy Coburn is screwed, and all Vaughn will be able to do for his cousin is to stand beside him, fight with him, champion his hopeless cause until the NTSB reaches its final conclusions and Eddy is forced to enter the next—and likely last, and short—stage of his life.

"Jesus."

More than anything right now, Vaughn wishes he were in his uncle's gym, hitting the heavy bag. Or sparring with someone as angry and frustrated as he is.

In the office, Vaughn asks Angie to print out the complaints that have been filed so far on behalf of the train-crash victims. He's had her checking the docket of the federal court for the Eastern District of Pennsylvania, where most of the cases are being filed, as well as the federal dockets in New York and New Jersey. His plan is to review the complaints over the weekend. He's not sure what he'll find in them, but you never know; maybe he'll come across a piece of information he doesn't have.

Susan comes into Vaughn's office and snipes at him for not getting her a brief she'd asked for earlier in the week. He apologizes and promises the brief, in final form, first thing the next morning. As soon as

Susan leaves, Angie buzzes and tells him Nelson Wexler is on the phone. Vaughn remains upset at what happened at the NTSB's interview of Eddy and has declined to answer a half dozen calls from Wexler. He's about to tell Angie to put Wexler off again, but changes his mind. He might need his help down the pike. Vaughn says he'll take the call and pushes the button that connects him to Wexler.

"Vaughn Coburn," he says.

"Mr. Coburn, thank you for picking up. I wanted to apologize for the adversarial tone taken by Mr. Bunting. Our interviews are not intended to be accusatory. He overstepped his bounds, and I told him so after you left."

"Thank you for doing that," Vaughn says, his voice flat.

"You're welcome. And to offer you another olive branch, I'm going to share something with you."

"You found out something about what caused the accident?" Vaughn asks, both hopefully and with trepidation.

"I wish that were the case. No, what I learned is that your district attorney is being pressured to bring criminal charges against your cousin."

"*What?* By whom?"

Wexler pauses. "Let's just say the pressure is coming from people who might have a lot to gain, financially, should your cousin's culpability rise to the level of a crime."

"Eddy's culpability? What about the track crew that left the machine on a live track? Why isn't anyone pressing to bring *them* up on charges?"

"We've questioned the crew members, and it's pretty clear to us that they didn't leave the TracVac on Track 2. It seems they left the machine on Track 1, and we're coming to believe that it may have been moved to Track 2 by vandals. The track crews' only malfeasance was in not properly securing the giant excavator against movement, which is being chalked up to their lack of experience in using the new machine. I would have told you all this had you taken my earlier calls."

Vaughn kicks himself for pushing Wexler off until now. Still, he goes on the offensive. "Really? The machine was moved by vandals who just happened to know how to maneuver a complex piece of railroad equipment?"

"We interviewed everyone on the track crew, and they all swear they left the machine on Track 1 the afternoon before. Other trains passed down Track 2 that afternoon and evening, and on the morning of the accident, before Train 174. More than a dozen. The TracVac had to have been moved during the thirty minutes before the crash, and we know the track crew was working out by Thorndale at that time."

"What about the foreman, Reggie Frye? The media are saying he claims he was out sick that day."

"The railroad confirmed Mr. Frye called out that morning. When we interviewed him, Frye gave us permission to obtain his medical records. They showed he'd gone to his physician that morning with a bad stomach virus. Nonetheless, to be thorough, we're in the process of re-interviewing the track crew, including Frye—once we succeed in reaching him."

"Reaching him?"

"He's not answering our calls, or the press's, either, from what I understand."

Vaughn thinks for a minute, then changes direction. "How did you find out about the pressure to charge Eddy?"

"The Philly DA called me himself to give me the heads-up and to ask if I had any information that would justify bringing your cousin up on charges."

"What did you tell him?"

"The truth. We know that your cousin failed to react to the presence of the TracVac, by either slowing down his train or throwing it into emergency, but we don't know why. Your cousin can't remember what happened in the moments leading up to the crash, and the inward-facing camera can't tell us because it was turned off. We do know your cousin wasn't talking on his cell phone, wasn't texting, so that can't be why he was distracted—if, in fact, he was distracted as opposed to unconscious. And on that score, we have no evidence of any medical conditions that would've caused your cousin to pass out. So, in my opinion—and this is what I told him—the record at this point isn't sufficient to lead to any firm conclusions one way or the other."

"And what did he say to that?"

"He mumbled something about being between a rock and a hard place. I got the impression that the people behind this are strong-arming him."

"How are they doing that?"

"Some are saying the DA's going to run for mayor next year."

"So?"

"Political campaigns are very expensive."

"So they're offering him *money*? To go after my cousin?"

Wexler sighs but doesn't answer.

Vaughn thanks Wexler for the tip, and they hang up. Vaughn jumps from his chair and paces his office, stewing. After a few minutes of doing this, he makes a decision.

Time to go on the offensive against these assholes.

Vaughn walks to his phone, picks up the receiver, and calls Tommy.

"Vaughn, how you doin'?"

"I'm pissed is how I'm doing." Vaughn tells Tommy about the call from Wexler, including that someone is pushing the DA to bring charges against Eddy and offering money to do so. "He didn't name names, but I'm sure it's those two carnival barkers, Day and Balzac. I want to find out everything I can about them. Can you poke around? Also, if you can use your contacts at Amtrak, I need to find out about Jack Bunting. He was the railroad-management rep on the go-team who interviewed Eddy."

"Why do you want to know about him?"

"Because unlike the others, he really went after my cousin in his questioning. It felt to me like he was planning a hatchet job from the outset." Vaughn realizes he probably sounds paranoid to Tommy, but he doesn't care. He *is* feeling paranoid. "And see what you can learn about the track-crew foreman, Reggie Frye. It seems he's gone underground."

"Got it. I know some guys. I'll find out what I can. And I'm glad to see you swinging the sword on this one and not just hiding behind a shield. You know what they say about the best defense."

Vaughn is glad that Tommy's down with his plan. Not that he's surprised. Tommy's never been one to hesitate. Unlike his brother, Mick, who is more careful about striking out, Tommy's been through a lot. He did a stretch in prison when he was younger. Vaughn would love to know the full story on that. But neither Tommy nor Mick has never offered the tale, and Vaughn knows not to press an ex-con about his past.

He spends the next three hours working on the brief for Susan. He focuses on the work, but even so, an idea percolates in the back of his mind.

If he really is going to go on the offensive, why shouldn't he hold a press conference of his own?

14

SATURDAY AND SUNDAY, JULY 12–13

It's Saturday morning just after eleven o'clock, and Vaughn sits at his kitchen table. He called the farmhouse the night before to check up on his cousin and Kate. They both said they were okay, but he could hear the strain in their voices. He did his best to allay their fears by saying he was making some progress in his investigation into the accident, but he doubted he sounded very convincing. He still hasn't told Eddy and Kate about the threat posed by Nunzio. It would be worse than pointless to do so; they couldn't do anything about Nunzio, so knowing would only add to their already unbearable stress. Nor would it help to relocate them again. Wherever he moved Eddy and Kate, Nunzio would surely find them. Hell, Johnny Giacobetti's probably watching his apartment at this moment. Hanging up the phone, he felt worse than before he called, and he was pretty sure his cousin and Kate did, too. Needless to say, he hadn't gotten much sleep.

Sitting before Vaughn on the table is the pile of complaints Angie printed out for him on Friday. It's been less than a month since the train crash, and already fifty civil cases have been filed. Thirty-five cases have been brought in the Eastern District of Pennsylvania by Day and Balzac. Six cases are pending in the Eastern and Southern Districts of New York. There are three cases in the District Court of New Jersey, and four other cases sitting in the district courts of Massachusetts, Maine, and Maryland. Two cases have been filed in state courts.

Every one of the complaints includes a count asking for punitive damages. The complaints condemn Amtrak based on the company's hiring of a locomotive engineer with a known or discoverable propensity for reckless and deadly operation of motor vehicles and a history of alcohol abuse and criminality. As to Eddy himself, the complaints assert that his failure to observe and respond to the TracVac constituted "outrageous and reckless" conduct. The complaints written by Day and Balzac appear to have been filed earliest, with the other lawyers' complaints coming later and parroting Day and Balzac's language almost word for word. Something about the allegations scratches at the back of Vaughn's mind, but he can't figure out what it is.

In addition to the complaints, Angie printed a motion by Day and Lockwood and the Balzac Firm to the United States Judicial Panel on Multidistrict Litigation. In the motion, Day and Balzac ask the multidistrict panel to centralize all pretrial proceedings in the federal court in Philadelphia, and to appoint the Day and Balzac firms as liaison counsel, putting them in charge of the entire litigation.

Vaughn finishes reading the material, then stuffs it into the leather satchel he uses as his briefcase. He puts his sweatpants on over his shorts, grabs his gym bag, and leaves his apartment. He's going to Northeast Philly to spend some time at his uncle's boxing gym, then have lunch with Eddy's side of the family. Forty minutes later, Vaughn pulls his old Jeep Wrangler Sport against the curb on Longshore Avenue in the Tacony section. Frank Coburn's Boxing Club is housed in a three-story brick pile built at the turn of the last century and looking, on the outside, every bit its age.

Vaughn climbs a set of stairs to enter the gym on the second floor. He pauses in the doorway to take it in and is immediately hit with a familiar smell—a suitcase full of socks that haven't been washed in a month. His ears take in the machine-gun-fast *thumpada-thumpada-thumpada* of the speed bag and the cracking of gloves against the heavy bags. Vaughn looks around. Fluorescent tube lighting hangs on the ceiling. Support beams run down the center of the room, from front to back. The walls are cheap paneling and drywall, overhung by boxing posters and photos of club boxers. Five Everlast heavy bags hang from the ceiling by thick chains.

The main attraction is a three-rope ring. Right now, two fighters are sparring. Vaughn walks past the bench press and bags and pauses to watch them. Both fighters are about Vaughn's size, five ten, mid-160s. One, in red trunks, is light on his feet; the other has a longer reach and hits harder. They must've been going at it for a while; they are drenched and tired. Vaughn envies them. It's been a long time since he's sparred in the ring.

"There he is," says a gruff, gritty voice.

"Uncle Frank." Vaughn turns, offers his hand. It disappears into Frank's huge paw. "I thought I'd come in, do some bag work before lunch."

"Make yourself at home," Frank says.

Vaughn smiles. Growing up, this place was like a second home to him.

"But first, let's talk a minute," Frank adds, nodding toward his office.

Vaughn follows his uncle into an eight-by-ten room off the gym. The space, enclosed by dark-paneled walls hung with photos of club fighters, is crammed with two gray filing cabinets, a black metal desk, a pair of worn swivel chairs patched with duct tape, a small table with a Mr. Coffee machine, and an assortment of trophies sitting on the floor against the walls.

Frank closes the door and motions for Vaughn to take one of the swivel chairs. Frank sits down in the other, and the men sit facing each other no more than two feet apart. "So," Frank says, "what's your plan?"

Plan? Vaughn doesn't say it, but Frank can read his face well enough.

"You need a plan, boy. A strategy. Isn't that the first thing I taught you and Eddy when you both started here?"

"Yes, sir." Vaughn remembers well his uncle telling him and Eddy that their most important weapon against an opponent wasn't their speed or their strength, but their battle plan: the strategy forged from a keen understanding of their opponent's strengths and weaknesses, and of their own. "Actually, right now, I am gathering information on the major players."

Vaughn tells his uncle about the surprise ambush by Jack Bunting, the missing track foreman, Reggie Frye, the NTSB's belief that vandals moved the track machine, and the pressure that Day and Balzac are putting on the district attorney to bring criminal charges. The last point seems to hit home with Frank. Seeing the stress etching his features, Vaughn decides not to tell his uncle about his meeting with Jimmy Nutzo and his men.

"I always hated lawyers," Frank says. "No offense."

"None taken." Vaughn forces a smile and looks away. He's made it sound to his uncle like he has been gathering intelligence on Day and Balzac and Jack Bunting as the first step in formulating a strategy. In fact, he's merely grasping for a clue as to what to do next.

Frank Coburn studies his nephew for a long minute. "You'll figure it out," he says, and Vaughn knows from the tone of the older man's voice that his uncle has seen through him. "Now go and work out some of your frustration."

Vaughn stands and thanks his uncle. He leaves the office and breathes a sigh of relief. Frank didn't bring up Vaughn's chit—the debt he owes to Eddy, to the whole family, because of what he'd done to his cousin. The liability that weighs on his heart every day, which, on his worst nights, wrenches him from sleep and shouts in his ear, *Coward! Deserter!* and forces him to relive his moment of profound personal failure.

An hour later, Vaughn is soaked in sweat. His arms are rubber, his lungs are on fire. His eyes sting with salt. It was only once he started attacking the heavy bag that he realized how frustrated and angry he really was. The more he cracked the bag, the more his rage seemed to overtake him. He lost track of time and was surprised when the alarm on his iPhone—set for sixty minutes—sounded.

Vaughn takes off his gloves, packs them into his gym bag, and heads to the locker room. Like the gym itself, it hasn't changed since Vaughn first starting boxing there. It has four sets of dented lockers, three slippery shower stalls, two worn benches, two chipped sinks, a pair of urinals, and one well-stained commode. On the floor, interlocking rubber tiles top concrete. The walls are, of course, covered with old boxing posters. Vaughn showers quickly and checks to see if his uncle is still in his office. He's not. Vaughn assumes he's already left for the lunch gathering at his house. Realizing he's late, Vaughn hurries out of the gym and hops into his Jeep.

Frank and Claire Coburn's house is a split-level sitting on a quarter acre at the end of a cul-de-sac. As he approaches the house, Vaughn is surprised by the number of vehicles parked in the driveway and along the perimeter of the street. He thought lunch was going to be a small get-together with Eddy, Kate, his uncle Frank and his aunt Claire, and maybe one of Eddy's sisters. It's obvious to him now that it is going to be a much larger affair.

Vaughn parks his Jeep and walks around the side of the house to the backyard. Half a dozen kids are playing on the cedar swing set and plastic slide that Frank and Claire erected for their grandchildren. The brothers Coburn—Frank and John—are up on the deck by the grill with two younger men Vaughn recognizes as the husbands of Eddy's sisters. A number of the women—including Eddy's two sisters—are seated around a table. Through the sliding glass doors, Vaughn sees more kids, cousins, and in-laws crowded around the island in the kitchen.

Vaughn climbs the three steps to the deck, walks to the cooler, and pulls out a Budweiser. He kisses the women on their cheeks then moves over to the grill and shakes hands with his father, uncle, and cousins-in-law, waving along the way through the window at his mother and Aunt Claire. Before long, Vaughn is immersed in conversation with the men. They talk about the Phillies, the president, bad traffic on the Schuylkill, taxes, this one's new roof, that one's new driveway, how Frank's gym is doing, how John's bar is doing. They talk about everything except *the* thing. Even when Eddy finally shows up—driven by Tommy—and takes his position by Kate's side, everyone treats Eddy as just another cousin or in-law. People do ask him how he's doing, how he's feeling or, more generally, how he's holding up. But no one asks any pointed questions about the crash, the NTSB investigation, or the status of Eddy's job at Amtrak.

Vaughn decides that some agreement must've been reached not to bring up the elephant in the room. Still, he feels its presence, and he can tell that everyone else does as well. Everyone seems to be smiling just a little too broadly, laughing just a little too hard. Two hours into the picnic, Vaughn thinks he's going to skate through it when he's approached by Jean, the older of Eddy's two sisters. Jean has always been a strong-willed woman, never accepting orders from anyone. Vaughn recalls that her temper and spiritedness got her into more than a little trouble in high school. But Jean made it through okay and now runs some sort of small business out of her house, which she commands like the captain of a whaling ship. Her husband, Tim, is a weak second mate.

"We need to talk," Jean says, approaching Vaughn with a beer bottle in her left hand, a sleeping infant in the crook of her right arm.

"Sure. What's up?"

"You know what's up. So does everyone. Are you sure you should be representing Eddy?"

Vaughn opens his mouth, but before he can answer, Jean resumes.

"I mean, you don't have any experience with NTSB investigations, right? Or railroads."

"I've done my homework. I'm getting to know the players, and I have a good handle on the whole process."

Jean studies Vaughn for a long minute. "Eddy's not a guinea pig. You shouldn't be learning a new area of the law on him."

This pisses Vaughn off. "That's not what I'm doing, Jean. And in case you're unclear, it was Eddy—through Kate—who came to *me*. I didn't seek him out as a client."

"You didn't turn him down, either."

"Nor would I, ever."

"Maybe that's the problem here. Maybe the old thing between the two of you is the only reason you didn't turn him down, given your lack of experience. What Eddy could be facing if it gets screwed up—think about it. Would you have agreed to represent some stranger who called and said he just crashed a train full of people, killing dozens, injuring hundreds? Especially if he couldn't pay you?"

"What does it matter *why* I'm representing him so long as I do a good job?"

"You're missing the point. Maybe you *aren't* doing a good job. You just don't know it because you're new to this area of the law, to this type of investigation."

"That's not fair."

"The other day, I was in the supermarket and two women were standing together, looking at me. And one of them said, 'She's the sister. You know, of that engineer.'"

Vaughn, confused by the non sequitur, furrows his brow.

"The point is," Jean continues, "it's not just Eddy you're fighting for. We're all in this, the whole family. My father almost came to blows with another retired cop who said the wrong thing to him on the street. Your own father has lost customers at his bar. I won't even tell you about the toll this thing is taking on my mother."

106

Vaughn takes a deep breath, considers what Jean is telling him.

"Just think about it. That's all," Jean says before turning and walking away.

Vaughn hears someone else approach and turns to see Eddy limping toward him.

"Don't pay her any mind," Eddy says. "Jean has an opinion on everything. Usually the wrong one."

Vaughn takes in Eddy's words. "She made some good points. Maybe you and I should have a real serious talk about this whole thing. Your first instinct, or Kate's, was to turn to me to help you through this. And I'm happy to do it. I'm proud to stand with you on this, Ed. I really am. But maybe neither of us has a clear head. I'm the only lawyer in the family, so it makes sense for you to look to me. And you're my cousin—more like my brother—so my instinct is to fight for you. But we have a history, and it's not a good one, thanks to me. So part of what's going on, with me, is to try to make up—"

"I want you in this with me," Eddy interrupts. "But not because you're a family member who happens to be a lawyer, or even because of how close we were growing up. You're wrong about that. But you're right about the other thing: we do have a past. And because of it, I know I can count on you to give everything you have to get me through this. No matter what happens. That you will not abandon me, no matter what comes out."

The hairs on the back of Vaughn's neck stand straight up at his cousin's words.

No matter what happens. No matter what comes out.

Eddy is hiding something.

Vaughn is about to ask him what's really going on when Kate sidles up beside him. She's uber-pregnant and looks miserable. The three of them exchange a few minutes of uncomfortable small talk before Vaughn excuses himself to walk back up on the deck and say his good-byes. It takes a good thirty minutes for him to extricate himself from the party. Just as he's through the threshold of the front door, his aunt Claire calls after him and follows him to the front walkway.

Vaughn sees worry in his aunt's eyes, but steel as well. She reaches out to him, takes both of his hands in her own, and gets right to the point. "Eddy can't go back to prison."

"Prison? Why—"

"You have no idea how hard it was on him the first time. The things he had to put up with. The things that happened to him—"

"Aunt Claire—"

"You have to promise me that you'll do whatever it takes to make sure that Eddy stays out of jail."

"Well, of course. I'll do everything in my power to—"

"No! That's not enough." Claire tightens her grip on Vaughn's hands. "I'm not asking you to do your best or try your hardest. I want a guarantee, Vaughn. A *promise*. Your word that you'll find a way—whatever you have to do—to see that Eddy doesn't get locked up again like an animal."

Vaughn stares into his aunt's eyes, which bore into him. He knows he can't give her the kind of promise she's asking for. No lawyer can guarantee a certain result. Only a fool would do so. Vaughn takes a long time, then slowly nods his head. "All right."

Claire Coburn throws her arms around her nephew and squeezes for all she's worth.

Driving home, the full weight of Jean's words and his promise to his aunt settles on Vaughn's shoulders.

If I fail, Eddy won't be the only one who pays the price. The whole family will be torn apart.

And it hits Vaughn that's the message he was supposed to take from the picnic. That was the whole point of the get-together. To show him who he was fighting for. Not just Eddy, but all of them.

15

Sunday, July 13

Balzac grunts. The final reps tax him of his last reserves of strength and will; he puts enough weight on the bar to make sure of it. He pushes it up the last few inches, until his arms are fully extended. Then he slowly lowers the dumbbell onto the holders. After a moment, he sits up, then lifts himself from the bench press and walks over to his towel hanging on a spike driven into the wooden support beam.

Balzac dries his face and upper body, rehangs the towel, and walks over to the full-length mirror leaning against the basement wall. His upper arms are thick as tree trunks. He has an eighteen-inch neck. His thigh muscles bulge from all the squat work.

Not bad for a sixty-year-old man.

Balzac stands on a worn pair of old-style Converse sneakers. He's wearing white gym socks with blue stripes, a wife-beater T-shirt, and cotton gym shorts that extend only two inches below his groin. None of that fancy, moisture-wicking workout wear for Benjamin Balzac. No ergonomically designed weight machines, either. Balzac lifts free weights. He's used the same set for almost thirty years.

And why not? he thinks. *Iron doesn't wear out.*

Balzac keeps his gym in the basement of his Gladwyne mansion. When he moved in fifteen years earlier, the space was fitted with a

$100,000 home movie theater. Balzac had it torn out. Not just the retractable screen, reclining leather seats, and Bose sound system, but the paneled walls, carpeting, and coffered ceiling. He had the contractors strip the cellar to the cinder-block walls and cement floor. *That's what a man's workout room should be like,* he told himself. *Primitive, rough, unrefined. A proper place for pain.* He'd felt that way ever since he'd seen Mr. T. doing pull-ups on a basement pipe while the champ pranced around his upscale gym in *Rocky III*.

Balzac climbs the basement stairs to the kitchen. Loki and Thor, his twin 150-pound English mastiffs, rise to greet him. He pulls a bottle of Pellegrino from the Sub-Zero refrigerator and walks down the hall to his study, the great beasts at his heels. The room is cavernous, more than forty feet long with fifteen-foot ceilings. Floor-to-ceiling windows look out onto a rolling lawn. The interior walls are fitted with bookcases made from the same dark mahogany as the flooring. The room's most prominent feature is the massive leather-topped desk, a $35,000 masterwork by local craftsman John Previti. Following Balzac's own design, Previti adorned the desk with intricate carvings of roaring bears. Balzac had always felt an affinity for *Ursus arctos*, particularly the enormous Alaskan browns. It's one reason he always kept a full beard.

Balzac sits quietly for a minute, then reaches for a briefcase leaning against the desk. He withdraws a memory stick and plugs it into the Apple laptop in front of him on the desk. He pushes the power button, and then, once the computer boots up, plays a video. It opens with an aerial view of a railroad track taken from about sixty feet off the ground. In the distance, a passenger train enters a curve. The train rounds the curve into a long straightaway, heading in the direction of the camera. As the train passes below, the camera turns to follow it. For a brief instant, two figures—walking quickly away from the track—are visible below. A few seconds after the camera turns, the ACS-64 crashes into a huge track machine. The car directly behind the engine crashes into it, compressing like an accordion. The cars behind the first car fly off the tracks, some to the left, others to the right.

It's all over in a matter of seconds. Then the screen goes black.

The memory stick containing the video arrived at Balzac's office a week after the crash. It was hand-delivered by a courier who'd been given strict instructions to turn it over only to Balzac himself. The sender was obvious to Balzac from the return address on the envelope.

"Idiot," Balzac says.

He knows Day's purpose in delivering him the video—to send a message. *I have something on you.*

The gesture has troubled him ever since he received it.

Balzac yanks the memory stick from the computer and walks to the fireplace, Thor and Loki following him. He presses a button and the gas flame ignites. For a long moment, Balzac and his beasts stare into the blue flames. Then Balzac tosses the memory stick into the fire and watches it melt.

"Idiot," he says again.

"Mr. Balzac?"

"Annika." Balzac turns toward the door to his study, where his twenty-four-year-old cleaning lady stands holding a bucket of cleaning supplies. He'd forgotten all about her. He shouldn't have. Sunday is her regular cleaning day—a sore point with her because she's a devout Catholic. But he insisted, and she stopped protesting. Not that she had much choice, since Balzac had agreed to be her sponsor toward getting permanent-resident status. Annika had emigrated to the United States four years ago with her mother, from some ex-communist shitzelvania. For reasons neither she nor her mother will get into, they are both deathly afraid of going back.

Balzac studies Annika as he moves back to his desk and sits down. The girl's own eyes are on Thor and Loki. She's told Balzac several times she's afraid of dogs, and terrified of those two, in particular.

"Thor. Loki. Where are your manners? Go say hi to Annika."

Balzac watches Annika stiffen as the dogs approach. They take their time sniffing her before moving away and sitting on either side of the door.

"Mr. Balzac, would it be possible for me to leave a little early today? I'm not feeling well."

"I'm sorry to hear that, but no. I may have some visitors this week, and it's important that the house be spick-and-span. That includes the garage. And the pool area."

Annika forces a smile. "Of course." She turns toward the door—and the dogs—and starts walking fast, arms glued to her sides to get out as quickly as possible.

Balzac calls out to her, "Don't forget to clean those two big rooms on the third floor. The dogs have been shitting there again."

16

MONDAY, JULY 14

It's 9:00 a.m., and Erin has been plodding through a defense brief for more than two hours. Her third cup of coffee sits empty on her desk. She's about to get up and walk to the kitchen for another when her phone buzzes. Its Geoffrey Day's secretary, Kristen.

"Erin? It's, uh, Kristen. Are you available?"

Erin hears stress in Kristen's voice. "Yes. Are you all right?"

"I'm not sure. You'll never guess who just showed up to meet with Geoffrey."

"Who?"

"James Nunzio," Kristen whispers. "The mobster. He's here to interview Geoffrey about representing his son's estate against Amtrak."

Erin's heart skips a beat.

"He wants you in on the meeting," the secretary says.

"Why would Geoffrey want *me* there?"

"Not Geoffrey. Nunzio. He told Geoffrey he wants you to be part of the conversation."

"But I'm not working on that litigation."

"I know. Geoffrey doesn't get it, either."

Erin takes a deep breath. "Okay. I'm on my way," she says, trying to keep her voice even.

Vaughn shared with her his fear for his cousin's life and told her about Jimmy Nutzo's enforcer being parked outside her building the other morning. And now the psychopath is at her firm, undoubtedly seeking to figure out what she's up to with Vaughn. She does not like this one bit.

Erin walks to the private conference room adjoining Day's office. She knocks on the door and enters. "Erin Doyle," she announces, extending her hand and looking directly into Nunzio's gleaming black eyes.

"Firm handshake," the mobster says. "I like that."

"Well, now that we're all here," Day says after Erin is seated, "let me say how honored I am that you're looking to Day and Lockwood to represent your son's estate—"

"I'm considering your firm, Mr. Day. I haven't made any decisions yet."

"Of course. You'll want to interview some other firms as well. I can certainly understand that."

Geoffrey Day is talking fast, and Erin can see that it's because he's nervous. She can tell that Jimmy Nunzio sees it, too.

Corey King opens the door and walks in. "Sorry I'm late, everyone. I had Judge Nyquist on the phone. He talks for*ever*."

"This is Corey King," Day says. "He's one our brightest attorneys. Mr. King was honored this year as a 'rising star' by the Pennsylvania Super Lawyers."

Nunzio looks King up and down. "Yeah. He can leave now."

Day and King exchange uncomfortable glances. Then Day nods toward the door, and Corey leaves, but not before glaring at Erin.

"So, let me tell you where we are with the litigation," Day begins. He explains the number of cases the firm is handling, the number of attorneys working the cases, and what the firm is doing to investigate the crash. "Of course, we're not satisfied to leave it to the NTSB. They're just a government agency. Well intentioned, certainly. But undermanned. No, in litigation of this magnitude, I prefer to do my own investigation . . ."

Day drones on, and Erin watches Nunzio study him, taking in the patrician haughtiness of Day's voice, the disdainful look in his eyes whenever he's speaking of someone other than himself.

The mobster's upper lip curls, revealing his canines as he turns to her.

"So, Ms. Doyle," says Nunzio, interrupting Day in midsentence. "What do you think? Do you believe the engineer really can't remember what happened?"

"Well—"

"Erin isn't part of the Amtrak litigation," Day interrupts. "She's not really up to speed on the matter."

Nunzio slowly turns his head in Day's direction and fixes his stare on the attorney, whose face seems instantly to drain of blood. "Maybe she should be part of the litigation," he says, before turning back to Erin. "Maybe she has some ideas about the crash. Who knows, maybe she has an inside *track*," he adds, smiling at his pun.

"Yes, well, there's always room for one more person on the team," Day says. "There's no such thing as overstaffing a case of this importance."

Erin and Nunzio ignore Geoffrey Day, who's oblivious to the subtext between them.

"Well, of course I don't know any more than what I see and hear in the news," Erin says. "And I promise you, from everything I'm told, the engineer truly doesn't recall the accident. I'm sure he wishes he could; it's probably eating him up that he has no answers for what happened."

Nunzio nods his head ever so slightly. "I hope you're right, Ms. Doyle. It would be a shame if it turned out that young man was holding back information. That he was lying."

Erin wishes she could look away from the mobster, but the gravity of his dark eyes grips her. The two of them stare at each other wordlessly for a long moment, until Day breaks the ice.

"I get the sense that the two of you know each other," Day says, trying to sound perky.

"We have friends in common," Nunzio says, still looking at Erin. Then, without more, he stands and says, "Well, this has been most interesting." The crime lord takes Erin's hand in both of his and smiles. "Ms. Doyle, it's been a pleasure meeting you. Please tell our friends I was asking about them, and that I haven't forgotten them. Not for a minute."

"Of course," Erin answers, forcing a smile. "And I'm certain that you're always on their minds as well."

The meeting concludes, and Geoffrey Day walks the city's most notorious gangster to the elevators, where he thanks Nunzio effusively for considering the firm.

A few moments later, Erin is in her office trying to catch her breath when Geoffrey walks in. "What was that all about? Between you and that . . . criminal."

"I have no idea."

"Who are these friends you share?"

Erin hesitates. "I . . . don't think he'd want me to mention their names."

"I have to say that I'm feeling very uncomfortable right now. This firm has a sterling reputation. I cannot afford to have it sullied by association with known villains."

"You, uh . . . don't want to be his lawyer?"

"There's nothing wrong with representing a person who's despicable. Being his friend is different."

Erin stares at her boss, folds her arms across her chest.

"You know what they say about birds of a feather." And with that, Day turns away.

In his own office, four blocks to the east, Vaughn dials his phone. Patrick Branch was the attorney who represented Dr. Matthew Anderson in the med-mal amputation case brought two decades earlier by Benjamin Balzac. Now in his seventies, Branch is retired. It took some work on Vaughn's part to track him down.

Branch answers the phone, and Vaughn introduces himself only as a Philadelphia lawyer. "I came across the Third Circuit's decision in the McCrory case, and I'm hoping you can tell me a little about it. Do you remember the case?"

"Remember it? I'll never forget it."

"The physician, Dr. Anderson, seems to have self-destructed on the stand. Did you know he was going to do that?"

"No. It took me by complete surprise. The whole way through the discovery period, he seemed perfectly reasonable and committed to defending himself. He insisted to me that it wasn't his fault he amputated the healthy leg; that his nurse had marked the wrong appendage. And he seemed truly upset for the girl, who ended up a double amputee. But then, when he got on the stand . . . Well, you read in the appellate decision what happened."

"Did you know why he said all those things? He had to know his testimony would inflame the jury."

"Did I know then? No."

Vaughn considers Branch's wording. "How about now?"

There is a long pause on the other end of the line. "Do you know anything about Dr. Anderson?" the lawyer asks.

"No. I never heard the name before I read the decision."

Another long pause. "Find out who he's married to."

And with that, the line goes dead.

Who he's married to?

Vaughn turns to his computer screen and googles the doctor. A list of links appears: hospitals.jefferson.edu, LinkedIn, a site called vitals. com, and others. There is also a collection of images of the surgeon showing him in a suit, wearing a lab coat, dressed in surgical scrubs, plus a YouTube video in which Anderson speaks at a medical conference. Toward the bottom of the first page is a category called "Related searches for Matthew Anderson," which includes a list of other links. One of them, amazingly, is entitled, "Matthew Anderson Wife."

Vaughn clicks on the "Wife" link. And there it is: Dr. Anderson standing next to his wife, Elizabeth *Balzac* Anderson.

"Holy shit." Vaughn says the words out loud. A few more clicks of his mouse confirm what he suspects—that Elizabeth is Benjamin Balzac's sister. Anderson, it turns out, married her about a year after the trial in the McCrory case. The implication strikes Vaughn like a mallet.

Turning back toward his phone, Vaughn calls Alexander Hogarth and tells him what he's learned. "Please tell me that what I'm thinking happened here *didn't* happen. That I'm missing something."

A-Hog snorts. "Missing something? I'd say you found it."

"But that would be terrible."

No answer.

"Would a surgeon actually deride a patient at trial like Anderson did just to help his future brother-in-law win a big verdict?"

"Son, if that's all you think happened there, then you *are* missing something."

"What are you saying?"

"Think about it. If you can't figure it out in two minutes, call me back."

Vaughn hears the phone click and replaces the receiver on the cradle. He sits back in his chair. It takes only a few seconds before Vaughn grasps what A-Hog was hinting at: *The surgeon and Balzac didn't just set up Dr. Anderson's trial testimony. They set up the whole case.*

"No. That can't be." Vaughn picks up the phone and calls Hogarth back. "That can't be right," he says as soon as A-Hog picks up the phone. "A doctor flushing his whole career down the drain just to help his future brother-in-law? That can't be what happened."

Vaughn hears Hogarth laugh on the other end of the line.

"You don't know anything about medical malpractice, do you? What happened is that Anderson's insurance carrier paid the verdict. The good doctor himself walked the plank . . . right to another hospital. Where he is now head of orthopedic surgery."

Vaughn hangs up again and closes his eyes. *Balzac is a monster who surrounds himself with other monsters. And Hogarth says Day is just as bad.*

This, Vaughn realizes, is who he and Eddy are facing. This is the enemy.

Now that he sees the opposition for what it is, Vaughn knows what the next question is and how to make use of it. And on that score, he knows one thing for sure. You have to fight fire with fire. Tomorrow, he will call the press conference he's been thinking about. He'll do his best to let the world see the real Eddy Coburn. The good guy, not the villain painted by Day and Balzac.

17

MONDAY, JULY 14, CONTINUED

It's 7:30 when Erin arrives at Vaughn's apartment with the takeout Chinese they agreed to have for dinner.

"Did you buy the wine?" she asks when he opens the door.

"A cheap bottle of sauvignon blanc," he says. "Just like you asked for."

It's the first time she's been at Vaughn's place on Spruce Street. Vaughn opens the door and leads her up the stairs to the second floor. She enters the apartment and pauses to take it in. Bare wood floors, no drapes, an Ikea wall unit, a mismatched coffee table, and a cheaply framed print of two boxers, one standing over the other. The only things Vaughn seems to have spent any money on are the oversize distressed leather couch and the 55-inch flat-screen TV.

"I love what you've done with the place," Erin says. "Or maybe *not done* is what I should say. Are you deliberately going minimalist?"

Vaughn struggles to find something clever to say. Before he can come up with anything, Erin asks, "Have criminal-defense firms stopped paying associates in actual money?"

"All right, now you're pissing me off." Vaughn takes the white cardboard boxes from Erin's hand and sets them on the coffee table, next to a pair of plates he's laid out. He walks to the refrigerator and pulls out the wine, screws off the top, and pours into a pair of glasses.

"Seriously," Erin says once they've started eating, "are you that hard up for cash that you have to live this way?"

"I'm saving up. Plus, I still have some student loans to pay off. And I don't mind this place at all. I'm almost never here, for one thing. For another . . . Let's switch the subject. How was your day?"

Erin chews a mouthful of lo mein noodles, then answers. "Interesting, to say the least. Your capo stopped by."

Vaughn stares, suddenly serious. "Tell me."

"He came in to interview Geoffrey about maybe hiring our firm to represent his son's estate. That was the cover story, anyway. I think he was really there to feel me out—about us. And Eddy."

"This is not making me happy," Vaughn says. He doesn't want Nunzio anywhere near Erin.

"Relax. I handled it quite well, if I do say so myself."

"This isn't a joke, Erin. Jimmy Nutzo is a killer. And he wants revenge for his son's death. He'll go after anyone he thinks is to blame. And I doubt he'll take pains to prevent collateral damage."

Erin sits back on the couch, suddenly serious herself. "I get it, Vaughn. Believe me. It scared me shitless to be in the same room with him. But I made it clear that I don't have any inside information on Eddy. And I think I also convinced him that your cousin is telling the truth about not remembering the crash. You should be thanking me instead of lecturing me."

Vaughn exhales, closes his eyes, then opens them. "I'm not trying to lecture you. I'm just . . . It worries me to think that you might wind up in Nunzio's crosshairs."

Erin considers this, then says, "Well, in any event, he won't be coming back to Day and Lockwood. I watched how Nunzio looked at Geoffrey during our meeting, and it gave me a hunch. I waited a few hours, then called my friend Laurie Mitzner. She works at Benjamin Balzac's firm. She confirmed what I suspected: Nunzio went right to

Balzac's office after he was done with Geoffrey and hired *him*. Laurie is part of Balzac's Amtrak crash team, and she sat in on the meeting. She said Balzac and Nunzio laughed about Geoffrey. Nunzio said his father taught him never to trust a man who smells better than his wife. Balzac had some choice words of his own."

"Figures that Nunzio would go with a roughneck like Balzac."

Erin furrows her brow as she piles some more lo mein onto her plate. "I'm a little worried for Laurie," she says. "She didn't sound right on the phone. I asked her what was up, but she brushed me off."

"You think she was shaken up by Jimmy Nutzo?"

"No. I got the sense that there's something else going on—with Balzac himself."

Vaughn thinks about this. "That wouldn't surprise me, based on some things I found out about him today."

Vaughn shares what he learned about Balzac from the defense attorney in the medical-malpractice case, and from Arthur Hogarth. Erin stares, mouth agape, as Vaughn confides his belief that Balzac and his future brother-in-law conspired to deform a young girl and get rich off it. He finishes and lets it all sink in.

"I don't even know what to say to that. It's so insane."

"It is insane, if it's true." Vaughn pauses, then asks, "Have you ever heard anything like that said about Geoffrey Day?"

Erin doesn't hesitate. "Never. And I wouldn't believe it if I did hear it. Geoffrey's driven by money, no doubt about it. But I can't see him actually physically injuring someone for a verdict, no matter how big. And didn't you tell me that A-Hog said Balzac's amputation case was his big break? That he'd been a small-timer before that? Geoffrey's always been rolling in dough, from the time he left Hogarth."

Vaughn nods his head, thinks for a minute. "Tell me about Relazac."

"That mess. It was a huge multidistrict litigation. Geoffrey had the inside track that the drug caused birth defects. He had the whole firm working on it. We filed cases all over the country. But it all fell apart when the first couple of cases went to trial. Our science turned out to be junk, and the cases were dismissed. We eventually had to scratch the entire litigation."

"Hogarth said Geoffrey was about to flounder when a white knight rescued him, financially."

Erin nods. "He was trying to keep it all a secret—how much trouble he was in. But word got around the firm. Lawyers were sending out résumés. Staff, too. Then, all of a sudden, everything was somehow fixed. Geoffrey called a big meeting and told everyone there was nothing to worry about. To prove his point, he hooked his laptop to the big screen in the conference room and linked in to the firm's operating account. It had millions in it. Millions and millions. You could hear everyone exhale. And that was the end of it. We all went back to our offices, and the firm continued functioning like nothing ever happened. Everyone tried to guess which bank had bailed Geoffrey out, but we never found out."

Vaughn mulls what Erin has told him. "A-Hog seemed to think that Day still needs money."

"If so, it's news to me. But even if he does need money, what does that have to do with your cousin?"

"I don't know yet. But somehow, I get the sense it's all tied together. I feel it in my gut. It's like one giant web. Day's money problems. The crash. The missing track foreman Frye. Bunting going after Eddy at the go-team interview. Day and Balzac joining up. The probable fact that they're pressuring the DA to bring Eddy up on charges. I can't close my eyes without feeling like I'm going to burst!"

Vaughn tosses his chopsticks onto his plate and sits back.

"I know this is hitting close to home for you."

"It's not *close* to home. It *is* home, for me."

Erin studies Vaughn closely, weighing whether to say what she's thinking. "Is it . . . possible . . . ," she begins, slowly, "that maybe you're *too* close to this?"

"Too close to be representing Eddy, because I can't be objective? That's what my cousin Jean thinks. But here's the bottom line: so long as Ed wants me to represent him, I'm going to. I owe him."

"You owe him? Why? Because he's your cousin?"

Vaughn doesn't answer. He purses his lips and looks away.

"What am I missing here?"

Vaughn turns to Erin, stares for a long minute. Then he takes a deep breath.

"Eddy and I were real close growing up. We're the same age, thirty-four, and were born two weeks apart. Eddy's father opened a boxing gym when we were teenagers, after he left the police force, and Eddy and I started taking lessons. We loved it. We both got very good. Not good enough to fight professionally, but neither of us wanted that anyway. We were going to college, going to get good jobs. Neither of us was sure what we wanted to do for a living, but we were both confident we'd figure it out.

"The summer after high school graduation, everything turned to shit for Eddy. We both had summer jobs, and we agreed to meet up after work one night at the Vet for a Phillies game. The game went way into extra innings, and it was late when we left the stadium—and even later when we left the lot after some postgame tailgating."

Vaughn closes his eyes. He can remember it like it was last night. It was an unusually cool evening for late July, the temperature in the mid-seventies. The sky was brilliant with stars. A perfect night for driving with the windows down. Eddy drove a red 1988 Ford Mustang. The car's fourteen-year-old body was dented, scraped, and patched, but the engine was pristine, thanks to Eddy's mechanical skills. Vaughn drove a black 1985 Chevy Camaro. It looked even worse than Eddy's car but ran just as well, thanks again to Eddy.

"I don't remember how long we drove around that night, but we covered a lot of ground. We went down I-95, then back up to 276, to the Schuylkill, to 476 past Allentown, then back down to 76. We took turns passing each other, and we sped the whole time, for sure. Any minute, I expected to see the colored lights flashing behind me, but I didn't care; it felt so great to open up the cars. Eddy must've felt the same way. But we never did get pulled over.

"Then, we were on Kelly Drive, going east, so we slowed down and drove smart. But after a few minutes, something came over me." Vaughn recalls the adrenaline surging through him as a Springsteen song blasted on his radio. "I crossed the double yellow line, into the westbound lane, pulled up next to Eddy on his driver's side." *Stupid move. Stupid, stupid move.* "We came to the curve, and the cop car appeared out of nowhere. He was in the westbound lane, headed right for me. Before I even had time to react, the cruiser veered hard to its left and ran onto the grass, cutting in front of Eddy, who panicked and did the same thing. The cop car . . ."

Vaughn pauses, closes his eyes, and Erin completes the sentence. "The cop crashed headfirst into a tree. And Eddy wrapped his car around another tree. It's the story that was reported in all the papers."

Vaughn nods. "I didn't know Eddy and the cop crashed their cars. They just disappeared in my rearview mirror. Still, I knew that I needed to go back and get ticketed with my cousin. Or arrested with him. That's what I should have done."

"But you didn't."

Vaughn exhales. "I kept right on driving until I reached home. I went to my room and closed the door. I was terrified. I figured the officer had arrested Eddy, and the cops would be pounding on my parents' front door any minute—I was certain of it. I didn't sleep a wink that night.

"The next morning, we all learned that Eddy and the officer were both taken to Hospital of the University of Pennsylvania. Eddy was under arrest, and the policeman wasn't expected to live. My parents pressed me, but I feigned ignorance. I told them Eddy and I had parted ways following the ball game. That I had no idea where he went or what he'd done after that.

"The patrolman did die, but not before telling the investigating officers that Eddy had been drag racing, that a second car was involved. All the officer saw of the second car—my car—were its headlights, so—"

"He saw your headlights because you were the one in his lane?"

"Yes."

"You were the one who really caused the crash."

Vaughn lowers his head.

"And Eddy covered for you."

"He told the police he didn't know who was in the second car, that some guy had come up behind him and tried to pass him on the left."

"But the cops knew he was lying. And they threw the book at him, didn't they?"

"The only thing Eddy had in his favor was that his father was a hero cop. That counts for a lot in this city, and that saved Eddy some serious time. Even so, he served three years in state prison."

Erin looks as though Vaughn has clubbed her with a haymaker. "You left him at the scene. Then you let him take the rap for a crash you'd caused."

Vaughn closes his eyes. "All I'd have had to do was come forward. He'd have gotten off a lot easier."

Erin stares at him, the air conditioner grumbling in the background. She tries to process what he's told her, looking for some way to harmonize it with her view of him as a good guy. A guy who can be counted on to stick with you when the storm rolls in. But she can't. "What a shitty thing to do."

That night is the first since they've started seeing each other again that they don't make love. Erin goes to bed as soon as the food is cleared away and pretends to be asleep when he joins her.

Vaughn leans on his elbow, studying Erin, watching the rise and fall of her breathing.

Is this what's going to end it for us? It would be a form of justice if it did.

The next morning, Vaughn gets out of bed to make coffee. When he returns to the bedroom with Erin's mug, he finds her up, dressed, and ready to leave.

They face each other, and he says, "Now you know. I have to stand with Eddy, no matter what happens."

Erin stares at him. "Yes. You damned well do." Then she brushes past him and leaves.

18

TUESDAY, JULY 15

The office swirls with activity. Vaughn has called his press conference for noon, and the local news channels are setting up in the large conference room. Reporters and cameramen from the local Fox affiliate and from all three network stations are there. They have no problem demanding that Angie bring them water, coffee, and soda. One reporter asks where the firm's greenroom is and expresses her disappointment at learning there is none. "Day and Lockwood has a greenroom," the journalist says. "They set out fruit and cheese and cakes."

"I think there are leftover soft pretzels in the kitchen," Angie replies. "Put 'em in the microwave."

Walking past Angie on his way to Vaughn's office, Tommy laughs at her retort, gives her the thumbs-up. When he gets to Vaughn's office, the door is closed. He knocks, then goes in.

"Man of the hour," Tommy says, sitting down in front of Vaughn's desk.

Vaughn looks up from his notes, the stress obvious on his face. Tommy sees it's not a good time for small talk and gets right to the point. "I found something out about Balzac. He knows Jack Bunting, that Amtrak guy who went after your cousin at the NTSB interview. They were good friends growing up."

Vaughn's jaw drops. "You're kidding me."

Tommy shakes his head. "I thought I'd start at the beginning with Balzac. I found out he grew up in Upper Darby, so I went to his high school and started asking around. Someone pointed me to a guy named Joe Dell, who was a basketball coach and gym teacher when Balzac went to school. You should see this guy—he's pushing seventy and runs marathons. Anyway, he agreed to meet me and gave me an earful about Balzac and two of his friends. He says they were bad news. The biggest of the three, Bunting, got kicked off two sports teams for beating people up. The other one, he said, was just creepy. The kind who didn't talk much, but you could tell he was fucked up in the head. Dell said he was a runt."

"What'd he say about Balzac?"

"He told a story about Balzac coming up to him in the parking lot after school. He thinks he gave Balzac a hard time about something that day, but he can't remember what it was. So Balzac follows him into the parking lot and complains. They must've been standing next to Dell's car, because Balzac makes some remark about it. Dell doesn't think anything of it, but a couple of days later, the car blows up in his driveway."

Tommy pauses, waits for Vaughn to say something, but Vaughn is speechless.

"Dell called the police, but there was nothing left of the car, so there was no way to trace who it was that tampered with it. I asked Dell if he confronted Balzac about it. He told me no way. Said he stayed away from him after that, he had a wife and two kids."

Vaughn takes some time to process it all. Then he tells Tommy about the missing track foreman, Reggie Frye, and the NTSB's current thinking that it must've been vandals who moved the TracVac into the path of Train 174. Tommy considers this, and Vaughn asks, "So, what's your next step?"

"I've put some feelers out about Bunting through a guy I know at Amtrak. I'm also going to talk to that third kid from Balzac's high school. Unlike Bunting and Balzac, he never made it out of Upper Darby. I'm hoping maybe there's a little jealousy there I can exploit."

Vaughn nods. "Let me know what you find out. Just be careful. Bunting or Balzac might still have ties to their old neighborhood."

"Don't worry. I'm not going to say who I really work for."

"Just watch your back," Vaughn says. But Tommy is already up and moving toward the door. He closes it behind him.

A few seconds after Tommy leaves, the door opens again. It's Mick.

"You're certain a press conference is a good idea?"

"I feel like I don't have a choice. Balzac and Day's smear campaign can't go unanswered, Mick. I have to go on the offensive. For Eddy. For my whole family."

"I get it," Mick says. "Just be careful not to say anything in Eddy's defense that can be shown to be false. If the NTSB digs up evidence that disproves something you say, your cousin will be worse off than if you'd kept quiet."

Vaughn purses his lips, stares at his boss. He knows the stakes. But the time for rope-a-dope is over. It's time to hit back.

Fifteen minutes later, Vaughn sits before the microphones and addresses the cackle of reporters. "First, I want to thank the members of the press for agreeing to be here and for listening to Mr. Coburn's side of the story. My client, too, wants to thank you, and to thank everyone who might be watching now. But, first and foremost, he wants me to express his profound sadness, his grief, and his horror over the suffering caused by this terrible tragedy. Engineering a train is an awesome responsibility—a responsibility that Mr. Coburn took very seriously. That such a terrible thing happened on his watch has left him heartbroken. He thinks about it night and day, and he knows that it will follow him for the rest of his life."

Vaughn pauses. "Like many of the passengers, Mr. Coburn suffered serious and painful injuries. They included significant trauma to the head resulting in swelling of the brain. A ruptured spleen. A bruised liver. Broken bones in his face. Badly broken bones in his right leg." Again, Vaughn pauses.

"Because of the head injuries—and the doctors tell us this is very common—Mr. Coburn cannot recall the actual accident. The last thing he remembers before the crash is taking the train into the curve. The next things he recalls is waking up inside the crumpled locomotive, being carried out, being transported in the ambulance. He shared this with the NTSB investigators, when he voluntarily agreed to be interviewed by them. An interview at which he answered all the questions put to him in good faith. An interview he wanted to continue even after a high-ranking Amtrak official started attacking him. An interview that I, as his lawyer, had no choice but to end. Since that time, at Mr. Coburn's insistence, I've continued to make myself available to the NTSB and have spoken with Mr. Wexler, the head of the go-team. Mr. Coburn's focus at this point, in addition to trying to recover from his injuries, is on helping the NTSB any way he can to find out what caused the train to crash."

Vaughn lifts his water bottle, takes a drink, and continues. "What we know as of now is this: Mr. Coburn had no drugs, no alcohol, no prescription medications in his blood. So he was not operating the train while under the influence.

"He was well rested, having made sure, as he always does, to get sufficient sleep. He has no medical conditions that would make him unfit to operate a train. And, importantly, Eddy Coburn has a sterling safety record with Amtrak." Here, Vaughn pauses to direct the cameras to a Lucite trophy in the shape of a tall pyramid. "This is an Amtrak President's Safety and Service Award for Safety Awareness, and it was bestowed on Mr. Coburn just last year. The fact is that Ed Coburn was a safe engineer, and was known to be a safe engineer by his peers and superiors at Amtrak."

Vaughn looks away from the trophy, back to the cameras. "Now, it's been speculated that Mr. Coburn had to have been distracted at the time of the crash. Some have suggested he was on the phone talking, or texting. But the fact is that the NTSB found his cell phone in the wreckage of the locomotive. It was zipped in his knapsack. And when the NTSB examined the phone, they found that it was powered off, and that no calls or texts had been placed to it or from it after the train departed from 30th Street Station. This is very important. There was another crash a few years back, of a Metrolink train in California. The engineer, who was killed, failed to stop at a red signal because he was texting on his cell. That didn't happen here."

Vaughn pauses, takes a sip of Smartwater. "Now, you've heard some things about mistakes that Mr. Coburn made many years ago, when he was a teenager. And it's true that he was involved in a tragedy that cost a police officer his life. Mr. Coburn offers no excuses for that terrible day. It was foolish, even for a teenager, to drive as he was driving. No question about it. And Mr. Coburn didn't fight any of the charges brought against him. He accepted his punishment, served time in prison. And for a period afterward, he struggled. But then Mr. Coburn turned his life around. He met Kate, the love of his life—an elementary-school teacher who works with special-needs children—and married her. They're expecting their first child in the coming days.

"Ed Coburn's family is proud of him. His father, Frank, is a hero Philadelphia police officer wounded in the line of duty. He now runs a boxing gym, where he offers special instruction to underprivileged kids. Ed's mother, Claire, is a retired trauma nurse who worked at Temple University Hospital, saving the lives of badly injured people. Ed's two sisters, Peg and Jean, are both working mothers, juggling careers while raising families of their own. They all stand by Ed.

"As do I. My name is Vaughn Coburn. I'm Ed's cousin. And like every other member of our family, I believe in Ed. And I stand by him. And, again, I want to thank everyone watching right now for keeping an open mind. For not rushing to judgment, as some members of my own profession, I'm sad to say, are baiting you to do. Thank you."

With that, Vaughn stands.

"What? No questions?" Vaughn hears the voice call after him but keeps on walking out of the conference room.

Behind him, the disappointed reporters give the "Cut" signals to their cameramen, and they, too, file out.

◆　◆　◆

"So, what did you think?" Vaughn asks as he walks into Mick's office and sits down. Behind him, the big wall-screen TV is still on.

Mick uses the remote to turn off the television. "You did a good job," he answers from behind his desk. "I did get the impression that the press were expecting something more. Like, maybe a new revelation about what caused the accident."

Vaughn nods, opens his arms.

"I've played the press myself," Mick says. "In our line of business, you have to, sometimes. But there's a price to pay, if they catch on."

"What, that they'll screw me?"

Mick smiles. "They'll do that anyway, if they think it will help them sell a story. But now, they'll be *looking* to screw you."

"Better me than Eddy."

Mick shakes his head no. "It's not that simple. You can't forget that your personal credibility can be the difference between victory or defeat for your client. In taking their measure of the client, jurors will look at you as much as they do him. Some judges, too. And the first question the public asks whenever the defendant's attorney makes his appearance is whether the lawyer is just a high-price mouthpiece brought in to find loopholes, or is a champion for the oppressed."

Vaughn stares but says nothing.

"The point is that the press can play a big part in shaping that image, either way."

Vaughn takes a deep breath, bites his lower lip. He wants to ask, *What was I supposed to do—let those two P.I. attorneys continue to paint Eddy as the bad guy without hitting back? And how was I supposed to get the press to show up without promising them something big?*

Instead, he takes another deep breath, counts to ten. "I hear you." He stands, looks at Mick, starts counting again, and leaves.

Across town, in a big brick building on Delancey Street, Benjamin Balzac sits at the end of his twenty-five-foot conference table, watching Vaughn's press conference. The table sits beneath a massive, rustic chandelier that Balzac bought from the owner of a Montana cattle ranch. The rancher hadn't wanted to sell, but Balzac offered a price too high to turn down. The table itself Balzac found in a Scottish castle. The owner, who claimed it was once owned by William II, seemed a little too eager to sell, so Balzac offered a miserly price and waited six months for the cash-strapped laird to cave.

Sitting around the table are eight of Balzac's associates, all members of his Amtrak-crash team. Five are men. Three are women, two of whom Balzac has slept with, one of whom—Laurie Mitzner—he intends to. The associates are holding their breaths, waiting to see how Balzac reacts to the press conference so they'll know how to react themselves.

On the television, Vaughn signals the press conference is over. The scene switches to the anchor desk, where an attractive female newscaster with dazzling white teeth and dead blue eyes does her best to juggle the emotions she believes her audience might be experiencing. "You've just seen Vaughn Coburn, the lawyer, and cousin, of engineer Edward Coburn. As you heard, the engineer, like many of the passengers, was badly injured, and the tragedy has affected the engineer's whole family." Here, the anchor pauses to realign herself. "Of course, none of that matters to the badly injured passengers or to the families of those who lost their lives. For them, what matters is that the engineer deliberately hid his history of alcohol abuse, violence, and a fatal driving record when he applied to Amtrak, and that the railroad failed to properly vet him before hiring him to drive its trains. And, of course, the biggest question still remains: Why didn't the engineer see the TracVac ahead and stop his train . . ."

The anchor continues, but Balzac turns off the TV.

Balzac looks around the table. "Damage assessment?"

"Too obvious," a male associate jumps in.

"Too little, too late," says another associate.

Balzac considers their input, then, "Laurie, what's your view? Did the lawyer make you like his cousin? Make you forgive him, or want to forgive him?"

Laurie stares at Balzac as he looks directly into her eyes. *Oh God, he knows.* Her heart races, but she does her best to keep her voice flat, measured. "He made some good points, albeit nothing new. The lack of drugs in the blood, the fact that the engineer volunteered to be questioned by the NTSB. I thought the safety-award thing was strong."

Balzac nods. "And, of course, the cell phone. It was turned off and locked away."

The associates glance at one another, and Laurie knows they're hoping someone will come up with an answer to the phone thing. That must be what Balzac is expecting.

"Any ideas?" Balzac asks, his voice rising. "Or are you all just going to sit there and wait for good news to drop into our laps? Laurie? Do you have any thoughts?"

Laurie can feel her face drain of blood. *He knows for sure. That's why he's torturing me.* "I . . ." She draws a blank.

Balzac sighs, waves her off. He takes his time looking around the table, giving the lawyers a few seconds each to read the disgust on his face. "Just leave. All of you." Balzac watches them slowly file out of the room. When the last is gone and the door is shut, he punches a number into his cell phone. "Did you watch?"

"I did," says Jack Bunting. "I think that young fool just hung his cousin."

"I agree. I think it's time the government boys find the second phone."

"I'm on it," Bunting says. He hangs up, waits five minutes, and places a call from his office phone.

"Wexler," the leader of the NTSB go-team answers.

"Nelson, this is Jack Bunting. I just received a strange call and thought I should tell you right away."

"A call? From whom?"

"He refused to say. But he claimed the engineer, Coburn, had a second cell phone." Bunting lets the words hang in the air.

"Sounds fishy," Wexler says. "It's not uncommon to get crackpot calls after a big accident. And the engineer's lawyer just held a press conference."

"And maybe the press conference spurred him to call. I thought that, too. But he didn't sound off balance. And I'm certain he's one of ours, that he works at Amtrak. He told me that two weeks ago he was in a crew room with Coburn and saw him using two cell phones: a company phone and a second one that looked like a cheap burner phone."

Bunting can hear Wexler breathing on the other end of the line, trying to decide what to do.

"I guess we could go to Bear, search the locomotive again," Wexler says. Amtrak's repair facility in Bear, Delaware, is where Amtrak is storing the crashed railcars until the NTSB releases them. Known by the employees who work there as Bearcatraz, the property is surrounded by chain-link fencing, and the only entrance is through a manned guardhouse.

"Probably wouldn't find the second phone, even if there was one," Bunting muses. "Still . . ."

"Still, we have to follow every lead. Especially in a situation like this, where we have no insight as to what was going on with the engineer."

"Agreed. So when are you looking to go to Bear?"

"No reason to delay. Let's say day after tomorrow."

"Thursday, sure. I'll make the arrangements and meet you there."

Right after I make a brief trip there by myself.

19

Friday, July 18

At 6:30 p.m. Royce Badgett leaves his house and walks across the street to the corner bar for his nightly suds and sandwich. Dark and cool, the bar is a welcome relief from the steamy July evening. It's a small place, only ten seats at the bar with a few tables in the back. Behind the bar, there's a decent-size TV for watching the ball game. The place is older than Royce himself and tended by Neil Mason, the grandson of the man who founded it. A year ahead of Neil in high school, Royce has known him forever.

Two regulars sit on the far-right side of the bar. They look up at Royce as he enters and nod. He nods back, then takes a seat in the middle, to the left of a stranger. The guy looks to be in his early forties. He's done time; Royce can tell from the prison tat peeking up from beneath his shirt collar. Probably saw some trouble inside, but not too much; through his T-shirt Royce can see the man has a powerful chest, and his arms look like granite. The man doesn't pay the least bit of attention when Royce takes the stool next to him.

The man is halfway through a cheesesteak. He orders another beer.

"Another Yuengling?" Neil asks the man, who nods.

Royce and the man sit side by side for twenty minutes, neither acknowledging the other until Neil brings Badgett's own dinner, a hot open-face turkey sandwich with fries.

"Need the ketchup?" the man asks, passing the bottle from his right to his left and setting it on the bar.

"Much appreciated," says Royce.

They sit in silence for another five minutes. Then Royce, still looking up at the Phillies on the TV screen asks, "So what do you think?"

"Outfield sucks," the man answers. "Hitting's weak."

"Herrera's not bad. And they're thirty-five and twenty-seven. Second place in their division."

"We'll see how long that lasts."

Tommy has been tailing Badgett for three days now. The guy seems to follow a set routine. The lights go on in his house at 7:00 a.m. He's out the door at 7:30, on his way to Newtown Square, where he works as a mechanic at a Cadillac dealership. He takes a half-hour lunch at noon, leaving the dealership and driving to Newtown Square Pizza or Wendy's. He's off work at 5:00, home by 5:30. He leaves his house around 6:30, walks across the street to the bar, where he eats dinner and drinks beer for a couple of hours. Then he goes back home, spends time in his basement or watching TV in the living room. The second night, he sat for two hours on his porch, smoking cigarettes and throwing back Buds, staring into space as he listened through the open window to the baseball game on the television. Badgett had no visitors, and the only person he said "Hi" to was the old lady who lives next door.

Today, Tommy made sure to be at the bar when Badgett entered and sat down. The plan was to strike up a conversation, see where it took him, hopefully find an opening to bring up Balzac. It's going okay so far. They talk about baseball for a long while. Then Badgett asks Tommy where he's from, what he does for a living, and Tommy feeds him a story about being out of work since GE closed its O'Hara solar-inverter plant near Pittsburgh. Tommy says he's here visiting his brother, who lives in Havertown. He introduces himself as Joe LaBrava.

"What's that, Italian?"

"Mutt," Tommy says, and they both laugh.

Just then, the ball game breaks for a commercial, and a tickler for the eleven o'clock news comes on. It's a story about the Amtrak train crash. The engineer's lawyer has given a press conference that day. "Tune in at eleven to see what he said," the anchorwoman says, an enticing gleam in her eye.

"That's fucked up," Tommy says. "That train crash. All those people who were killed."

Badgett nods but doesn't say anything.

After a moment, Tommy tells him, "A good buddy of mine was on that train. He got hurt pretty bad. I told him he should get a lawyer, but he says he's not ready yet." If Badgett is connected to Balzac, Tommy figures, this will give him the perfect opening to suggest Balzac as an attorney for Tommy's friend.

Again, Badgett says nothing, just shakes his head.

"My brother told me there's a lot of big-time lawyers working that accident," Tommy says. "He sees them on the news."

"Lawyers." Badgett says the word like he's spitting something out. "Never met one I didn't not like." Badgett smiles at his twist of the old Will Rogers saying.

"They make a lot of money, some of them."

"Money they haven't earned, which they spend on things they don't need to impress people they don't like."

More Will Rogers.

Tommy drains his mug and asks the bartender for another. A political ad plays on the TV screen and Tommy says, "Country's going to hell in a handbasket, you ask me."

"That's a fact," Badgett says, and they go back and forth agreeing with each other on immigration, trade policy, jihadists, and corporate greed.

Every now and then, Tommy interjects something relevant about lawyers, personal injury, and that damned government-owned Amtrak, but Badgett doesn't bite. After a lull in the conversation, Tommy asks Badgett where he grew up, where he went to school.

"You keep in touch with anyone from the old days?" Tommy asks. "I tried to, but it got real tough once I moved across the state."

Badgett gets a sour look on his face. "Most of the guys I grew up with either went to jail, overdosed, or got too snooty for my tastes."

"Not so many of my people got sent up," Tommy says. "But way too many got uppity. Doctors and lawyers."

The sour look is back on Badgett's face, but he doesn't add anything.

"I think one of my old friends works for that Balzac. My brother told me that. I wonder what it's like to work for that guy."

"Balzac." Badgett almost chokes on the name. "I went to school with that one. Had some good times, too. Not that he'd ever admit it. He's one of them got too fuckin' big for his britches."

Tommy hears the venom in Badgett's voice and decides he was right about the man; he's obviously jealous of his rich former schoolmate who likely wouldn't give Badgett the time of day. He wonders whether Badgett feels the same about Jack Bunting, but he can't figure out how to work that name into the conversation without tipping his hand.

They talk for another hour, but Tommy can't get Badgett to offer any real insight into Balzac. He senses that Badgett is holding back, but he isn't sure whether it's information that Badgett's holding on to or just more venom. Tommy pays his tab and says good night. He leaves the bar and walks to his pickup, which is parked on the street outside.

◆ ◆ ◆

As soon as the stranger walks out the door, Neil Mason walks up to Badgett. "Who the fuck was that?"

"No idea," Royce says. "Any chance you got his license plate?"

Mason smiles. "Wrote it down when I went out for a smoke," he says, sliding a torn sheet of paper across the bar.

◆ ◆ ◆

Fifteen minutes later, Badgett is back home, sitting on his front porch. He pulls out his cell, makes a call.

"I was right," Badgett says. "I *was* being followed."

"By whom?"

Badgett laughs. "By Joe LaBrava."

"What's funny?"

"Name's from an old Elmore Leonard novel. You know I read all his stuff, right?"

"Yeah, but it's about all you read," Benjamin Balzac chuckles.

"Can you get your guy at DMV to run a plate?"

Balzac asks for the number. "What do you think this guy wants with you?"

"It's not me he wants at all. It's you. He must've come at me a dozen ways about you."

"What'd you tell him?"

"The truth," Badgett answers matter-of-factly. "That you're a son of a bitch."

Badgett and Balzac share a good belly laugh. Then, when they quiet down, Balzac tells Badgett to call him if the guy shows up again, though that likely won't happen before Balzac gets the info back on the plate and finds out who the prison-tatted asshole really is.

Balzac hangs up and leans back in his leather chair, smiling at the thought of Royce Badgett and his other best friend, Jack Bunting. They shared so many good times, pulled so much shit, Balzac can't imagine how any group of guys could've had more fun growing up together.

Bunting was the toughest and meanest of the three. On the basketball team, he fouled so often and with such gusto that he rarely made it into the second period. In tenth grade, the coach finally kicked him off the team for unnecessary violence. The next year, after Jack had gained forty pounds, he went out for football. He was kicked off that team, too, halfway through the season, again for excessive violence—an amazing feat considering that Bunting was a lineman.

Royce Badgett was the crazy one. Nicknamed "Badger," Royce would do anything—literally anything—that Balzac told him to do. Or anything he *thought* Balzac might want him to do. One time, Balzac mentioned to Royce that a family living on Balzac's street had a mean-looking Doberman that stood on the porch and growled every time he walked past. The next week, the dog went missing. The family was bereft and had the whole neighborhood looking for the animal. They even offered a large cash reward. When Balzac mentioned it to Royce, Badgett smiled and said, "Let me know if they change the reward to dead *or* alive. They do that, and I might just see to it that Rover makes an appearance."

Balzac's own role in the trio was unspoken but clear: he was the leader. He was neither as strong as Jack nor as unrestrained as Royce. But he was the smartest. Balzac was the one who found ways to sneak them into ball games and concerts. The one who learned to fabricate photo IDs to get them into bars and frat parties. And it was Balzac who figured out what drugs you could use to slip into a woman's drink to make her pass out and not remember anything after.

Balzac met Bunting and Badgett in ninth grade, when legal troubles made it prudent for his old man to move as far from Oakland, California, as he could. Balzac senior settled the family in Upper Darby, a small township bordering West Philadelphia. Balzac's parents enrolled him in Upper Darby High School, where he banded with Jack and Royce. Back then, Balzac was more chubby than solid, and he was subjected to bullying. Until Bunting stepped in. One time—and it was a story Balzac, Bunting, and Badgett always chuckled at when they reminisced—an eleventh-grader named Jimbo Strunk pushed Balzac to the ground and held him there, slapping and taunting him. Balzac couldn't get up to fight back and so had to lie there and take it until a teacher came along and broke it up. When Bunting and the Badger found out, they were furious. The three boys concocted a scheme to get even. Strunk worked weekends at the McDonald's on Sixty-Ninth Street. One Saturday after quitting time, Balzac and Bunting were waiting for him. They snuck up on Jimbo as he was about to get into his car and threw him down so hard they knocked the wind out of him. Then, Bunting rolled him onto his stomach and held him down while Balzac twisted his right arm until he tore the shoulder tendons and Jimbo started screaming.

Later, Strunk insisted to the police that Balzac was one of the guys who attacked him, but Balzac and Bunting had worn masks so Jimbo couldn't identify them with sufficient certainty to satisfy the police. And since both boys claimed they were at the movies and had the tickets to prove it—thanks to Royce—nothing could be done.

Balzac walks to the bar he keeps in his office and pours himself a glass of Bombay Sapphire. He takes a hefty gulp, then smiles. "Glory days."

20

WEDNESDAY, JULY 23

Vaughn kisses Erin, who's still sleeping, on the forehead and leaves her apartment. It's been more than a week since their troubling conversation, when he shared with Erin the secret underlying his relationship with Eddy. Erin made plain her disappointment in him, and, for a couple of days, he worried that things between them would cool permanently. But Erin had softened, and they were back on track. Most nights, they met up with each other right after work and didn't separate until the next morning, when Vaughn left Erin's apartment or she left his.

Vaughn's family seems to be breathing a little easier. Eddy and Kate, Uncle Frank and Aunt Claire, and Vaughn's own parents, all called, congratulating him on the press conference and thanking him for standing up for Eddy. Even Cousin Jean had nice things to say. Their optimism is an illusion, of course, and would crash to the ground if they knew what he did: that a sociopathic mobster was chomping at the bit for revenge, that the most powerful P.I. attorneys in the city were pressing the district attorney to bring charges against Eddy, and that one of those attorneys actually has a high-ranking connection at Amtrak.

The only real bright spot for Vaughn is that all the stress is motivating him to get back in shape. He's returned to his uncle's gym half a dozen times for some bag work. And on one of those occasions, he sparred a few rounds for the first time in a long while. He even started jumping rope and running again.

Tommy told Vaughn about his bar conversation with the cagey Royce Badgett. Tommy's conclusion that Badgett may harbor hard feelings for his former friend, Benjamin Balzac, seems sound. But Badgett likely isn't going to be a source of usable information. Still, the investigation into Balzac and Day may prove unnecessary if, as Vaughn hopes, the district attorney doesn't decide to lower the hammer on Eddy despite the two attorneys' insistence that his cousin be criminally charged.

Two hours after he leaves Erin's apartment, Vaughn walks into his office and sits behind his desk. He empties his leather satchel of a motion and supporting legal brief when the phone rings. It's Erin, who's now at her own office.

"Hey," Vaughn says, smiling over the phone.

"Something's happening," Erin says, her voice serious. "Day is in the big conference room with his whole Amtrak crash team, and they're watching the television. It's tuned to CNN, or MSNBC, I think. Day and Corey King are both smiling like Cheshire cats. I don't like the feel of it."

Vaughn bites his lip, thinks for a minute, then tells Erin he'll call her back. He walks toward Mick's office, but the door is closed, so he turns back to the main conference room, which has its own TV. He turns it on, waits for the shoe to drop. It doesn't take long.

"We're getting word," says Mika Brzezinski, "that the NTSB is planning to hold a press conference this morning on the crash of Amtrak Train 174. It's not confirmed, but sources have told MSNBC that the engineer may have had a second cell phone on board at the time of the crash, and may have been talking on it."

"Jesus Christ." Vaughn jumps from his seat and sprints to his office, where he opens his contacts file, then calls the number for Nelson

Wexler. The call is sent directly to voice mail. His next thought is to call Eddy, but he decides to wait until he knows more. He returns to the conference room, where the television screen displays an empty podium.

After a few moments, NTSB board member Richard Olin walks to the lectern and begins to speak. He introduces himself and Nelson Wexler, who has moved up beside him. Then he gets to the business at hand.

"Last Tuesday, Mr. Wexler, leader of the Train 174 go-team, was notified that one of the Amtrak members of the team had received information that the train's engineer was in possession of a second cell phone. Two days later, on July 17, members of the go-team conducted another inspection of the locomotive cab. The locomotive, as well as the other railcars, have been stored since the accident at a secure Amtrak facility in Bear, Delaware. The inspection of the locomotive was extremely difficult, given the extensive nature of the damage caused by the crash. Nonetheless, after several hours of searching, go-team members did find a second cell phone. The device was immediately taken to NTSB headquarters in Washington for detailed inspection and testing by the NTSB's Vehicle Recorder Division. The cell phone was not registered in anyone's name, but was a prepaid phone, sometimes referred to as a 'burner phone.'"

Vaughn feels his whole body go numb. He knows what's coming. He wants to counterpunch, swing, fight. But he cannot. He is frozen in place. All he can do is wait for the body blows.

Olin continues, "Engineers from the NTSB's Vehicle Recorder Division downloaded information from the cell phone, and determined that the phone was used twice during the run between 30th Street Station in Philadelphia and the crash. The first call was placed *from* the cell phone to a private number. It lasted one minute and thirty seconds, from 12:08:10 to 12:09:41. The second phone call was placed *to* the cell phone at 12:17:50, and lasted through the time of the crash twenty-eight seconds later, at 12:18:18. That second call was placed from another cell phone, another so-called burner phone. We do not know who owns that phone, or who placed that call."

Here, Olin pauses, takes a deep breath. "The phone number to which the first call was placed from the cell phone was the home number of engineer Edward Coburn. Fingerprints were taken from the cell phone, and we expect they will match those of Mr. Coburn." Olin pauses again, then resumes. "The Board will shortly be reaching out to Mr. Coburn's attorney to find out whether Mr. Coburn is willing to be interviewed a second time. We have also served Mr. Coburn's home-phone carrier, Verizon, with a subpoena for the home records."

Olin continues for a few minutes more, then leaves the podium. The news coverage switches back to the studio, where the *Morning Joe* hosts and guests take turns skewering both Eddy and Vaughn. One guest accuses Vaughn of using his own press conference to "sell us a bill of goods." Another accuses Vaughn of conspiring with his cousin to mislead NTSB investigators by failing to disclose the second phone. "Certainly, his cousin/client would have told him about the second phone. Yet in his press conference, attorney Coburn pretended there was only one cell phone and represented that the engineer wasn't on the phone at the time of the accident when, clearly, he was."

Vaughn changes channels to Fox and then CNN, only to hear more of the same.

Sensing someone behind him, Vaughn turns to see Susan Klein standing in the doorway. Her eyes, fixed on the TV screen, are filled with anger. Seeing Vaughn turn to face her, she lowers her gaze to him. Her nostrils flare, and Vaughn sees her fight to control herself. He opens his mouth to say something, but his boss waves a palm.

"Don't," she says. Then she turns and walks away.

Vaughn closes his eyes for a moment, then opens them and slams his hand against the conference-room table. An instant later, he's racing for the elevator. Ninety minutes after that, his Jeep is kicking up dirt on the road leading to the farmhouse where his cousin has been holed up for the past three weeks.

Eddy walks onto the front porch even before Vaughn's car is stopped. Vaughn is out of the car and walking fast toward the porch before the dust settles.

"What the fuck, Eddy?" Vaughn takes the steps two at a time and gets right up in his cousin's face.

"It's not what it seems!" Eddy backs up until he's against the front door.

"A second cell? And you let me stand in front of the whole damn world and say you weren't on the phone? That you couldn't have been because your phone was tucked away in your knapsack!"

Eddy drops his head. "I'm sorry. I'm sorry."

"Do you have any idea what you've done? By not telling me?"

Eddy's eyes are filled with anguish. "I messed up. I know, I know."

Vaughn takes a deep breath, then backs away. "Why, Eddy? Why didn't you tell me? And why did you have two phones to begin with?"

Eddy exhales and closes his eyes. After a long moment, he opens them. "It was for Kate. I wanted her to be able to reach me. In case . . . She was eight months pregnant. And our next-door neighbor was just beaten up and robbed, inside her house. The railroad won't let us have phones on our runs, but what about emergencies? What if something happened with Kate and she couldn't get ahold of me?"

Vaughn shakes his head. The words come out almost as a whisper. "Why didn't you just tell me this?"

"I was afraid you'd tell the NTSB and Amtrak. They didn't find the burner phone the first time, but I knew they might find it if they looked again. And they'd know I talked to Kate during the run. I'd never get my job back then. And—"

"Your *job*?" Vaughn interrupts. "Eddy, what aren't you getting here? No matter what happens with the investigation, you're *never* going to work for Amtrak again. Or any other railroad. You crashed a train, and thirty-six people died. Hundreds more were injured. No one's going to touch you, man."

Vaughn sees Eddy's eyes fill with water, sees them searching his own eyes.

He really doesn't understand. He thought he was going back to Amtrak.

"I'm sorry, Ed. I'm . . . Come on, let's go inside and sit down."

They take their places at the kitchen table and sit facing each other. Neither one says anything for a while, then Vaughn breaks the silence. "Tell me about the calls. The NTSB says there were two calls, the first one to your house."

"That was me calling Kate, just to tell her I had started the run and to check in on her. It only lasted a minute."

"What about the second call?" asks Vaughn. "They say it happened seconds before the crash. And came from a burner phone. What the hell, Eddy?"

Eddy looks him straight in the eye. "I have no idea. That's the truth. I don't remember it at all. I don't know who it could've been from."

"Well, who knew the number of the second phone? How did you even know how to buy a burner phone?"

"I didn't buy it. Another guy gave it to me. He'd be the only one who knew the number."

"What guy was that?"

Eddy stops breathing. He stares at Vaughn. "It was Reggie. Reggie Frye."

Vaughn leaps from his chair. "*The track foreman?* Are you *kidding* me? The guy in charge of the TracVac? The one who's disappeared?"

Eddy sighs. "That's the other reason I didn't say anything. I didn't want to be connected to him. I knew it would look bad."

Vaughn tries to rein in his anger, but he can't. "Of course it would look bad! Two Amtrak employees sharing a secret phone. One of them is in charge of a TracVac that somehow winds up where the other one can crash his train into it?" Vaughn pauses and Eddy stares at him. "Did the two of you have some kind of suicide pact?"

"That's crazy!" Now it's Eddy's turn to lose his temper. "I'm married. I have a kid on the way. *I don't leave people behind!*"

The remark stops Vaughn cold. He and Eddy, now both standing, square off. Neither moves for a long time. Then Vaughn lowers his own head and takes his seat. After a bit, Eddy sits down as well.

"This is just awful," Eddy says. "This whole thing. What am I going to do? What's going to happen now?"

Before Vaughn can answer, Eddy's new cell phone rings. He glances at the number. "It's Kate," he says, pressing the button to answer. Eddy says hello, listens for a few seconds, then stands up fast. "This is it! Kate's on the way to the hospital. She's having the baby."

Without another word, the two of them are racing for Vaughn's Jeep. Eddy spends the ride into Center City on the phone with Kate, with her mother, with his own mother, Vaughn's Aunt Claire. The two older women are keeping Kate company until Eddy gets there. He'll take over then, and stay with Kate through the birth. It's all planned out; it's why Kate and Eddy had started weekly birthing classes before the crash.

Vaughn is speeding north on 222 when he sees a black Cadillac Escalade heading south. He thinks of Johnny Giacobetti, and his heart beats faster. Could that be Johnny G.'s Escalade? Has Nunzio—in a fit of rage over the disclosures about the second cell phone—dispatched his enforcer to the farm to dispatch Eddy? It's going to happen, sooner or later, unless he can find a way to clear his cousin.

The ringing of Vaughn's cell phone pulls him from his thoughts. He recognizes Tommy's number on the display and answers.

"Where are you?" Tommy asks.

"I went to see Eddy. Now we're on our way back to Philly. Kate's about to deliver. What's up?"

"I'm not sure, but I just found out that the DA and a whole army of cops spent the last few days reaching out to the victims of the crash and their families. They've been calling them in or going to their houses and hospital rooms, collecting birth and death certificates, medical records, affidavits. Something big's going down. You know what it could be?"

"I've a pretty good idea," Vaughn says. "Shit." The district attorney's going to charge Eddy criminally. His burner was just what Day and Balzac needed to push the DA to act. The prosecutor and police have probably been working to get their ducks in a row since the minute the NTSB found the second phone. "I'll call you later, tell you what I think," Vaughn tells Tommy before hanging up. He doesn't want Eddy to hear.

Forty minutes later, Vaughn pulls up to the hospital and lets Eddy out. Then he drives the car to the parking garage. Ten minutes later, Vaughn is walking down the hall on the maternity floor. When he turns the corner, he's thrown into confusion. Just ahead of him, Eddy is on his knees, held there by two men. His hands are cuffed behind him. He's shouting Kate's name. Vaughn can hear Kate's own screaming from the doorway. Kate's mother and Aunt Claire are shouting, too, cursing at the men restraining Eddy. Nurses, doctors, patients, and family members crowd the hallway, staring.

"Just let me see her!" Eddy pleads.

"Just let him see her!" the two mothers shout.

Vaughn calls out to the two men restraining his cousin, demanding to know what's going on. They turn toward him, and when they do, Vaughn's stomach drops. One of the men he doesn't recognize, but the other one is all too familiar: Detective John Tredesco. A lanky, stoop-shouldered man with a potbelly and limp black hair, Tredesco has bad history with Vaughn's boss Mick. The detective did everything he could to prosecute Mick's old friend in the Hanson murder case, including persuading a key witness to perjure himself. Mick found a way to win the case despite Tredesco's efforts, and Vaughn can tell from the gleam in the detective's eyes that he's thinking he's found a way to get even.

"Attorney Coburn . . . ," Tredesco intones. "Just in time for your client's arrest."

"On what charges?" Vaughn asks, as if he can't guess.

"Well, let's see. There's thirty-six counts of involuntary manslaughter, two-hundred-plus counts of aggravated assault, and a list of other charges longer than a donkey's you-know-what."

"For crying out loud. His wife's in labor. Do you have to do this now?"

"Have to? Nah, probably not. But, hey . . ." Tredesco and his partner pull Eddy off the floor and start to march him away.

"At least let him see her!"

Tredesco looks at his partner, then at Eddy, then back to Vaughn. "No," he says matter-of-factly. And with that, the two detectives squeeze Eddy's arms and drag him away.

Vaughn's aunt Claire begins screaming again. "Vaughn! Vaughn! You promised! You promised Eddy wouldn't go to jail!"

Vaughn stands, paralyzed, in the middle of the hall. As though through a fog, he sees his aunt screaming, hears Kate's own cries through the doorway. He wants desperately to console the women, but there is no time. Clearing his mind, he turns and runs toward his cousin, shouting after him and the two cops.

"He invokes his right to counsel! You hear that, Tredesco? You can't question him."

Tredesco and his partner ignore Vaughn and continue marching their prisoner past the stunned faces gathering in the hall and doorways.

"Don't talk to anyone, Ed!" Vaughn shouts. "Don't say anything other than to demand to see your lawyer."

Vaughn follows the officers and his cousin until they reach the elevator, where Tredesco forbids his entry. As the doors close, Vaughn races down the stairs, reaching the elevator bay just as Eddy and the two detectives exit. He follows them to the hospital entrance. His heart sinks when he sees what's waiting on the other side of the large windows: a cackle of reporters. Someone made sure to alert them that Eddy was going to be arrested.

Eddy and Vaughn are assaulted with questions as soon as they all leave the building. The reporters follow them, encircle them, the whole way to the waiting police car. Vaughn shoves against them, and it takes all his willpower not to start throwing roundhouses.

Tredesco and his partner load Eddy into the back seat, then pull away. Watching it unfold, Vaughn feels like he's been gut-punched. He wants to double over, catch his breath. But he remains standing. He feels his stomach tighten, feels his hands form into fists, his eyes narrow. The reporters, still surrounding him, fade into the background as his mind focuses and his chest fills with rage.

Vaughn turns back to the hospital, back to his aunt and to Kate and her mother. They'll be desperate, he knows. It'll be his job to calm them down, get them to concentrate on the immediate task at hand: the birth. "I'll take care of Eddy," he'll tell them, then watch as their eyes fill with doubt. He's been doing his best to take care of Eddy since the crash, but the press has trampled his cousin just the same. And now, it's clear: the wheels of justice are going to run over Eddy Coburn like a goddamned freight train.

21

Thursday, July 24

The preliminary arraignment takes place at eleven o'clock the next morning in the basement of the Criminal Justice Center. The arraignment court magistrate, Delia Smick, sits at her bench, which is cluttered with file folders and a computer screen. Her courtroom is positioned behind a wall of Plexiglas through which spectators sitting in the waiting area can watch the proceedings. Both the hearing room and waiting area have gray walls, gray carpeting, and low ceilings. The waiting area itself has five rows of black benches, split down the middle by an aisle. This morning, the benches are filled.

Sitting at the defense table in the hearing room, Vaughn glances to his right. Across the room at the prosecutor's table is Assistant District Attorney Christina Wesley. Vaughn remembers her from the Hanson trial. She was first chair to the lead prosecutor, Devlin Walker. She looks different now, harder—in the eyes and body—and, frankly, more attractive. Her face, though, still carries its permanent scowl. Vaughn wonders if the woman ever laughs.

Vaughn turns toward the back, looks through the Plexiglas to take in the scene behind him. A number of the benches are taken up by members of the press. Some in the crowd have casts and crutches—clearly injured crash passengers. A pair of Amtrak police officers have shown up to watch. Half a dozen well-dressed young men and women are seated in one of the back rows, and Vaughn decides they must be associates from Day and Lockwood, the Balzac Firm, and one or two others sent to gather intelligence. Finally, Vaughn spots Eddy's parents and his own. Vaughn hasn't forgotten for a second that his entire family has been drawn into this tragedy with his cousin.

Vaughn is about to turn toward the bench when he sees two men walk into the back of the waiting area. One of the men is solidly built, with jet-black hair; he wears an expensive Italian suit and tie. The second man, in a suit jacket and black-collared shirt, is enormous.

James Nunzio and Johnny G.

Nunzio spots Vaughn and glares at him, his black eyes radiating hostility. Giacobetti's eyes are more matter-of-fact, though no less frightening. Vaughn holds their stares until he sees everyone's eyes dart suddenly toward the bench. He turns to see that his cousin has now appeared on the big, freestanding flat-screen TV to the magistrate's left. Eddy is being held in a cell at the Roundhouse, the Philly police headquarters and jail at Eighth and Race Streets. His image is broadcast to the hearing room, via closed-circuit TV.

The charge: thirty-six counts of involuntary manslaughter, defined under Pennsylvania law as causing the death of another person as a result of performing an otherwise-lawful act in a reckless or grossly negligent manner. Thirty of these counts are misdemeanors of the first degree. Six are felonies of the second degree, because the victims were under the age of twelve. The felonies, Vaughn knows, are each punishable by up to ten years in prison. Each of the misdemeanor charges carries up to five years. For the passengers injured but not killed, Eddy is charged with 205 counts of felony aggravated assault, the complaint asserting that he recklessly caused serious bodily injury to another under circumstances manifesting extreme indifference to the value of human life. The import of all the charges, Vaughn knows, is that if Eddy goes to trial and is convicted, his newborn daughter will be old enough to retire by the time he gets out of prison.

"What is your position regarding bail, Ms. Wesley?" asks Delia Smick over top of the black-rimmed glasses sitting on the end of her nose.

"This is a Mass. Homicide. Situation." Christina pauses after each word. "The defendant has a prior criminal conviction for recklessly causing the death of a police officer. There is no question that the defendant must be held over for trial." Short and simple.

"Mr. Coburn?" the magistrate asks.

"We believe the court should grant bail. The most serious charges against Mr. Coburn are involuntary manslaughter, not murder. He vehemently denies that he caused the accident and very much wants his day in court, to clear his name. He is no flight risk; he has strong ties to the community, has no prior history of flight, and he lacks the means to flee. He doesn't even have a passport. And," Vaughn adds with emphasis, "Mr. Coburn and his wife just became parents. Yesterday." Saying the words makes Vaughn's blood boil. Eddy missed the birth of his own daughter. "Mr. Coburn's arrest robbed him and his wife of his right to be there while she gave birth. He needs to be present for his wife and child during this critical time."

Vaughn pauses to watch Delia Smick considering the issue. Politically, the smart thing to do would be to keep Eddy in prison until his trial. Hell, politically, Delia Smick would be best served by ordering Eddy's keepers at the roundhouse to string him up right now, in his cell. But maybe, as a wife and mother, she's feeling empathy for Eddy's own wife and newborn.

"Mr. Coburn, you say that your client lacks the means to flee? How would he raise money for bail, were I to set it?" Without waiting for Vaughn to answer, she looks through the Plexiglas. "Are any members of Mr. Coburn's family present?"

Frank Coburn shoots immediately to his feet. "I'm his father, Your Honor. And we'll put our house up." Vaughn's own father, John, rises, too. He doesn't speak, but Vaughn knows that his parents would put up their own home, if need be. Vaughn glances at Jimmy Nutzo and feels a shiver of dread.

There's no way I can let them bet all their money on Eddy's showing up for trial, because if he's released, he'll disappear long before he ever makes it to court.

"Very well," says the magistrate. "What I'm going to do here is to set bail at one million dollars."

Christina Wesley protests, but Delia Smick refuses to change her mind. At this point, the magistrate gives her speech about the right to a preliminary hearing, and Vaughn tells her that his client does indeed want a preliminary hearing. Smick sets the date for Friday, August 1, eight days hence.

After the hearing, Vaughn stands with his family in the waiting area as everyone else clears the room. James Nunzio makes a point of catching Vaughn's eye before he leaves. When Vaughn is alone with his family, Frank and John Coburn tell him that they'll start making the arrangements for Eddy's bail. Vaughn nods but doesn't say anything to this, telling them instead that he's going down to the Roundhouse to talk to Eddy before they load him onto the bus for the trip to county lockup.

Vaughn does his best to reassure them, especially his aunt Claire, whom he promised Eddy wouldn't go back to prison. He keeps his voice strong, tries to project an image of confidence. But in Frank and John Coburn's eyes, he sees their awareness of the truth. Eddy's in big trouble, and Vaughn is flailing helplessly.

An hour later, Vaughn is sitting with Eddy in a cell in the Roundhouse. He explains to his cousin that he'll be taken by bus to the county prison, Curran-Fromhold, in Northeast Philadelphia.

"That's where they'll keep you until the preliminary hearing. At the hearing, the prosecutor has to present testimony and other evidence sufficient to convince the judge to hold you over for trial."

The word *trial* seems to strike Eddy hard. The reality of what he's facing is sinking in.

"The judge set bail," Eddy says. "She said a million dollars. But I only have to come up with a part of that, right? Like ten percent? My parents could borrow against the house."

Vaughn pauses before answering. This is going to be very hard. "The magistrate set it as straight bail, so you would need the full amount, in cash or secured by real estate. Your parents, and my own, could put their houses up as collateral. And your father's gym, and my dad's bar. There's enough property to cover the bail."

Eddy brightens, but Vaughn raises his hand. "But that would be a mistake."

"A mistake for me to get out of jail?"

Vaughn sighs. "You know that James Nunzio's son was on that train, don't you?"

Eddy stares.

"Nunzio was sitting in the spectator's section today. Watching the arraignment."

Eddy's mouth slowly opens.

"You can't be out on the street, Ed."

"What are you saying? He's going to kill me?"

It's Vaughn's turn to stare.

"Jesus." Eddy lowers his head, puts it into his hands. "I'm fucked. Kate, too. And little Emma."

"There's time between now and the trial. To investigate. Find evidence that it wasn't your fault."

"*Was it* my fault? I don't even know anymore."

"I'm going to be working on it night and day, Ed. If there's information out there that will clear you, I'll find it."

His hands now covering his face, Eddy slowly shakes his head. "I can't let my baby grow up without a father, Vaughn. You have to find a way. You have to . . ." Eddy's voice trails off.

22

Thursday, July 24, continued

By the time Vaughn gets back to the office, it's close to four o'clock. From behind the reception desk, Angie looks up, her eyes filled with concern. "We heard what happened. It's all over the news. Mick is in his office. He said he wanted to see you as soon as you got in."

Vaughn closes and then reopens his eyes. He hasn't called in since Eddy's arrest, and he knows Mick is going to be angry at him. He also knows there's a good chance that Mick and Susan will order him to drop the case, tell him to refer Eddy to another attorney. Representing his cousin will require vast amounts of attorney time and the outlay of large amounts of cash, none of which Eddy can cover. Susan likely wants to see Eddy sent to jail for a long time. Vaughn has no idea how he's going to convince his bosses to let him move forward.

"There's a box on your desk," Angie says, pulling him from his thoughts. "Your uncle dropped it off about an hour ago."

Vaughn takes a deep breath and walks back to his office. He sits down behind his desk and pulls the box toward him. Made of brown cardboard, old and dented, the box is tied shut with twine. Vaughn wonders where his uncle has kept the box all these years. The gym? His garage? A bedroom closet?

Vaughn unties the twine and lifts off the lid. And there they are: his old sixteen-ounce Everlast training gloves. Black. Always black. Eddy always used red. Vaughn inspects the gloves, smells the leather, which is cracked from use and age and sweat. Holding them now stirs something deep inside him.

A few minutes later, Vaughn enters Mick's office carrying the gloves. He lowers himself into one of the visitor's chairs. Susan is in the other. Tommy is leaning against the window.

"Whose gloves?" asks Tommy.

"Mine, from a long time ago," Vaughn answers.

"This about Eddy?" asks Mick.

Vaughn nods, and exhales. He tells them how he and Eddy grew up close and got into boxing together. Then he tells them the same story that he told Erin, the tale that made her look at him differently.

"The night before Eddy stood in front of the judge, there was a knock at my parents' door. It was my uncle Frank, Eddy's father. My dad called me into the living room, and the two of them sat me down. My dad had put my boxing gloves on the coffee table. My uncle looked at them, then looked at me, and then he . . ."

Vaughn would never forget the look in Frank's eyes.

"He told me that there was never a chance Eddy was going to rat me out. 'That's not how we do things in this family,' he said.

"'But now there's a debt,' my father said. 'You owe your cousin. Your aunt Claire and uncle Frank, too.' Then he picked up the gloves, handed them to my uncle. 'These gloves are your chit. There ever comes a time he hands them back to you—he, or anyone in the family—you honor your debt. Whatever you have to do. Whatever it takes.'"

Vaughn looks down at the gloves. After a while, he looks up at Mick, then at Susan. "I know you don't want me to represent my cousin in the criminal case. And given how much I feel like I've botched things so far, a part of me would love to hand his defense over to someone else. But I can't leave Eddy hanging in the wind, and I won't turn him over to someone else. I have to stick by my cousin. No matter the price. If that means I have to leave the firm, I'll do it, and I won't complain or raise a fuss. I live pretty simply, and I've got some money socked away. Enough to support myself for a couple of years. As for the costs of defense—expert witnesses, court costs, subpoena fees—my family will find a way to raise the money. That's it. Now you know. I'm sorry."

Vaughn stands and turns to leave.

"Where are you goin'?" It's Tommy's voice, low and gravelly.

Vaughn turns back. He stands and watches as something passes between Tommy and Mick.

So much goes on beneath the surface with those two.

"Family doesn't abandon family," says Mick. "You're sticking by your cousin. And you're staying here. As for the costs of defense, Susan and I came into a windfall from the Hanson case. We've barely touched it, and it's more than enough to cover Eddy's defense."

Vaughn looks at Susan. She stares back at him, bites her lower lip, and nods. "Just make damn sure you don't do anything to shame this firm."

Ten minutes later, Vaughn leaves Mick's office, his stomach still fluttering, hands shaking. He feels like he's just boxed ten rounds. He calls his uncle Frank to arrange a meeting at the gym. Before he can leave the office, though, Vaughn has hours of catch-up work to do on his other cases. He's there until after nine.

On the drive to Northeast Philly, Vaughn recalls attending Eddy's sentencing. The hearing took more than an hour, during which Vaughn sat between his uncle and his father. Eddy sat at a table in front of them with his attorney.

At a podium at the front of the courtroom, just below the bench, Eddy officially pled guilty to the charge of involuntary manslaughter. Vaughn could tell that his cousin was nervous; Eddy kept shifting on his feet, and his voice wavered. While Eddy talked, his mother gripped her husband's forearm. Frank covered Claire's hand with his own and gently patted it. Vaughn knew his uncle was trying to stay strong for his wife, but he sensed something go out of the man as he watched his only son stand before the judge and admit to a serious crime.

The worst part for Vaughn was when they took his cousin away. Eddy looked back at his parents, and Vaughn could see anguish in his eyes. And fear. He only glanced at Vaughn for an instant. But an instant was all it took. Vaughn has never been able to find the word for what he saw on his cousin's face, but it ran him through like a sword. If he hadn't been sitting, he might have fallen in pain. That's how deeply it cut.

After the sentencing, Vaughn, burning with shame, stayed in the building while his and Eddy's parents left the courthouse. He sat in the hall outside the courtroom for a long time. Eventually he got up and walked into another courtroom. Inside, a nineteen-year-old defendant was being tried for assault. Listening to the charging officer's testimony, Vaughn was quickly convinced the defendant was a bad seed. Then the defense attorney went to work. In a matter of minutes, it became clear that the cop had a hard-on for the kid. It was also obvious that the officer's animus was rooted in bad blood between him the defendant's father, a result of something that had happened over a woman. For years, this same officer had arrested the defendant multiple times . . . for disturbing the peace, creating a nuisance and other minor—and, it became plain, trumped-up—charges. Time after time, the kid had been hauled into court, made to stand in front of a judge, and deflect the legal blows thrown at him by this one rogue cop. The prosecution tried to paint the defendant as a predator who made the city's streets a dangerous place. But, in fact, it was the cop who made the streets unsafe for the young kid.

A classic David-and-Goliath story. Except in this tale, the kid had a giant of his own: his relentless defense attorney. He gave the kid in court what he could never have out on the streets—a fair fight.

It was then and there that Vaughn decided to become a lawyer.

◆　◆　◆

Vaughn parks the Jeep in front of his uncle's gym and walks inside. It's dark, but Vaughn can see the light on in his uncle's tiny office. He knocks on the door frame and takes one of the two beat-up chairs as Frank turns his own chair to face him. He knows his uncle has been making plans to raise Eddy's bail, and Frank clearly thinks he's there to start walking him through the process. In fact, he's here to shut it down.

"I've spoken with Eddy," Vaughn starts. "I told him what I have to tell you now. He has to stay inside until the trial."

Frank's face turns scarlet, and Vaughn can tell he's about to lay into him. Vaughn raises his hand. "Uncle Frank, please. Just listen."

His uncle sits back, and Vaughn tells him everything that's transpired with Jimmy Nunzio.

"It'd be easier for Nunzio to get to Eddy in jail than outside, with us," his uncle argues. "We could protect him. I could protect him. Hide him."

"Maybe. But he found him once already, and if he does it again, there'll be collateral damage. A friend or family member who Eddy holes up with. Or a separate attack on one of *us*, just because."

Frank pushes and Vaughn pushes back. They go at it until Vaughn says what he was hoping not to have to. "If Nunzio gets Eddy on the street, he'll make him disappear. He won't show up for his preliminary hearing, and your bail will be forfeit. You'll lose everything."

Frank's shoulder's slump, and Vaughn knows he finally gets it. "But if he's whacked inside, there'll be a body."

Frank's face turns gray, and Vaughn thinks this is the first time he's ever seen his uncle afraid.

Frank leans forward, steeples his huge hands, and rests his forehead on them. "How did it come to this?"

23

FRIDAY, JULY 25

Well after midnight, Vaughn sits in the ring, his back against the ropes, wearing only his suit pants and training gloves. His uncle left the gym an hour earlier, and Vaughn immediately went to work on the heavy bag. He punched himself out, then practiced visualization and footwork in the ring. He's exhausted now, and drenched with sweat. The two front windows are open, but the July night air is stifling. Vaughn has the overhead lights turned out, but the gym glows pale with moonlight washing through the skylight.

Vaughn moves away from the ropes, sits cross-legged, and focuses on his breathing. He tries to clear his head, but worry and fear push their way inside. It won't be enough for him to simply stand by his cousin and fight for him. Frank Coburn made that clear.

"My bosses have agreed to let me keep representing Eddy," he told his uncle before the older man left him alone. "And I'm going to. Whatever happens—trial, appeal, retrial—I'm going to stand by Eddy. I got the gloves . . . and the message."

Frank Coburn stood in the doorway of his office. He looked down at Vaughn, still in the chair. "That's not the message, son. Yes, you'll stand with Eddy, fight the full twelve rounds. But that won't make things even for leaving him before."

Vaughn stared up at his uncle.

"Those gloves have been gathering interest, Vaughn. For sixteen years. If you think that just sticking around this time is going to pay your debt, you're wrong. You have to *win*, son. You have to find a way to get Eddy out of this mess. You have to *save* him."

Vaughn looked into Frank Coburn's flat steel-blue eyes and opened his mouth, but nothing came out. What could he say? *Sorry, Uncle Frank, can't make any promises. First rule of lawyering.* Of course not. And besides, he knows his uncle is right. What he owes his cousin is nothing less than victory. And with it, salvation. He owes Eddy the life he'd struggled so long to rebuild after Vaughn left him wrapped around that tree on Kelly Drive.

Vaughn stands and climbs through the ropes. He takes off his gloves, puts on his shirt, socks, and shoes, then makes his way to the stairs leading to the roof. From the top of the building, he can see in the distance the towers of Center City: One and Two Liberty Place, the two Comcast towers, Mellon Bank Center, and the Cira Centre buildings.

Vaughn stares at the structures for a long time. Despite their cheery, colored lights, the towers seem cold. And their size is less evocative of grandeur than of bigness. They don't tower; they loom. And it strikes Vaughn that what the buildings stand for is power. The type of power held by men like Benjamin Balzac and Geoffrey Day, and the district attorney/would-be mayor whom they pressured and probably bribed into bringing charges against Eddy.

"Who can stand against the likes of us?" the towers seem to ask.

"Who can beat us?" boast the Days and Balzacs and their political cronies.

Vaughn takes a deep breath. "Fuck you," he says aloud. "I can."

Twenty minutes later, Vaughn is in his Jeep heading south on I-95. His cell rings, and he wonders who's calling him at 1:30 in the morning. He glances down at the phone, sees that it's Erin. He's been ducking her calls all day—he's been ducking everyone's calls—and he debates whether to answer now. But given the hour, her reason for calling may be too important to put off.

"Hey," he says.

"You have to get over here right away." Erin's tone is serious, even strained.

"What's wrong? Are you all right?"

"I can't explain over the phone. My friend Laurie Mitzner is here. The one who works for Balzac. She brought something. You have to see it."

"Is it something good? Will it help Eddy?"

"If it's what I think it is, it's not good at all. It's horrible. But it might help your cousin. Just get here as fast as you can." And with that, Erin hangs up.

By the time he knocks on Erin's door, Vaughn's heart is racing. He cannot imagine what Laurie might have that could help Eddy, or what could be as terrible as Erin thinks it is.

Erin opens the door, then immediately turns and walks into the living room. Laurie is sitting on the sofa. A pretty woman with dark hair and olive skin, Laurie's eyes are red—and afraid. Vaughn sees at once that she's a wreck.

Vaughn sits next to Laurie on the couch, takes her hands in his. "Tell me what's wrong," he says.

"It's the crash," Laurie answers, her voice quavering. "He had a video of it. Balzac. I saved it on my phone."

Vaughn glances at Erin. He doesn't understand what Laurie is trying to tell him.

"Start from when you were in his office," Erin says to Laurie. "Tell Vaughn how you found it. Like you told me."

Laurie inhales. "Okay. It was about a week after the accident. Balzac wanted a memo on his desk first thing in the morning, and I was working really late to finish it. He was working late, too. He had his door closed for a long time, then he opened it and came to my office and started talking to me. Nothing important, just small talk. I got the impression he'd been drinking. He does that sometimes when he works late. He has a little bar in his office."

Vaughn's glance at Erin asks, *Where is she going with this?* Erin's look tells him to be patient.

"He started to creep me out, and maybe he could tell, because he stopped talking and went back to his office. I think all he did was pick up his jacket because he left almost right away. I kept working until I finished the memo. Then I took it to his office and laid it on his desk. I must've bumped his mouse, because his computer screen lit up. It opened to an image of a train. I was curious, so I clicked the mouse to play the video."

Laurie stops here to gather herself. "It was the crash. The video showed the crash."

Vaughn is totally confused. "I've seen dozens of videos of the crash. A hundred. So has everyone else who owns a television."

"Not like this one," Erin says. Then she leans over to her laptop, open on the coffee table. "Laurie taped the video from Balzac's monitor using her cell phone. After she showed it to me tonight, I had her e-mail it to me, and I saved it on my computer." Erin presses a button on the MacBook Air, and the video begins to play. It shows an aerial view of the track, the train rounding the curve in the distance, then racing down the straightaway, past and beneath the hovering camera, which turns to follow it. There it catches two figures moving quickly away from the track, followed by the train crashing into the TracVac, pulverizing the engine and sending the cars flying off the track behind it. The screen goes black.

Vaughn is stunned. "It shows the actual crash," he says, his voice barely audible.

"Which means," Erin says, "that whoever took the video *knew* the train was about to crash. And there's only one way that's possible."

"They caused the crash *themselves*," says Laurie.

No. It can't be.

It takes a moment before Vaughn can speak. "Could it be the railroad's? Like those highway traffic cams?" But even as he asks, he knows this video is different.

"Look more closely," says Erin, playing the video again. "It's too floaty. The camera is gaining and losing altitude. Only a few inches, but it's definitely moving up and down. The camera's not on any tower."

"And it turns," Laurie says. "It's following the train. Remote-controlled."

"Balzac had a drone?" Vaughn asks Laurie.

"Maybe, maybe not," says Erin. "But Geoffrey Day sure as hell did. He had the firm buy it about a week before the accident. He showed it off to everyone, even flew it around the office."

Vaughn looks from Erin to Laurie. "You're telling me your bosses worked together to crash the train?"

Inconceivable. And yet.

Balzac, with the help of his future brother-in-law, turned a young girl into a double amputee to win a big verdict. And Geoffrey Day lost tens of millions in a failed class-action suit at the same time he forked over untold millions to buy Penn Law. And . . . something pecks at the back of Vaughn's mind . . .

"The websites."

Erin and Laurie look at each other, and Vaughn explains.

"The night of the train wreck, I was doing research on the computer and saw that a bunch of plaintiff firms had put up paid Google Ads about the crash. The ads linked directly to the law firms' websites. And each law firm's website had blurbs about the train crash, or train law, or the train industry. Except that Balzac's website and Day's website didn't just have blurbs—they had multipage compendiums that covered all things railroad. I wondered how your firms could have generated such erudition in such a short time. Except now, it turns out, those articles weren't written in the few hours after the accident; they were written in the days and weeks before. This whole thing was planned down to the *n*th degree."

Erin's eyes are wide. "I never even thought to look at how our website handled the train crash. I'm sure none of the other lawyers at the firm did, either. We have nothing to do with the website ourselves; Geoffrey's PR and marketing people run it."

"I'm so scared," Laurie blurts. "He knows, I'm sure of it."

"Knows what?" asks Vaughn.

"That I was in his office. That I saw the video. After I watched it, I tried to rewind it back to the exact spot where I found it. But I'm not sure I did. What's worse is that I left my memo on his desk. He would have known that next morning that I had been in his office. And he'd know as soon as he touched his laptop that the video was right there, waiting to pop up."

"You're being paranoid," Erin says.

"No, I'm not. He's been acting weird toward me ever since. Being real nice, and solicitous. I wasn't even on the crash team when I saw the video. But two days later, he brought me on board. He said it was the firm's most prestigious litigation, and he wanted me to be a part of it."

No one talks for a long while. Then, Laurie asks, "What are we going to do?"

Vaughn looks at Laurie, then at Erin. "We're going to bring them down."

24

Friday, July 25

It's 9:00 a.m., and Geoffrey Day sits behind his desk, around which are gathered the heads of Day and Lockwood's website, PR, and marketing departments. Spread on the desk are draft advertisements, press releases, and mock Web pages. Each features the image of some form of rising or risen sun. Some pieces include sketches of trains or cars or planes or stethoscopes or pills, encompassing the various instrumentalities through which individual and corporate villains inflict harm on the innocent. The name of the campaign—arrived at with the aid of online surveys, interviews, and focus groups—is "A New Day."

"The triumph of justice—" begins Irvin Sloan, the head of PR.

"Over corporate greed," interjects Cindy Schlemming, who runs the website.

Reading Day's mood, John Shein, the overall head of marketing, remains silent.

Day turns first to Sloan and then to Schlemming, the look on his face sending a clear message: *You must be kidding me.*

They go back to the drawing board, and after thirty minutes that pass like thirty hours, Day summarily dismisses the Three Marketeers (his nickname). He rises and walks to the one nonwindowed wall of his office. It's adorned with photographs. Day and Clinton. Day and Bush

I. Day and Bush II. Day and Obama. Day and several sitting justices of the United States Supreme Court. Day and Sting. There are also a dozen framed awards from various humanitarian associations. Geoffrey Day scans it all and sighs. Then he walks to the windows behind his desk, looks out at the vast landscape forty floors below, and considers the path that led him here.

For as long as he could remember, he'd strived to be the best. And in America, to be the "best," as best he could figure it, meant to be the most successful. He started by being the most successful student. He had perfect grades and graduated as valedictorian in both high school and college. At Penn Law, he was editor-in-chief of the Law Review and graduated summa cum laude. None of that was especially difficult for him; according to standardized testing, his IQ was off the charts.

Success in the actual practice of law was only a little more challenging, requiring, in addition to intelligence, a modicum of political acumen. Once he hired on with Arthur Hogarth's firm—the most successful P.I. firm in the city—it hadn't taken him long to realize that the quickest way to advance was to eliminate his competition and marry into A-Hog's family. He accomplished the former by exposing Benjamin Balzac for the bad actor he was. The latter he achieved by winning the heart of Hogarth's niece, Bethany—a sweet if unimaginative girl. Shortly thereafter, Hogarth made him partner and assigned him the biggest cases in the firm. A few years later, he took his book of business and formed his own firm.

He quickly won several huge verdicts and used the money to build out marquis office space, poach top associates from major P.I. firms, and draft a stable of politicians. In the years that followed, through careful maneuvering and the nurturing of select relationships, he won the top office in the city trial lawyers' association, then the state association, then the national association. At the same time, he was recognized as one of the top-ten trial attorneys in the country. The "Super Lawyer of Super Lawyers," he'd been called.

Finally, he'd won his crowning achievement: persuading Penn president Amy Gutmann to let him buy Penn Law. He still couldn't believe how much she'd charged him. A hundred million dollars.

"But, Geoffrey, it's *Penn*," she repeated over and over. "I'm sure you could get Villanova for a steal."

Smug little bureaucrat.

But the end result, he knows, is worth it: the Commonwealth's only Ivy League law school is now his personal billboard, making him, undeniably, the most successful attorney in the state.

It was all going smoothly until the Relazac blunder and his deal with the devil. But he'd get out from under that rock soon enough, thanks to the train crash. Yet, despite his confidence in his ultimate victory, he still carries with him the same vague sense of unease that troubled him throughout his largely friendless childhood. The feeling that there is something not quite right with him.

Meanwhile, at the Balzac Firm, its own leader isn't in such a good mood himself. It had taken only a few hours for his contact at the Pennsylvania DMV to run the license plate of the man who'd spoken with Royce Badgett inside Badgett's neighborhood bar. The driver's name is Thomas McFarland. He works as an investigator at his brother's law firm, McFarland and Klein. The firm representing Amtrak engineer Edward Coburn.

As soon as he found out, Balzac phoned Badgett and told him to have McFarland followed, and to tail Vaughn Coburn himself. For Tommy's tail, Balzac suggested that Badgett employ "the usual suspects," meaning Coraline Demming, a local girl Badgett used to do in high school. Badgett has paid her a few times to do odd jobs on Balzac's cases.

Now on the phone with Badgett, Balzac is learning the results of his and Coraline's efforts.

"Coraline says the investigator mostly goes between the law firm and a little house he lives in near Chestnut Hill. He served some subpoenas, visited some people who are probably witnesses in other cases, went to a couple of bars—including a cop bar—and bent his elbow with guys he seemed to know. He usually eats alone or with his brother."

Balzac is about to yawn when Badgett says, "Now for the interesting stuff. McFarland's tailed *me* a couple of times since the bar. He also tried to strike up some conversations about me with my neighbors, but he got nothing. And he has a couple of friends who work for Amtrak that he visited."

"Who are these friends?"

"One's a car repairman. Another works with the Bridges and Buildings Department. I checked them out, and they have no connection to our guys."

Badgett pauses for a moment, and Balzac thinks he hears the man grunt. "Are you okay?"

"Just a little heartburn," Badgett says unconvincingly.

"So, tell me about the lawyer."

"Nothing earth-shattering. On the day of the arraignment, he went to county lockup and met with his cousin. Then he went back to his office and worked until late. From there, he drove to his uncle's boxing gym—that would be Frank Coburn, the engineer's father. The old man left, but the lawyer remained in the gym until late, like one in the morning. Then he drove to the same building in Center City where he's been spending the night since I started tailing him. This time, after he went in, I waited a few minutes, then had the security guard let me in, too. I introduced the guard to my friend, Ben Franklin—actually, three Ben Franklins—and found out that Coburn is hot and heavy with another lawyer who lives in the building. Her name is Erin Doyle, and . . ."

As Badgett talks on, Balzac pulls up Martindale.com on his computer and types in Erin's name. He does a double take when he sees who she works for.

"Fuck me," he says.

"Say what, boss?"

"That bitch works for Geoffrey Day."

"Oh." Badgett grunts again. "That's not good."

"Not even a little." Balzac takes some time to think, and Badgett doesn't interrupt. "It may be time to start tying up some loose ends. Speaking of which, how is our nervous friend?"

Balzac is referring to track foreman Reggie Frye. Jack Bunting told Balzac that Frye had been a jittery mess during his interview with the NTSB go-team. So Balzac had Bunting drive Frye to a cabin in the Poconos to hide out until things blew over. Frye was happy to escape the scrutiny, at first. But, according to Bunting, Frye was getting cabin fever and demanding a better arrangement, along with the money he'd been promised. Bunting had been pushing for weeks to have Reggie disappear on a more permanent basis. Balzac realizes now that Bunting was right.

"Still nervous," answers Badgett.

"That makes me nervous."

"Message received."

Balzac hangs up, smiling. Feeling much lighter than he had a few minutes earlier, he leans forward and opens the large humidor sitting on his desk. He pulls out a Stradivarius Churchill. Then he ignites his S.T. Dupont Black Lacquered Ligne 2 lighter and carefully toasts the cigar, keeping the flame one inch below the foot while holding the Churchill at a forty-five-degree angle and rotating it. Once the foot begins to smoke, he places the cigar in his mouth and begins taking short puffs until the tip glows.

Balzac removes the cigar. He knows that his secretary, Edna, will have a shit fit when she smells the smoke. *Who cares? It's not like I'm planning to nail her. Again.* Speaking of which, Balzac's thoughts drift to Laurie Mitzner. He's at the awkward stage of the seduction process. The point at which he shows increasing interest in the woman. They never know how to take it at first, and things become uncomfortable for a while. After a point, though, the woman begins to grasp that he views her as special. More intelligent than her peers. More interesting. More worthy of his precious time. Once she becomes comfortable with his attention, he stops cold. The woman becomes confused, then a little angry. When that happens, he again showers her with attention, takes the time to explain that his sudden aloofness had nothing to do with her, but with some pressing problem he's facing. He'll repeat this hot-and-cold dance a few times, speeding up the cycle, until the woman becomes so fearful of losing his mercurial favor that she throws herself at him.

It's a simple process. Crude, actually. But he knows it will work with Laurie, just as it worked with the other two women on his Amtrak crash team. And the two before them, and the five before them, and the ten before them.

Benjamin Balzac takes a deep drag off the Churchill. Then he leans his head back and blows out a thick column of smoke. On the other side of his door, Edna coughs theatrically.

Hearing her, Balzac laughs.

Ten blocks away, at 1515 Market Street, four people sit in a conference room. Laughter is the last thing *they* have on their minds. Mick and Tommy McFarland and Susan Klein sit with their mouths agape, staring at Vaughn Coburn. He's just shown them Laurie Mitzner's videotape and explained his theory that Geoffrey Day and Benjamin Balzac caused the crash. Without revealing Erin's name, he's told them what she said about Day's drones. He's also shown them printouts of the detailed railroad-law sections from the Balzac and Day and Lockwood websites.

"And then, there are the complaints," Vaughn says. "Balzac and Day were the first to the courthouse, and all the complaints filed after theirs are almost verbatim copies. The important thing is that Balzac's and Day's complaints refer to my cousin's deadly operation of a motor vehicle and his history of alcohol abuse and crime. But if you compare dates, you realize that none of that information came out in the press until *later*."

Mick, Susan, and Tommy look at one another.

"Day and Balzac knew about Eddy all along. I think they *chose* him as the engineer they wanted to set up."

"His past makes him the perfect patsy," says Tommy.

Susan leans forward. She starts to speak, then stops herself, then begins again. "This is . . . unthinkable."

"Yes, it is," Vaughn agrees. "Until you start thinking about it. Then it all adds up."

Next, he shares what he knows about Balzac's amputation case and Day's financial troubles. Mick asks about his sources, and Susan wants to know who gave him the video taken in Balzac's office. "A-Hog tipped me off to the amputation case and Day's financial troubles from the failed class-action cases."

"And the information about the drones—the source of the video?" Susan presses.

Vaughn takes a deep breath. "I'm dating an associate who works for Day. Her friend, who works for Balzac, recorded the video on her iPhone as it played on Balzac's computer."

"Jesus Christ," Mick says. "You have lawyers passing you confidential information, betraying their bosses, their law firms?"

It's Vaughn's turn to stare. "We're talking about two monsters who crashed a train. Mass murderers. Who the hell cares about them, or their firms?"

Mick seems momentarily taken aback by the venom in Vaughn's voice. Then he nods. "What do you want to do with all this?"

"We have to take this right to the FBI," Susan declares before Vaughn can answer.

"*No!*" Vaughn practically shouts the word. "Day and Balzac are too politically connected. They'd be tipped off in an hour. And any evidence that might be out there that could inculpate them and clear my cousin would disappear."

"He's right," says Tommy. "And one of my guys on the railroad says he has something for me. I'm going to meet him this afternoon. Who knows what's out there?"

Mick and Susan look hard at each other, then Susan turns to Vaughn. "At some point, we have to take this to the government."

"I don't think we'll need to," says Vaughn. "If the preliminary hearing goes as I hope, the government will come to *us*."

Mick studies Vaughn. "You're planning to present evidence at the preliminary hearing?"

Ordinarily, preliminary hearings are where the prosecution presents just enough evidence to convince the judge that it's more likely than not that a crime has been committed and that the defendant is the perpetrator. Defense attorneys use the hearings to find out what they can about the prosecution's case. Sometimes, they'll cross-examine witnesses. Although they have the right to present evidence of their own, they hardly ever do; in all but the rarest cases, it's a foregone conclusion that the judge will bind the defendant over for trial. So there's no reason for the defense to tip its own hand by showing its cards to the prosecution.

"You actually think there's a chance you can get the judge to let Eddy go?" Susan asks, incredulous.

"Right now, I have the video, and the prescient complaints and websites," Vaughn answers. "That won't be enough. But if I find more . . ."

Susan sighs. "I know you want to do right by your cousin. And if you're right about Day and Balzac, I want them to hang. But I just can't envision a scenario where the judge won't bind the case over for trial, no matter what you find."

Vaughn nods. "You're probably right. But I have to try. I have to get Eddy out from under this as fast as I can. And not just because of the law."

"Jimmy Nutzo," Tommy says, catching Mick's eye.

"He's going to kill Eddy, I have no doubt of it. Unless I give him one helluva reason not to. And soon," he adds, recalling Nunzio's warning: *Sometimes soon isn't soon enough.*

Royce Badgett clicks off his cell phone, then starts dialing.

"Whatcha doin'?" Coraline asks over her shoulder.

"I'm making a call."

"You just made a call."

"No. I received a call. From the boss. Now I got to make one."

"You have to do it right now?" Coraline is annoyed. Royce is sitting on his La-Z-Boy. Coraline is on his lap, facing the other way. They are both naked.

"Just sit still. It'll only take a minute."

"A minute my ass," says Coraline.

"If that's what you want, just slide me in."

"You're disgusting, you know that?"

He puts a hand on her back. "Now turn around." He likes fornicating with Coraline well enough, but only if she's facing the other way. She's got an okay body, but even with the dental work, her face is nasty. Her nose looks like a beak. She's jowly, and she has a wandering eye. He doesn't remember her having the eye thing in high school. He wouldn't be surprised if Coraline's husband, Denny, hit her on the head and knocked it loose. First, because Denny is a rough-ass son of a bitch. Second, because Coraline can be really annoying.

"Jack?" Badgett says when Bunting answers the phone.

"Hey, Badger. What's up?"

"Boss says it's time to take care of the track foreman."

"We should've gotten rid of him three weeks ago. What's the plan?"

"Just bring him to my place."

"On what pretext?"

"Who gives a shit? Tell him you're taking him to pick up his money. That we're getting him down to some Caribbean island for a few months and I need to take his picture for a fake passport."

Bunting smiles. "I like that."

"I'm good on my feet." He kills the phone and grabs Coraline's hair. *And on my La-Z-Boy.*

25

FRIDAY, JULY 25 THROUGH SATURDAY, JULY 26

It's 8:00 p.m., and Tommy is nursing his Miller Lite in the back room just off the bar. The guy he's supposed to meet, George Haley, is already half an hour late, and Tommy is getting nervous that he won't show. Haley is an Amtrak track supervisor. Tommy met George five years earlier, when Mick represented his brother, Dave, in a bar-fight felony-assault case. Tommy worked hard to drum up witnesses to testify that George's brother wasn't the aggressor, and George was grateful. So when Tommy wanted background information on Amtrak, George was the first person he called. But Haley has stood Tommy up twice now, and it's obvious he's scared of something. Probably why he insisted they meet at a rundown tavern in Essington, ten miles south of the city.

Tommy lifts his cell phone to call Haley when he sees the big man pausing in the doorway, looking around. Tommy waves his hand, and Haley walks across the bar to the back room. Haley looks like an older Orson Welles and has the actor's baritone voice. What he lacks is Welles's confident demeanor. Haley's eyes, Tommy notices, dart back and forth like he expects someone to grab him at any moment.

The two men shake hands, then sit down at the long table that takes up most of the back room. A waitress comes in and asks Haley if he wants something to drink. He waves her off, says no.

"George, thanks for doing this," Tommy says. "We have a tough fight on our hands with this Coburn kid."

Haley looks around the room, behind him, and through the doorway to the bar. "Okay."

"Let's start with a little background. What do you know about the track foreman, Reggie Frye? The one who's gone missing."

"Pain in the ass. Always bitching."

"He worked under you?"

"Worked? More like he put in time. He's the kind who never does more than he has to."

"Then why'd he join the track department? You guys work harder than anyone."

"That's part of his problem. He didn't start out in track. He was an engineer. Thinks he's better than the guys on the ground."

"So how'd he end up working track?"

"I heard he tested dirty, twice, while he was an engineer. Drugs or booze, I don't know which. That happens, and a guy gets bounced from the railroad. But he found a way to stay with the company."

Haley reaches into his pocket, pulls out a pack of cigarettes, and lights one up. Smoking in a public restaurant is illegal, but since they're in the back room, it's allowed anyway.

Tommy chews on what Haley's told him. "Any idea whether Frye knew Eddy Coburn?"

Haley shakes his head. "Not that he ever mentioned to me. But if they were both engineers working the corridor, they probably ran into each other, at the very least."

Tommy pauses before asking the big question. "Any chance Frye was unhappy enough with his job that he'd want to wreck a train?"

George Haley stares at Tommy.

"Right now," Tommy says, "the official theory is that random vandals moved the TracVac onto Track 2 after Frye and his crew left for the day. Any chance it wasn't vandals?"

Haley sits back in his seat. "What are you saying here?"

Tommy shakes his head. "Not saying anything. I'm asking, that's all."

"If you're *asking* me whether Reggie Frye would have deliberately caused a train crash, my answer is, how the hell should I know?"

Tommy picks up the anger in Haley's tone and switches gears.

"So tell me about Jack Bunting. I know he was one of Amtrak's representatives on the NTSB go-team."

"He was the first one in the locomotive after the crash. He downloaded the information from the black box. He said there was nothing to download from the video recorders because the cameras were on hold until the railroad and the union ironed out their differences."

"What's he like?"

Haley takes another deep drag of his cigarette, then looks to the door to make sure it's closed.

"World-class SOB."

"How so?"

Haley thinks for a minute, then answers. "Before he got bumped up to management, we worked together as track supervisors on a couple of big jobs. From what I saw, he worked his men like dogs. Wrote them up for infractions every chance he got. If one of 'em got hurt, Bunting would make sure the guy was charged with ten different rules violations and blamed for his own accident."

Haley lights another cigarette, takes a deep drag. "One time, I heard, he kept his men working even after one of them *died*. They were laying track out near Paoli. It was the middle of summer, hot as hell. One of the older guys keeled over. Haley ordered the crew to move the body away from the track, put a shirt over the dead guy's face, then told everyone to get back to work."

"You're shitting me."

"Ask around. Everyone's heard about it."

"You know whether there was anything between Bunting and Eddy Coburn?"

Haley pauses. "I don't know if those two even knew each other."

Tommy hears hesitance in Haley's voice. "What aren't you telling me?"

George Haley checks the door again. "I don't know whether Jack knew that engineer or not. But he knew Reggie Frye."

Haley pauses again, and Tommy nods, signaling him to keep going.

"When I told you that Frye found a way to stay on the railroad, maybe I should have said he found a *who*. The only way he could've saved his ass from getting kicked off the property was if he had someone watching out for him. Someone with clout."

"Like a division engineer."

"Jack Bunting barely had time for his men when he was a foreman and a track supervisor. He didn't joke around with anyone. He didn't even eat with them. And when he started moving up, he got even more aloof. But I saw him more than a few times talking with Reggie Frye. Struck me as kinda unusual, him giving a guy with less than a year of department seniority the time of day."

Tommy watches Haley take a deep drag off his Pall Mall. Then a second.

"So you think Bunting is how Reggie Frye stayed on the railroad."

"I don't think nothing. I'm just telling you what I saw."

Tommy sits back. He's confused. "You told me over the phone you might have something for me. So here we are, and you tell me that Bunting knew Frye and that someone high up on the railroad helped Frye keep working at Amtrak even after his piss test came up positive. But you won't commit that it was Bunting. What gives?"

Haley looks away.

"There's something else, isn't there?"

Haley bites his lower lip. "A rumor, that's all."

Tommy opens his hands. *Out with it.*

"It's the inward-facing camera. I know a guy who thinks he caught Bunting watching a video from the inward-facing camera. Says he was at 30th Street real early one morning—like 4:30—and he passed a little conference room, one with a video setup. The conference room has those vertical windows on either side of the door so you can see inside if you're out in the hall. Bunting was sitting at the conference table, watching a video. And on the video was that kid, Coburn, sitting in the engineer's chair."

"But how could there be a video if Amtrak had the cameras off?"

Haley laughs. "Amtrak *said* they'd keep the cameras off during contract negotiations. Doesn't mean they *did*."

"You're telling me Amtrak welched on the agreement?"

"Welcome to the railroad."

Tommy and Haley look at each other for a long moment, until Tommy says, "This guy who saw all this—you think he'd testify to it?"

"No way."

"But—"

"Not a chance he'll go public. Unh-uh."

"Will he talk to *me*, at least?"

Haley smashes his cigarette in the tin ashtray on the table as he shoots up from his seat. "He just did." He turns toward the doorway, takes a step, then turns back. "None of this gets back to me, right?"

"We never met."

Tommy watches Haley move through the bar and out the door. *Could Haley really be that afraid of Jack Bunting?*

Vaughn paces the bedroom while Erin watches him from the bed. It's close to midnight, and both are too wired to sleep. They thought sex would tire them out, but it only amped them up more.

"We have to get our hands on the locomotive-cab video," Vaughn says. Tommy had shared what he learned from George Haley—about Jack Bunting having the engine video despite Amtrak's claim that the video cameras were turned off pending contract negotiations. "The drone video is powerful, and the websites and the complaints will help. But the judge isn't going to buy our claim that Day and Balzac caused the crash unless we can explain *how* they did it. The cab video could be the key, because it would show exactly what was going on inside the engineer's cab leading up to the crash. And presumably will show Eddy doing nothing wrong."

"Agreed, on all points. But how do we get the video? We have no access to Amtrak's offices at 30th Street Station, and Bunting wouldn't produce it even in answer to a subpoena, because he's said it doesn't exist."

"There's only one chance: we have to go on a fishing expedition. Two expeditions."

Erin knows instantly what he means. "Balzac's office. And Day's? You think they'd have copies? That Bunting wouldn't have just destroyed the video?"

"He hadn't destroyed it as of the time Tommy's contact saw it. And who knows what the arrangement was between him and the lawyers? If they knew about the video, they might have demanded he make them copies."

Vaughn stops pacing and looks at Erin. "Laurie can search Balzac's office, and—"

"And I can search Day's." Erin steels herself. "All right, I'll do it. Geoffrey flew out to the West Coast for the weekend. I'll go tomorrow—I mean today," she corrects herself after looking at the clock and seeing it's after midnight. "Early enough that no one else will be there."

Vaughn smiles. He's impressed that Erin didn't have to be convinced to make the bold play.

A gutsy woman.

"I'm not sure we can count on Laurie, though," Erin says. "She's too spooked."

"Then let's ask her to let us in, and you and I can search Balzac's office ourselves."

"And how could we explain our being there if we get caught?"

Vaughn considers the question. "We don't get caught."

It's Erin's turn to smile.

26

SATURDAY, JULY 26

Erin arrives at the firm at 4:30 a.m. The lobby and hallway are dark, which tells her that no one else has arrived yet. Still, she walks the floor, checking all the offices to ensure that they are unoccupied. Then she goes to her own office, where she turns on her computer and opens a legal brief she's been finalizing to make it seem as if she's working in case someone else shows up.

Vaughn's plan was to root through Day's office for the engine-cab video and any potentially relevant documents she might find. But on her way out the door of her apartment, she decided to try something else as well. She pulled her midsize Tumi suitcase out of her front closet.

She now wheels the suitcase through the hall to the elevator and descends one floor to the large evidence room where the firm stores the paper documents, broken products, and demonstrative evidence developed for trial. Erin pulls the Tumi to a wall of metal shelves. There she finds the silver, hard-shell aluminum case that contains the firm's drone. The box says it's a DJI Phantom 3 Professional Quadcopter equipped with a 4K camera. All Erin knows is that when Day flew it around the office, it was creepily futuristic-looking in a scary, Big Brotherish sort of way. Her thought in securing the drone is that perhaps the machine leaves digital fingerprints on its videos, the same way the rifling of a gun barrel leaves distinctive markings on a bullet fired from it.

Erin opens the carrying case to make sure the drone is inside, then closes it again and packs it into the Tumi. She returns to her own floor and parks the suitcase next to her desk. Then she walks to the kitchen and uses the Keurig, because no one will believe she's working this early unless she has a cup of hot coffee next to her laptop.

Erin sits for a minute behind her desk to gather herself, then sets off for Day's office. She hates that the interior walls are made of glass; anyone walking by will see her inside.

All right, let's get this done and get out of here.

Day's desk—designed by the same architect who planned out their offices—is made of stone and teak, with chrome embellishments. Unlike Erin's cluttered desktop, Day's is immaculate—bare of pens, paper, books, or any other evidence of work. The few objets d'art that adorn the desk are precisely ordered. The drawers themselves appear to be organized. Everything in the top side drawers—business cards, stapler, scissors, calculator, Scotch tape, eyeglass cleaner, Aleve, toothpaste, Tic Tacs, personal grooming kit—is neatly positioned.

In the bottom drawers, all the files are arranged in clearly labeled hanging folders. Erin quickly riffles through the folders, lifting each out of the drawer, opening it on the desktop, turning the pages, and then replacing it. After about ten minutes, she hits pay dirt: a folder containing versions of the new railroad sections of the firm's website, heavily edited in Day's own hand. Erin takes the folder, races to the copy room, and copies the contents. She takes the copies to her own office and hides them in her desk. Then she returns to Day's office and replaces the folder.

Erin turns her attention to the center drawer, where Day keeps more business cards along with his collection of obscenely expensive pens and his gold-plated Pez dispenser. She's about to close the drawer when something tells her to lift the carved ivory drawer tray. Beneath it lies a manila envelope. Erin withdraws it, places it on the desk, and opens it. Inside is a single piece of stationery. It's from 2020 Marketing, a company out of Manhattan that runs focus groups for Day. Erin met its CEO once in connection with an automobile-products liability case Day was about to take to trial. The CEO was a sketchy little man in a shiny suit who wore sunglasses even when he was inside. He leered at Erin the whole time she was in the room and kept asking her what there was to do in Philly at night.

The piece of stationery is blank except for a single line: "You're a dead man. Bang, bang, motherfucker. Bang, bang."

What the hell?

Erin stares at the writing, trying to figure out what it means. Because there's only one page, Erin decides to photograph it with her iPhone rather than walk it to the copy room. Once she's done, she returns the document to the center drawer and pushes it shut.

"Erin!"

Erin gasps as her heart stops. Standing in the doorway is Geoffrey Day. She tries to form words to answer him, but nothing comes out.

"What are you doing?"

Erin's heart, stopped for an instant, now races like it's going to explode.

"I'm . . . I'm . . . Oh, this is so embarrassing. I'm . . . *imaging*."

Day glares.

"It's very important to set goals."

Day stands still as stone.

"That's what my life coach tells me."

He cocks his head at the term *life coach*, clearly not a term he's familiar with. "What does that have to do with sitting at my desk?"

"They call it 'sitting on the throne.'" Erin says "throne," but what she's actually envisioning is Geoffrey strapped into the electric chair. "The idea is that you think of someone great, or heroic, and you envision yourself in their place. I thought . . . Well, I thought . . . Oh, I know this sounds corny, but you're everyone's hero. Not just in the firm. But the whole city. That's what I want to be . . . someday."

Day's glare softens to his normal disapproving gaze. "You can't just go into someone's office—especially my office—without asking. It's an invasion of privacy."

Erin lowers her head, makes her lips pouty. The scolded child. "I know. But . . . Oh, I'm sorry. I have no excuse."

"You disappoint me."

"It's unforgivable, I know." Erin stands and walks around the desk as Day—eyeing her warily—takes his seat.

She moves toward the doorway, but turns around before she reaches it. "Can I say something? It's been on my mind for several weeks. The Amtrak crash is the firm's biggest litigation. I've been with the firm for nine years, and yet you didn't ask me to be on it. How am I supposed to learn if I can't work side by side with you?"

Day narrows his eyes, studies her. After a moment, he forms his mouth into an unconvincing half smile. "I'll consider it. The case is fully staffed, but you are an exceptional attorney. Perhaps we could make room for you."

She's about to leave when he raises a hand for her to wait, then asks why she's in the office so early. On sheer instinct, she says she's going to visit her parents for the weekend but needed to get some work done first. Her boss's silence is disconcerting enough that Erin adds that she thought he was supposed to be on the West Coast over the weekend, to which he replies that he's flying out a little later and had to pick up some files from the office.

Erin thanks him for being so understanding and forgiving. Day gives her a curt nod, then abruptly dismisses her, eyeing her suspiciously as she walks out.

Erin pretends to work for an hour, then turns off her computer and leaves her office. She walks straight to the elevator, pulling the small Tumi suitcase behind her. She's nervous that Day will see her and demand to see what's inside the suitcase. The elevator doors begin to close, and she breathes a sigh of relief. But just before the doors close completely, a hand juts inside and the doors open again.

It's Geoffrey Day, toting his own suitcase.

"Going to the airport, right? I'll give you a lift."

"That would be great."

Shit, shit, shit.

Reggie Frye squirms in the front passenger seat of the Buick Regal as it cruises down 476. Jack Bunting is at the wheel. Frye is restless, having been holed up in a little cabin in Pocono Pines.

"This should've happened a long time ago, you ask me," Reggie says.

"I couldn't agree more," says Bunting.

"I did everything you asked me to."

"You didn't have much choice, seeing's how I saved your job."

"I pretended to like Coburn, which wasn't easy, seeing how I can't stand him. He only had a month's seniority on me, and he kept bumping me for better runs."

"So you've told me—a hundred times."

"If it wasn't for me, you'd never have gotten that burner phone into his hands."

Bunting sighs, but Frye ignores him and presses on.

"And what about me single-handedly moving that TracVac to Track 2 in ten minutes flat? And without throwing up signals that the track was occupied? That was some A-plus railroading, you ask me. But did I ever hear a thank-you?"

"You'll get your thanks soon enough."

"Twenty-five thousand. It better all be there."

"Stop worrying. You're getting your money and the passport."

"Are you sure this guy's good?" asks Frye. "The one doing the passport?"

"Best in the city."

"And he has my money?"

"I have the money right in the trunk."

"Oh." Frye perks up, sits taller in the seat.

That shuts him up for the rest of the ride. An hour later, they park in front of a block of row houses. Frye follows Bunting to the back of the car, where Bunting opens the trunk and withdraws a black duffel bag.

"That for me?" Reggie asks.

"You'll get it inside."

They walk up the pitted concrete steps leading to a wooden porch. The front door opens.

"You the ones here for the passport?" asks Royce Badgett.

"It's for him," Bunting says, angling his head at Frye.

"Hurry on in. Some of my neighbors have prying eyes."

They stand in the living room, where Badgett nods at the black duffel. "Is that for me?"

"You wish," Bunting says. "*This* is for you." He pulls a white envelope from his sport coat.

Badgett opens the envelope so Frye can see what's inside. He counts. "Fifteen hundred." He turns to Frye. "Let's go downstairs. The passport and driver's license are ready to put the pictures on. The camera's set up. I'll snap off a few and finish up."

Reggie descends the narrow stairwell into the musty cellar. It's dark, so it takes his eyes a few seconds to focus. Once they do, he's confused by what he sees in addition to the furnace and hot-water heater. There's an impressive array of handguns, bolt-action rifles, and automatic weapons hanging on the wall; a large work table littered with trays of upright empty brass cartridge cases; and various small devices and tools, including a Forster case trimmer, a powder dispenser, powder scale, calipers, a Lyman Turbo Sonic 6000 case cleaner, and a Hornady Lock-N-Load Auto-Progressive reloading press.

What Reggie doesn't see is a camera. Or any form of equipment that looks like it might be used to make passports or drivers' licenses.

The scene doesn't make any sense to Reggie until he sees the hole in the basement floor. Not a hole, actually, but a concrete chamber embedded in the dirt floor. The chamber has a perfectly square, shoulder-width opening and looks like the vaults they slide caskets into at mausoleums, except that it's vertical rather than horizontal. Reggie stares at the opening, suddenly understanding what he's seeing.

"Oh, man." The last two words Reggie Frye will ever say.

Tommy passes Royce Badgett's house just as Jack Bunting and Reggie Frye are standing by the open trunk. He followed Bunting from his house to the hunting cabin and back to Philadelphia. It was tricky going, especially once they got to the Poconos. Traffic on 476 and 80 was heavy enough that he could find cars and trucks to hide behind. But once he got onto the back roads, he had to stay well back of Bunting's Buick and almost lost him a couple of times.

Tommy never actually saw Reggie Frye until he was standing behind the Regal in front of Badgett's house. Once he did, he recognized the track foreman immediately from the photos he'd seen on the TV news.

"Another piece of the puzzle," Tommy says, turning the corner.

Reggie Frye goes down like a puppet with cut strings when he's hit with the dual prongs of Badgett's X26C Taser. Quickly, Badgett binds Frye's hands and feet with Safariland Double Cuff plastic restraints and wraps his mouth with gray duct tape. He has done this before.

Badgett knew as soon as he saw Frye that he was going to have some difficulty stuffing the track foreman into the vertical, concrete-lined vault in his basement floor. Frye's shoulders are broad, and Badgett strongly suspects they are wider than the diagonal span of the vault. Badgett's concerns are confirmed when he drags Frye to the opening and lowers him feetfirst into the vault. Sure enough, the man's shoulders wedge so tightly he gets stuck.

Royce steps back and tries to figure out what to do. He faced a similar problem with the seventy-two-year-old truck driver in the second vault, the one who'd broadsided the Chrysler minivan with his BP tanker truck, wiping out a family of four. The boss secured a $30 million settlement when the trucker testified in his deposition that he'd been distracted because he was watching porn on his cell phone. Happily, the man, though broad-shouldered like Reggie Frye, was so old and decrepit that Royce was able to shove him into the vault by simply pushing down on his shoulders. The old fart's clavicles splintered like chicken bones. The ill-fated Frye is younger, so Badgett knows it's not going to be that easy.

Badgett is wrenched from his thoughts by Reggie's sudden squealing. The track foreman is awake now, in pain, and fully cognizant of what awaits him. Needless to say, he is not taking it well. Badgett has heard the squeals before, seen the pleading eyes. It's old hat. He considers explaining this to Reggie Frye, telling him not to waste his time trying to beg his way out of it. But he doesn't bother. Instead, he walks to his work table and retrieves the instrument of Frye's demise. It's not a gun or a knife. Either of those would spray blood all over the floor. Rather, it's a clothespin.

Badgett kneels down to the level of Frye's head and places the clothespin over his nose. With his mouth already sealed shut by the duct tape, there is no way for Frye to breathe. He shakes his head violently, trying to dislodge the pin, but it's a sturdy, old-fashioned wooden number with a galvanized steel spring, and it goes nowhere.

Reggie's eyes bulge and his squealing increases in volume until he runs out of steam—actually, air—and stops. Badgett waits until the show is over, then calmly positions himself above the body. He raises his hands above his head and grabs hold of a small-diameter pipe running along the ceiling. He uses it to steady himself as he jumps up and down on Reggie Frye's shoulders, slowly pounding him deeper into the vault. He stops when his head is three inches below the level of the opening.

27

Saturday, July 26

The late-night meeting of Vaughn, Tommy, Laurie, and Erin in Erin's apartment is tense. Laurie Mitzner's fear is palpable. She fights hard against the idea of searching Balzac's office, but finally agrees when Erin convinces her that if they are right about the crash video and the websites and the complaints and the drone, then Benjamin Balzac and Geoffrey Day are mass murderers, and it's worth risking their careers—and maybe more—to bring them to justice.

"I just took the same risk at my own firm," Erin says. And what a nerve-racking fiasco that turned into. She hadn't been able to avoid accepting Day's offer to drive her to the airport, so she ended up sitting next to him in his Lexus LS 460, making up details—time, terminal, carrier—of her imaginary flight and praying that her boss didn't later pull up the airline on his cell to see whether there actually was such a flight. The worst part was when Geoffrey lifted her suitcase—containing the drone—first into and then out of his trunk. Her heart was racing so fast she thought she might pass out. She was saved, in the end, only because Day was flying out of Terminal A while her own fictitious flight left from Terminal C, so she was able to separate from him before ticketing.

"So, let's agree on what we're going to be looking for," Vaughn says, wrapping up the meeting. "First, the crash video Laurie pulled up on Balzac's computer. We need to find the video and then *retape it*, capturing Balzac's office." When Laurie had initially taped the video, she didn't include any footage corroborating that she'd taped it off Balzac's computer. This time, after the recording ended, the cell-phone camera would pan out to include Balzac's computer, desk, and office. This would prove that Balzac himself had been in possession of the crash video. It would also arguably make the video *self-authenticating*, meaning that it could be introduced into evidence without Laurie having to testify—a long shot, but one Vaughn might have to take should Laurie develop cold feet.

"The second thing we're looking for," he continues, "is the inward-facing locomotive video. Of all the possible evidence, the inward-facing video will likely go the farthest in explaining what happened to cause the crash. It would show what was happening inside the engine with Eddy leading up to, and through, the wreck." Of course, there was always the risk the video would inculpate Eddy, but that was a chance he'd have to take. Either way, he'd know the truth about what happened.

"Don't forget the 'bang, bang note' I found in Day's desk," Erin interjects. "I'd love to find a copy of the same thing in Balzac's office. Or something explaining what the hell it means."

"Absolutely," Vaughn agrees. "So, that's number three. Number four is anything linking Balzac or Day to Reggie Frye. Or linking Balzac's friend Bunting to Frye. Number five would be rough drafts of the website language, like Erin found in Day's office."

"What about Eddy's car crash and criminal records?" asks Tommy.

"Yes," says Vaughn. "Especially if there's something showing that Balzac had the records *before* they were reported on by the press."

At this point, everyone falls silent for a while. Finally, Laurie says, "Do you really think the judge at the preliminary hearing is going to let you get any of this into evidence?"

Hearing the question posed that way makes Vaughn's heart sink. His whole plan is a long shot, he knows—that the judge will let him blame the crash on two of the city's most prominent members of the bar, attorneys fighting for the victims and their families. "It's Eddy's only hope. If he gets held over for trial, if we fail to be convincing that Eddy didn't cause the crash . . ." Vaughn trails off; he doesn't want to complete the thought.

But Erin picks it up anyway, just as Tommy had when Vaughn met with him and Mick and Susan. "Convincing to whom? I'm guessing it's not only the judge you're worried about."

Vaughn turns to Erin and simply says, "We have to make this work."

Twenty minutes later, just before ten o'clock, Tommy, Vaughn, and Erin are in Tommy's F-150 crew cab. The pickup is parked in the alley behind the Balzac Firm's office building on Delancey Street. Laurie Mitzner arrived at the firm fifteen minutes earlier to make sure no one else was in the building. The plan is simple: Vaughn, Erin, and Laurie will search Benjamin Balzac's office as swiftly as possible while Tommy remains in the truck, in case Balzac shows up. Laurie said that Balzac uses the alley to access his personal parking space behind the building, so Tommy will wait on the cross street that Balzac would have to use to access the alley.

Erin's cell phone rings. It's Laurie. "Coast is clear," Erin says.

"Let's go," Vaughn says, opening his door.

Laurie lets Vaughn and Erin in the back door, then leads them through the firm's kitchen and down the hall to the broad stairway. Balzac's office is a suite of rooms on the second floor. There's an outer office shared by his secretary and his personal assistant, a small conference room, and Balzac's private office and bathroom.

Wordlessly, the three pass from the outer room into Balzac's office and get to work opening drawers, or trying to. Most of Balzac's desk drawers have locks, as do the drawers built into the wall shelving. The only drawers that can be opened are the center drawer of the desk—a glorified junk drawer—and those on the minibar.

Frustrated, Vaughn turns his attention to the papers on the desktop. All he finds are some legal briefs, the "Super Lawyer" edition of *Philadelphia* magazine, and a highlighted appellate decision addressing issues of admissibility in a products-liability case.

Erin and Laurie aren't having any more luck, and in short order they all find themselves standing around Balzac's desk, staring at his closed laptop. Vaughn glances at Laurie—who looks like she's about to faint—and then to Erin. Then he leans forward, opens the laptop, and presses the "Power" button. The computer boots up to the opening page, which asks for a password.

"Shit." Vaughn says. Then he looks at Laurie. "Any ideas?"

Laurie shakes her head no, but leans forward and starts pressing keys. The computer informs her that she's entered the wrong password.

"What'd you type?" asks Erin.

"Balzac."

Laurie tries a number of variations on her boss's name: Benjamin Balzac; B. Balzac; Balzac Firm; The Balzac Firm; and so on. To no avail. She even types in the names of her boss's two hellhounds, Thor and Loki. Again, it doesn't work.

"This is making me nervous," Laurie says. "What if his computer sends him an e-mail that someone is trying to hack into it?"

"Is your firm's system programmed to do that?"

"I have no idea. Balzac is pretty secretive about the computers."

"And everything else, apparently," says Erin, pulling on one of the locked desk drawers. "Come on, we should get out of here. We're not going to find anything."

Vaughn starts to protest, but realizes Erin is right. "All right, let's go."

Back in the truck, the mood is pensive. Everyone knows the stakes. Everyone hears the clock ticking on Eddy Coburn. And everyone's thoughts revolve around the same two words: James Nunzio.

◆　◆　◆

Benjamin Balzac's swimming pool sits fifty feet beyond the terrace that runs the length of the back of his mansion. Just off the pool is a twenty-foot cedar pergola supported by stone columns. The pergola covers Balzac's outdoor kitchen—fitted with a K1000 Hybrid Fire Kalamazoo grill and its attendant sink, cooktop, warming cabinet, and refrigerated drawers, all of which are built into marble-topped stone cabinetry. An identical pergola sits above Balzac's U-shaped, ten-seat bar. The pool, grill, and bar—along with a two-story pool house, cabanas, and a ten-seat dining table—make up Balzac's large outdoor-entertainment area. The flagstone-paved space is surrounded by a ten-foot wooden fence that's hidden behind twelve-foot skip laurels.

Balzac is there now. So are Jack Bunting and Royce Badgett. The three friends are having a roaring good time, enjoying Ketel One, Macallan 25 Year, Zino Platinum Crown cigars from Holt's, and fat Kobe steaks flown in from Japan and grilled to perfection by Balzac himself. Benny Balls is especially ebullient over the news regarding the cap on damages. Earlier that day, thanks to pressure from him and Day and their well-placed Washington cronies, Congress actually repealed the statutory cap, paving the way for a punitive-damages award that could rise into the billions.

"Hey!" calls Badgett from the floating pool lounger, pointing to his crotch. "When does the entertainment arrive? Little Badger's getting impatient."

Balzac laughs and shakes his head. "If you moved out of that rowhouse shithole and took more of my money, you could actually get some pussy on your own."

"I don't need no Wayne fuckin' Manor to get tail," Badgett shoots back. "I got the moves."

The three men laugh again, but Badgett is only half joking. He really *doesn't* need a big house like the boss's, or want one. He never has. That's why he only accepted $5,500 for causing the train crash, why he accepts even less for whacking guys like Reggie Frye—shmucks who agree to help the boss with one of his plans, then try to fuck things up by having an attack of conscience, or by demanding more than they agreed on, or by just being a pain in the ass. Badger's dad once told him that there are two kinds of people in the world: those who need to live high on the hog, and those who are satisfied just to live.

No soul searching is necessary for Badgett to know which he is. He accepts his place in the world and is happy with it. The little row house suits him just fine. A used car is no problem; he has the know-how to keep a car running with three hundred thousand miles on it—even a Chrysler. And women? He doesn't need runway models with their stuck-up attitudes, porcelain faces, and rock-hard asses. He'll take a good-natured skank with a few dents and dings any day.

Well, most days, anyway. Even the steadiest salt-of-the-earth man—and that's how Badgett sees himself—needs prime beef sometimes. Benny knows that, which is why he splurges two or three times a year to fly in some top-shelf talent, usually Asian and Eastern Bloc girls brought in via Dallas or Vegas or LA.

Speaking of which, Badgett sees Dave Devine, the Boss's part-time driver and errand boy, leading three lovelies through the wooden gate. One of the women is a tall redhead with massive boobs. She would be for Bunting. The Jap would be the boss's date. That leaves the third woman, a Ukrainian blonde with a perfect button nose and sparkling blue eyes, for Badgett.

"Hey, sweetheart, over here!" Badgett shouts to blue eyes as he waves.

Everyone looks in Badgett's direction, and when they do, the little Ukrainian's eyes bulge, and she covers her mouth with her hands.

"Don't worry," Balzac says. "He only *looks* like Putin."

The three men burst into laughter.

"Yeah," says Bunting. "Our government was going to smuggle him into Russia and substitute him for the real thing, but they just couldn't teach him any Russian."

"Seems he has the IQ of a russet potato," Balzac says, and he, Bunting, and Badgett laugh some more.

Suddenly, Balzac stops smiling. His cell phone, sitting on the bar, has begun buzzing and flashing blue. He knows that can mean only one thing: someone has set off the motion detectors in his office. "Jack! Royce! Get over here," he shouts. "Something's up." As his two friends make haste, Balzac opens the cabinet doors under the large television screen above the bar. He presses some buttons, and the TV turns on.

"You three," he says to the women, "on the ground, facedown." He doesn't want the hookers seeing whatever is going to appear on the screen.

Bunting and Badgett move up to the bar to get a good look at the television. They're just in time to see black-and-white images of Vaughn Coburn, Laurie Mitzner, and Erin Doyle.

"That's them," Badgett says. "The lawyer Coburn and the one he's seeing. I don't know who the third one is."

"I do," Balzac says, his blood pressure rising. "She works for me."

"Fuck," says Jack Bunting.

"What are they looking for?" Badgett wonders aloud.

"I wish I'd installed sound," says Balzac.

The three men watch silently for the next ten minutes as Vaughn, Erin, and Laurie try in vain to open the desk drawers, then scour every nook and cranny of Balzac's office and try to access his laptop. It's clear that their search yields nothing, which is some relief to Balzac, but not much. The very fact that they're searching his office and that Coburn's investigator has been tailing Royce tells him they're onto something. There's no way they can know how the train crash went down, of course, or that he and Day were behind it. But they know *something*, and something always leads to something else. Balzac turns to Badgett.

"I think the search-and-rescue stage of the mission is over. It's time you switched over to retrieving bodies. Just don't do anything until I figure out the order and timing. We can't have a bunch of disappearances happening all at once. It'll look suspicious."

"Sounds like what needs to happen are accidents, not disappearances." Bunting puts his two cents in.

Balzac nods. "Maybe a couple of each."

"I don't have any more vaults in my cellar," says Badgett.

"You might have to do some seeding," says Balzac. Meaning march them into a cornfield and plant them in a hole.

Badgett looks away and sighs. He doesn't like the cornfield routine. Too many logistical problems, too much risk. If you walk them from the car to the burial site, there's always a chance they'll break and run, even if you have a gun pointed at them. If you plasticuff their legs so they can't run, the long walk takes forever. If you have them dig their own grave, you have to free their hands and risk them trying something with the shovel. If you dig the grave yourself—well, that's a huge pain in the ass. It's why Royce decided to construct the vaults in his basement.

"Aw, cheer up," Balzac says. "That's all for another day. As for tonight . . . girls, on your feet!"

28

Sunday, July 27

Laurie Mitzner sits at her desk, pretending to work on a legal brief. Pretending to check her e-mail. Pretending not to be an electrified bundle of nerves. *What on earth,* she asks herself, *was I thinking, coming here this morning after ransacking Balzac's office last night? How could I expect for a minute that I'd be able to concentrate? What force impelled me to show up here today? How could I forget that returning to the scene of the crime is a criminal's mistake as old as crime itself? As old as the moth and the flame?*

Close your eyes and take some deep breaths.

Inhale, hold for ten seconds, exhale. Again.

There's nothing unusual about her being in the office before nine on a Sunday morning. She's a senior associate with a heavy caseload. And Balzac has just pulled her into the Amtrak thing, so she has plenty of catching up to do.

But what's up with that?

The train-crash litigation is already fully staffed. And why has Balzac been paying so much attention to her all of a sudden? There's only one possible explanation for all of it: he knows she saw the crash video, and he's toying with her.

Oh God, please let that not be it.

Laurie is pulled from her thoughts by the sound of feet in the hallway. *Is that him?* Laurie holds her breath as the footfalls get closer. She exhales when she sees that it's Ginny Lenfest, another one of the associates. Ginny stops in Laurie's doorway, and they trade small talk for a few minutes before she moves on.

I can do this, Laurie thinks, determined to conquer her fear and get some work done. But no sooner has she begun editing a brief than she hears the growl of Balzac's BMW 750Li as it pulls into the small lot behind their building. She hears car doors open and close, followed by wet, heavy breathing, and the quick clumping of eight massive paws.

He's brought the hounds.

The stampede progresses directly toward Laurie's office. In short order, Laurie is being glared at by four gleaming black eyes. And then another pair appears.

"Laurie!" Balzac practically shouts her name.

Laurie's eyes bulge, her jaw drops, and she issues a squeak so thin that only the dogs hear it.

"I need you in my office, right now," Balzac continues, using the same voice she's heard him use to melt opposing witnesses. It's the voice Patton used when he dressed down soldiers—fakers, he called them, and cowards—paralyzed by shell shock.

Balzac turns and heads down the hallway. Thor and Loki remain until Laurie stands and starts walking toward the door—as though Balzac had them stay behind to ensure her compliance.

Laurie does her best to compose herself. She climbs the stairs to the second floor and walks through the outer office to Balzac's inner sanctum, just as she did last night.

He knows!

No, he doesn't!

Laurie pleads to herself. There's nothing to fear but her own guilt. She tells herself that all she has to do is keep her cool and she'll be fine.

Laurie takes one of the guest chairs in front of Balzac's massive desk and waits for Balzac to tell her what he wants. But he says nothing, just stares, for what feels to Laurie like hours.

Sometimes when Laurie stands up too fast, the blood rushes from her head and she'll feel faint. That's what she feels like now. *Calm down,* she tells herself. *It'll all be fine as soon as he starts talking, explains why I'm here.*

"My office was broken into last night."

"Oh God. Really?"

"Now, now, it's nothing to keel over about." Balzac's voice is gentle now, almost nurturing. "There's really nothing in here worth stealing," he says. "Still, I wanted you to know because you're going to have a special role to play."

"A role—"

"A very special one. You see, I'm not going to share this with anyone but you. Not the other attorneys. Not the staff. I'm telling you alone."

"What? Why?"

"Because I trust you, Laurie. I'm a good judge of people, and out of everyone who works here, I can tell that you have the highest character. You're the last person I could ever imagine betraying me, betraying the firm."

"Uh, thank you?" Laurie's stomach churns. A small amount of vomit boils up the back of her throat. She chokes it back down.

"Don't thank me yet. We haven't gotten to the special-role part yet. You see, I need you to keep an eye out for me."

"An eye out?"

He nods, still staring at her. "Be alert to how other people behave. Study them and ask yourself if anyone is acting like they have a guilty conscience. Like they're afraid because they've done something they know would really piss me off? Something that would cause me to retaliate in some terrible fashion?"

Laurie gulps.

"I can spot guilt and fear in a person from a mile away. But I can't be everywhere, and I'm just too busy." Balzac stops and looks hard at Laurie for a long minute. "Can you do this for me?"

Laurie stares back, her eyes wide. "Yes." It's all she can get out.

"I knew it." Balzac beams. "I knew I could put my faith in you." He stands, smiling at first. Suddenly, his face clouds over.

"Damn it!"

Laurie flinches, takes a half step back.

"Loki!" Balzac looks toward the back of the room and shakes his head. The dog has urinated on the floor. "Laurie, be a dear and get some paper towels and clean that up for me."

Laurie rushes out of Balzac's office toward the hallway bathroom. She takes a roll of paper towels from the cabinet beneath the sink. Then she stands up, doubles over the toilet, and evacuates the contents of her stomach.

29

Monday, July 28

Vaughn stares at Eddy's casket, ready to be lowered into the ground. He glances at Eddy's wife, Kate, holding their newborn daughter. He looks at the other bereaved on the folding chairs directly in front of the coffin—Aunt Claire and Uncle Frank, their daughters, Peg and Jean. Vaughn's own parents and siblings stand behind them, along with other relatives, neighbors, and some of Eddy's friends from the railroad.

Vaughn stands by himself, on the other side of the coffin.

Suddenly, Aunt Claire leaps from her seat, thrusts her finger at him. "This is all your fault!"

As she screams at him, all the other mourners turn away . . .

Vaughn wakes with a start, soaked in sweat. Another nightmare, the latest in a long series. He's alone in Erin's guest bedroom. His tossing and turning the past two nights made it unfair to ask that he share her bed.

He throws off the sheet. He stares at the ceiling, then rolls onto his side, then onto his stomach, then onto his back again. But sleep doesn't come. It's not enough—the scant evidence he's been able to muster in Eddy's defense. Laurie can swear up and down that she phone-taped the crash video directly from Balzac's computer. But her word will not be enough. His theories about Day's and Balzac's prescient website train-law compendiums and the complaint allegations about a fatal driving history and criminal record? Theories and nothing more. Day and Balzac will claim they were planning to branch into train law before the crash and were in the process of drafting their website passages when the train wrecked. And how did they know about Vaughn's driving and criminal histories? They didn't. The language was boilerplate.

The hours drag on, and Vaughn finally falls into the black.

He opens his eyes to find Eddy sitting in a warehouse, tied to an old wooden chair. Next to the chair is a metal table. On the table are hand tools—a drill, a hammer, a hacksaw, pruning shears, a blowtorch. Jimmy Nutzo and Johnny Giacobetti stand next to the table, trying to choose which one to use first, and on which part of Eddy's body. Eddy screams through the gag. Nunzio picks up the drill as Vaughn, tied to his own chair, struggles to tear free.

"You look and you look, but you just don't see," Nunzio says to Vaughn.

"It's all about picking the right tool," says Johnny G.

"That's it!" Vaughn vaults out of bed, walks to Erin's bedroom, but stops himself at the threshold; he'd better think this through. The moral implications are too great to make the leap in haste. He walks to the kitchen, pulls a Smartwater from the fridge, and drinks. The clock on the oven reads 3:47 a.m. He walks through the living room and out onto the balcony. It's cooler than it has been, and a fresh breeze is blowing. Vaughn leans over the railing and stares into the night sky. He senses something behind him and turns his head. It's Erin. She smiles, but he can see the worry in her eyes. She waits for him to talk. After a moment, he does.

"I've been looking at this the wrong way," he says. "Nunzio isn't the problem. He's the solution."

At 9:00 a.m., Eddy Coburn stands in the shower, scrubbing himself as fast as he can. He suffered some bad experiences in prison showers when he was incarcerated before, and he wants to get done quickly. Not that he thinks anyone is going to bother him. When they first brought him to Curran-Fromhold, he was put into a private cell. A guard—Quaid—told him it was because he was a target for prisoners wanting to build their cred by attacking someone notorious. For the same reason, he wasn't allowed to eat or exercise or even socialize with the other inmates. Then, two days ago, everything changed. He was kept in the private cell, but was taken for his meals to the prison cafeteria. He was also allowed to socialize in the yard with other inmates. Not that it mattered; no one would talk with him. No one wanted to be anywhere near him. He tried to strike up conversations with other prisoners, but they turned away. When he sat to eat, the table emptied.

He didn't understand. He asked Quaid what was going on, but the guard just shrugged his shoulders. Finally, Quaid quietly confided that, "You're off-limits. No one's allowed to lay a hand on you."

"My lawyer do that?" Eddy asked.

Quaid smiled sadly. "Be better for you that way. But it's not. You're off-limits because you're being saved for someone." Quaid shook his head and walked away.

Eddy shakes his head now, as he showers. He hates this place. It's not as bad as the state prison he served time in for killing the patrolman, but it's still awful. The claustrophobic cells, the orange jumpsuits that make grown men look like clowns at a kid's birthday party, the animal smells, the hopelessness. And most of all, the loneliness. Eddy's been here five days and has had no visitors other than Vaughn. That's because, with the exception of their attorneys, inmates are allowed visitors only one day each week. For names that begin with C, that day is Monday, and Eddy was admitted on Wednesday. He desperately hopes Kate will come with the baby. He'd like to see his parents, too, and Vaughn.

Eddy closes his eyes as he washes the shampoo from his hair and face. When he opens them, two inmates are standing outside the shower stall. The taller of the two has a bald head and a full beard. The shorter one, also bald, is very muscular, and his whole head is covered with tattoos. The two prisoners glare at Eddy, neither saying anything. Eddy starts to ask them what they want but stops when he realizes suddenly that there is no one else around. No prisoners. No guards. Just these two. It's then that Eddy notices that the tall one is holding a plastic jug filled with some liquid. The shorter man has a small metal object. A Zippo lighter.

The tall man pulls the lid off the plastic jug, and Eddy smells gasoline.

Eddy quickly looks around him to see if there's any way of escape, but the shower walls prevent it. The only way out would be through the two hardened men.

Eddy's shoulders slump as he's overwhelmed by sadness. He's never going to hold his little girl, never see her grow up. He's never again going to hug the only woman he's ever loved. Never say goodbye to his parents, tell them he loves them. Never see another sunrise. Eddy thinks of the run-down little farm he shared for a few days with Kate before he rushed to the hospital in his ill-fated trip to join her for the birth of their child. And it hits him that he wants nothing more than to be back on that farm with Kate, and the baby.

Eddy hears a click as the shorter of the two inmates standing outside the shower stall flips open the lid of the Zippo.

Eddy closes his eyes.

Vaughn strides through the lobby of the modern office building. He takes the elevator to the third floor and walks quickly down the hallway toward the offices of Modern Innovations, Inc. Through the glass doors, he sees Johnny Giacobetti leaning over the reception desk, apparently flirting with the receptionist. The young woman looks Vaughn's way, says something to Johnny G., who rises to his full height and stares through the doors at Vaughn.

"You gotta be kidding me," Giacobetti says as Vaughn opens one of the doors and enters.

"I need to see your boss."

Without a word, Johnny G. moves to Vaughn and searches him. When he's done, he tells Vaughn, "Wait here." Then he turns and walks down the hall. In short order, Giacobetti returns. "Let's go."

Vaughn follows the big man to James Nunzio's office. The mobster is sitting behind the desk when Vaughn enters. He follows Vaughn with his eyes as Vaughn takes one of the visitor's chairs.

"Remember what I told you about lying to me?"

Vaughn opens his mouth to answer, but Jimmy Nutzo cuts him off. "If you're here to plead for your cousin, don't bother. I have a very simple business model, Mr. Coburn. I reward my friends, I punish my enemies. That's the way it is with me because that's the way it has to be. If I don't reward my friends, I'll end up without friends. If I fail to punish my enemies, they will lose respect for me. In my business, not having friends bodes ill. Not having respect bodes dead."

"That's not why I'm here. I—"

"But, of course, this isn't just business. This is personal. My son, my Alexander, is dead. And that means that the *punishment* must be taken to a whole other level. Which brings us back to your cousin, the fuckup driving the train when my boy was killed—"

"Your son wasn't killed in that train crash, Mr. Nunzio. He was *murdered*."

This stops Nunzio cold. His whole body seems to freeze in place.

"The train accident was no accident." Vaughn's right hand is closed. He extends it over Nunzio's desk and opens it to reveal a memory stick.

"The fuck is that?" Nunzio demands.

"A video of the crash, taken by the people who caused it."

Nunzio lets Vaughn put the memory stick into his laptop, and Vaughn plays the crash video. When it's finished, Vaughn tells the mobster about Geoffrey Day's drone, and about the complaints and the websites. He describes the connections between Balzac and Jack Bunting and between Bunting and Reggie Frye. He tells Nunzio that Frye gave Eddy the burner phone Bunting recently "found" on the locomotive, that Eddy remembers calling his wife from the train but has no memory of the second call, the one placed *to* the burner phone. Finally, he tells Nunzio what George Haley told Tommy about Jack Bunting having a copy of the locomotive-cab video.

"That engine-cab video could be the key to how they pulled it off, to this whole thing," Vaughn says. "It will certainly show what happened to Eddy." Vaughn pauses here. He steels himself. He's thought about what his next sentence will mean, for him, as a person. He's about to cross a threshold, into the dark lands. But there's no choice.

"The reason I'm here is that I need your help getting that video. Bunting denies it exists, so a subpoena would be useless. I've searched Day's office, and Balzac's, but couldn't find a copy."

Nunzio studies Vaughn, hits him with a hard look. "You know what you're asking?"

Vaughn stares back, equally firm. "There's no other way."

"Fork in the road . . ."

"No other way," Vaughn repeats.

As Jimmy Nutzo sits back in his chair to consider Vaughn's request, his secretary buzzes him. He picks up the receiver, listens. His face registers surprise. He thanks the secretary, hangs up, looks to Giacobetti. "We have another guest. Bring him back."

Johnny G. leaves, and Jimmy Nutzo leans forward, toward Vaughn. "If a single word of what you've told me is bullshit, I will rip your beating heart from your chest. And, Mr. Coburn, so that there is no misunderstanding between us: I'm not speaking metaphorically."

Vaughn swallows. He tries to think of an answer, but before he can, the door opens again and Giacobetti walks in, with Tommy behind him.

"Tommy?" Vaughn says. Then, with his eyes: *What are you doing here?*

"I was in the neighborhood."

"This your muscle?" Nunzio asks. He and Johnny G. chuckle.

Tommy stiffens. His eyes ignite with a ferocity that Vaughn has not seen before. Johnny G. squares off with him. The tension in the room increases fivefold.

"It's okay," Vaughn tells Tommy. "We're all on the same side now."

"We're all on the same side *for* now," says Nunzio. Then, as though he's suddenly remembered something, he turns to Giacobetti. "You better make a call. Hurry."

Giacobetti pulls his cell phone from his jacket pocket, puts it up to his ear. After a moment, he says, "You do it yet? Well, don't. Yeah. Change of plan." Johnny G. hangs up, turns to his boss. "Nick of time."

Ten minutes later, Vaughn is riding in the passenger seat of Tommy's pickup. Tommy tells Vaughn that Erin called him, told him what Vaughn was up to, said she was worried. After that, neither says anything most of the way up Broad Street.

When they reach South Street, Tommy turns to Vaughn. "You know what they'll do to Bunting to make him turn over that video, right?"

Vaughn's mind returns to the news footage of the train crash, the injured people limping away from the railcars, their faces fixed in stunned, faraway gazes. He recalls the two men kneeling over the body of the dead woman, sees the photos of the deceased in the *Inquirer*— young faces, and old. White, black, Latino, Asian. He remembers Susan's description of the blind woman sitting in the overturned car, calling out for her dog. He looks at Tommy.

"I can live with that."

◆　◆　◆

Eddy Coburn closes his eyes and waits for the end, waits for the tall guy to splash him with gasoline and the short one to toss the lighter. Then a cell phone rings, and he opens his eyes. The tattooed inmate, holding the lit Zippo in his left hand, pulls a phone from his orange jumpsuit with his right. He lifts the phone to his ear. "No," he says. "Okay." He puts the cell phone away, closes the lighter. "Come on," he says to the tall man with the plastic jug, whose disappointment shows in his eyes. "Mission canceled."

It's just before four o'clock and Vaughn is sitting on a black, wire-mesh seat next to Eddy in the visitation room of the prison. The room is crowded with inmates in orange jumpsuits, their friends, wives, and girlfriends. Uniformed prison guards casually patrol the space, keeping an eye out. Eddy tells Vaughn about the two inmates who appeared outside his shower stall, about the gasoline and the Zippo, and about the phone call that stopped them from immolating him.

Vaughn takes in what Eddy's told him; then it's his turn. He shares everything he's learned about Balzac and Day, Balzac and Bunting, Bunting and Frye. The drone video, and the engine-cab video he hopes to be able to see soon. The websites. The complaints. And last, but most important, Jimmy Nunzio.

Eddy sits back in his chair. His eyes have a faraway look to them, and it seems to Vaughn that his cousin isn't getting it, that he's hearing the words, but some part of him simply cannot accept that the crash was planned. Or that a mobster has him in his sights.

"If I'm right," Vaughn says, "there's only one real mystery remaining. How they did it. How they actually set it up so you wouldn't stop or slow the train. The engine-cab video is the key to answering that question."

It has to be . . . or Eddy's a dead man.

"I sure want to see that tape," Eddy says. "I need to know what happened."

"You still can't remember anything?"

Eddy shakes his head. "It's right there. The memory. I can feel it. Like it's on the other side of a curtain that I can't see through."

They sit in silence for a while. Then Eddy says, "What if that video doesn't clear me? What if I never remember what happened, if there's no answer for why I didn't see that track machine, didn't slow the train down?"

Vaughn imagines Jimmy Nutzo and looks away.

"You know what I thought when those two guys came for me? I thought that what I wanted more than anything in the world was just to go get Kate and the baby and take them to that little farm." Eddy's eyes well up. "Just a run-down little house in the middle of a field. Right now, man, that seems like heaven on earth to me."

Vaughn looks away. He doesn't want his cousin seeing the tears in his own eyes. "Don't worry," he says. "I'll get you there."

30

TUESDAY, JULY 29

At 10:01 a.m., Balzac sits behind his massive leather-topped desk. Shifting impatiently in his chair, he watches the second hand on his Rolex Oyster Perpetual as he waits for Geoffrey Day to pick up the phone. It's already been a full minute, and Balzac is getting pissed. He'd have hung up by now if he weren't looking forward to the call.

"Hello, Ben. How can I help you?"

Balzac snorts. The very idea that he would need help from Geoffrey Day is insulting. "You're not running a very tight ship, are you?"

On the other end of the line, Geoffrey Day sighs. "What is that supposed to mean?"

"You have an associate named Erin Doyle. She went to law school with the engineer's lawyer. Coburn."

"What of it?"

"What of it, Geoffrey, is that she's been meeting with him. And they've been nosing around, looking for information about you and me. Along with Coburn's investigator." He doesn't mention Laurie Mitzner's role.

"Why should Coburn be interested in us?"

"Maybe because we crashed a trainful of people and framed his client for it."

Silence from the other end of the line.

"Are you there?"

"I don't like the idea of some investigator trying to dig up dirt on us," Geoffrey says, carefully avoiding any admission of guilt in case of recording devices. "Something needs to be done about that."

Balzac lets the words hang in the air, then says, "What type of *something*?"

"Do you really want me to spell it out, Benjamin? On the phone?"

"You want me to have them rubbed out? Including your associate?"

"I'm hanging up now."

"You hang up on me and I'll call in your loan right now."

"Ben—"

"I'll walk the damned complaint and confession of judgment to the courthouse myself and—"

"Oh, all right. Just do it!"

"Including your associate?"

"Yes. Yes. Just leave me out of it."

The phone goes dead, and Balzac smiles. He'll never forget the night that Philly law's golden boy showed up at his office, hat in hand. It was pouring down rain. Day looked like he'd been wandering in the deluge for hours—his $100 haircut, $1,000 shoes, and $10,000 suit were all sopping wet.

Balzac knew as soon as he saw Day why his nemesis was there. Day's Relazac multidistrict litigation had collapsed in spectacular fashion, leaving the fool with tens of millions in unrecoverable legal expenses. Balzac also knew that Day had just forked over $50 million as his down payment on Penn Law and indebted himself at least as much on the balance. Day's bank had refused to increase his firm's line of credit, and no other bank in town would touch him. Balzac had learned all this from a source he'd cultivated inside Day's own law firm.

Day looked pitiful, standing in the reception area of Balzac's building. A startling contrast to the haughty Ivy Leaguer who'd joined Arthur

Hogarth's firm the same year as Balzac and set about immediately to drive him out.

Before Day could open his mouth to make his plea, Balzac smiled at him and said, "No."

"Ben, please. This could work out very well for both of us."

"What could work out better for me than watching you flounder and then snatching up all of your cases?"

"Don't be shortsighted. That would just be killing the goose that laid the golden egg."

Balzac smiled, took a sip of Bombay Sapphire from the glass he'd carried with him from his office to the firm lobby when he'd heard the doorbell ring. In his other hand, he held the lit Churchill. It had been close to ten o'clock when Day showed up. Nights were Balzac's favorite time at the office.

"Think about it, Ben. By investing in my firm, you could have a percentage of every one of my cases. You'd make back your investment in no time. But if my firm fails now, you'd get some of the cases, sure, but not all of them. Probably not even most."

Balzac took a deep drag off his cigar (yes, he inhaled; fuck the surgeon general) and shrugged his shoulders, unconvinced. Day seemed to be unraveling by the second.

"You could monitor the cases," Day continued, choking on the words. "Make tactical suggestions. I would let you look at the firm's P-and-L once a quarter—"

"I would have real-time access to all of your firm's financials and bank accounts. And I don't make 'suggestions' on cases. I give orders."

Day's face was ashen at this point. He looked like he was about to pass out. But he closed his eyes and slowly nodded his head.

Balzac took another drag on his Churchill, the ember at the end glowing bright red. After a moment, he exhaled, then took a healthy gulp of gin. "It does sound somewhat interesting," he said. "Not as much fun as watching you hauled off to debtor's prison. But more lucrative." But it wasn't the money he was thinking about; it was the power. If he saved Day and Lockwood, he would do something no other P.I. lawyer had ever done. He'd run the top *two* firms in the city.

Balzac sighed. "I guess we could flip a coin."

"A coin?"

"Heads, I go along with it. Tails, you stand on the sidewalk while the bankruptcy trustee auctions off your artwork and underwear." With that, Balzac pulled a quarter from his pocket.

Geoffrey Day stood numbly as Balzac flipped the coin and watched it land on the crimson oriental carpet.

"Looks like this is your lucky day," Balzac announced. "It's heads."

Day clutched his chest and exhaled.

"It will all have to be put down on paper, of course," said Balzac. "And there will be a confession-of-judgment clause."

"Confession of judgment?"

"Absolutely. I want to be able to race into court and destroy you on a moment's notice if you try to welch on me."

"I would never—"

Balzac raised his hand, cut Day off. "There's no one who would never."

The two men stood in the center of the reception area, each waiting for the other to speak. A smile slowly spread across Balzac's lips. "There is one other thing . . ."

Day raised his chin, asking the question silently: *What?*

"Beg."

Day looked stricken. Now he said it aloud: "What?"

"Drop to your knees, you popinjay patrician, stick-up-your-ass son of a bitch. Pull your nose from the air, and plant it on my rug."

Geoffrey Day stood frozen in shock and outrage for a full minute. And then he slowly lowered himself to the floor.

Thinking back on it now, Benjamin Balzac feels warm inside. He walks to the minibar, pours himself a tumbler of Bombay Sapphire, and takes a generous sip. Then he lights up a cigar and lets his mind drift to the afternoon when Day dropped the first hints about crashing a train. It was the same week that a passenger train crashed in Germany, killing a hundred people, the accident all over the news. Day mentioned the crash and mused aloud about something similar happening here. He brought up the Metrolink accident in California and the Metro-North crash in New York.

Balzac could see that Day thought he was being clever, that he was planting the idea into Balzac's head in a way intended to make Balzac think it was his own idea. Day would never admit *he* was up for a train crash. But weeks later, when Balzac had informed Geoffrey that Amtrak Train 174 would be crashing soon, and told him how it would happen, Day leaped in with both feet, offering suggestions as to how to fine-tune the plan.

And now, Geoffrey is perfectly willing to go along with killing the engineer's attorney and investigator, plus his own associate. Just so long as he doesn't have to do the dirty work himself.

"Coward."

Forty floors above street level, Geoffrey Day lowers the receiver and glares at the phone. *Numbskull. Talking about rubbing people out over the phone.*

It was the same with the train crash. Balzac was alert enough to take his bait and set it in motion, but Balzac's rudimentary scheme lacked a critical element: he'd planned to have a sniper fire at the train to scare the engineer away from his controls. But that would only work if the engineer instantly grasped that he was being *shot at*, that his life was in immediate and deliberate peril. Otherwise it would take too long for him to figure out what was happening—if he understood at all—which meant that he'd surely see the track machine ahead and throw the train's emergency brake. No, it was essential that the engineer realize instantaneously that someone was shooting at him so that he would duck away from the controls and stay down as the train raced toward the track machine. Any fool could see that this required someone to phone the engineer and signpost what was about to happen. Of course, the caller's wording would have to be effective to do so, and that required that a behavioral psychologist and focus groups be brought on board—without knowing why, obviously—to help craft a short and intense word burst that would accomplish the desired effect. Balzac had foreseen none of this.

Day opens his top drawer, removes the drawer tray, and retrieves the envelope. He stares at the wording beneath the 2020 Marketing letterhead: "You're a dead man. Bang, bang, motherfucker. Bang, bang."

He'd kept the original for himself and given Corey King the copy to read to the engineer over the cell phone. In the back of his mind, he knows it's probably not the greatest idea to keep the paper, but he can't bring himself to get rid of it. Some things are too good to part with.

31

TUESDAY, JULY 29

Vaughn gets the call just before noon. Angie buzzes him, and when he picks up, he hears the strain in her voice.

"What's the matter?"

"Uh, someone's here to see you. It's, it's . . ."

"Never mind. I can guess. I'll be out in a minute."

Vaughn turns the corner to the hallway leading to the reception area. Sure enough, standing by the leather couches is James Nunzio. With him is Johnny Giacobetti. Approaching them, Vaughn glances at Angie, whose face is white with fear. *It's okay,* he tells her with his eyes. It doesn't do any good.

"Nice place," says Nunzio. "Your bosses must be doing well. After that Hanson trial, I would expect so."

Vaughn doesn't answer. Nunzio probably has an inch-thick folder on Mick and Susan and the firm. Probably knows every case they ever tried, the names of the prosecutors. The verdicts.

"I have something you may want to see," Nunzio says.

"Your friend Jack Bunting gave it to us," adds Giacobetti.

Knowing what likely happened to Bunting, Vaughn winces.

"Don't worry, counselor," Giacobetti says. "It won't get back to you. That's one stone that will never be unturned."

Vaughn cringes, then leads them down the hall to the big conference room. When he shuts the door, Nunzio nods to Giacobetti, who pulls a memory stick from his breast pocket. Vaughn accepts it, plugs it into the system, and the three of them watch what happens with Eddy in the moments leading up to the crash.

The video starts at 12:06:05, the time Eddy pulled the train out of 30th Street Station. Eddy is positioned in the engineer's seat, which is on the right-hand side of the locomotive—the same side drivers sit on in the UK. Judging from the video, the camera must be positioned in front of and above Eddy. For two minutes, nothing unusual happens. Then, at 12:08:10, Eddy pulls a cell phone from his shirt pocket and dials a number. He waits for the person at the other end to answer, then says a few words. There's no sound, so Vaughn can't hear what Eddy says, but he knows that Eddy placed the call to Kate, so he figures his cousin is just asking how she's doing. For ninety seconds, Eddy listens some and talks some. Then he hangs up and puts the phone back in his pocket.

For the next eight minutes, Eddy remains seated, mostly looking out the front window, sometimes glancing out the side, sometimes looking at his control console. Every few moments, with his left hand, he presses forward on a small handle. This, Vaughn knows from talking to Eddy, is the "dead-man's switch." It's a safety device meant to ensure that a train doesn't go speeding down the track with a dead engineer at the helm. The lever has to be pushed every thirty seconds, otherwise the train automatically goes into emergency mode, its brakes fully applied until it comes to a stop.

At 12:17:50, Eddy glances down at his shirt pocket and withdraws the cell phone. He doesn't look to see who's calling before he answers. As soon as he hits the "Receive" button, his face contorts with a mixture of surprise and confusion. After a second, Eddy, looking angry, says something into the phone. Then he listens for a moment, his eyes widening at what he hears. Suddenly, at 12:18:03, he leaps up from his seat. He covers his face and stumbles backward, and down. He disappears from view, and remains that way until the tape goes black, at 12:18:18.

Vaughn looks at Nunzio, who opens his hands to signal, *That's it.* Vaughn turns off the TV. "It doesn't make sense," he says. "It seems like Eddy sees the TracVac and jumps up. He covers his face and goes down. But it takes fifteen seconds before the video goes black, which would've been when the train hit the TracVac."

"Plenty of time to apply the brakes," Johnny G. says.

The comment makes Vaughn's heart stop. He struggles to come up with some explanation for why Eddy cowered under the control panel rather than brake the train, but he comes up empty.

The video hasn't saved Eddy; it's doomed him.

"Maybe it wasn't the track machine he was responding to," Nunzio says.

Vaughn studies him for a moment, glances at Johnny Giacobetti, then returns his gaze to Nunzio. "Sounds like you have it figured out."

"Let's just say I've seen guys react to certain things the way your cousin did."

They sit quietly for a moment, until Vaughn asks a question he already knows the answer to.

"Jack Bunting?"

A smile spreads across Johnny G.'s lips. "We Theon Greyjoyed him," he says, explaining what Ramsay Bolton did to the luckless scion of the Iron Islands on *Game of Thrones.* "But we didn't *finish* by cutting off his dick; that's how we started. And things went downhill from there. For him." Johnny G.'s eyes sparkle as he says this.

Vaughn shudders. His dream about Nunzio and Giacobetti and the table loaded with power tools obviously wasn't too far off. He'd like to be able to lie to himself and say that he's surprised how things turned out for Jack Bunting. But, of course, he knew exactly what could happen. His setting up Bunting was the threshold he knew he'd have to cross to move forward. The fork in the road that Nunzio referred to.

"He would have been more helpful to us as a witness than as a corpse," Vaughn says.

Giacobetti blows air. "That guy? He wasn't going to testify for you."

"I have to hand it to him," Nunzio says. "He was a tough son of a bitch. Didn't cop to anything about causing the crash. Just decided when he'd had enough and told us where to find the download. It was right in his glove compartment."

"So that's one down and what—three, four—to go?" Giacobetti asks his boss.

"Starting with my lawyer," says Nunzio. "Balzac."

"Wait!" Vaughn shouts. "There can't be any more killing. I'm not sure yet who I'll need at the preliminary hearing. Look, I know you have your own endgame here. But so do I. This is all for nothing if I can't get the charges against Eddy dismissed. That's what we have to focus on. What we have to—"

"*Have* to?" Nunzio says. He leans across the conference table and points at Vaughn. "Boy, don't ever tell me what I *have* to do."

"I'm sorry," Vaughn says, desperate to win Nunzio over. "I apologize. But I'm guessing you can reach out and take your vengeance anytime you want. My cousin has one chance. And that's for me to lay it all out at the preliminary hearing. Convince the judge, and the press—hell, everyone—that Eddy isn't to blame for what happened."

"I'd be more concerned about convincing *me*," says Nunzio.

"But you saw both the videos. You said you had a hunch—"

"A hunch, that's right. But a hunch isn't the same as knowing. Your cousin is still on my list."

Vaughn's in full panic mode now.

"I need to talk to him myself," Nunzio continues. "I need to watch him watch that video and see if it makes him remember. See if it went down like I'm thinking it did."

"But there's no way I'll be able to get the video through prison security to show it to him."

Nunzio and his enforcer exchange glances and laugh.

"Prison security." Johnny G. practically spits out the words.

Nunzio stands. "Come on."

"What? Where?"

"We just went over this," says Nunzio. "We're going to meet your cousin. The car's waiting outside."

Everyone stands, and Vaughn leads Nunzio and Giacobetti toward the lobby. Mick is there, talking to Angie. He looks hard at the two mobsters, then fixes his eyes on Vaughn. "My office, when you get back from wherever it is you're going."

Vaughn nods and keeps walking.

Outside the building, Nunzio opens the back door to an Audi A8 L, then looks to Giacobetti. "You made the arrangements?"

"All set."

"Call and tell them we're on our way."

Nunzio motions to Vaughn to climb into the car, then gets in after him. Johnny G. remains on the curb.

It's a twenty-minute drive north on I-95 to the prison. Another fifteen minutes checking in and passing through security, during which Vaughn and Nunzio are disencumbered of their cell phones. They are led to a small room used for private inmate-attorney confabs. When they enter, a guard hands Nunzio an Apple 6s Plus, then turns and leaves.

"Video's on the phone," the gangster tells Vaughn.

Eddy is brought into the room, and his cuffs are removed. He glances at Nunzio, then looks to Vaughn.

"This is Mr. Nunzio," Vaughn explains.

Eddy's eyes widen.

"He's on our side now."

"We'll see," says Nunzio.

"We have something we want you to look at," Vaughn says. "We found a way to get our hands on the video from the locomotive cab."

Eddy looks confused. "What video? The railroad wasn't supposed to be taping us. That was the deal with the union."

"They welched on the deal," Nunzio says.

"The video runs the whole way through the crash," Vaughn says.

"What does it show?"

"That's what you're going to tell us," Nunzio says. He slides the phone across the gunmetal-gray table between them and pushes the button to play the video. Then he and Vaughn watch Eddy watch the video.

Eddy's face remains frozen for the first two minutes. Then, when the video gets to his call to Kate, he brings his left hand to his mouth and slowly nods his head. He keeps it there as the video shows him clicking off the call and replacing the phone in his shirt pocket. His eyes widen when the video shows him reaching for the phone a few minutes later. His jaw drops when he sees himself talking to the person on the other end, and his whole body begins to shake. He utters a low cry when the video shows him leaping out of his seat and covering his face. A louder cry when he falls backward, out of sight.

"I remember! I remember! He said he was going to shoot me! Then he *did* shoot! That's why I went down. That's why . . ." Eddy puts his elbows on the table, buries his face in his hands, and rocks back and forth. "Oh God. Oh God."

Vaughn glances at Nunzio, who nods. The mobster's hunch, Vaughn realizes, must've been that Vaughn's reaction was that of a man being fired upon—something Jimmy Nutzo has certainly seen before.

Vaughn waits until Eddy drops his hands and lifts his head. Then he asks, "What exactly did he say to you? Do you remember? Take it slow."

Eddy looks up, closes his eyes. "He said . . . he said I was a dead man. Then he said he was going to shoot me. No, wait! He made shooting *sounds*. Then, all of a sudden the windshield cracked, and I knew it was a bullet. I went down, and the shots kept coming. I could hear the windshield being hit again and again."

"Why didn't you stop the train?" Nunzio asks.

"I knew I didn't have to. Coming out of that curve, it's a straight-away for ten miles. All clear, or it was supposed to be. Even if the shooter was firing from a half mile away, I knew I'd pass him pretty quickly. The worst thing that could have happened was for the train to automatically set its emergency brake because I hadn't pushed the dead-man's switch."

Vaughn turns to Nunzio to make sure Eddy's explanation sits well with him.

"It was all on purpose," Eddy says, the emotion in his voice thickening to anger. "They put that TracVac on the rail and found a way to get me down so I wouldn't see it. They *wanted* the train to crash. They wanted all those people to die. To get injured. Oh my God."

Eddy Coburn looks to Vaughn, then to Nunzio, then back to Vaughn. "What are we going to do?"

"We're going to get justice, Ed. For all those people. And for you. We're going to get justice."

"And then some," says Nunzio.

It's just before five o'clock, and Vaughn is sitting in one of the visitor's chairs in Mick's office. He's told Mick about the engine-cab video, about his meeting with Nunzio, and their meeting with Eddy. Mick listens without speaking. When Vaughn is finished, Mick stares at him for a long minute. Then, "You got the video how?"

Vaughn takes a deep breath. "Nunzio got it, from Jack Bunting."

"How'd he know Bunting had it?"

Vaughn skips a beat. "I told him."

Mick nods, looks away for a minute. Then he looks back at Vaughn and waits.

"It was the only way."

Mick says nothing.

"Bunting would never have turned it over voluntarily. He denied it even existed."

Mick stares.

"I was out of time."

Still nothing from Mick.

"Nunzio was blaming Eddy. He'd have been murdered in jail by now if I didn't get the video. It was the only way to convince Nunzio that the crash wasn't Eddy's fault."

"And did it? Does Nunzio no longer blame your cousin? Even a little?"

"He knows the whole thing was a setup. That Eddy was their stooge."

"So it was worth it?"

Vaughn shoots to his feet. "Fuck Jack Bunting! He was part of it. He planned for Eddy to take the fall. If Eddy even lived. They all probably thought Eddy would be killed on impact." Vaughn collects himself, sits again. "Are you saying you wouldn't have traded Bunting for Tommy if you were in my place?"

It's Mick's turn to think. "No, I'm not. I just want you to be very clear with yourself about the decision you made. To own it. And, hopefully, to find ways to avoid ever having to repeat it."

Vaughn studies his boss. Something in the tone of his voice makes it clear that Mick has been in his shoes. "Believe me, Mick, I didn't do this lightly," he says. "I thought about it. About what it would mean about me. And then I thought about all those people on that train. The ones Jack Bunting, and Balzac, and Day killed and mangled. I thought about their families—the husbands and wives, fathers, mothers, sons and daughters left behind."

Vaughn turns away from Mick, then looks back. "You talk about finding ways not to repeat it. But I can look you in the eye, Mick, and tell you I'd do it again, a hundred times, to save my cousin. To get justice for all those people." With that, Vaughn turns and leaves.

◆ ◆ ◆

It's close to midnight. Vaughn and Erin are sitting on the balcony of her eighth-floor condo at Independence Place. Vaughn is wearing only his boxers. Erin has on short shorts and a white wife-beater T-shirt. Her thick hair is pulled up into a ponytail. The heat and humidity have returned, with a vengeance. Vaughn's beer bottle is dripping with sweat. Erin's skin has a sheen. For a long time, they sit quietly, listening to the sounds of the city—the beeping of a car horn, people laughing as they walk by the building, a far-off siren.

Erin reaches over, takes Vaughn's hand in hers.

Vaughn smiles, lifts his beer with his other hand, takes a swig. "I realize I'm asking too much of you."

That she testify about the drone. Admit she rummaged through Day's desk and found the *bang-bang* note.

"Hey, I volunteered for this, remember? I only wish I'd have taken the original of that note, not just a picture on my phone. And that the drone thing had worked out."

Erin's hope that perhaps the drone would leave digital fingerprints on its videos was shot down by the technology expert Vaughn hired. "No," the expert had said flatly. "And even if it were otherwise, you'd need the original of the video, not just a copy recorded secondhand on a cell phone."

Vaughn shrugs. "It's still going to be dramatic when you march into the courtroom carrying the drone."

"For sure." Erin smiles, throws back her own bottle. "Maybe I can get a job with one of those tech-support companies that helps lawyers present evidence in the courtroom. My career at Day and Lockwood will certainly be over. Actually, if we're successful, Day and Lockwood will be over."

"Which brings me back to my original point: I'm asking way too much."

Erin's smile disappears. "You can stop that, right now," she says, an edge to her voice. "What we're doing here is a whole lot bigger than my job. I'm not doing this because you asked. I'm doing it because it's the right thing. I'll be paying a price, yes. But it'll damn well be worth it."

Vaughn accepts the rebuke. "I still apologize," he says. "But you're absolutely right."

They sit silently again, until Erin brings up Laurie Mitzner. "I'm worried about her. I spent the whole time at dinner with her tonight talking her off the ledge. She insists that Balzac is onto her. She even thinks he knows she searched his office. He cornered her the next day. Said he knew his office was ransacked, and said she was the only one at the firm he was telling about it. He told her he wanted her to be his lookout."

"Sounds like he trusts her, not that he suspects her."

"She said it felt like he was toying with her."

Vaughn chews on what Erin has told him. "We absolutely need Laurie to testify. Without her to authenticate the crash video, the judge won't let us admit it. It's as simple as that."

Erin goes inside and brings out two more bottles. Handing one to Vaughn, she asks how his cousin is holding up.

"When I first saw him inside, he looked thin to me, like he'd already lost weight. His original prison stint destroyed him for a decade. I can't imagine what it would do to him to serve hard time again." Vaughn pauses here. "And today, when Nunzio showed him the video—it really rocked him. When Eddy realized that the train wreck had been planned, he looked like a person whose whole worldview was shattered. He told me all he wants to do is to round up Kate and Emma and move back to that dingy little farmhouse."

"Have you talked to your family?"

"Just my uncle Frank. I brought him up to date on everything, and told him about Nunzio being with us now. That last part was a huge relief for him."

Erin studies Vaughn. "What's your feeling going into this?"

Vaughn thinks for a minute. Then he stands and faces Erin. "I'm not optimistic, but I'm not pessimistic, either. I don't really know how it's going to turn out. But I know this: I've never been looking forward to a fight more than this one. I want to look those bastards in the eye, see the shock in their faces when I lift the rock they've been crawling under, and watch them fry in the sun."

32

WEDNESDAY, JULY 30

Benjamin Balzac paces his office, nervously fingering an unlit cigar. He's spent the past two days obsessing over Laurie Mitzner's betrayal. His original thought was to have fun with her, toy with her for a while. But her disloyalty has proved too distressful for him to bear. It's always been his practice to have infiltrators inside the large defense houses and major plaintiff's firms. He's planted moles, and he's co-opted existing employees. To his thinking, spies are a normal part of business. But the idea that someone else has turned one of his own employees enrages him. Laurie must be made to pay, as a matter of principle. But first, he has to find out what, if anything, she and her conspirators have learned about the train crash.

Balzac lifts his cell and dials. "Badger," he says when Royce answers, "I've given this a lot of thought, and I want my associate taken right away."

"No problem. Uh, but there's that issue with disposal. There's no more room in my basement."

"That won't be a problem. I want you to bring her to my place. I want to interrogate her."

"Interrogate? Is that what they're calling it these days?" Badgett chuckles. "All right, then."

◆　◆　◆

It's just before noon, and Vaughn is exhausted. He's been on the phone for four hours with Assistant District Attorney Christina Wesley, finalizing the scores of evidentiary stipulations she will read into the record at the preliminary hearing. Stipulations as to the identities of the crash victims, the causes of deaths of those killed, and the nature of the survivors' injuries. And stipulations concerning details of the crash itself.

The purpose of the stipulations is to save time by avoiding the need to present legions of witnesses to testify to each and every one of a thousand facts about which there is no dispute. Without the stipulations, the preliminary hearing would take weeks—something neither side wants and the court would never tolerate. Preliminary hearings are not meant to be drawn-out affairs. On a typical day, a Philly judge could run through three or even four homicide prelims.

Still, Vaughn is far more cooperative with Christina Wesley than he would be on a typical case. He can tell that she's wary of his easy compliance. She assumes it's some sort of ploy. And, in a way, it is. Unlike in a normal case, Vaughn wants as much damning evidence admitted onto the record—both the official record and the public record—as possible. That's because his cousin's fate will not hinge on the contours of the prosecutor's evidence, but on the testimony and evidence Vaughn himself presents. Vaughn's plan is to let the prosecution's fires burn, then fan the flames himself, let them explode into the laps of Balzac, Day, and their cronies.

"E-mail me the stipulations," Vaughn says. "I'll sign them, and you can submit the writings for the record. That way, you won't have to read them all. The judge wouldn't be happy with you if you did that."

Christina pauses. "Okay. But I'm going to read some of the stipulations aloud."

"I get it," Vaughn says. "The press will be there. But we both know the judge is going to cut you off."

"And I'm still going to present the witnesses I told you about."

"Again, the press will be there, so of course you will." While being cooperative, he still has to rattle her chain a little bit.

"This isn't about the press," Christina says. Vaughn doesn't answer, so she continues. "I don't know what game you're playing here, Vaughn. But this isn't the type of case to play fast and loose with. This was a real tragedy. A lot of people lost their lives and loved ones."

Vaughn considers saying something snarky, but holds himself back. Instead, he takes the high road with Christina. An advocate to the court, she fights hard on every case and believes she's doing the right thing. He respects her. "You're right. Everything you said is true. And you're just doing your job. So I'm going to give you a heads-up. You think this case is big. And it is. You think all those people were victims, and they were. But you don't know the half of it."

"The hell I don't."

Vaughn hears the heat in Christina's voice, and he knows right away that's she's taking this case personally. And how could she not? Scores dead and hundreds injured—all seemingly because the engineer entrusted with their lives was talking on his phone as his train raced down the track. The scenario is a paradigm for how vulnerable everyone is, how each and every one of us depends for his life on the care and diligence of people we don't even know: the thousands of drivers traveling with or against us on the road to and from work each day; the pharmacists who fill our prescriptions; the manufacturers who design and produce our cars, planes, trains, boats, lawn mowers, and four-wheelers. And most of all, the people whose jobs involve assuming physical possession of our bodies: pilots, bus drivers, limo drivers, and engineers. For this last group, especially, there must be consequences—criminal consequences—when they betray our trust and place us in peril.

To any good prosecutor, *Commonwealth v. Edward Coburn* would be a personal mission. To a true believer like Christina Wesley, it's a holy crusade.

"Look, Christina," Vaughn says, his voice quiet and even, and devoid of all sarcasm or irony, "I don't expect you to believe me or even understand me yet, but I'm going to tell you anyway. You and I are on the same side." With this, he gently hangs up the phone.

For a long while, Vaughn sits, almost motionless, at his desk. He thinks about the monstrous crime perpetrated against the train passengers and the injustice being imposed on his cousin, and his blood starts to boil. It's time to face down these pricks . . . or at least one of them.

Twenty minutes later, Vaughn enters the Comcast Technology building and walks to the security desk. "I'm here to see Erin Doyle, with Day and Lockwood," he tells the guard. "I'm not on the list, so you'll have to call up."

The guard places the call and tells Erin that Vaughn Coburn is in the lobby. Vaughn's cell phone rings while the guard is still on Erin's office line, and Vaughn realizes she must be calling him from her cell.

"What are you doing here?" Erin asks.

"I came to take you to lunch."

"Why didn't you call ahead so I could meet you somewhere?"

"Where's the fun in that?"

"Well, you can't come up here."

Vaughn says nothing.

"Vaughn?"

"The guard is waiting for you to clear me."

"Are you crazy? Everyone here knows who you are. I can't have them see me with you. It would . . . it would . . ."

"What? Spell the end for you at Day and Lockwood?"

Erin doesn't answer, and Vaughn can hear her thinking. Then he hears her talking to the guard, from her office line.

"You're good to go," the guard tells Vaughn. "Fortieth floor. Middle elevator bank."

The elevator doors open to Day and Lockwood's reception area, and Vaughn is dazzled by the sunlight washing through the fifteen-foot floor-to-ceiling windows. The marble floor and blond wood walls reflect the light, which bounces brilliantly off the sparkling crystal statuettes and cut flowers positioned throughout the area—and the Monets and Manets hanging on the walls.

"Well-done forgeries," Erin says quietly, following his eyes as she meets him. "The originals are in one of Geoffrey's houses. Come on, let's go to my office before a crowd forms."

She leads Vaughn down a series of broad hallways lined with secretarial surrounds on the one side and, on the other, glass walls through which Vaughn can see to the external windows and—far below—the city.

"Home sweet home," she says as they reach her office. She turns to her assistant, who's pretending to be busy shuffling documents. "Marie, this is Vaughn Coburn. We went to law school together."

"Oh, hello. It's nice to meet you," Marie says, lifting her head.

Before he has a chance to answer, Vaughn spots Geoffrey Day moving toward him. He recognizes Day's rigid posture, bald pate, and ready-to-scold look from the press conferences.

"Well, if it isn't Mr. Coburn," Geoffrey says. "I'd have expected you'd be hunkered down, getting ready for the preliminary hearing."

Vaughn pauses to size up his adversary, look him in the eye the way two boxers do before a fight. He wonders if Geoffrey Day has figured out that's why he's here. Wonders whether the man even thinks in those terms.

"Vaughn just stopped by to pick me up for lunch," Erin says.

"Is that right? I didn't know you were friends with Mr. Coburn, too."

"Too?" Erin furrows her brow.

"Mr. Nunzio," Day says. "You must have a very large social circle." Day's thin smile fails to disguise his disapproving gaze. He turns to Vaughn. "I must say that this seems more than a little inappropriate—your being here. You know I represent many of the train-crash victims."

Vaughn leans into Day. "I represent one of them myself."

At this moment, Corey King hurriedly approaches. "It's gone," he says. "The drone. Somebody's taken it."

Vaughn turns, and King's jaw drops.

"Wow," Vaughn says, "you guys have your own drone? Like the CIA uses to kill people in Afghanistan?"

Corey casts Vaughn a furious glance and is about to say something when Day jumps in.

"That's impossible," Day says. "Why would anyone want to steal our drone? And how could they get it out without being noticed?" A queer look forms on his face. He turns to Erin and stares.

"What's *he* doing here?" asks Corey, now also looking at Erin.

"He's picking me up for lunch. Speaking of which, we're late." Erin grabs Vaughn's arm and pulls him to the elevator.

Day watches them leave, then strides quickly to his office and places a call. Balzac keeps him on hold for a full five minutes.

"Unacceptable," Day mumbles, watching the minutes tick off.

"What's unacceptable?" Balzac says, having picked up the phone.

"He had the gall to come to my office—"

"Who are you talking—"

"The engineer's lawyer. Coburn. And you were right about him and my associate. They're thick as thieves. Speaking of which, my drone is missing, and I believe that she—Erin Doyle—took it."

"You and that fucking drone."

Day hears something crash in Balzac's office. "Something has to be done, Benjamin. I'm concerned those two are digging far too deeply."

The silence feels like a tangible thing as Balzac broods on the other end of the line.

"Did you hear me, Benjamin? Something must be done."

"I'm working on it," Balzac growls, and the line goes dead.

33

THURSDAY, JULY 31

In Philadelphia, preliminary hearings in homicide cases are held in Courtroom 306. It's a high-security space, the visitors' gallery separated from the well of the court, where the judge and lawyers preside, by a wall of bulletproof Plexiglas. Because of this, Courtroom 306 is known as the "fishbowl." Entry to the well may only be gained through a metal security door that must be buzzed open from the inside.

Vaughn is sitting at the defense table, which, from the perspective of the gallery, is on the left side. The prosecutor's table is on the right, and between the two is the podium. A door in the wall to Vaughn's left opens, and Eddy, wearing the prisoner's garb of white T-shirt and jeans, is led to the defense table by a sheriff's deputy. Vaughn reaches over to his cousin, clasps Eddy's forearm, and speaks near his ear.

"You ready?"

Eddy nods.

Vaughn straightens the papers on the table, then looks behind him, through the Plexiglas partition. The gallery is a dark space with gray walls, no windows, and dim high-hat lighting. Eight rows of pew-style seats finished with scratched and dented black lacquer are jam-packed with members of the press, crash victims, and their families. Sitting in the pews behind the defense table are Eddy's and Vaughn's own family members: Frank and Claire Coburn; Vaughn's parents, John and Kathy; Eddy's sisters, Jean and Peg. And, of course, in the front row, Kate, holding baby Emma and bookended by her two parents. Vaughn looks through the glass and acknowledges the family.

Directly across from Kate, behind the prosecution table, on a two-person pew, are Geoffrey Day and Benjamin Balzac. Day sits with his head tilted back, nose in the air. Balzac scowls. Looking through the glass, Vaughn tosses each of them a hard look, then starts to turn away when he spots, directly behind them, two more familiar faces: James Nunzio and Johnny Giacobetti. Vaughn does a double take, and it troubles him that they are sitting behind the prosecution. He also doesn't like that they register nothing when he looks at them.

Vaughn turns toward the front of the courtroom in time to see the judge enter and take the bench. Regina Johnson is a no-nonsense African American woman in her late forties. She was a career prosecutor before ascending to the bench. Vaughn has appeared before her in the past, and although some defense attorneys criticize her as having a prosecutor's mind-set, he's always found her to be fair. Judge Johnson can affect a folksy demeanor, but she's sharp as a whip and brooks no disrespect. Vaughn is glad she's been assigned to the hearing.

"Counsel, announce your names," the court clerk says, and Vaughn and Christina Wesley do so.

Judge Johnson looks to the prosecutor.

"The Commonwealth would like to introduce exhibits C-1 to C-36."

"And those exhibits are?" asks the court.

Christina pauses for impact. "Death certificates."

Judge Johnson looks to Vaughn. "Objections?"

"None, Your Honor."

The judge accepts the exhibits, and Christina moves on to the stipulations she and Vaughn have agreed to.

"Stipulation one: Joseph Underhoffer, age twenty-three, was removed from railcar number 5702 of Amtrak Train 174 on Monday, June sixteenth, at 1:45 p.m. He was transported to Germantown Hospital, where he was pronounced dead at 2:20 p.m. His remains were taken to the medical examiner's office, where the ME, Dr. Weintraub, determined to a reasonable degree of medical certainty that the cause of death was crush injuries to the head and torso, sustained in the crash.

"Stipulation two: Marie Johns, age fifty-one, was removed from railcar number 5702, of Amtrak Train 174 on Monday, June sixteenth, at 2:00 p.m. She was transported to Temple University Hospital, where she was pronounced dead at 3:15 p.m. Her remains were taken to the medical examiner, where Dr. Weintraub determined to a reasonable degree of medical certainty that the cause of death was exsanguination from traumatic amputation injuries to both legs, sustained in the crash.

"Stipulation three—"

"Ms. Wesley, excuse me," Judge Johnson interrupts. "How many stipulations are there regarding the deaths and injuries?"

"There are thirty-four more stipulations regarding the deceased victims, and two hundred and five stipulations regarding the injured."

"Uh-huh. These stipulations have all been reduced to writing, I assume, and defense counsel has seen them?"

"Yes, Your Honor."

"Mr. Coburn." The judge is now looking at Vaughn. "Do you have any objection to the Commonwealth simply placing the written stipulations onto the record?"

"No, Your Honor. So long as the public has access to those stipulations. My client and I want to make sure that the public is fully apprised of the full scope of the human suffering caused by this tragedy."

Judge Johnson raises her eyebrows at this but says nothing, then looks back to the prosecutor.

"As our next exhibits," says Christina Wesley, "the prosecution offers C-37 to C-300. Photographs of the deceased and injured, showing the terrible injuries inflicted on the victims."

At this point, Vaughn would normally object, arguing that the photographs are too inflammatory and, with the nature of the injuries already stipulated to, serve no purpose in the task at hand, which is simply for the judge to determine whether there is enough evidence to bind the defendant over for trial. The prosecution would normally argue that the judge can be trusted to dispassionately review the photographs, not be swayed by emotion. And the normal thing would be for the judge to sustain the objection and decline to look at the photos.

The judge waits for Vaughn's objection. When it doesn't come, she looks at him. "Mr. Coburn?"

"Your Honor?"

"Objections?"

"None. Again, my client and I want to ensure that the full nature and scope—"

"No speeches, Mr. Coburn. First warning."

"I apologize."

Judge Johnson sighs. "I will admit the photographs but will not view them or consider them in my decision." Then, to Christina, "Continue."

The assistant district attorney begins the witness testimony by calling Albert Cruise, the rail-accident investigator on the NTSB go-team. Vaughn stipulates to Cruise's expertise, and the witness walks the judge through the train crash. Cruise testifies to the nature of the data gathered and recorded by the train's event recorder, or "black box," including train speed, brake pressure, throttle position, distance, and time. He says that, based upon data from the train's black box, it was traveling at eighty miles an hour going into the curve. And it continued at that speed right up to the time of the crash.

"How much distance did the train travel from the time it cleared the curve to the time it crashed into the TracVac?"

"Eighteen hundred feet."

"How much time elapsed between the time the train cleared the curve and the time it struck the track machine?"

"Fifteen seconds."

Christina pauses to let the fact sink in that there was plenty of time for the engineer to have reacted to the presence of the TracVac on the track ahead.

"Between the time the train cleared the curve and the time it crashed into the TracVac, was there any attempt by the engineer to decrease throttle speed?"

"No. The data from the black box makes clear that the throttle position remained constant."

"Was there any attempt by the engineer to apply the train's normal service brakes, or its emergency brakes?"

"No."

"Did the data from the black box indicate any action whatsoever on the part of the engineer to avoid the collision?"

"None."

Christina Wesley has Cruise identify the printout from the train's black box, and she moves it into evidence, with no objection by Vaughn. Christina says, "Nothing further."

Vaughn begins his cross-examination.

"Mr. Cruise, if I understand you correctly, the train rounded the curve and the engineer had a full fifteen seconds to see the TracVac on the track ahead and react to it, either by pulling back on the throttle or applying the brakes. But he did neither."

"Exactly."

"Why didn't you just look to see why he didn't react?"

Cruise frowns. "I don't understand."

"The locomotive was equipped with an inward-facing video camera, wasn't it?"

"Yes, but it wasn't turned on yet, in accordance with an agreement between the railroad and the engineers' labor union."

"Who told you that?"

"Ah, well, it was Amtrak itself. Its division engineer, Mr. Bunting. That's why we didn't attempt to download the video. There wasn't any."

"Mr. Bunting? I see. I'm going to make a mental note to remember that name." Vaughn looks up at the judge. "Nothing further."

As her next witness, the prosecutor calls Nelson Wexler, head of the NTSB go-team.

Christina establishes Wexler's credentials, and Vaughn stipulates to his expertise and competence to testify.

"Were you present when the defendant, Mr. Coburn, was interviewed by the NTSB?"

"I was."

"Was he questioned about how the crash happened?"

"Yes."

"What did he say?"

"He said he didn't remember anything after heading into the curve at Torresdale."

"Was he asked if there was any medical reason he would have lost consciousness?"

"Yes, and he said there was none."

"Was he asked why he wouldn't have seen the TracVac on the track ahead, if he were facing forward?"

"Yes. He said he couldn't think of any possible reason."

"As part of your investigation, did you yourself inspect the curve and the track between the curve and the place where the train crashed into the TracVac?"

"Yes. It's a straightaway."

"Was there anything, any structure or object, that would have prevented engineer Coburn from seeing the TracVac on the track ahead once he rounded the curve?"

"No, there was not."

Christina pauses, then switches topics. "Let's talk about his phone. What did he tell you about his phone?"

"He said he had a cell phone and kept it in his knapsack. He said the phone was turned off, and he made no calls during the run."

"Did he confess to you that in fact he had two phones on the train?"

Vaughn looks up at the judge. "Objection to the term *confess*."

"Sustained." Judge Johnson tells Christina to continue, and she does.

"Did there come a point when you learned the defendant had a second phone on the locomotive?"

"Yes. We were alerted by Amtrak that they were tipped off to the fact that the defendant did have a second phone. So we went to Amtrak's facility in Bear, Delaware, where the train cars were being stored. We went in and found the second phone."

"And what did the phone show when the NTSB electronics division examined it?"

"It showed that the engineer was on the phone twice during the run. Once when he placed a call, and once when he received a call."

"What were the times and duration of those calls?"

"The first call lasted a minute and a half, from 12:08:10 to 12:09:41. The second call, the one he received, lasted from 12:17:50 the whole way through the crash."

"So he was talking on the phone during the critical fifteen seconds leading up to the crash?"

Wexler declines to answer the question, telling the judge that, per federal statute, the NTSB does not testify as to its conclusions, only its factual findings. The way he explains it, though, makes clear to everyone that the NTSB believes Vaughn was talking on the phone.

"Even if he were on the phone, the engineer would still have been able to see through the windshield to the track ahead."

"Of course."

"So he wasn't just talking on the phone, he was facing away from the windshield?"

Vaughn objects and Wexler again tells the judge that the NTSB does not testify to its conclusions. And, again, he does it in a way that tells everyone he thinks Eddy wasn't looking ahead like he was supposed to.

Christina asks a few more questions, then has Wexler identify and authenticate the transcript of the NTSB's interview of Eddy, which she moves into evidence.

Judge Johnson gives Vaughn permission to cross-examine.

"Your team's examination of the second cell phone shows that it was turned on during the time leading up to the crash," Vaughn says to Wexler, "but it didn't show that my client was talking on the phone, correct?"

This gives Wexler pause. "I don't understand what you're saying."

"May I approach the witness, Your Honor?"

Judge Johnson nods.

Vaughn walks up to Wexler, holding two cell phones. He uses the one to dial the other, presses the button on the other phone to accept the call, then lays them both down on the witness stand. After a moment, he asks, "Both phones are on?"

"Yes."

"But no one is talking into them?"

Wexler doesn't answer.

"That my client's cell phone was on during the seconds leading up to the crash doesn't prove he was talking into the phone at that time, does it?"

Wexler hesitates.

"I suppose not."

"And if—"

"You've made your point, Mr. Coburn," the judge interrupts. "Move on."

Vaughn turns back to the witness. "Who at Amtrak told you about this tip that Mr. Coburn had a second phone?"

"Mr. Bunting."

"Bunting again. And who went into the locomotive and found the second phone?"

"Mr. Bunting."

"Bunting," Vaughn repeats the name. "But isn't he the Amtrak representative who went into the locomotive the first time, right after the crash?"

"Yes."

"But he didn't find a second phone then, did he?"

"Well . . . we weren't expecting to find a second phone. So after he found the first one, I suppose he stopped looking."

"And Bunting's the one who told the NTSB the recording device for the inward-facing camera was *not* turned on?"

"That's correct."

"Had the camera been on, it would have shown us exactly what Mr. Coburn was doing in the seconds leading up to the accident, wouldn't it?"

"That's the whole point of the inward-facing camera."

"Yes, Mr. Wexler, it is."

"Objection." It's Christina Wesley. "Counsel's testifying."

"Sustained," says the judge.

"Nothing further," says Vaughn.

The judge calls a short recess, and Balzac marches out of the courtroom and down the hallway. He finds a quiet place and makes a call. Jack Bunting's voice mail answers, and Balzac curses under his breath. *Where the hell is he?* Balzac listened carefully to Coburn's questions on cross, and he didn't like what he heard. The engineer's lawyer either knows or has intuited that Bunting is at the heart of things. Balzac wonders whether Bunting, like Laurie, has turned. He quickly dismisses the notion; Bunting would never betray him. Any more than Royce would. Which reminds him: Badgett should be well on his way to securing Laurie Mitzner. He lifts his cell phone and makes another call.

◆　◆　◆

Back in the courtroom, Vaughn is holding his own cell to his ear, his heart racing.

"Slow down, Erin. Say it again."

"Laurie's gone. We were supposed to meet this morning and spend the day together going over our stories. She was going to stay at my place overnight and come with me to court tomorrow. But she never showed up. I've called her home phone and her cell half a dozen times, and I keep getting thrown to voice mail. I called her office to see if she chickened out and went to work. Her assistant said she didn't show up and didn't call out sick, either. They have no idea where she is."

"Damn." Vaughn's mind is spinning. He absolutely needs Laurie's testimony; everything hinges on the court's seeing the crash video and tying it to Balzac. Without Laurie to authenticate the video, it won't get into evidence and his plan will fall apart.

Has she gotten cold feet? Or come to harm at the hands of Balzac?

"Go to her apartment," he tells Erin. "Have the doorman let you in. Tell him you're a relative and it's an emergency. And keep calling her. Text me with what you find. I can't talk on the phone because I'm in court, but I can glance down at my phone to see what you've written."

Vaughn hangs up. He turns to see his cousin staring at him.

"Someone went AWOL on us, didn't they?" Eddy says.

"No," Vaughn says firmly. "No one's leaving you behind this time, Eddy. Not if I have to drag them back myself."

34

THURSDAY, JULY 31, CONTINUED

The judge resumes the bench and tells Christina Wesley to call her next witness.

"The Commonwealth calls Melissa Nash."

Vaughn watches the witness enter the rear door, walk through the gallery, and then into the well of the courtroom. She's young, in her midthirties. And attractive—thin, fit, with long blonde hair and large blue eyes. It's obvious why Christina has chosen Nash to be her first passenger witness.

Christina establishes that, at the time of the accident, Melissa Nash lived in Germantown with her husband, Tim, a neonatology resident at Children's Hospital. They were on their way to New York for some much-needed respite.

"Tim had been working crazy hours for a long time, and I told him he needed a break, even if it was only for a day. He didn't want to, at first—there were two preemie babies he was caring for, and they were both struggling—but I strong-armed him." Here, Melissa pauses to gather herself and everyone reads the guilt on her face. "I tried to make it special by getting tickets to see *Hamilton*, the musical. It was a big splurge for us, but I wanted Tim to have a good time, and he'd been talking about getting up to New York to see it."

"Tell us about the crash, and what happened to your husband."

"We were moving along and everything seemed fine. It was bright and sunny. Tim was reading the paper, and I was texting one of my girlfriends. All of a sudden, it felt like the whole world exploded. There was a huge crashing sound, and the car went sideways and everyone and everything went flying. Windows were shattering. Stones came flying up into the car. I felt my body tossed around like laundry in a dryer. After what seemed like forever, it stopped, and I was lying on the side of the railcar, which was now the floor. I couldn't find Tim, so I started screaming his name and crawling around looking for him. I found him about twenty feet away. He was awake and said his leg hurt. I looked, and his right leg seemed okay, but most of his left leg was out of the window, out of the railcar, against the ground. It was pinned. I tried to pull him free, but he was jammed too tightly. I told him to hold on, that help would come and they'd lift the car and he'd be okay. I sat there with him, holding his head in my lap. We talked, at first. He even made a joke about missing the play. Then, after a while, he closed his eyes and stopped talking. I called his name, but he wouldn't answer."

Melissa's eyes glaze over, and everyone can see that she's back on the train. After a minute, she steels herself and resumes. "I thought he was in shock, but . . ." Melissa pauses again. "It seemed to take forever for the rescuers to reach us. There was a police officer and an EMT. They lifted me off Tim and checked his pulse. The policeman told me I needed to get out of the train. I said I was going to wait until they got Tim out, but he wouldn't let me; he said it was unsafe. He walked me to the end of the car, which was ripped wide open, and helped me to the ground, where some other people got me onto a bus." Melissa's voice trails off.

"And your husband?"

"They told me he bled to death, because of his leg." Melissa's eyes are far away again.

"Thank you," Christina says.

"Cross?" Judge Johnson asks Vaughn, her tone making it clear that he'd be a fool to challenge the witness in any way.

Vaughn stands. "I'm sorry for your loss, Mrs. Nash."

Melissa holds Vaughn's eyes for a long moment. He takes the time to search them, finding neither hate nor anger, only grief. Bottomless grief.

Everyone waits quietly, respectfully, while the young widow slowly leaves the witness stand and exits the courtroom. When she's gone, the judge turns to Christina Wesley.

"How many more passengers do you intend to present?"

"Just one, Your Honor."

"You know you don't need them. The deaths and injuries have all been stipulated to, as has their being caused by the accident."

"Just one," Christina repeats.

The judge nods. "All right. This is an unusual case. So I'll give you the leeway, for now."

"Thank you, Your Honor. The Commonwealth calls Brian Stewart."

The account offered up by the twentysomething computer technician is no less moving than Melissa Nash's. Brian, his wife, Elizabeth, and their two-month-old daughter, Reagan, were traveling in the third car. One minute, everything was fine. The next minute, they were thrown into hell.

"When I came to, I saw Lizzy a few feet away. She was mangled. Her face was . . . I only knew it was her from what she was wearing. I looked for the baby until they forced me to leave the train." Brian pauses, and everyone sees the same glazed look Melissa Nash had taken on. "It wasn't until later, after nine, that I got the call about Reagan. They told me to go to the medical examiner's office . . . They had her laid out real nice on a table for me. Wrapped in a blanket. But she was . . ."

Brian Stewart closes his eyes, lowers his head. At that moment, almost as if she's conjuring the spirit of the dead baby, Emma Coburn starts to cry, bringing many in the gallery to tears.

The baby's wailing has a profound effect on Brian Stewart, who stares at Emma, his mouth wide open. Then, something inside him snaps, and his eyes fill with fire. He points at Eddy Coburn and shouts, "You should be ashamed of yourself. Taking chances like you did with other people's children, when you had one of your own!"

The witness's anger is infectious, and Eddy and Vaughn can both feel the crowd heating up behind them. And they can see the hostility in the eyes of the judge's clerk, and court reporter, and even the bailiff—an old court dog who's been around long enough to have heard it all.

The last thing Vaughn wants to do is rise and face the suffering man on the witness stand, but he does so. "Mr. Stewart, my client and I are both very sorry for your loss."

The fury flares again in Brian Stewart's eyes, but in an act of will and grace, he restrains himself. "Thank you," he says, forcing the words.

Watching Stewart leave the stand, Vaughn can't imagine that he'd have handled himself with half as much restraint if he were in the man's place.

"Does the Commonwealth have any other evidence to offer?"

"No, Your Honor," answers Christina Wesley.

"Then we'll take a short recess before hearing argument from defense counsel."

"Your Honor?" It's Vaughn. "The defense has witnesses."

This surprises Judge Johnson. Defendants have the right to offer testimony at preliminary hearings but rarely do so. For a defendant, the safe play is to use the hearings to learn the prosecution's case and cross-examine its witnesses to uncover dirt or inconsistencies, laying a foundation to undermine the witnesses when the case goes to trial. Offering one's own defense witnesses only serves to tip off the district attorney to the defense strategy and give the prosecution the chance to probe for weaknesses.

"What witnesses?" asks the judge.

"To begin with, the defendant. Mr. Coburn."

Now the crowd is really buzzing. And the judge is stunned. If defense attorneys rarely offer witnesses at preliminary hearings, they *never* put on the defendant.

Judge Johnson stares down from the bench at Vaughn, who doesn't flinch. She slowly shakes her head. "All right. We'll have that recess, and when we come back, the defendant will be at bat."

Fifteen minutes later, Eddy Coburn is sitting on the witness stand, and everyone seems to be holding their breaths. The bailiff has Eddy state his name, raise his hand, and take the oath.

"Your witness," the judge tells Vaughn.

"Mr. Coburn, would you begin by telling the jury where you live?"

Eddy looks confused. "Uh, jail?"

The remark draws some chuckles from the gallery, and the judge's staff, too. Vaughn smiles and asks Eddy where he lived before he was arrested, and with whom.

"I lived in North Jersey with Kate. That's my wife."

"Is she in court today?"

"Yes," Eddy says, nodding toward the gallery. "She has Emma."

"Emma is your newborn?"

A sad expression crosses Eddy's face. "Yes."

"Who are Kate and Emma sitting with?"

"With the rest of the family. Her parents. My parents, and sisters—"

"And my own parents—your aunt and uncle?"

"Yes, we're cousins," says Eddy.

"More like brothers." A statement, not a question, from Vaughn.

"Objection," says Christina. "Touching as it is, this family reunion is irrelevant."

"Move on," says the judge.

Vaughn nods and gets to it. "Mr. Coburn, were you the engineer driving Amtrak Train 174 on Monday, June the sixteenth of this year, when it crashed into a TracVac just after the Torresdale curve?"

"I was."

"Did you yourself suffer physical injuries as a result of the crash?"

"Swelling of the brain, head and face lacerations, ruptured spleen, and a broken leg."

"Please tell the court, and everyone, what happened during that run—the whole run, through the time of the crash."

"Objection." Christina, still sitting, leans across the prosecution table. "He's already told the NTSB that he doesn't remember what happened after the train rounded the curve. He's not competent to testify to anything that happened after that point."

Judge Johnson turns to Vaughn, who says, "He remembers now."

The comment draws moans from the gallery. They're all thinking, *How convenient.*

Christina rolls her eyes. "You must be kidding."

Judge Johnson arches her eyebrows. "For real?"

"Yes, Your Honor," Vaughn answers. Then, turning back to the witness stand, he tells Eddy to continue.

"We left 30th Street a little after noon. About ten minutes later, I called Kate."

Vaughn raises a hand to stop him. "Wasn't it against Amtrak procedures to make a call from the locomotive? Even to have your cell phone on?"

"Yes. I broke the rules. There had been some break-ins in our neighborhood, and I was worried. Kate was eight months pregnant at the time. I had a burner . . . a prepaid cell phone to talk with her on in case of emergency. I just wanted to see that she was all right."

"Where did you get the prepaid cell phone?"

"Reggie Frye gave it to me."

"Who is Reggie Frye?"

"He's an engineer—or was an engineer. He works in the track department now. We were talking one day, and I told him about the break-ins. He said I should have a burner phone. He told me lots of engineers have them. That way, if something happens during a run and supervision asks to see your cell to make sure you weren't on it, you can just show them your company phone and it'll be clean. He gave me his own burner phone that day and told me he'd buy himself another one."

"What about the inward-facing cameras? Weren't you concerned you'd be recorded using the burner phone?"

"No. The cameras weren't supposed to be turned on for another three months."

Vaughn pauses, then asks, "Isn't Reggie Frye the track foreman who was in charge of the TracVac your train crashed into?"

The question triggers memories in the gallery and causes a stir.

"Yes."

"Do you know where he is now?"

"No. I haven't talked to him since that day he gave me the phone."

"Did you know that Reggie Frye lost his job as an engineer because he twice tested positive for alcohol, and that he'd have been fired outright from Amtrak except that he was being protected by someone high up in the company?"

"Objection." It's Christina Wesley. "There's no evidence on the record of any of that. And it's hearsay, at best."

"Sustained."

Vaughn pauses, then asks, "Is Jack Bunting someone pretty high up at Amtrak?"

"Objection—"

"Sustained," says Judge Johnson even before Christina finishes. "Stay focused, Mr. Coburn. No detours."

Vaughn says, "Yes, Your Honor. Eddy, tell us about the second call. The one that continued up until the time of the crash."

Eddy Coburn takes a deep breath, and everyone leans forward in their seats.

"It was between five and ten minutes after I hung up with Kate. I was approaching the curve when the phone rang. I assumed it was Kate again, so I didn't look at the screen to see the number. But it wasn't Kate. It was a man's voice. He said I was dead—"

"Be exact. What *precisely* did he say?"

"He said . . . he said, 'You're a dead man.' And I said, 'Who the hell is this?' And then he said, 'Bang, bang. Motherfucker. Bang, bang.'" Eddy looks sheepishly at the judge. "I'm sorry for the language. That's what the caller said."

"You say he used the words 'bang, bang'?"

"He said it twice. The second time with a lot of emphasis."

"And then?"

Eddy raises his hand to his chest. "He started shooting at the train."

Christina Wesley leaps to her feet. "Objection! Objection!"

"What's the nature of your objection?" asks the judge.

"It's just too much. First, he suddenly remembers the accident. And now he's being shot at? It's beyond incredible."

"That may be, Ms. Wesley," the judge says, "but it's his story, and if he wants to lock himself into it at a preliminary hearing, he has the right to do so. Of course," she adds, turning to Vaughn, "whether that is a wise thing to do is another question. Mr. Coburn, are you sure you want to continue with this?"

"Absolutely," Vaughn says.

Judge Johnson dismisses him with a wave of her hand: *So be it.*

"Tell us," Vaughn says, "about the shooting, and what you did."

"Well, as soon as he said the 'bang-bang' thing, the first shot hit the windshield. It was right in front of me. It was like a loud smack, and the windshield cracked. I jumped up out of my seat, and as soon as I did, another shot hit the windshield. So I threw myself down on the floor to wait it out."

"Wait it out?"

"Yes. Since the bullets were hitting the windshield in front of me, I knew the shooter had to be ahead of the train somewhere, and not too far away. At eighty miles an hour, I knew I'd pass him quickly. And I knew there was nothing on the track ahead. Just the curve, followed by a long straightaway. At least that's what I thought."

"Why did you think that? Explain it to the court."

"Well, my track was in service, and there were no speed restrictions or notices of work being done. The track should've been clear."

"Okay. So you know you're being shot at, you believe there's nothing on the track ahead, and you decide to lie low inside the engine. What happens?"

"The shots keep coming. I hear the bullets hit the windshield. *Smack. Smack. Smack.*"

"And then what?"

Eddy's gaze turns inward. "And then . . . nothing. I mean, the train hit the TracVac, obviously, and I must've been thrown around pretty hard inside the locomotive, but I don't remember any of that. At first, I didn't even remember that second phone call, or the shooting, until . . ." Eddy pauses here for dramatic effect, as Vaughn instructed him to do. "Until I saw the video. From the inward-facing camera."

"Objection!" Christina is on her feet again. "What video? There is no video from inside the train."

"That's what my client thought, too," says Vaughn.

"And Mr. Cruise testified to it," the judge says.

"Yes, he did," Vaughn agrees. "Because that's what he was told by Jack Bunting—the same person who claimed he didn't find my client's cell phone the first time he went onto the engine but somehow did find it the second time."

"What did I say about speeches, Mr. Coburn? Now, please tell me what's going on with regard to this video."

"It turns out that the inward-facing camera *was* on, and it did record Mr. Coburn. I showed him the video this morning, before trial, in his holding cell."

"And when did you come into possession of this video?" asks the judge.

"Late last night. A memory stick containing copy of the video was hand-delivered to me at my apartment—"

"By whom?"

"I don't know. The messenger didn't say when he dropped it off. Just told me that it was a video I'd want to see right away. I pressed him for more information, but he rode off on his bike."

"If that's the case, then the video can't be authenticated and can't be admitted, or watched by the court," says Christina Wesley. "I object."

"But it *can* be authenticated, by the defendant," Vaughn counters. "He can positively say it shows him on the locomotive leading up to the crash. And it corroborates what he's just told Your Honor about what happened. As a backup, I'm having Mr. Bunting served at 30th Street Station with a subpoena to appear tomorrow. Though, legally, I think it's unnecessary."

Of course, Vaughn knows Bunting won't be there to receive the subpoena.

Judge Johnson sits back in her chair and thinks. Vaughn can feel the excitement in the gallery behind him. Everyone, he knows, is chomping at the bit to see the video, itching to learn whether Eddy's fantastic tale about being shot at could be true.

The judge leans forward. "All right, Mr. Coburn. I'm going to let you play the video. I'll decide what to do with it afterward." She directs the bailiff to turn on the court's video system, and he positions the large flat-screen TV so that it faces the attorneys and the gallery behind them. She will watch the video on her own small screen. Her staff will watch on two other small screens positioned on the desks below the bench.

"While they're setting up, we'll take a short break."

The judge leaves the bench and exits the courtroom through a side door. After she leaves, Vaughn turns around to the gallery and acknowledges the members of his and Eddy's family, who nod back, smile, and give him the thumbs-up. Finally, they all believe, Eddy is going to be vindicated, and this nightmare will be over.

Vaughn also looks to Geoffrey Day and Benjamin Balzac. Day looks like he's going to be ill. Balzac's eyes burn with fury. Behind the attorneys, James Nunzio's face is expressionless, and neither he nor Johnny G. acknowledges Vaughn when he glances their way. That troubles Vaughn, as does the fact that they are still sitting behind the prosecution.

Is it possible that, even now, even knowing what he does, Jimmy Nutzo is still out for Eddy's blood? Could he be involved in Laurie Mitzner's disappearance?

When the equipment is set up and the judge is back on the bench, she gives Vaughn the signal to play the video. It runs just under twelve minutes from start to finish, and the whole time, everyone is glued to their screens. In the gallery, everyone from seasoned reporters to Vaughn and Eddy's family members to crash victims sits on the edge of their seats.

The video shows Eddy throughout the run. It shows him sitting in the engineer's chair, periodically pushing the red button known as the "dead-man's switch" with his left hand, operating the throttle, looking ahead. It shows him placing the first call, to Kate. It shows him receiving the second call. It shows his mouth moving, and although there's no sound, his lips are easily read: "Who the fuck is this?" The video shows Eddy listening for a moment, then flinching and leaping out of his seat, then throwing himself to the floor. It plays on for another fifteen seconds or so. And then it goes black.

When the video stops, no one moves for a long time, or so it seems to Vaughn. A sea change has come over the hearing—he feels it, and he's certain everyone else does, too. He looks at the judge, her clerks, the court reporter, and the bailiff, and he sees they are all studying Eddy. He imagines they are asking themselves whether the system hasn't gotten it all wrong. Maybe Eddy is as much a victim here as the other people injured and killed in the crash.

Christina rises. "Your Honor, I renew my objection. The video doesn't show anyone shooting at the train. It doesn't show any bullets entering the train. It doesn't show pieces of glass being blown into the cab from the windshield, and there were no bullets found inside the locomotive. Not by the NTSB. Not by Amtrak. The video shows nothing corroborating the defendant's story that he was shot at. And its origin is suspect. I move the court to deny its admission."

Vaughn would like nothing more than to throttle Christina Wesley. A rush of heat pushes its way up through his shirt collar, and he knows his neck and face are turning red. Instead, he breathes deeply, looks down, and waits for the judge to make her ruling. He begins counting to ten. When he gets to eight, Regina Johnson leans forward on her seat.

"I'm going to reserve ruling on the admissibility of the video until all of the evidence is in. Mr. Coburn, you may continue with your witness."

Vaughn finishes with a short series of questions in response to which Eddy confirms that the video does indeed show what happened during the ill-fated run, and that seeing the video is what triggered his memory of the two phone calls and shots fired. Then Vaughn thanks Eddy and tells the court he's finished.

Judge Johnson turns to Christina. "Your witness."

"Your Honor, the defendant's story is a complete surprise to the prosecution. I was not apprised of it before court today, and it flatly contradicts what the defendant told the NTSB. With the court's permission, I'd like to reserve my cross until the defense has called all of its witnesses."

"A fair request, under the circumstances. Court is adjourned. I will see you all at eight o'clock tomorrow morning. Sharp. Ms. Wesley, after the defense has put on the rest of its witnesses, and you have had a chance to question the defendant, do you plan to present any additional witnesses of your own? How about this Mr. Bunting we've been hearing about?"

Christina pauses. "We, uh . . . we're looking for him."

"And Mr. Frye? The one who gave the extra phone to the defendant?"

"We're looking for him, too."

Vaughn sees the judge hold the prosecutor's eyes for a long time, and he can tell that Regina Johnson is starting to smell something rotten.

"As for you, Mr. Coburn, you put on a good show. That video was gripping, to say the least. But I have no idea who gave it to you, or why they gave it to you, or how they got it. I'm sure the media will have a field day with this video, but given the things that special-effects people can do with digital recordings these days, I wouldn't be too optimistic, if I were you, that I'm going to accept it into the record. Even if I do, I might not give it much weight. So, if you're hoping I'm going to buy the idea that your client was actually being shot at, you have a long way to go. And if you're hoping that I buy into it enough not to hold him over, well, you'll need more than a Pixar movie for that. Court dismissed."

The judge's words are a stinging comedown for Vaughn. As high as he was after the video played, he realizes that he's only started down the path to convincing the court of Eddy's innocence. And that is precisely what he has to do. The purpose of a preliminary hearing is only to determine whether the prosecution has come up with enough evidence to justify a conviction—*if believed by a jury*. A defendant's showing that he has enough contrary evidence in his favor to potentially justify a verdict of not guilty doesn't justify letting him go. In case of a tie, the defendant is bound over for trial. So the only way Eddy is going to walk is if Regina Johnson comes to believe with certainty what Vaughn knows to be true: that Geoffrey Day and Benjamin Balzac engineered the crash and set up Eddy as their fall guy. And for that, he's going to need Laurie's testimony to get the drone video into evidence and tie it to Balzac. Erin's testimony about Day's drone and the "bang, bang note" in Day's drawer is critical as well. Erin's ready to go, but Laurie has gone AWOL.

35

THURSDAY, JULY 31, CONTINUED

It's five o'clock and Balzac is back in his office. Coburn's playing of the video has unnerved him. There's only one source from which they could have obtained the video: Jack Bunting. And Jack's not answering his calls. *Maybe he's turned after all.*

Balzac paces his office, pours himself a glass of Bombay Sapphire to soothe his nerves. He tells himself to focus. The video itself is nothing. The judge said as much. And the idea that someone would shoot at a train to deliberately derail it is so far-fetched that no one's going to swallow Coburn's tale without irrefutable evidence.

So what else could Coburn have up his sleeve? He's gone this far down that road, so he must have more.

Balzac's mind zeros in on Geoffrey Day's associate, Erin Doyle.

Who knows what kind of evidence that moron Day left lying around for her to find.

As for Laurie Mitzner, Balzac knows he left no evidence for her to uncover—if he'd had any doubts about that, they were erased when he saw the live feed of Laurie, Doyle, and Coburn rooting around his office and turning up nothing. Still, Laurie is a loose end that has to be tied off. Balzac raises his cell phone to call Royce, but before he's able to dial, the phone rings. The ringtone is the Empire's theme music from *Star Wars*. Darth Vader's song. Balzac assigned the tune to Royce.

"What do you have for me?" Balzac says.

"In a few hours, I'll have your associate."

"A few hours?"

"Yeah. I was waiting for her this morning, outside her house. You know, she has that town house and usually walks to work. But today she drove out of her garage, and I've been following her since. Five and a half hours so far. We're on I-80, just outside of Youngstown, Ohio, heading toward Akron. I thought for sure she'd have had to stop by now, but that girl sure can hold her pee. Or maybe she's wearing a diaper like that female astronaut who drove fourteen hours to her boyfriend's house to kill him. Anyway, I'm going to follow her until she stops, which she'll have to sooner or later, then zap her with the stun gun. I'll toss her into the trunk and head back."

Balzac breathes a big sigh of relief. "Good man," he says. "Just don't let her get away."

"How'd that hearing go today? With the engineer?"

"Not good. He remembers that he was being shot at. And they had Jack's video from inside the cab."

"Fuck me," Badgett says, drawing out the words.

"Fuck us all, if the engineer's lawyer has anything else up his sleeve."

"What's Jack say?"

"I can't reach him."

This clearly shocks Badgett. "You don't think there's any way he—"

"I can't imagine it," Balzac cuts him off. "But . . ."

Balzac wonders whether Coburn could have Bunting in the wings, ready to testify tomorrow. He mulls this and realizes it can't be the case; if Jack had turned coat, he'd have been the *first* witness the defense put on the stand. Coburn would simply have had Bunting lay it all out, in detail, for the court: the plan, the participants, how it was actually done.

And that would have been the end of it. The judge would have released the engineer and taken him and Day into custody.

No. Coburn didn't put Bunting on because he doesn't have him. The best he had was the engineer's fantastic claim and the video showing him talking on his phone when he shouldn't have been, and diving to the floor, God knows why.

Those were the strongest cards in Coburn's deck, which is why he led with them. Which means that from here on out, his evidence is going to get weaker and weaker.

An hour after Balzac hangs up with Badgett, Vaughn is sitting on his couch at home, channel surfing the local six o'clock news. They all lead with what they call Eddy's "bombshell" testimony that he was shot at, and the "dramatic" video showing him diving to the floor. It's exactly what Vaughn was hoping for. In the media, at least, this is no longer a clear-cut case of a train crash caused by a criminally reckless engineer. To the contrary, it seems Eddy the Villain might in fact be Eddy the Victim.

But vindication in the press is a hollow victory. Other than Nunzio, there is only one audience that matters here: Regina Johnson. And she's made it clear that Eddy's testimony and the videotape haven't convinced her of anything.

Vaughn lifts his cell and dials Erin's number, again. She's been on the phone for an hour, and he keeps getting thrown to voice mail.

Why doesn't she just put the other person on hold and answer me?

"Vaughn?"

"Finally."

"I've been talking with Laurie, and—"

"Where is she?"

"Will you let me talk?" Erin huffs and then goes on. "Her brother lives in Toledo. She'd planned to drive there but got too tired to go on and stopped for the night, just outside of Youngstown, Ohio—"

"Ohio! What the f—"

"Stop! She's afraid, Vaughn. She's worked with Balzac for nine years, and she has a good sense of what he's about. And she told me that if he's willing to crash a trainful of people, he's willing to hurt her as well. And I really couldn't disagree with her on that."

Vaughn exhales loudly. "But we need her. Without Laurie, there's no crash-in-progress video. No link to Balzac. No tie-in to Geoffrey's drone."

"I get it. That's why I'm going to find her."

"You can't leave. I need you to testify yourself tomorrow."

"I have to go. Laurie's not going to listen to anyone but me. Call Tommy and tell him to pick me up at my place, ASAP. We'll drive to her hotel, and, hopefully, I can convince her to come back."

"But Akron has to be six hours away. The hearing starts at eight tomorrow."

"That gives us fourteen hours. If we drive fast, we can make it there and back in time."

"I don't believe this," Vaughn says, rubbing his forehead.

"Call Tommy." Erin hangs up.

Midnight. Royce Badgett sits in the driver's seat of his Cadillac CTS—a present forced on him by the boss six years ago for his work on a truck-on-bus accident. He's parked behind the Fortune Garden Restaurant, which shares a parking lot with the Motel 6 on Belmont Avenue, off exit 229 from I-80. His car faces the motel, a two-story '70s-style structure where the cash-strapped can rent a room for fifty bucks a night. Not the kind of place you'd expect to find a hotshot Philly lawyer pulling down $200K a year. Which, he figures, is why Laurie Mitzner is staying here on her way to who-knows-where.

Mitzner pulled in just after 5:30 p.m., Badgett right behind her. While she checked in at the office building, he parked across from her car, in front of Fortune Garden. She exited the office after about ten minutes and moved her car to the main building. Royce watched her pull her suitcase through a first-floor doorway, then reappear on the second-floor balcony. The motel was one of those places where the doors to the rooms were on the outside—a fact that Badgett knows will be helpful when the time comes to take the young lawyer.

Badgett positioned his car so he could keep an eye on Laurie's door, make sure she didn't leave. He watched for two hours, until he was satisfied that she was going to stay the night, then drove across the street to the Station Square Ristoranti, where he wolfed down the broiled stuffed-shrimp appetizer, spaghetti con funghi, and Granny's apple pie.

Now, sitting in his car, Badgett is about ready to make his move. His plan is simple: he'll walk over to the hotel, go up to the girl's door, quietly pick the lock, enter, point a gun at her head, and tell her to keep her mouth shut. He'll walk her to his car, open the trunk, stun-gun her, and push her inside. Tape her mouth, bind her hands and feet—maybe feel her up a little—then head back down the pike to Philly.

He'd have gone in a lot sooner, but there was too much activity at the grungy motel. *Surprising for a Thursday night,* he thought, *but who can figure out Ohio? You know what they say about Ohioans . . .* Badgett chuckles to himself. *On the great trek westward, they were the first ones to quit.*

Badgett starts to open his car door when he sees a Ford F-150 pull into the lot in front of the hotel. *Shit, another delay,* he thinks. *Wait a minute . . .* Badgett leans forward to make sure his eyes aren't deceiving him. Getting out of the pickup is Day's associate, the one who's screwing Vaughn Coburn. And with her is the big hard case who followed him for a while, then tried to ply him for information at the bar. Coburn's investigator.

"Trifecta," he says out loud. *The boss'll be as happy as a pig in doo-doo.*

Badgett reformulates his plan. He'll barge into the motel room with his sawed-off shotgun to show them he means business. Then he'll have one of the girls bind the big guy's hands behind his back so that the investigator can't make trouble. He'll march them all to the car and drive off to some secluded place, get them out of the car, and stuff them all into the trunk. He'll put a couple of slugs in the investigator's head and maybe Coburn's girlfriend's head, too. He can't hurt the boss's associate because the boss wants her for himself.

Standing outside the hotel, Tommy asks Erin, "Now what?" This is because, although Laurie told Erin what hotel she was staying in, she didn't share the room number. Erin didn't ask because she didn't want Laurie to know that she intended to show up. Which might've caused her to scram. But Erin knew that her only chance of persuading Laurie to change her mind and come back to Philadelphia was a face-to-face meeting.

Erin thinks for a moment, then says, "*Streetcar Named Desire*."

"What?"

"Laur-ie!" Erin shouts the name. "Laurie! Laurie!"

Tommy joins in.

A door opens on the second floor of the motel. Laurie runs out, leans over the balcony, and whisper-shouts down to Erin and Tommy. "Do you want the whole world to know where I am? Why don't you just run a newspaper ad?"

Laurie turns and walks back to her room but leaves the door ajar. Taking the hint, Tommy and Erin race into the hotel and up the stairs.

Ten minutes later, Tommy is doing his best to keep the two women from coming to blows. Erin has cajoled, begged, and cursed, but Laurie refuses to budge. Now the two lawyers are facing off across the bed, yelling at each other.

"You can't leave Vaughn in the lurch," insists Erin. "You can't let his cousin get sent to prison for something that's not his fault. And you can't let those two murderers walk free!"

"Balzac will *kill me* if I go back. He knows. Somehow, he knows that I copied the crash video and gave it to you."

"And tomorrow, the whole world will know. That's the whole point. The news is carrying the story about the video already. This is how you get safe. You testify to clear Eddy Coburn and sic the legal system on Balzac and Day."

"They'll find a way out of it, Erin. You know they will. They're smart. They're slick. And they have all the money in the world. They'll find some way to turn it all around, and I'll end up holding the bag, or worse. And if—" Laurie is about to say, *And if you think I'm going back with you, you're crazy*, but she stops short when she sees the man standing in the open doorway—Erin and Tommy must not have locked the door—holding a sawed-off shotgun.

The first thought that flashes through Laurie's mind is this: *Why is the president of Russia staying at a Motel 6?*

Then she realizes what's happened.

Royce Badgett closes the door behind him and smiles. "Well, well. The gang's all here."

At the same time Royce Badgett enters the hotel room, Vaughn picks up his cell to call Erin. It's been a half hour since he last spoke with her, and she'd told him she and Tommy were almost at the hotel. They should've been there by now, met with Laurie, and called him.

Vaughn has spent the past two hours pacing his apartment. The past two hours, and the two hours before that. This is already the longest night of his life, and it's not even half over.

Erin's phone starts to ring, and Tommy warns her with his eyes.

"Don't even think about it, sweetheart," Badgett says. He orders Laurie—the more terrified of the two women—to come to him, and he hands her a set of Safariland double cuffs. He nods toward Tommy and tells Laurie to secure Tommy's hands behind his back. "Nice and tight," he says.

Standing next to Laurie, on the far side of the bed from the door, Tommy takes in the room, the furniture, and all the players, searching for a way to avoid being restrained and to take out that scrawny crook Badgett. But the sawed-off is insurmountable. He could leap left, or right, or dive across the bed, but it would be impossible not be ripped apart by the shotgun blast, which would certainly catch Erin and Laurie as well.

"Fuck," Tommy says.

Badgett chuckles, and gestures with a nod for Laurie Mitzner to get busy. As Laurie moves away from the door toward Tommy to apply the plastic cuffs, Badgett sees Tommy and Erin look behind him. Before he has the time to figure out why, his right wrist—the wrist of his trigger-finger hand—is splintered by what feels like an iron vise grip, and he's lifted off the floor. When Badgett looks down at the vise grip, he sees that it's a huge human hand. Despite himself, he starts to scream as his shotgun hits the carpet.

Laurie Mitzner turns around and sees her captor being held—like a schoolboy holds his books—against the hip of the biggest man she's ever laid eyes on. Badgett is wriggling and writhing maniacally, like a cat held over a tubful of water.

Johnny Giacobetti balls his free fist and smashes it squarely into Royce's nose. The sound of crunching nasal cartilage is sickening, and Laurie and Erin wince. Still, they're all relieved when the Putin dop-pelgänger loses consciousness and stops moving.

Tommy stares, amazed, and says, "How in the hell—"

"I was following you. Well, not you. Her." He nods to Erin. "I was outside her apartment building when she ran out to your truck. I tailed you the whole way here. It wasn't long before I noticed this joker was tailing you, too. Who is he?"

"He grew up with Balzac," Erin answers for Tommy. "My guess is he's working for him." Erin pauses, then demands to know, "Why were you following me?"

"To get to the bottom of this."

Erin is taken aback. "What the hell does that mean? You *know* what's at the bottom of this. And who: Balzac and Day. You and your boss saw the video of Eddy inside the train."

"Yeah, we saw the video. And we heard the judge say it didn't really mean shit. Bunting handed it over, but he didn't admit anything about the scheme your boyfriend says was cooked up by those two P.I. lawyers. Your boyfriend, who looked the judge in the eye and sold her a bullshit story about some messenger giving him the video."

"Are you saying you don't trust us?"

"Trust?" This draws a snort from Johnny Giacobetti.

"What are you going to do now?" Tommy interjects.

The big man smiles but says nothing. His boss will soon be on his Gulfstream G650 headed for a nearby private airport. Jimmy Nutzo has the plane equipped with a special "fun" room, in which Royce Badgett will have no fun at all.

Laurie Mitzner collapses on the bed. "I don't feel so good."

"Laurie, stand up!" It's Erin. "We're going back to Philadelphia, and you're coming with us. You said you were afraid of Balzac? Look at this giant, then look at Balzac's little toad. Still afraid?"

Laurie shifts her gaze back and forth between Johnny G. and Royce Badgett. Then she slowly lifts herself from the bed and looks Johnny G. in the eyes. "Do it again," she says.

Giacobetti furrows his brow until he figures out what Laurie wants. Then he smiles and punches the unconscious Badgett in the face.

"Thank you," Laurie says. Then, to Tommy and Erin: "Come on. Let's get those bastards."

36

Friday, August 1

An absolute disaster. That's what Vaughn is thinking. It's almost eight o'clock, and Judge Johnson will take the bench minutes from now. And Vaughn has no witnesses. Erin, Laurie, and Tommy took off from Youngstown shortly after 12:30 this morning. That gave them seven and a half hours to get to Philly. Just enough time. But Erin called at 5:30 and told Vaughn they were caught in a massive traffic jam on the Pennsylvania Turnpike. A tractor-trailer overturned and blocked both lanes. Nothing was moving. Vaughn called back at 6:00 and 6:30, and nothing had changed. At 7:00, there was some movement, but not much. At 7:30, things were clearing and they were making good time, but they were still two hours out. With court starting at 8:00, Vaughn now has ninety minutes of trial time to fill.

Eddy is nervous. He fidgets, shifts in his seat, taps his feet. Vaughn is nervous, too, though he's doing his best not to show it. He looks back at Kate, Vaughn's parents, and the rest of the family, and smiles. His bosses, Susan and Mick, are present today, and he nods at them. With the revelation of the video, Susan has done a 180-degree turn and now fully supports Vaughn in his efforts to save his cousin and to nail those who caused the crash.

"Good morning, everyone." It's Judge Johnson. Vaughn turns and sees that she's already on the bench. The judge briefly discusses some administrative matters with her staff, then addresses Vaughn. "Present your first witness."

Vaughn stands. "Your Honor, we have an issue with our witnesses. They are caught in transit and won't be here until about nine thirty."

This doesn't sit well with Regina Johnson. "Well, then, your client's at bat." She nods at Eddy. "Mr. Coburn, please take the stand for cross-examination," she adds, turning to Christina Wesley.

Christina stands. "Your Honor, as you may recall from yesterday, it was my hope to call the defendant *after* the defense had presented all of its own witnesses."

"And it was my hope to be rich and retired by now," Regina Johnson says, drawing laughter. "I told you that you'd have your shot at the defendant. Well, here it is. Are you going to take it or not?"

"Absolutely."

Until now, Christina has remained seated while questioning witnesses. But for Eddy, she's going to stand. She walks to the podium between the prosecution and defense tables, and Vaughn still cannot get over her transformation since the Hanson case. Back then she'd been soft, maybe even a little flabby. Now, Christina's arms, visible in her sleeveless blouse, are cut. Her leg muscles are well defined. Her eyes are predatory, her movements ferociously feline.

Christina pauses at the podium and stares at Eddy. He holds her gaze for a moment, then looks away. As soon as he does so, Christina starts in on him.

"As an experienced engineer at the time of the crash, you knew all about the 2008 Chatsworth crash, correct?"

"Sure."

"Twenty-five people killed, dozens injured, all because the engineer was on his cell phone and didn't see a red signal."

"Yes."

"It was to prevent something like that from ever happening again that Amtrak instituted its rule prohibiting engineers from having live phones in locomotive cabs?"

"I guess so."

"You *guess so*?"

"I mean, I knew the rule. I didn't know why Amtrak instituted it."

"Are you serious? You didn't know that the purpose of the rule was to prevent engineers from being distracted and causing train crashes?"

Eddy's eyes dart to Vaughn, then back to the prosecutor. "No, I knew that it was to prevent you from being distracted."

"To prevent train crashes, to save lives?"

"Yes."

"And yet . . ." Christina pauses. "And yet you brought a second cell phone into the cab for the express purpose of making and receiving calls *during your run*."

"Calls with my wife only, because of the break-ins, beca—"

"And when questioned about it by the National Transportation Safety Board, you lied to them."

"Well . . ."

"Does this sound familiar to you? 'I always kept my cell phone in my knapsack, turned off.' Didn't you tell that to the NTSB when they interviewed you?"

"Yes."

"And how about this: Question, 'So, your phone was off, and it was in your knapsack?' Answer: 'Yes.' That was you again, to the NTSB?"

"Yes."

"And it was a lie, wasn't it, Mr. Coburn?"

Eddy looks down. "Yes."

"Oh, and here's another question: 'When was the last time you were on the phone before the accident?' Answer, 'I called Kate, my wife, *just before* I boarded the train.' Another lie?"

Eddy's shoulders slump. "Yes."

"I'm sorry, I didn't hear you."

"Yes!"

"You tried to deceive the NTSB—you tried to deceive the whole world—into believing that you had only one cell phone with you, and that it was turned off."

"I was worried about my wife, the baby. I—"

"Is there a wife exception to the Amtrak rule prohibiting cell-phone usage on the engines?"

"No."

"Now, Mr. Coburn, you had made this run before many times, isn't that right?"

"Sure."

"And you would have known that there would have been more than two hundred souls sitting behind you on that train?"

"There would be a lot of passengers, yes."

"You knew there'd be men and women and even children?"

"Yes."

"Some of them probably going to business meetings, others to attend shows or concerts?"

"Okay."

"Probably some college kids going back to school after a weekend with their parents?"

"That could happen."

"Young couples taking a day off, like Mr. and Mrs. Nash."

"Yes."

"And you knew, Mr. Coburn, that every single one of those people was dependent on you to get them there alive and safe."

"Absolutely." Eddy says the word proudly, sits up in his seat. "That's my job."

"Dependent on you not allowing yourself to become distracted for any reason."

"Any reason that I could prevent."

"That you could *prevent*? Is that what you said?"

"Yes, meaning—"

"You're not claiming you had no power to *prevent yourself* from bringing a second phone into the locomotive, are you?"

"What I mean is . . . No, I'm not saying that."

"You're not claiming that you had no power to prevent yourself from turning the phone on? That you had no power to prevent yourself from talking into the phone? That you had no power—"

"Objection." Vaughn is standing now. "Badgering the witness."

"Sustained. You're beating the proverbial horse, counselor. Move on."

Christina smiles. "Yes, Your Honor." She walks back to her table, pours water from the pitcher into her glass, and takes a slow sip. She glances at Vaughn, who spots the gleam in her eyes. He's given her an opportunity rarely accorded a prosecutor—the chance to question the defendant at a preliminary hearing—and she's making the most of it.

She returns to the podium. "Now, let's run through this story of yours about the shootout at the O.K. Corral."

"Objection." It's Vaughn.

"Sustained," says the judge, but she's smiling at the prosecutor's metaphor.

"You claim you were being shot at?"

"Yes."

"When you told us about your injuries yesterday, I don't remember you saying you'd been shot. Were you hit by any bullets, Mr. Coburn?"

"No."

"You said it was more than one shot. It was shot after shot after shot."

"Like, three or four. More, maybe."

"Yet neither Amtrak nor the NTSB found any bullets inside the locomotive. Did you know that?"

"No. I don't know what they found."

"Can you explain that to me? How can shot after shot be fired at the glass windshield and none of the bullets makes it inside the cab?"

"I've never even fired a gun. I don't know anything about that."

Christina smiles. "For that second call, who was on the other end of the phone?"

"Like I said, I didn't know—"

"What is the real reason you squatted down on the floor?"

"I didn't squat. I dove. I thought I was going to be killed."

"Your friend, Reggie Frye, the man who oversaw the TracVac you crashed your train into. He's the same one who gave you the phone."

"Just like I said, yes."

"When, exactly, did you and Reggie plan this whole thing?"

"Objection!" Vaughn is angry now. "There is no basis for a question like that. It doesn't even make sense—why would anyone plan to crash a train they were on themselves? Move to strike!"

The judge sustains the objection.

Christina is moving beyond recklessness to intentional conduct. Nothing would ever come of it at trial; there's no fair basis in the evidence to support even asking this line of questions. But Christina isn't doing this for the legal proceedings. She's doing it for sport. She's tasted blood. She likes it, and she's getting carried away. It happens to trial attorneys all the time.

Christina's torture of Eddy Coburn continues for another thirty minutes, until the judge shuts it down. "You've moved beyond beating the horse, Ms. Wesley, to stomping it. One more question."

Christina Wesley glares at Eddy. "Mr. Coburn, can you imagine anything more reckless for an engineer to do while driving a train carrying hundreds of people at eighty miles an hour than to knowingly put himself in a position where he can't see the track ahead and can't reach the controls to stop the train?"

His shoulders stooped, his voice weak, his head lowered so that he's looking into his lap, he answers, "Someone was shooting at me."

By the time he voices the words, Christina is halfway to her seat. She has no interest in his answer. And Vaughn senses that no one else does, either.

"Present your first witness," Judge Johnson says to Vaughn.

Vaughn glances at his cell phone and sees that Erin has not called or texted while Eddy's been on the stand. He has no idea where she and the others are, or when they'll arrive. He glances at the gallery, hoping to see—what? He doesn't know. No one in the audience can help him now. Not the press corps, which now includes some familiar faces from the national cable networks. Not his family members. Not the sheriff's deputies the judge has placed to ensure order. Certainly not Day or Balzac or their cadres of associates, including Corey King, who's shown up to watch Vaughn go down in flames. Not even Mick or Susan. *Unless* . . . It would be a dangerous move, he knows, because the testimony would only help to bury his cousin if, in the end, he hasn't convinced everyone that the accident wasn't Eddy's fault. Still, he must buy time for Erin and Laurie to testify. And the theme of his defense—hell, the *truth*—is that Eddy didn't do it.

In for a penny.

Vaughn turns to face the judge. "The defense calls Susan Klein."

Vaughn can hear the murmurs from the gallery. He turns to look at Susan and Mick, whose faces are painted with confusion. Finally, Susan shakes her head, stands, and walks toward the security door. The guard opens the door, and as Susan passes through it, she glances at Vaughn, who has no problem reading her thoughts: *I hope you know what you're doing.*

"Who is this witness, Mr. Coburn?" asks the judge.

"My boss, Your Honor. Susan Klein of McFarland and Klein."

"Excuse me?"

"She was on the train."

"You're calling a passenger as a witness?"

"Yes, Your Honor."

"Was she injured?"

"Oh, yes."

"And she's an attorney at your firm?" Regina Johnson tilts her head. "What am I missing here? An attorney representing a party can't also be a witness in the case."

"Ms. Klein doesn't represent the defendant," Vaughn says. "I do."

"But you work at McFarland and Klein. Your firm represents the defendant, and Ms. Klein owns the firm."

Vaughn lowers his head, closes his eyes. Then he looks up at Susan. "I quit."

"What?" says Susan.

"Are we good now, Your Honor?"

Regina Johnson shakes her head back and forth, plants her elbows on the bench, and spreads her hands. "Good? That's not a word I'd use about any of this. But if you're asking me if you can proceed now that Ms. Klein no longer represents the defendant, you may." The judge sits back in her chair, her face sending him the same message sent by his ex-boss: *I hope you know what you're doing.*

Vaughn spends a few moments having Susan explain for the record who she is, where she lives, and what she does for a living. Next, he has Susan establish that she was on Train 174 and asks her to explain what happened that day.

Susan takes a deep breath. "I took an Uber from my apartment to 30th Street Station. I was late calling the car and got there just in time to catch the train. I sat in the second car, the quiet car, because I wanted some time to think, gather myself. You see, the reason I was traveling to New York was to see my mother. Our relationship is . . . not an easy one." Susan pauses here and looks out at the gallery, where all the women who have mothers nod and smile.

"My mother had invited me up to see her. She said she had something she wanted to discuss."

"Not to put the cart before the horse, but did you ever find out what your mother wanted to talk to you about?"

Susan pauses and seems to look inward. Then she nods and says, "Her doctors found a spot, on her pancreas."

"I'm sorry to hear that. Please, when you're ready, go on. Tell us what happened on the train."

"For the first ten or so minutes, nothing happened. We pulled out of the station, made our way through the city. The sun was shining into the car. People were reading newspapers, typing on laptops, sleeping, or listening to headphones. Then, in an instant, everything was chaos." Susan describes the same nightmare scenario recounted by the earlier witnesses—the world turned on its side, people and belongings flying through the air, shattering glass, ballast stones ricocheting around the car. And when it stopped, the moaning and crying. Bones protruding from shredded clothes. Blood-soaked faces. People limping and crawling over the debris and one another. The blind woman shouting, "Clyde! Clyde!"

"But her dog, the German shepherd, was gone," Susan says.

Vaughn pauses, looks around. The court reporter is crying. Some of the men are fighting not to. In the gallery, he's sure, the same thing is happening. "Thank you," he says.

Judge Johnson turns to the prosecution table. "Questions?"

Christina Wesley thinks for a moment, glances at Vaughn, who can see that her mind is spinning furiously, trying to figure out why on earth he'd have presented a passenger witness. Trying to decipher his angle—for, surely, there must be one. Finally, no other course left, she looks at Susan and asks, "Why are you here?"

Susan leans forward on the witness stand. "To see that justice is done."

To everyone in the gallery, Susan's words wrap themselves around Eddy Coburn's throat like a hangman's noose. Eddy feels it. Vaughn does, too.

Judge Johnson waits for Susan to return to the gallery, then calls both attorneys to the bench. "Mr. Coburn, I have no idea what you're up to. But if those people weren't ready to crucify your client before, they sure are now. And none of what your witness said has any bearing on my decision whether to bind your client over for trial or not. Quite frankly, that little sideshow you just put on may be the worst case of legal malpractice I've ever seen."

"Your Honor, I—"

"I'm ready to rule, Mr. Coburn. Unless you have some more witnesses to reinforce the prosecution's case."

Vaughn glances through the glass wall to the gallery, where he sees Tommy and Erin walking in. "I do have more witnesses, Your Honor. But they won't help the prosecution one bit."

Judge Johnson purses her lips. This isn't what she wanted to hear. "I set aside the whole morning for this matter, Mr. Coburn. That's the only reason I'm going to let you continue. But I warn you. You keep this train moving in the same direction, and you're going to crash your client just as surely as he crashed the 174." Regina Johnson looks at the court reporter. "That last part isn't for the record. Understand?" The court reporter nods.

"Call your next witness, counselor."

37

FRIDAY, AUGUST 1, CONTINUED

Vaughn looks behind him, ecstatic to see Erin standing by the open door to the hallway. She looks exhausted but manages a smile. He nods, amazed at her guts and determination for crossing the state twice, overnight, to retrieve their key witness, save their case, save his cousin.

Vaughn announces Laurie's name and glances at Balzac, whose eyes widen and then narrow into a glare. Laurie walks through the gallery, making sure not to look at Balzac, and passes through the security door into the well of the courtroom. She takes the witness stand, then swears the oath, keeping her eyes glued to Vaughn the whole time.

Vaughn begins his questioning by walking Laurie through her background—where she was raised, where she went to college and law school. When he asks her where she works, she answers, "The Balzac Firm," and this generates interest in the room, including from the judge.

"You work for Mr. Balzac?" Regina Johnson asks from the bench. The judge is acutely aware of Balzac's presence, and of Day's; they're the most powerful gods in the city's P.I. pantheon. She's surely mingled with them at bench-bar conferences and charity events. Both of them have no doubt contributed to her campaign for the judgeship.

"Yes, Your Honor," Laurie answers.

"Well, I hope you do a good job, because he's watching," Judge Johnson says, and Laurie gets a sick look on her face.

"Your Honor," Vaughn says, putting an end to the exchange, "I'd like to begin the heart of the testimony by showing a minute of crash video."

Regina Johnson rolls her eyes. "Haven't we all seen enough newsfeed, Mr. Coburn? Is another run-through really going to be helpful?"

"I think it will, Your Honor. And it's only a minute." Vaughn is playing fast and loose here. First, he's misled the judge into believing that she's just going to see familiar footage. Second, he's putting the cart before the horse with respect to getting the video on the record. The right way to do this would be to have Laurie lay the foundation for the video's admissibility before playing it. But he doesn't want to tip his hand as to what's coming because he wants to take no chance of Regina Johnson excluding it before it's shown.

"All right, then. Let's get it done." The judge has her bailiff set up the big screen again.

When it's ready, Vaughn hands up the memory stick, and the bailiff starts the video. The railroad track is the first thing that comes into view, taken from sixty feet above. In the distance, the train enters the curve, rounds it, and moves into the straightaway. After a few seconds, it passes directly below the camera and speeds down the track. In the distance sits the TracVac.

Vaughn sees a frown form on Regina Johnson's face. It's dawning on her that she's seeing something vastly different from what has been aired before. She pulls her eyes from her screen just long enough to glance at Vaughn, then looks back at the video.

Vaughn turns his seat and looks out the corner of his eye into the visitor's gallery. Everyone is leaning forward in their seats. Mouths are agape. Eyes wide open, or clenched shut. He hears someone start to cry, probably a crash victim.

"Oh, no!" someone behind him shouts.

"My God!"

"No, no, no!"

The voices are raised now, and Vaughn knows they're seeing the locomotive crash into the TracVac, watching the cars behind it fly from the tracks, landing every which way.

As the screen goes black, Vaughn turns his head to Christina Wesley, who looks confused. He sends her a message with his eyes: *I told you this isn't what you think.* He holds her gaze for a long moment, then addresses the court.

"That's the end of the recording, Your Honor."

Regina Johnson is silent for a moment, then asks, "Do you mind telling the court what we just saw?"

"The train crash, Your Honor. Actually, the train *crashing*."

"And you got this how?"

"That's what the witness will testify to." Then, without waiting for more from the court, Vaughn addresses Laurie. "Please explain to Her Honor how you obtained this video."

Laurie takes a very long, very deep breath. "I was at work late one night . . ."

Balzac is glaring directly up at Laurie, his teeth bared, looking like he's ready to smash through the glass, race to the stand, and tear her apart. But she stays strong, and it doesn't take long to tell the tale. How she went into her boss's office late one night to deliver a legal brief. How the computer screen came on when she laid the brief on the desk, probably because she bumped the computer mouse. How she watched the video, uncomprehendingly at first, then in horror.

"And what did you do when you realized what you were seeing?" Vaughn asks.

"I knew I had to do something, tell someone. But I didn't know what, or who. So I made a video with my cell phone. A video of the video. And then, I . . . I did nothing for a long time. More than a month. But it was eating at me, what I saw. And what it meant. And I was afraid that Mr. Balzac knew I'd seen the video. So I told my friend Erin, Erin Doyle, and she had me show it to you."

"When was that?"

"It was last week."

"You said that what the video *meant* was weighing on you. What did you mean by that?"

"It was obvious. The video showed that Mr. Balzac knew the crash was going to happen. How else would he know to have the drone there, to videotape it?"

"Wait! *What?*" It's the judge, who looks at Vaughn. "Are you trying to persuade me that Mr. Balzac was somehow involved in causing the crash?"

"That's exactly what I'm saying," Vaughn answers, his voice rising with each word. "And what the evidence will prove. And not just him, but Geoffrey—"

"Objection!" shouts Christina.

"This is ridiculous!" It's Balzac, now standing, his face almost up against the glass. "I've never seen that video before in my life! This is perjury! I want her cited for contempt!"

"Outrageous!" declares Geoffrey Day, standing next to Balzac.

The gallery is in full-blown pandemonium now. Half the people are out of their seats. Some of the crash victims are weeping openly. Others are shouting angrily. Members of the press corps disregard courtroom rules and talk excitedly into their cell phones.

On the bench, Judge Johnson smashes her gavel. "Order! Order! I will have order, or I'll clear the courtroom."

It takes some time, but Regina Johnson finally regains control. She looks at Vaughn and, through clenched teeth, says, "If you think I'm going to let you—"

Christina sees the judge is about to shut it all down and jumps to her feet. "I want her!" she interrupts loudly. "I want cross-examination. I'm entitled to—"

"The witness isn't done testifying, Your Honor," Vaughn interrupts. "I'm not finished questioning her."

Regina Johnson glares at Vaughn, then at the prosecutor. "You're half-right, Mr. Coburn. Your witness isn't done testifying. But you are done questioning her."

"But—"

"No buts, counselor." The judge turns to Christina. "All right—have at it."

The ADA almost runs to the podium. "So this tape you just showed us—it came from your cell phone?"

"Yes, I—"

"It's not the original tape, or even a tape downloaded from a computer?"

"No. It's—"

"And all we have is your word that it came from Mr. Balzac's computer?"

"Well, it did—"

"Do you have proof of that? Corroboration of any kind that this video was recorded from Mr. Balzac's computer?"

Laurie closes her eyes. "No."

"How did Mr. Balzac get it?"

"How? I guess—"

"You guess? Do you know?"

"No, I—"

"When did he get it?"

"I'm not sure."

"Who took this video?"

"How would I know that?"

"So you don't know who took the video, or when they gave it to Mr. Balzac?"

"That's right."

"Do you know *why* it was given it to Mr. Balzac, assuming you're telling the truth?"

"You'd have to ask him—"

"Did you?"

"What?"

"What do you mean, 'What?' You say you came across a video showing the train actually crashing. Didn't it cross your brilliant legal mind, even for a second, to go to Mr. Balzac and say, 'Hey, I accidentally saw a crash video on your computer. What's up?'"

Laurie lowers her head.

"I'll take that as a no." Christina pauses to let it all sink in, to the judge, the press, the victims. Then, it dawns on her to ask, "Were you alone when you went into Mr. Balzac's private office?"

"That time, yes."

"*That time*? There were others? And people were with you?"

"One other time."

"And when was that, and who all was in on it?"

Laurie glances at Vaughn: *I'm so sorry.* "Mr. Coburn and Erin Doyle."

"Don't make me call for order again," Judge Johnson calls out to the gallery, which, once again, is in turmoil. "Proceed."

"Who is Erin Doyle?"

"A friend. She works at Day and Lockwood."

"And her relationship with Mr. Coburn?"

"They're . . . dating."

"Hold on a second," Judge Johnson interrupts. "Are you telling me that you and Mr. Coburn and his girlfriend broke into Mr. Balzac's office?"

"Well, I let them in. I work there."

"But you didn't have your boss's permission to be in his office."

"No, Your Honor."

"When was this?"

"Saturday."

"Last week?"

"Yes."

"At night, I suppose? So Mr. Balzac wouldn't be there to catch you?"

"Yes, Your Honor."

Vaughn lowers his head.

Eddy is leaning over the table, head in his hands.

Behind them, Eddy's mother, Claire, and Kate are crying. The men sit stone-faced.

"I've heard enough from this witness," says the judge. "I'm calling a recess. When we come back, barring some miracle, I'm going to rule."

Vaughn and Eddy stand as the judge leaves the bench. The deputies take Eddy out the side door and into the holding cell. Before they do, Eddy searches Vaughn's eyes for something to hold onto. He finds nothing.

"I'm sorry," Vaughn says under his breath. But Eddy's already gone.

On the other side of the security glass, Geoffrey Day winces. His stomach is in knots. "I just want this to be over," he says quietly to Balzac.

"Shut up, you idiot," Balzac shoots back. He resolves to buy Badger a second house, with a really big basement. And the first one to go in it will be this witless debutante. Him and his drone. Balzac takes a deep breath. Then another one.

Badger, where are you?

Balzac stands and leaves the courtroom, finds some members of the press conferring in the hallway, who ask him for a comment. Balzac pauses, then says, "I've sued some of the biggest corporations in this country. Sued them hard. But I've never sued someone as hard as I'm going to sue that little insect. Him and his girlfriend. And my fired-as-of-right-this-instant *former* associate."

Balzac affects a tone of outrage, and he is mighty pissed, but inside he's sporting a rueful smile, too. What young Coburn failed to see coming was that the story he planned to peddle could never be sold—it was too implausible. The idea that a pair of personal-injury attorneys would crash a train just to drum up cases is so fantastic it just couldn't be true. No reasonable person could accept it as a possibility. And therein lies the core genius of the whole plan: its audacity. Then again, audacity is at the heart of all great plans.

Balzac pushes past the reporters, takes the stairs down a floor, and finds an empty hallway. He still can't believe Laurie Mitzner showed up in court. Something went terribly wrong with Royce's plan. He needs to find out what. He's tried reaching Badger all morning, but all he gets is Royce's voice mail. He wonders whether his old friend suffered a heart attack and is lying in some hospital. Or morgue.

Vaughn waits until the judge's staff has cleared the courtroom, then walks over to Christina Wesley, who's still at counsel table. "I really need to talk to you," he says.

"I think you've said quite enough. You and your witness. The two of you, and your girlfriend, make quite a little threesome, though I'd expect you could have thought of something a lot more fun than ransacking Balzac's office in the dead of night. That part of her story, by the way, I believe. As for the video and the lunatic notion that Balzac—and Day, too, did I hear that right?—conspired to crash a train? Well, I think there's something wrong with you, Vaughn."

"Christina—"

"Look, I get it. He's your cousin. You want to free him. But a preliminary hearing is not the place to do it. And your story . . . Jesus Christ, man, it's like you've become unhinged. What are you *thinking*?"

"But it's true. All of it. Please!" he says, putting up his hand to stop her from interrupting. "Just listen. There's a lot more than the video. Laurie found a note in Day's desk drawer. It's from a marketing firm in New York. And guess what's written on the note: 'You're a dead man. Bang, bang, motherfucker, bang, bang.'"

"So you molded your client's testimony to fit the note—"

"Then there's Day's and Balzac's websites. The very day of the crash, within hours, they put up long, detailed sections on their sites about the history of train crashes and railroad law. Stuff that would have taken days, at least, to write and prepare." Vaughn continues, spitting out every ounce of evidence they've found: the complaints that allege Eddy's criminal history long before it came out in the press; Balzac's link to Jack Bunting; Bunting's likely link to Reggie Frye, who gave Eddy the cell phone; Day's purchase of a drone. As he lays it out, Vaughn sees Christina studying him for any hint of bullshit, any clue that he doesn't believe what he's telling her.

"Vaughn, I don't even know how to respond to all that, other than to say that you need help. And I'm not saying that to be mean. I'm saying it as a colleague. You need to take a break. Give this case over to someone who can be objective about it. And find a good therapist."

38

FRIDAY, AUGUST 1, CONTINUED

Vaughn watches Christina pass through the security door, then looks at Erin and Laurie, who are waiting together for him at the back of the gallery. He nods but doesn't join them. He has nothing to say. The fight is over. He sits at counsel table and waits.

Five minutes later, Vaughn is pulled from his thoughts by the sound of someone knocking on the security glass behind him. He turns and sees Tommy, who points to James Nunzio and Johnny Giacobetti, now sitting in the second row. Tommy waves several pages of white copy paper and signals that he got them from the mobsters. Vaughn walks to the security door, buzzes it open, and takes the pages, then stands by the door and reads them.

Holy shit. Holy. Effing. Shit.

Vaughn turns to Nunzio and Giacobetti, a huge smile on his face. They ignore him, but he smiles nonetheless. He sits and studies the pages in detail. It's all set out for him: what questions to ask the witness and what the answers will be. Vaughn's hands are shaking. He struggles not to hyperventilate.

Fifteen minutes after she called the break, Judge Johnson is back on the bench. Before she has the chance to say she's reached her decision, Vaughn is on his feet. "The defense has one more witness, Your Honor."

"It's a little too late for—"

"The defense calls Royce Badgett," Vaughn announces over the judge.

"Absolutely not!" Balzac's stentorian voice booms from behind the safety glass. "I forbid it!" He's on his feet, fists pressed against the glass.

Vaughn turns immediately to Christina Wesley, his eyes pleading: *Don't object—help me do this.*

But Christina isn't looking at Vaughn. She's staring directly at Balzac. And Vaughn realizes what's happening: Christina is having an *Oh shit!* moment. She's thinking, *What if it's true? What if Balzac really* was *behind the crash?* In Vaughn's mind's eye, Christina is mentally reviewing the in-cab video showing Eddy diving for the floor, the drone video showing the crash. She's trying to recall what he told her about the complaints and the websites and the "bang, bang" letter in Day's desk, and the relationships between Balzac and Bunting and Frye.

Christina turns from Balzac to Vaughn. Her eyes are wide, her mouth hanging open. They stare at each other until the judge's voice pulls them apart.

"Sit that man down!" Regina Johnson is angry, and the sheriff's deputies rush toward Balzac and push him into his seat. Then, to Balzac: "I will make the decisions as to who testifies and who doesn't." Turning to Vaughn, she demands to know who the witness is.

"He's a personal friend of Mr. Balzac, Your Honor, and he has first-hand information into *exactly* what caused the crash." Vaughn pauses, looks at Christina, and says, "I've spoken with the prosecution, and she does not object."

"Is that true?" the judge asks from the bench.

Christina Wesley looks hard into Vaughn's eyes. Her message: *You better not screw me on this.*

"The Commonwealth has no objection."

"Then you may proceed, Mr. Coburn. But get this done fast. I'm ready to rule."

Vaughn turns to the gallery, signals to Tommy, who is at the back door. Tommy opens the door, and through it passes Royce Badgett—or what's left of him. Badgett's dominant right hand is wrapped in gauze. Beneath the gauze is a nailless thumb and four stumps where his fingers used to be. He's limping badly, thanks to drill holes in his left kneecap and an anal orifice so wide it could accommodate more traffic than the German autobahn. His face is purple and swollen.

It takes Badgett quite a while to pass through the gallery and court-room. He grunts as he shuffles, moans as he climbs the witness stand, and whimpers as he slowly, oh so slowly, sits.

"Mr. Badgett, you look like you're in a great deal of pain." Regina Johnson leans down from the bench. "Mind telling me what happened?"

Royce thinks for a moment. "I fell."

"You suffered all those injuries in a fall?"

"It was a nasty fall, Your Honor. Plus, I was carrying hedge trim-mers," he adds, holding up his right hand. "And there was bees, a whole swarm of 'em," he says, motioning toward his face. "I'm allergic to bees. And nuts."

"You were carrying nuts when you fell?"

"No. Don't get near 'em. I'm allergic."

The judge rolls her eyes. "Just . . . get on with this," she says to Vaughn.

Vaughn waits a beat, then gets right to it. "Mr. Badgett, where were you and what were you doing at 12:18 p.m. on June sixth of this year?"

Royce Badgett glances into the gallery, where his eyes fix for a moment on the faces of James Nunzio and Johnny Giacobetti. Then he looks to Balzac.

"Mr. Badgett? Answer the question."

Badgett's shoulders slump. He closes his eyes, then opens them. "I was kneeling next to Track 2, about eighteen hundred feet north of the Torresdale curve, aiming my semiautomatic M25 at Amtrak Train 174, firing bullets at the windshield at two-second intervals."

The gallery explodes.

"Order! Order!" Judge Johnson, almost shouting, bangs her gavel—something that almost never needs to be done during a preliminary hearing.

Vaughn takes the opportunity afforded him by the uproar to glance back at Benny Balzac. The monster's eyes are filled with rage, his face is purple, the veins in both temples throbbing. His fists are balled. Vaughn can tell the only reason Balzac hasn't already smashed his way through the security glass is because both his shoulders are being held down by the meaty hands of sheriff's deputies.

Order is finally restored, not because of Regina Johnson's gavel banging, but because everyone wants to hear what's coming next. The judge gives Vaughn the go-ahead, and he resumes his questioning.

"Why were you firing at the train?"

"The boss asked me to."

"Who is the boss?"

Badgett glances past Vaughn. He hesitates again, and it becomes clear to Vaughn that what Badgett's about to do is killing him. He suspects that Badgett would rather die than betray his lifelong friend. Judging from Badgett's injuries, Vaughn guesses that Badgett begged to do just that on Nunzio's jet.

"Ah, that'd be Benny. Mr. Balzac."

"How do you know Benjamin Balzac?"

"We grew up together."

"And Jack Bunting?"

"Him, too. Me, Benny, and Jack were best friends. Then, and now."

"That's a lie!" It's Balzac. He's managed to free himself from the deputies, and he's on his feet again. "That man's not my friend. I haven't seen him in almost thirty years! He's nothing to me!"

Badgett shrinks, his heart clearly broken. After a moment, he looks up at the judge. "You remember that music from *Star Wars*?" he says. "What they played whenever Darth Vader showed up? The Empire's theme?" Judge Johnson nods, and Badgett hands her his cell phone. "Press 'Star,' then 'One.'"

Regina Johnson takes the phone and hits the keys. After a few seconds, those sitting near Balzac hear the muffled music.

Someone in the gallery stands, points to Benjamin Balzac, and yells to the judge, "It's coming from him!"

The judge orders the deputies to remove Balzac's cell phone from his suit jacket. When they do, Darth Vader's theme is heard in the gallery and courtroom proper. One of the deputies looks at the phone and shouts up to the judge. "The screen identifies the caller as 'Honey Badger.'"

"My nickname," Badgett tells the judge.

Regina Johnson cringes.

"Was anyone with you when you were shooting at the train?" asks Vaughn.

"That tall guy, in the tan suit," Badgett says. "Behind Mr. Balzac and Mr. Day."

"Let the record reflect the witness has identified Corey King, an associate at Day and Lockwood." Vaughn pauses long enough to enjoy the horror in Corey King's eyes. Then he asks, "What was Mr. King doing?"

"He was on the phone with the engineer."

"What was he talking about?"

"He wasn't really talking. He was, like, scaring him."

Vaughn pauses. "You're a dead man. Bang, bang, motherfucker. Bang, bang?"

Badgett nods.

"Answer out loud, please," says the judge.

"Yeah, that's what he said."

Vaughn drags Badgett through Reggie Frye's role in getting the cell phone to Eddy and moving the TracVac onto Track 2, and Bunting's role in getting Frye to do so. Royce testifies that he first fired a weapon in the army, where they told him he was a natural and made him into a sniper.

"Eighty-seven confirmed kills," Royce says proudly. "Maybe not Chris Kyle numbers, but almost all of mine were head shots."

On a hunch, Vaughn asks Badgett about the break-ins in Eddy's neighborhood, and Royce confirms that Balzac thought up the idea, and he—Royce—made it happen. "Not me personally, but some guys I hired."

"What was the purpose of the drone?"

"Oh, Benny—Mr. Balzac—was so pissed about that. He said that other one, Day, was a friggin' idiot to film the crash. He didn't use the word *friggin'*, though."

Geoffrey Day is on his feet as soon as his name is mentioned. He hisses at Badgett, firing off the words *outrageous*, *slander*, *libel*, *infamy*, and *scurrilous*. Balzac finally has enough and pulls Day into his seat.

Vaughn waits while the judge cautions Day and Balzac. Then he asks, "Why not just park the TracVac in the middle of the curve itself? There'd be no chance for the engineer to see it in time to stop before hitting it."

"Blame," Badgett answers. "The whole point was to set up the engineer. Make it look like he could have stopped the train in time but wasn't paying attention. The boss said that would be recklessness, and there'd be punitive damages, which are a lot more than regular damages."

Vaughn glances up at Regina Johnson, who looks like she's about ready to have a stroke. As a judge in Philadelphia's criminal-justice system, she's certainly seen her share of villains. But he doubts she's ever witnessed evil as matter-of-fact, even cavalier, as what she's witnessing now.

"Mr. Badgett, do you know where Reggie Frye is?"

Another glance at Jimmy Nutzo and Johnny G. "He's in my basement."

"What's he doing there?"

"Not much."

Vaughn pauses. "What's his condition?"

"Dead."

"I see. And how did he get that way?"

"I may have helped."

"Nothing further."

Regina Johnson looks at Christina. "Cross?"

The young prosecutor stares at Royce Badgett like someone watching aliens walk out of a spaceship. If she's heard the judge, she's showing no sign of it.

"Ms. Wesley, do you have questions for this witness?"

"Huh? Oh, yes, Your Honor." Christina stands and walks to the podium. "Mr. Badgett, there were no bullets found inside the locomotive. How could that be?"

"Frangible bullets."

"Frangible?"

"They disintegrate on impact. Most are made of powdered copper and tin, or copper and nylon, and have no jacket. They only disintegrate on impact with metal, normally. I had to make my own special recipe to get them hard enough to fire out of my rifle but soft enough to disintegrate when they hit the locomotive's glass windshield. That was a lot of work. I'd say I earned my fifty-five hundred."

"Fifty-five hundred?"

"Dollars. That's how much the boss paid me."

Christina is, momentarily, speechless. Everyone watching is stunned and silently asking the same question: *This little monster killed and injured all those people for five grand?*

"Five thousand, five hundred dollars?"

"That's more than I normally ask from the boss."

"Normally? You mean you've done this kind of thing before for Mr. Balzac?"

Badgett's shoulders slump, and everyone in the courtroom can read what he's thinking: *Oh shit.*

"Yes."

"Give me an example."

Badgett doesn't answer.

The judge leans across to him. "An example, Mr. Badgett. Now. Or plead the Fifth."

Badgett sighs. "You remember that big crash a few years back, ·on the Schuylkill Expressway, when that tractor-trailer hit that bus? I helped set that up. But the driver started pressing Benny for more money than they agreed to, and I had to put him in the basement. He's in the vault next to Reggie Frye."

"Vault?"

"I built it myself," Badgett says. "I don't know if you've ever had to bury someone in a field, but let me tell you, it's a pain in the ass."

"Just how many bodies are buried in your basement, Mr. Badgett?"

"Four." Badgett turns to the judge. "It's a small cellar."

Christina Wesley blinks and stands perfectly still. She stares at the man on the stand, seemingly reaching for more words, but none will come. Behind her, on the other side of the security glass, everyone else is reacting the same way. No one is talking. No one is moving. The shuffling on the uncomfortable wooden benches has ceased. The reporters have stopped typing on their iPads and tablets. Everyone is simply staring at Royce Badgett.

Everyone, Vaughn realizes, except Benny Balzac and the man that Benny must sense looking at him from the other side of the aisle. When Balzac turns his head to the left and sees James Nunzio's dead, black eyes boring a hole through him, the lawyer clearly no longer cares about the press, or the crash victims, or the sheriff's deputies, or even the judge. All that matters to him is . . .

"I didn't know!" Balzac shouts. "I didn't know your son was on that train, I swear!"

Vaughn learned in science class about black holes in space. Spheres so dense they emit no light whatsoever. He sees two of them now, occupying the spaces where Jimmy Nutzo's eyes used to be.

"You can't blame me for that!" Balzac, now half standing, continues his plea. "Jimmy, please. I . . ."

Suddenly, Balzac turns to his right, where Geoffrey Day is sitting, leaning away, trying to distance himself. Balzac lunges at Day, puts a hand around his throat. "You idiot! You had to have a drone!"

Balzac is a thick man, and strong, and it takes some time for the sheriff's deputies to pry him off Geoffrey Day. When they do, Day collapses in a heap on the floor, massaging his throat and gasping.

Judge Johnson pounds her gavel, orders the deputies, "Take those two men into custody. And that tall one behind them."

As the deputies cuff Day and Balzac and Corey King, another man, very large, approaches them.

"Who are you, sir?" The judge addresses him through the security glass.

"Your Honor, my name is Ed Iwicki. I'm the chief of police for Amtrak. And I sure would be happy if you'd let me assist in taking these motherfuckers into custody."

Regina Johnson's neck snaps back, and her eyes widen. Then she leans forward and smiles. "Deputies, please let Captain Iwicki help you with the motherfuckers."

The pronouncement causes the room to erupt. People cheer and clap and shout, "Hear, hear!" Half a dozen reporters run from the gallery into the hallway. Crash victims and their families surround the Coburn clan, hugging them, shaking their hands, crying with them.

The judge watches from the bench and shakes her head. "What is this crazy world coming to?" she mutters under her breath.

"That's a fact," says Royce Badgett, who looks pale and spent.

Regina Johnson turns to the small man in the witness stand. "I forgot all about you." Then she has more deputies take hold of Badgett and tells them to walk him to the holding cells. "Just don't put him in with Mr. Balzac," she says. "I don't think he'd last a minute."

Once he's removed from the courtroom, Judge Johnson addresses everyone else. "I'm going to take a short break. Then I'll come back and announce my ruling."

Vaughn wishes the judge would just announce her decision now. *It can only be one thing, can't it?* He feels sure of it, but he's felt sure so many times through this ordeal and been wrong about almost everything. But the judge's ruling can wait. Right now, there's something more important. He turns to embrace Eddy.

But Eddy isn't in his seat. He's standing behind counsel table, his forehead and both palms pressed against the security glass, on the other side of which is Kate—holding Emma—her own forehead pressed against the glass.

A dagger pierces Vaughn's heart. *Please, God . . .* He doesn't complete the sentence; God already knows what he's praying for.

Twenty minutes later, Regina Johnson retakes the bench. She doesn't waste time, and she doesn't mince words. "This case—the whole thing—the train crash, the pain and death suffered by so many people, these proceedings—what happened and what almost happened here—is the biggest disaster I've ever had the misfortune to be a part of. Mr. Coburn," she says, looking directly at Eddy, "this court finds insufficient evidence to bind you over for trial. Go back and join your family, and get out of here. That goes for the rest of you, too. Get out. I want this courtroom cleared in ten minutes."

Now Vaughn gets his hug. Eddy embraces him with such force that Vaughn thinks he can feel his ribs crack.

Eddy kisses Vaughn on his cheek as he holds him. "I knew you'd do it! I knew it!"

Vaughn laughs as his eyes tears up. "That makes one of us." He hugs his cousin and slaps his back. Then he steps away and turns toward the prosecution table. Christina Wesley is gone, and he doesn't blame her. He'll have to thank her later for taking an enormous risk.

Eddy brushes past Vaughn and races to the security door. The whole family surrounds him the minute he enters the gallery. Vaughn waits a few minutes, then joins them. His uncle Frank takes Vaughn's face in his meaty paws and looks him in the eye. Frank tries to push the words out, but he chokes up, and Vaughn jumps in to save him.

"Uncle Frank, don't. It's okay. I get it." Before he can say more, Aunt Claire and Eddy's sisters are all over him with hugs and kisses of their own. Vaughn sees his parents nearby, watching and smiling. He joins them as soon as Eddy's mom and sisters release him.

In the back of the courtroom, Tommy, Erin, and Laurie stand together, waiting to catch Vaughn's eye. As soon as they do, they motion that they're leaving and will talk to him later. He shoots them the "okay" sign. He smiles at Mick and Susan, and they smile back, Mick like a proud mentor, Susan in gratitude.

Vaughn spends a few minutes accepting thanks from a dozen or so crash victims, then rounds up his family and leads them past the press stalking the hallways, to the elevators, then the building lobby and the pavement outside. Once his parents, aunt, uncle, and cousins are all safely in the underground parking garage, Vaughn hails a cab.

Ten minutes later, he walks through the open door into Erin Doyle's apartment, and into her arms.

39

Friday, August 29

It's 8:30 a.m., one month exactly since the preliminary hearing. The weeks since Vaughn's victory have been good ones, and busy. Mick and Susan gave him his job back before he even had the chance to ask. He's been interviewed on local and national news shows, and potential clients are lining up to hire him. His relationship with Erin feels stronger every day.

Eddy, Kate, and baby Emma moved back to the farm, which is being rented for them by Eddy and Vaughn's family, with McFarland and Klein chipping in a little as well. Eddy's promised Kate that once he gets a job, he'll find a nicer farmhouse to rent. They both know he'll never be an engineer again, which hurts because he came to love the railroad. Still, someone will hire him—though who, and when, is anyone's guess.

As for the perpetrators, whose plan almost landed Eddy in prison for the rest of his life, things turned out much worse. Royce Badgett never made it out of the Criminal Justice Center. An hour after the preliminary hearing wrapped up, the sheriff's deputies escorted Badgett to the elevators for the trip to the basement and then, via bus, to county lockup. Badgett and his honor guard stood by a pair of closed elevator doors next to an open pair of elevator doors protected only by a plastic yellow Out of Service sign and yellow caution tape—a familiar site at the CJC. Terrified that Jimmy Nutzo would not honor his agreement to kill him quickly, Royce Badgett saw his opening and took it. He broke free of the deputies—though, to be fair, they probably weren't really holding him that tightly—and threw himself down the open shaft. Sadly for Royce, it wasn't the three-story fall that killed him, but the elevator that'd been parked just above, on the fourth floor. At the exact moment the Badger dived into the open shaft, a repairman signaled the elevator to descend to the basement. The deputies stood helplessly as Royce's screams were replaced by the sounds of crunching bone.

Badgett's death was good for Jimmy Nunzio, of course. It's not wise to keep someone around who could tip the cops off to the kill room on your jet. The DA didn't miss Badgett, either, because everything he said on the stand was corroborated. The police found the bodies in his basement, which included two former truck drivers and an eyewitness to a small plane crash. Also found were Badgett's own hand-drawn diagrams of his sniping assignment—Honey Badger, it turned out, was a meticulous planner. His cell phone had pictures of him, Balzac, and Jack Bunting on fishing trips and sitting at a tiki bar in the Caribbean—unidentified but no doubt high-priced escorts on their laps at both locations. There were also pictures from a hunting lodge sans female companions, though the men weren't smiling quite as broadly in those.

In Geoffrey Day's office, the authorities found the original "bang, bang note," a copy of which they also found in Corey King's office. Directions for flying the drone were found in the office of another associate as close to Day as King was.

Two days into his stay at the Curran-Fromhold correctional facility, Geoffrey Day was approached in the shower by two men. One of them held a plastic bottle containing some sort of accelerant, the other a silver, metallic Zippo lighter. Twenty minutes later, the rising sun of the plaintiff's P.I. bar was medevaced to Crozer Burn Center, where he died in screaming pain late the following week. Geoffrey's nurses were convinced he would have passed much sooner were it not for the constant ministrations of his brilliant burn-treatment specialist, Stephen F. X. Nunzio, MD, brother of reputed mobster James F. X. Nunzio.

Benjamin Balzac remains alive and in custody, though Vaughn has heard via the criminal-defense-attorney grapevine that Benny Balls is in poor spirits and worse health. According to a lawyer representing an inmate in Balzac's part of the prison, the once-proud attorney spends all day and night curled in a fetal position next to his stainless-steel toilet and refuses to leave the cell for any reason, including nourishment or hygiene. As a result, he's lost twenty-five pounds and is subjected to force-feeding.

For a long while, Vaughn harbored fears of retaliation by Jimmy Nutzo. He called the mobster at his office the day after the preliminary hearing. The underboss kept him on hold for five minutes. Vaughn didn't dare hang up.

"I called to thank you," Vaughn said when Nunzio finally got on the line. "Your man saved my whole team at that motel. And you saved my cousin at the preliminary hearing." Vaughn paused and waited for a response. When none came, he got to the real point of his call. "So you saved us, and I got you justice for your son."

Vaughn waited again, and counted silently. When he reached ten, Jimmy Nunzio, his voice flat, matter-of-fact, said, "You think that makes us even?"

"Well—"

"Don't call me again. And do not come to my office."

The line went dead, and Vaughn sat at his desk with a racing heart.

And then . . . nothing. Weeks went by, and Vaughn heard nothing from the mobster. Finally, this week, he began to breathe easier. Obviously, the mobster had come to accept that Eddy was not the cause of his son's death and to realize that, to the contrary, he was as much a victim as Alexander Nunzio.

Vaughn sits now on the front stoop of his apartment building, waiting for the tow truck to carry away his Jeep. He was going to drive Erin to Stone Harbor that morning for a long weekend leading into Labor Day; Erin had a lot of free time on her hands now that Day and Lockwood is closed and being wound down by a court-appointed receiver. But Vaughn's Jeep wouldn't start. So Erin is going to pick him up in her own car as soon as the Jeep is hauled off to get fixed. At least that was the plan an hour ago. He's called her twice since then and keeps getting kicked to voice mail.

Vaughn pulls his cell phone from his pocket to call Erin again when a black limousine with gangster-tinted windows stops on the street just to his left. The rear door opens, and Johnny Giacobetti rises out of it like Jack's beanstalk, uncoiling until he reaches his full height. He walks up to Vaughn, his face a study in seriousness.

"Mr. Nunzio wants a word."

Vaughn looks up and down the street, then follows Giacobetti to the limo. He reaches the rear passenger door and, before he has the chance to see inside, is pushed hard from behind. He flies into the back seat, and Johnny G., getting in behind him, shoves Vaughn the whole way across to the driver's side. Vaughn tries to open the door, to escape, but it's locked.

Vaughn turns to Giacobetti. "What the *hell*?"

"I told you," Johnny answers. "Mr. Nunzio wants a meeting."

"A meeting. Where?"

"On a little farm in Lancaster County."

Vaughn's mind flashes to his cousin, to Kate, and the baby.

"But . . . there's no reason . . . Eddy wasn't to blame for that crash. You know that. And so does your boss."

"Not what the new lawyers are saying. He let himself get played. Lost his 'situational awareness.'" Giacobetti skips a beat, then says, "I was there when the boss explained his business model to you. Rewards and punishments. I don't know how he could have been any clearer."

"And Kate and the baby? Where do they fit into your boss's *business plan*?"

"You know anyone who served overseas? Friends of mine did. Came back with all sorts of interesting terms. *Fog of war. Collateral damage.*"

Vaughn balls his fists. The car's racing now, making light after light. He can't open his door, but maybe if he gets into it with Johnny G., the driver will stop the car and he can jump over the front seat.

"Don't even think about it," Johnny G. says. "You'd be lights-out before you got the first punch off."

Vaughn bares his teeth but leans back in the seat. His only play is with Jimmy Nunzio himself. The man's a bloodthirsty savage. But he's smart. He's capable of listening to reason.

The driver takes the limousine west on 76, then south on 222, through the town of Lancaster, past New Providence, past Quarryville, deep into farmland. No one says anything until Johnny Giacobetti, enjoying the distress on Vaughn's face, says, "You heard the story, right?"

"The fiancée, the boss, and the coffin? Who hasn't?"

Johnny smiles and Vaughn's stomach drops as he realizes what Nunzio is doing. He's planning on writing another story, going to use him and Eddy, maybe their whole family, to send a message. Like the myth about Keyser Söze, except the Nunzio legend is real.

The car pulls off the two-lane road onto the dirt-and-gravel driveway. Parked in front of the dilapidated farmhouse are the black Escalade, a blue Escalade EXT pickup with two enormous dogs in the flatbed, and a cherry-red convertible Porsche 911 Carrera. Half a dozen men, all in dark clothes, are milling around.

"Let's go," says Johnny G., pulling Vaughn out of the car by his shirt collar.

As soon as Vaughn's out of the car, the farmhouse door opens and James F. X. Nunzio makes his appearance. He leads Eddy and Kate, holding the baby, out of the door, onto the porch, and down the steps. Vaughn's mind is spinning as he tries to figure out what to say—what reasoning to use, what bargain to offer, what form of begging will be most effective—to persuade the mobster not to exact his vengeance. Then, in an instant, everything changes. Before Vaughn has a chance to open his mouth, she walks out from behind Nunzio. Erin. She's not smiling. She's not frowning. Her face is unreadable.

I'll kill you, Vaughn thinks, looking at Nunzio. *If you lay a hand on her, I'll find a way.*

Jimmy Nutzo positions Vaughn, Eddy, Kate, and Erin in a semi-circle in front of him. His men take up positions behind them.

Nunzio takes his time, studying their faces one by one, until he comes to Eddy. "Those others, the lawyers, set the whole thing up. But you're the one who let himself *get* set up to be the patsy, the one who brought the phone, made it all work."

Vaughn sees Eddy stiffen, getting ready for what's coming. Ready to fight, for himself and his family. Vaughn gets ready, too, clenches his fists. He'll lunge at Nunzio, take him down. Giacobetti and the others will rush to pull him off. In the confusion, Eddy, Kate, and Erin might be able to make a run for it. Eddy has a rifle in the house. The odds are overwhelmingly against them. But they'll have a shot.

Nunzio takes a deep breath. "Tell me why. Why you brought the second phone. You told the judge at the trial. But I want you to tell *me.*"

Eddy keeps his eyes glued to Nunzio. "There were break-ins where we lived. Kate was alone in the house. And eight months pregnant. I needed that phone, for my family."

"Your family."

Nunzio stands motionless as a stone, and Vaughn can see that he's looking both at Eddy and inside himself. After a while, the mobster closes his eyes. His whole body stiffens, then relaxes, then stiffens again. Everyone watches and waits. It seems to Vaughn that no one is breathing.

"Family." Nunzio repeats the word. After a minute, he sighs and relaxes his muscles, and it seems to Vaughn like he's let something go.

"Go inside," Nunzio tells Eddy. "Take your wife and your baby."

Eddy doesn't waste time. Before Vaughn can count to three, his cousin and his little family are halfway up the steps.

Vaughn watches Nunzio watch Eddy.

"Wait," Nunzio says, and everything seems to stop again. Nunzio walks toward the steps, puts his hand inside his jacket. When he gets to Eddy, he removes his hand, now holding a slim silver pen. He reaches into his pants pocket and pulls out a business card. He writes something on it, then hands Eddy the card. "Here. Guy I know runs a short-line railroad. Looking for a good engineer."

Eddy hesitates but takes the card. "Thank you." He stares at Nunzio for a long minute. Then, without more, he turns and takes his family into the house.

Vaughn stands stupefied as Erin moves up behind him and takes his hand.

Nunzio approaches them. "Your turn."

Vaughn tenses, remembering the last time he was on the phone with Nunzio.

Nunzio reaches into his pocket and pulls out a set of keys. Car keys.

Vaughn glances at the Porsche. "You're shitting me."

"Don't wet your pants, counselor," Nunzio says, handing Vaughn the keys. "It's a lease. You have the car for three years."

"But when I called you, you made it sound like—"

"Like we weren't even? Well, we weren't. I owed you. Rewards and punishments. Everyone forgets the rewards part." Nunzio turns and heads for the Escalade, his soldiers moving with him.

"Hey!" It's Erin. "You forced me to come here. What do I get?"

Nunzio nods toward Vaughn. "You get him. Whether that's a reward or a punishment . . ." He shrugs.

Vaughn waits until Nunzio is in the Escalade, then walks over. Nunzio lowers the window and Vaughn says, "The plane, the cars, all these men—you're not just an underboss, are you?"

The corner of Nunzio's mouth stretches into the thinnest hint of a smile, then he rolls up the window.

Johnny G. walks to the blue Escalade EXT pickup, pets the two gigantic dogs.

"Part of your crew?" Vaughn asks.

"Recent additions. Thor, Loki, say hello to Mr. Coburn."

The dogs turn their heads toward Vaughn, their eyes full of menace.

"They look pissed," Vaughn says.

Giacobetti shrugs. "No wonder. Their owner abandoned them. Got his ass thrown in jail."

"Balzac?"

Johnny G. smiles. "I'm working on a *Game of Thrones* thing for him."

"Ramsay Bolton." Erin, a huge fan of the show, translates.

Johnny G., still smiling, says, "The more enlightened prisons are introducing comfort dogs to uplift the inmates' spirits. I hear Balzac is down in the dumps."

Vaughn's face shows he has no idea what they're talking about.

"Ramsay Bolton's dogs eat him alive," Erin explains. Then she turns back to Johnny G. "I haven't heard from Laurie. Should I be worried?"

"Your friend's on her way to Paris, in the jet. She said I should join her in a couple of days."

Erin's eyes widen. She looks the big man up and down. "Oh my."

Giacobetti gets into the pickup and leads the caravan off the farm.

As the cars drive away, Eddy emerges from the house, walks over to Vaughn. The two cousins stand across from each other for a long moment. Then Eddy reaches out for Vaughn's hand, and they shake. Nothing more is needed. All debts have been repaid. The fallen, redeemed. The bonds reforged, in steel.

"We'll be looking for godparents soon," Kate says, rocking Emma in the doorway.

Vaughn turns to Erin. "We'd be honored."

They say their goodbyes, and Vaughn and Erin walk to the Porsche. They climb in and Vaughn starts the car. He's about to pull out when Erin holds up an envelope. "What do you think's in this?"

"One way to find out," Vaughn says, signaling Erin to open it.

She does, and finds a sheet of white copy paper with a single line. She reads it, smiles, and hands it to Vaughn.

He feels a chill when he sees what it says: *No drag racing.*

Vaughn shifts into first, kicks up some dirt, and an instant later, all that's left of them is the fading sound of Springsteen's "Born to Run."

ACKNOWLEDGMENTS

This book is the result of the insights, effort, and generosity of a great many people. First is my wife, Lisa Chalmers, to whom I've dedicated the book. She motivated me to create a worthy companion to *A Criminal Defense* and supported me as I worked to do so. My early readers gave me great feedback and suggestions, so thank you to Jill S.H.S. Reiff and Neil Reiff, Andrea and Rob Sinnamon, Lauren and Naumon Amjed, and Jill and Greg Cunningham.

To Cynthia Manson, my agent and guide through the publishing world, thank you for your attentiveness and direction. You've opened the door to this brave new world and continue to show me the way forward.

To editor extraordinaire Ed Stackler, you are a true alchemist, transforming base metal into gold.

To Gracie Doyle, I extend huge and heartfelt thanks for the personal interest you've taken in my books and for being so accessible and easy to work with. You make me glad I chose Amazon as my publisher. You and your whole Thomas & Mercer team: Jeffrey Belle, Mikyla Bruder, Galen Maynard, Clint Singley, Sarah Shaw, Dennelle Catlett, Ashley Vanicek, Gabrielle Guarnero, Laura Costantino, and Laura Barrett.

ABOUT THE AUTHOR

Photo © Todd Rothstein

William L. Myers, Jr. is a Philadelphia lawyer with thirty years of trial experience in state and federal courts up and down the East Coast. A graduate of the University of Pennsylvania School of Law, he has argued before the United States Supreme Court and still actively practices law. Myers was born into a proud working-class family and now lives with his wife, Lisa, in the western suburbs of Philadelphia. He is the author of *A Criminal Defense*.